DREAMS

CRUCIFIED

D1167005

SELECTED WRITINGS
OF JOE R. LANSDALE

NOVELS

Act of Love (1980)

Texas Night Riders (1983)

Dead in the West (1986)

Magic Wagon (1986)

The Nightrunners (1987)

Cold in July (1989)

Batman: Captured by the Engines (1991)

Batman: Terror on the High Skies (1992)

Tarzan: The Lost Adventure
    (1995, with Edgar Rice Burroughs)

The Boar (1998)

Freezer Burn (1999)

Waltz of Shadows (1999)

Something Lumber This Way Comes
    (1999)

The Big Blow (2000)

Blood Dance (2000)

The Bottoms (2000)

A Fine Dark Line (2002)

Sunset and Sawdust (2004)

Lost Echoes (2007)

Leather Maiden (2008)

SHORT STORY COLLECTIONS

By Bizarre Hands (1989)

Stories by Mama Lansdale's Youngest Boy
    (1991)

Bestsellers Guaranteed (1993)

Electric Gumbo: A Lansdale Reader (1994)

Writer of the Purple Rage (1994)

A Fistfull of Stories (and Articles) (1996)

The Good, the Bad, and the Indifferent:
    Early Stories and Commentary (1997)

Private Eye Action, As You Like It (1998)

Triple Feature (1999)

The Long Ones: Nuthin' but Novellas
    (2000)

High Cotton (2000)

For a Few Stories More (2002)

A Little Green Book of Monster Stories
    (2003)

Bumper Crop (2004)

Mad Dog Summer and Other Stories
    (2004)

The King: And Other Stories (2005)

The Shadows, Kith and Kin (2007)

Sanctified and Chicken-Fried (2009)

The Best of Joe R. Lansdale (2010)

HAP COLLINS AND
    LEONARD PINE MYSTERIES

Savage Season (1990)

Mucho Mojo (1994)

Two-Bear Mambo (1995)

Bad Chili (1997)

Rumble Tumble (1998)

Veil's Visit (1999)

Captains Outrageous (2001)

Vanilla Ride (2009)

The Drive-In series

The Drive-In: A "B" Movie with Blood
   and Popcorn, Made in Texas (1988)
The Drive-In 2: Not Just One of Them
   Sequels (1989)
The Drive-In: A Double-Feature (1997)
The Drive-In: The Bus Tour (2005)

Ned the Seal trilogy

Zeppelins West (2001)
Flaming London (2006)

Graphic novels and comic books

Lone Ranger & Tonto (1993)
Jonah Hex: Two Gun Mojo (1993)
Jonah Hex: Riders of the Worm and Such
   (1995)
Blood and Shadows (1996)
The Spirit: The New Adventures #8 (1998)
Red Range (1999)
Jonah Hex: Shadows West (1999)
Conan and the Songs of the Dead (2006)
Marvel Adventures: Fantastic Four #32
   (2008)
Pigeons from Hell (2008)

Anthologies edited

The Best of the West (1989)
New Frontier (1989)
Razored Saddles (1989, with Pat Lobrutto)
Dark at Heart (1991, with Karen Lansdale)
Weird Business: A Horror Comics
   Anthology (1995, with Richard Klaw)
West That Was (1994)
   (co-ed: Thomas Knowles)
Wild West Show (1994)
   (co-ed: Thomas Knowles)
Lords of the Razor (2006)
Cross Plains Universe: Texans Celebrate
   Robert E. Howard
   (2006, with Scott A. Cupp)
Retro-Pulp Tales (2007)
Son of Retro-Pulp Tales
   (2009, with Keith Lansdale)

CRUCIFIED DREAMS

EDITED BY
JOE R. LANSDALE

CRUCIFIED DREAMS
© 2011 BY JOE R. LANSDALE

THIS IS A WORK OF COLLECTED FICTION. ALL EVENTS PORTRAYED IN
THIS BOOK ARE FICTITIOUS AND ANY RESEMBLANCE TO REAL PEOPLE OR
EVENTS IS PURELY COINCIDENTAL. ALL RIGHTS RESERVED, INCLUDING THE
RIGHT TO REPRODUCE THIS BOOK OR PORTIONS THEREOF IN ANY FORM
WITHOUT THE EXPRESS PERMISSION OF THE AUTHOR AND THE PUBLISHER.

COVER DESIGN BY ANN MONN
INTERIOR DESIGN BY JOHN COULTHART

TACHYON PUBLICATIONS
1459 18TH STREET #139
SAN FRANCISCO, CA 94107
(415) 285-5615
WWW.TACHYONPUBLICATIONS.COM
TACHYON@TACHYONPUBLICATIONS.COM

SERIES EDITOR: JACOB WEISMAN
PROJECT EDITOR: JILL ROBERTS

ISBN 13: 978-1-61696-003-2
ISBN 10: 1-61696-003-5

PRINTED IN THE UNITED STATES
OF AMERICA BY WORZALLA
FIRST EDITION: 2011
9 8 7 6 5 4 3 2 1

Introduction © 2011 by Joe R. Lansdale.

"The Whimper of Whipped Dogs" © 1973 by Harlan Ellison. Renewed, 2001 by the Kilimanjaro Corporation. Reprinted by arrangement with, and permission of, the Author and the Author's agent Richard Curtis Associates, Inc., New York. All rights reserved. Harlan Ellison is a registered trademark of the Kilimanjaro Corporation.

"The Monster" © 1986 by Joe Haldeman, first published in *Cutting Edge*, edited by Dennis Etchinson (Doubleday, New York).

"The Mojave Two-Step" © 1999 by Norman Partridge, first published in *Future Crimes*, edited by Martin H. Greenberg and John Helfers (DAW, New York).

"Front Man" © 1997 by David Morrell, first published in *Murder for Revenge*, edited by Otto Penzler (Delacorte Press, New York).

"Interrogation B" © 2007 by Charlie Huston, first published in *A Hell of a Woman: An Anthology of Female Noir*, edited by Megan Abbott (Busted Flush Press, Houston, Texas).

"The Quickening" © 1981 by Michael Bishop, first published in *Universe 11*, edited by Terry Carr (Doubleday, New York).

"The Evening and the Morning and the Night" © 1987 by Octavia E. Butler, first published in *Omni*, May 1987.

"Love in Vain" © 1988 by Lewis Shiner, first published in *Ripper!*, edited by Gardner Dozois and Susan Casper (Tor Books, New York).

"Beast of the Heartland" © 1992 by Lucius Shepard, first published in *Playboy*, September 1992.

"Coffins on the River" © 2003 by Jeffrey Ford, first published in *Polphony, Volume 3*, edited by Deborah Layne and Jay Lake (Wheatland Press, Wilsonville, Oregon).

"Game Night at the Fox and Goose" © 1998 by Karen Joy Fowler, first published in *Black Glass: Short Fictions* (Henry Holt, Inc., New York).

"Copping Squid" © 2009 by Michael Shea, first published in *Copping Squid and Other Mythos Tales* (Perilous Press, California).

"Access Fantasy" © 2004 by Jonathan Lethem, first published in *Starlight 2*, edited by Patrick Nielsen Hayden (Tor Books, New York).

"Singing on a Star" © 2009 by Ellen Klages, first published in *Firebirds Soaring: An Anthology of Original Speculative Fiction*, edited by Sharyn November (Firebrand/Penguin USA, New York).

"Quitters, Inc." © 1978 by Stephen King, first published in *Night Shift* (Doubleday, New York).

"Nightbeat" © 1975 by Neal Barrett, Jr., first published in *Epoch*, edited by Roger Elwood and Robert Silverberg (Berkley, New York).

"Window" © 1980 by Bob Leman, first published in *The Magazine of Fantasy & Science Fiction*, May 1980.

"The Pit" © 1978 by Joe R. Lansdale, first published in *The Black Lizard Anthology of Crime Fiction*, edited by Edward Gorman (Black Lizard Books, New York).

"Loss" © 2008 by Tom Piccirilli, first published in *Five Strokes to Midnight*, edited by Gary A. Braunbeck and Hank Schwaeble (Haunted Pelican Press, Oklahoma).

CONTENTS

INTRODUCTION
Joe R. Lansdale

THIS IS ONE good book.

Let me tell you a little about it.

When I was approached by Tachyon Publications to edit an anthology, the original idea was that we would do something along the lines of the kind of stories I might write or like to read.

Jacob Weisman, the publisher of Tachyon, said that the field had caught up with me. Meaning, I guess, that some of my stories, thought to be extreme in the eighties, and for that matter the nineties, and even recently, were becoming more the norm. I think he meant my taste in fiction as much as my own fiction.

Frankly, I'm not sure what was meant by that line about time catching up with me, but I'm going to take it as a compliment and not some comment on my age. I'm going to decide that what he meant was I was working on stories that were ahead of their time in acceptance and taste, and now there are others writing extreme stories for which the readership has finally arrived. It's not entirely accurate, but I like it, and accept it, at least until the next few paragraphs where I deny it.

The idea was to find a bunch of writers who were doing whatever it was I was doing. Stretching the limits. But some of those writers were actually doing it before I was. Like Harlan Ellison, for example. I, and many other writers, was influenced by his audacity, and then there were writers who were in turn influenced by another generation of writers, and another generation, of which I was one.

I think that is more accurate. A generation of writers of which I was one. For certainly there were writers well ahead of us. The aforementioned Ellison, and David Morrell, included here, and ahead of them: Ray Bradbury, Theodore Sturgeon, Leigh Brackett, Cyril Kornbluth, Henry Kuttner, Cordwainer Smith, C. L. Moore, everyone from Hemingway to Flannery O'Connor, to Faulkner and Fitzgerald, to Steinbeck and William S. Burroughs, to Charles Bukowski. Everyone stands on someone else's shoulders at some point, and many of those shoulders are certainly much broader than mine.

So, in spite of the compliment, I not only can't take credit for these changes in taste or attitude, I freely point out it's a process. It doesn't begin with any one person, or any one group.

That said, these stories are certainly working The Now. These writers, earlier, middle, and present, are kicking some serious literary butt. This is one fine collection of reprints. They are each inimitable in their own way, and in fact, this book might well serve, and should serve, as an inspiration to up-and-coming writers who want to do something more than coat the literary wall with the same old paint.

Not that I'm suggesting anyone copy the writers here, but that instead they should be inspired by their innovation. The only thing these stories share is a certain climate under which they all exist: a climate of originality.

A quick explanation of the title:

Crucified Dreams was the title I had planned for the book Tachyon published in 2010, which Jacob called *The Best of Joe R. Lansdale*. Somewhere, we got our wires crossed, and *Crucified Dreams* became *The Best of,* and my title was applied to a kind of memoir/essay I wrote for the introduction to that book.

But the title stayed with us. We liked it. And for some odd reason, we thought it fit this anthology of short stories. For what are stories but dreams?

Dreams that have elements of nightmare.

Dreams gone pleasantly haywire.

Dreams hot-wired and tortured, whipped into shape by freshness and passion; some staggering down from the bloody cross of imagination, wounded and scarred, tattooed and hoodooed and full of strange excitement.

All manner of dreams are here.

Some bright.

Some shadowy.

Some a blending of light and shadow.

All entertaining.

Enjoy.

THE WHIMPER OF WHIPPED DOGS
Harlan Ellison®

ON THE NIGHT after the day she had stained the louvered window shutters of her new apartment on East 52nd Street, Beth saw a woman slowly and hideously knifed to death in the courtyard of her building. She was one of twenty-six witnesses to the ghoulish scene, and, like them, she did nothing to stop it.

She saw it all, every moment of it, without break and with no impediment to her view. Quite madly, the thought crossed her mind as she watched in horrified fascination, that she had the sort of marvelous line of observation Napoleon had sought when he caused to have constructed at the *Comédie-Française* theaters, a curtained box at the rear, so he could watch the audience as well as the stage. The night was clear, the moon was full, she had just turned off the 11:30 movie on Channel 2 after the second commercial break, realizing she had already seen Robert Taylor in *Westward the Women,* and had disliked it the first time; and the apartment was quite dark.

She went to the window, to raise it six inches for the night's sleep, and she saw the woman stumble into the courtyard. She was sliding along the wall, clutching her left arm with her right hand. Con Ed had installed mercury-vapor lamps on the poles; there had been sixteen assaults in seven months; the courtyard was illuminated with a chill purple glow that made the blood streaming down the woman's left arm look black and shiny. Beth saw every detail with utter clarity, as though magnified a thousand power under a microscope, solarized as if it had been a television commercial.

The woman threw back her head, as if she were trying to scream, but there was no sound. Only the traffic on First Avenue, late cabs foraging for singles paired for the night at Maxwell's Plum and Friday's and Adam's Apple. But that was over there, beyond. Where *she* was, down there seven floors below, in the courtyard, everything seemed silently suspended in an invisible force-field.

Beth stood in the darkness of her apartment, and realized she had raised the window completely. A tiny balcony lay just over the low sill; now not even glass separated her from the sight; just the wrought-iron balcony railing and seven floors to the courtyard below.

The woman staggered away from the wall, her head still thrown back, and Beth could see she was in her mid-thirties, with dark hair cut in a shag; it was impossible to tell if she was pretty: terror had contorted her features and her mouth was a twisted black slash, opened but emitting no sound. Cords stood out in her neck. She had lost one shoe, and her steps were uneven, threatening to dump her to the pavement.

The man came around the corner of the building, into the courtyard. The knife he held was enormous—or perhaps it only seemed so: Beth remembered a bonehandled fish knife her father had used one summer at the lake in Maine: it folded back on itself and locked, revealing eight inches of serrated blade. The knife in the hand of the dark man in the courtyard seemed to be similar.

The woman saw him and tried to run, but he leaped across the distance between them and grabbed her by the hair and pulled her head back as though he would slash her throat in the next reaper-motion.

Then the woman screamed.

The sound skirled up into the courtyard like bats trapped in an echo chamber, unable to find a way out, driven mad. It went on and on...

The man struggled with her and she drove her elbows into his sides and he tried to protect himself, spinning her around by her hair, the terrible scream going up and up and never stopping. She came loose and he was left with a fistful of hair torn out by the roots. As she spun out, he slashed straight across and opened her up just below the breasts. Blood sprayed through her clothing and the man was soaked; it seemed to drive him even more berserk. He went at her again, as she tried to hold herself together, the blood pouring down over her arms.

She tried to run, teetered against the wall, slid sidewise, and the man struck the brick surface. She was away, stumbling over a flower bed, falling, getting to her knees as he threw himself on her again. The knife came up in a flashing arc that illuminated the blade strangely with purple light. And still she screamed.

Lights came on in dozens of apartments and people appeared at windows.

He drove the knife to the hilt into her back, high on the right shoulder. He used both hands.

Beth caught it all in jagged flashes—the man, the woman, the knife, the blood, the expressions on the faces of those watching from the windows. Then lights clicked off in the windows, but they still stood there, watching.

She wanted to yell, to scream, "What are you doing to that woman?" But her throat was frozen, two iron hands that had been immersed in dry ice for ten thousand years clamped around her neck. She could feel the blade sliding into her own body.

Somehow—it seemed impossible but there it was down there, happening somehow—the woman struggled erect and *pulled* herself off the knife. Three steps, she took three steps and fell into the flower bed again. The man was howling now, like a great beast, the sounds inarticulate, bubbling up from his stomach. He fell on her and the knife went up and came down, then again, and again, and finally it was all a blur of motion, and her scream of lunatic bats went on till it faded off and was gone.

Beth stood in the darkness, trembling and crying, the sight filling her eyes with horror. And when she could no longer bear to look at what he was doing down there to the unmoving piece of meat over which he worked, she looked up and around at the windows of darkness where the others still stood—even as she stood—and somehow she could see their faces, bruise-purple with the dim light from the mercury lamps, and there was a universal sameness to their expressions. The women stood with their nails biting into the upper arms of their men, their tongues edging from the corners of their mouths; the men were wild-eyed and smiling. They all looked as though they were at cock fights. Breathing deeply. Drawing some sustenance from the grisly scene below. An exhalation of sound, deep, deep, as though from caverns beneath the earth. Flesh pale and moist.

And it was then that she realized the courtyard had grown foggy, as though mist off the East River had rolled up 52nd Street in a veil that would obscure the details of what the knife and the man were still doing…endlessly doing it… long after there was any joy in it…still doing it…again and again…

But the fog was unnatural, thick and gray and filled with tiny scintillas of light. She stared at it, rising up in the empty space of the courtyard. Bach in the cathedral, stardust in a vacuum chamber.

Beth saw eyes.

There, up there, at the ninth floor and higher, two great eyes, as surely as night and the moon, there were *eyes*. And—a face? Was that a face, could she be sure, was she imagining it…a face? In the roiling vapors of chill fog something lived, something brooding and patient and utterly malevolent had been summoned up to witness what was happening down there in the flower bed. Beth tried to look away, but could not. The eyes, those primal burning eyes, filled with an abysmal antiquity yet frighteningly bright and anxious like the eyes of a child; eyes filled with tomb depths, ancient and new, chasm-filled, burning, gigantic and deep as an abyss, holding her, compelling her. The shadow play was being staged not only for the tenants in their windows, watching and drinking of the scene, but for some *other*. Not on frigid tundra or waste moors, not in subterranean caverns or on some faraway world circling a dying sun, but here, in the city, here the eyes of that *other* watched.

Shaking with the effort, Beth wrenched her eyes from those burning depths up there beyond the ninth floor, only to see again the horror that had brought that *other*. And she was struck for the first time by the awfulness of what she was witnessing, she was released from the immobility that had held her like a coelacanth in shale, she was filled with the blood thunder pounding against the membranes of her mind: she had *stood* there! She had done nothing, nothing! A woman had been butchered and she had said nothing, done nothing. Tears had been useless, tremblings had been pointless, she *had done nothing!*

Then she heard hysterical sounds midway between laughter and giggling, and as she stared up into that great face rising in the fog and chimneysmoke of the night, she heard *herself* making those deranged gibbon noises and from the man below a pathetic, trapped sound, like the whimper of whipped dogs.

She was staring up into that face again. She hadn't wanted to see it again—ever. But she was locked with those smoldering eyes, overcome with the feeling that they were childlike, though she *knew* they were incalculably ancient.

Then the butcher below did an unspeakable thing and Beth reeled with dizziness and caught the edge of the window before she could tumble out onto the balcony; she steadied herself and fought for breath.

She felt herself being looked at, and for a long moment of frozen terror she feared she might have caught the attention of that face up there in the fog. She clung to the window, feeling everything growing faraway and dim, and stared straight across the court. She *was* being watched. Intently. By the young man in the seventh-floor window across from her own apartment. Steadily, he was looking at her. Through the strange fog with its burning eyes feasting on the sight below, he was staring at her.

As she felt herself blacking out, in the moment before unconsciousness, the thought flickered and fled that there was something terribly familiar about his face.

It rained the next day. East 52nd Street was slick and shining with the oil rainbows. The rain washed the dog turds into the gutters and nudged them down and down to the catch-basin openings. People bent against the slanting rain, hidden beneath umbrellas, looking like enormous, scurrying black mushrooms. Beth went out to get the newspapers after the police had come and gone.

The news reports dwelled with loving emphasis on the twenty-six tenants of the building who had watched in cold interest as Leona Ciarelli, 37, of 455 Fort Washington Avenue, Manhattan, had been systematically stabbed to death by Burton H. Wells, 41, an unemployed electrician, who had been subsequently shot to death by two off-duty police officers when he burst into Michael's Pub on 55th Street, covered with blood and brandishing a knife that authorities later identified as the murder weapon.

She had thrown up twice that day. Her stomach seemed incapable of retaining anything solid, and the taste of bile lay along the back of her tongue. She could not blot the scenes of the night before from her mind; she re-ran them again and again, every movement of that reaper arm playing over and over as though on a short loop of memory. The woman's head thrown back for silent screams. The blood. Those eyes in the fog.

She was drawn again and again to the window, to stare down into the courtyard and the street. She tried to superimpose over the bleak Manhattan concrete the view from her window in Swann House at Bennington: the little yard and another white, frame dormitory; the fantastic apple trees; and from the other window the rolling hills and gorgeous Vermont countryside; her memory skittered through the change of seasons. But there was always concrete and the rain-slick streets; the rain on the pavement was black and shiny as blood.

She tried to work, rolling up the tambour closure of the old rolltop desk she had bought on Lexington Avenue and hunching over the graph sheets of choreographer's charts. But Labanotation was merely a Jackson Pollock jumble of arcane hieroglyphics to her today, instead of the careful representation of eurhythmics she had studied four years to perfect. And before that, Farmington.

The phone rang. It was the secretary from the Taylor Dance Company, asking when she would be free. She had to beg off. She looked at her hand, lying on the graph sheets of figures Laban had devised, and she saw her fingers trembling. She had to beg off. Then she called Guzman at the Downtown Ballet Company, to tell him she would be late with the charts.

"My God, lady, I have ten dancers sitting around in a rehearsal hall getting their leotards sweaty! What do you expect me to do?"

She explained what had happened the night before. And as she told him, she realized the newspapers had been justified in holding that tone against the twenty-six witnesses to the death of Leona Ciarelli. Paschal Guzman listened, and when he spoke again, his voice was several octaves lower, and he spoke more slowly. He said he understood and she could take a little longer to prepare the charts. But there was a distance in his voice, and he hung up while she was thanking him.

She dressed in an argyle sweater vest in shades of dark purple, and a pair of fitted khaki gabardine trousers. She had to go out, to walk around. To do what? To think about other things. As she pulled on the Fred Braun chunky heels, she idly wondered if that heavy silver bracelet was still in the window of Georg Jensen's. In the elevator, the young man from the window across the courtyard stared at her. Beth felt her body begin to tremble again. She went deep into the corner of the box when he entered behind her.

Between the fifth and fourth floors, he hit the *off* switch and the elevator jerked to a halt.

Beth stared at him and he smiled innocently.

"Hi. My name's Gleeson, Ray Gleeson, I'm in 714."

She wanted to demand he turn the elevator back on, by what right did he *presume* to do such a thing, what did he mean by this, turn it on at once or suffer the consequences. That was what she *wanted* to do. Instead, from the same place she had heard the gibbering laughter the night before, she heard her voice, much smaller and much less possessed than she had trained it to be, saying, "Beth O'Neill, I live in 701."

The thing about it, was that *the elevator was stopped.* And she was frightened. But he leaned against the paneled wall, very well dressed, shoes polished, hair combed and probably blown dry with a hand drier, and he *talked* to her as if they were across a table at L'Argenteuil. "You just moved in, huh?"

"About two months ago."

"Where did you go to school? Bennington or Sarah Lawrence?"

"Bennington. How did you know?"

He laughed, and it was a nice laugh. "I'm an editor at a religious book publisher; every year we get half a dozen Bennington, Sarah Lawrence, Smith girls. They come hopping in like grasshoppers, ready to revolutionize the publishing industry."

"What's wrong with that? You sound like you don't care for them."

"Oh, I *love* them, they're marvelous. They think they know how to write better than the authors we publish. Had one darlin' little item who was given galleys of three books to proof, and she rewrote all three. I think she's working as a table-swabber in a Horn & Hardart's now."

She didn't reply to that. She would have pegged him as an anti-feminist, ordinarily, if it had been anyone else speaking. But the eyes. There was something terribly familiar about his face. She was enjoying the conversation; she rather liked him.

"What's the nearest big city to Bennington?"

"Albany, New York. About sixty miles."

"How long does it take to drive there?"

"From Bennington? About an hour and a half."

"Must be a nice drive, that Vermont country, really pretty. They went coed, I understand. How's that working out?"

"I don't know, really."

"You don't know?"

"It happened around the time I was graduating."

"What did you major in?"

"I was a dance major, specializing in Labanotation. That's the way you write choreography."

"It's all electives, I gather. You don't have to take anything required, like sciences, for example." He didn't change tone as he said, "That was a terrible thing last night. I saw you watching. I guess a lot of us were watching. It was a really terrible thing."

She nodded dumbly. Fear came back.

"I understand the cops got him. Some nut, they don't even know why he killed her, or why he went charging into that bar. It was really an awful thing. I'd very much like to have dinner with you one night soon, if you're not attached."

"That would be all right."

"Maybe Wednesday. There's an Argentinian place I know. You might like it."

"That would be all right."

"Why don't you turn on the elevator, and we can go," he said, and smiled again. She did it, wondering why she had stopped the elevator in the first place.

On her third date with him, they had their first fight. It was at a party thrown by a director of television commercials. He lived on the ninth floor of their building. He had just done a series of spots for *Sesame Street* (the letters "U" for Underpass, "T" for Tunnel, lowercase "b" for boats, "c" for cars; the numbers 1 to 6 and the numbers 1 to 20; the words *light* and *dark*) and was celebrating his move from the arena of commercial tawdriness (and its attendant $75,000 a year) to the sweet fields of educational programming (and its accompanying descent into low-pay respectability). There was a logic in his joy Beth could not quite understand, and when she talked with him about it, in a far corner of the kitchen, his arguments didn't seem to parse. But he seemed happy, and his girlfriend, a long-legged ex-model from Philadelphia, continued to drift to him and away from him, like some exquisite undersea plant, touching his hair and kissing his neck, murmuring words of pride and barely submerged sexuality. Beth found it bewildering, though the celebrants were all bright and lively.

In the living room, Ray was sitting on the arm of the sofa, hustling a stewardess named Luanne. Beth could tell he was hustling; he was trying to look casual. When he *wasn't* hustling, he was always intense, about everything. She decided to ignore it, and wandered around the apartment, sipping at a Tanqueray and tonic.

There were framed prints of abstract shapes clipped from a calendar printed in Germany. They were in metal Bonniers frames.

In the dining room a huge door from a demolished building somewhere in the city had been handsomely stripped, teaked and refinished. It was now the dinner table.

A Lightolier fixture attached to the wall over the bed swung out, levered up and down, tipped, and its burnished globe-head revolved a full three hundred and sixty degrees.

She was standing in the bedroom, looking out the window, when she realized *this* had been one of the rooms in which light had gone on, gone off; one of the rooms that had contained a silent watcher at the death of Leona Ciarelli.

When she returned to the living room, she looked around more carefully. With only three or four exceptions—the stewardess, a young married couple from the second floor, a stockbroker from Hemphill, Noyes—*everyone* at the party had been a witness to the slaying.

"I'd like to go," she told him.

"Why, aren't you having a good time?" asked the stewardess, a mocking smile crossing her perfect little face.

"Like all Bennington ladies," Ray said, answering for Beth, "she is enjoying herself most by not enjoying herself at all. It's a trait of the anal retentive. Being here in someone else's apartment, she can't empty ashtrays or rewind the toilet paper roll so it doesn't hang a tongue, and being tightassed, her nature demands we go.

"All right, Beth, let's say our goodbyes and take off. The Phantom Rectum strikes again."

She slapped him and the stewardess's eyes widened. But the smile remained frozen where it had appeared.

He grabbed her wrist before she could do it again. "Garbanzo beans, baby," he said, holding her wrist tighter than necessary.

They went back to her apartment, and after sparring silently with kitchen cabinet doors slammed and the television being tuned too loud, they got to her bed, and he tried to perpetuate the metaphor by fucking her in the ass. He had her on elbows and knees before she realized what he was doing; she struggled to turn over and he rode her bucking and tossing without a sound. And when it was clear to him that she would never permit it, he grabbed her breast from underneath and squeezed so hard she howled in pain. He dumped her on her back, rubbed himself between her legs a dozen times, and came on her stomach.

Beth lay with her eyes closed and an arm thrown across her face. She wanted to cry, but found she could not. Ray lay on her and said nothing. She wanted to rush to the bathroom and shower, but he did not move, till long after his semen had dried on their bodies.

"Who did you date at college?" he asked.

"I didn't date anyone very much." Sullen.

"No heavy makeouts with wealthy lads from Williams and Dartmouth... no Amherst intellectuals begging you to save them from creeping faggotry by permitting them to stick their carrots in your sticky little slit?"

"Stop it!"

"Come on, baby, it couldn't all have been knee socks and little round circle-pins. You don't expect me to believe you didn't get a little mouthful of cock from time to time. It's only, what? about fifteen miles to Williamstown? I'm sure the Williams werewolves were down burning the highway to your cunt on weekends; you can level with old Uncle Ray...."

"Why are you like this?!" She started to move, to get away from him, and he grabbed her by the shoulder, forced her to lie down again. Then he rose up over her and said, "I'm like this because I'm a New Yorker, baby. Because I live in this fucking city every day. Because I have to play patty-cake with the ministers and other sanctified holy-joe assholes who want their goodness and lightness tracts published by the Blessed Sacrament Publishing and Storm Window Company of 277 Park Avenue, when what I *really* want to do is toss the stupid psalm-suckers out the thirty-seventh-floor window and listen to them quote chapter-and-worse all the way down. Because I've lived in this great big snapping dog of a city all my life and I'm mad as a mudfly, for chrissakes!"

She lay unable to move, breathing shallowly, filled with a sudden pity and affection for him. His face was white and strained, and she knew he was saying things to her that only a bit too much Almadén and exact timing would have let him say.

"What do you expect from me," he said, his voice softer now, but no less intense, "do you expect kindness and gentility and understanding and a hand on *your* hand when the smog burns your eyes? I can't do it, I haven't got it. No one has it in this cesspool of a city. Look around you; what do you think is happening here? They take rats and they put them in boxes and when there are too many of them, some of the little fuckers go out of their minds and start gnawing the rest to death. *It ain't no different here, baby!* It's rat time for everybody in this madhouse. You can't expect to jam as many people into this stone thing as we do, with buses and taxis and dogs shitting themselves scrawny and noise night and day and no money and not enough places to live and no place to go to have a decent think…you can't do it without making the time right for some godforsaken other kind of thing to be born! You can't hate everyone around you, and kick every beggar and nigger and *mestizo* shithead, you can't have cabbies stealing from you and taking tips they don't deserve, and then cursing you, you can't walk in the soot till your collar turns black, and your body stinks with the smell of flaking brick and decaying brains, you can't do it without calling up some kind of awful—"

He stopped.

His face bore the expression of a man who has just received brutal word of the death of a loved one. He suddenly lay down, rolled over, and turned off.

She lay beside him, trembling, trying desperately to remember where she had seen his face before.

✠   ✠   ✠

He didn't call her again, after the night of the party. And when they met in the hall, he pointedly turned away, as though he had given her some obscure chance and she had refused to take it. Beth thought she understood: though Ray Gleeson had not been her first affair, he had been the first to reject her so completely. The first to put her not only out of his bed and his life, but even out of his world. It was as though she were invisible, not even beneath contempt, simply not there.

She busied herself with other things.

She took on three new charting jobs for Guzman and a new group that had formed on Staten Island, of all places. She worked furiously and they gave her new assignments; they even paid her.

She tried to decorate the apartment with a less precise touch. Huge poster blowups of Merce Cunningham and Martha Graham replaced the Brueghel prints that had reminded her of the view looking down the hill toward Williams. The tiny balcony outside her window, the balcony she had steadfastly refused to stand upon since the night of the slaughter, the night of the fog with eyes, that balcony she swept and set about with little flower boxes in which she planted geraniums, petunias, dwarf zinnias, and other hardy perennials. Then, closing the window, she went to give herself, to involve herself in this city to which she had brought her ordered life.

And the city responded to her overtures:

Seeing off an old friend from Bennington, at Kennedy International, she stopped at the terminal coffee shop to have a sandwich. The counter—like a moat—surrounded a center service island that had huge advertising cubes rising above it on burnished poles. The cubes proclaimed the delights of Fun City. *New York Is a Summer Festival,* they said, and *Joseph Papp Presents Shakespeare in Central Park* and *Visit the Bronx Zoo* and *You'll Adore Our Contentious but Lovable Cabbies.* The food emerged from a window far down the service area and moved slowly on a conveyor belt through the hordes of screaming waitresses who slathered the counter with redolent washcloths. The lunchroom had all the charm and dignity of a steel-rolling mill, and approximately the same noise level. Beth ordered a cheeseburger that cost a dollar and a quarter, and a glass of milk.

When it came, it was cold, the cheese unmelted, and the patty of meat resembling nothing so much as a dirty scouring pad. The bun was cold and untoasted. There was no lettuce under the patty.

Beth managed to catch the waitress's eye. The girl approached with an annoyed look. "Please toast the bun and may I have a piece of lettuce?" Beth said.

"We dun' do that," the waitress said, turning half away, as though she would walk in a moment.

"You don't do what?"

"We dun' toass the bun here."

"Yes, but I *want* the bun toasted," Beth said firmly.

"An' you got to pay for extra lettuce."

"If I was asking for *extra* lettuce," Beth said, getting annoyed, "I would pay for it, but since there's *no* lettuce here, I don't think I should be charged extra for the first piece."

"We dun' do that."

The waitress started to walk away. "Hold it," Beth said, raising her voice just enough so the assembly-line eaters on either side stared at her. "You mean to tell me I have to pay a dollar and a quarter and I can't get a piece of lettuce or even get the bun toasted?"

"Ef you dun' like it.... "

"Take it back."

"You gotta pay for it, you order it."

"I said take it back, I don't want the fucking thing!"

The waitress scratched it off the check. The milk cost 27¢ and tasted going-sour. It was the first time in her life that Beth had said *that* word aloud.

At the cashier's stand, Beth said to the sweating man with the felt-tip pens in his shirt pocket, "Just out of curiosity, are you interested in complaints?"

"No!" he said, snarling, quite literally snarling. He did not look up as he punched out 73¢ and it came rolling down the chute.

The city responded to her overtures:

It was raining again. She was trying to cross Second Avenue, with the light. She stepped off the curb and a car came sliding through the red and splashed her. "Hey!" she yelled.

"Eat shit, sister!" the driver yelled back, turning the corner.

Her boots, her legs and her overcoat were splattered with mud. She stood trembling on the curb.

The city responded to her overtures:

She emerged from the building at One Astor Place with her big briefcase full of Laban charts; she was adjusting her rain scarf about her head. A well-dressed man with an attaché case thrust the handle of his umbrella up between her legs from the rear. She gasped and dropped her case.

The city responded and responded and responded.

Her overtures altered quickly.

The old drunk with the stippled cheeks extended his hand and mumbled words. She cursed him and walked on up Broadway past the beaver film houses.

She crossed against the lights on Park Avenue, making hackies slam their brakes to avoid hitting her; she used *that* word frequently now.

When she found herself having a drink with a man who had elbowed up beside her in the singles' bar, she felt faint and knew she should go home.

But Vermont was so far away.

Nights later. She had come home from the Lincoln Center ballet, and gone straight to bed. Lying half-asleep in her bedroom, she heard an alien sound. One room away, in the living room, in the dark, there was a sound. She slipped out of bed and went to the door between the rooms. She fumbled silently for the switch on the lamp just inside the living room, and found it, and clicked it on. A black man in a leather car coat was trying to get *out* of the apartment. In that first flash of light filling the room she noticed the television set beside him on the floor as he struggled with the door, she noticed the police lock and bar had been broken in a new and clever manner *New York* magazine had not yet reported in a feature article on apartment ripoffs, she noticed that he had gotten his foot tangled in the telephone cord that she had requested be extra-long so she could carry the instrument into the bathroom, I don't want to miss any business calls when the shower is running; she noticed all things in perspective and one thing with sharpest clarity: the expression on the burglar's face.

There was something familiar in that expression.

He almost had the door open, but now he closed it, and slipped the police lock. He took a step toward her.

Beth went back, into the darkened bedroom.

The city responded to her overtures.

She backed against the wall at the head of the bed. Her hand fumbled in the shadows for the telephone. His shape filled the doorway, light, all light behind him.

In silhouette it should not have been possible to tell, but somehow she knew he was wearing gloves and the only marks he would leave would be deep bruises, very blue, almost black, with the tinge under them of blood that had been stopped in its course.

He came for her, arms hanging casually at his sides. She tried to climb over the bed, and he grabbed her from behind, ripping her nightgown. Then he had a hand around her neck and he pulled her backward. She fell off the bed, landed at his feet and his hold was broken. She scuttled across the floor and for a moment she had the respite to feel terror. She was going to die, and she was frightened.

He trapped her in the corner between the closet and the bureau and kicked her. His foot caught her in the thigh as she folded tighter, smaller, drawing her legs up. She was cold.

Then he reached down with both hands and pulled her erect by her hair. He slammed her head against the wall. Everything slid up in her sight as though running off the edge of the world. He slammed her head against the wall again, and she felt something go soft over her right ear.

When he tried to slam her a third time she reached out blindly for his face and ripped down with her nails. He howled in pain and she hurled herself forward, arms wrapping themselves around his waist. He stumbled backward and in a tangle of thrashing arms and legs they fell out onto the little balcony.

Beth landed on the bottom, feeling the window boxes jammed up against her spine and legs. She fought to get to her feet, and her nails hooked into his shirt under the open jacket, ripping. Then she was on her feet again and they struggled silently.

He whirled her around, bent her backward across the wrought-iron railing. Her face was turned outward.

They were standing in their windows, watching.

Through the fog she could see them watching. Through the fog she recognized their expressions. Through the fog she heard them breathing in unison, bellows breathing of expectation and wonder. Through the fog.

And the black man punched her in the throat. She gagged and started to black out and could not draw air into her lungs. Back, back, he bent her further back and she was looking up, straight up, toward the ninth floor and higher....

Up there: eyes.

The words Ray Gleeson had said in a moment filled with what he had become, with the utter hopelessness and finality of the choice the city had forced on him, the words came back. *You can't live in this city and survive unless you have protection...you can't live this way, like rats driven mad, without making the time right for some godforsaken other kind of thing to be born...you can't do it without calling up some kind of awful....*

God! A new God, an ancient God come again with the eyes and hunger of a child, a deranged blood God of fog and street violence. A God who needed worshippers and offered the choices of death as a victim or life as an eternal witness to the deaths of *other* chosen victims. A God to fit the times, a God of streets and people.

She tried to shriek, to appeal to Ray, to the director in the bedroom window of his ninth-floor apartment with his long-legged Philadelphia model beside him and his fingers inside her as they worshipped in their holiest of ways, to the others who had been at the party that had been Ray's offer of a chance to join their congregation. She wanted to be saved from having to make that choice.

But the black man had punched her in the throat, and now his hands were on her, one on her chest, the other in her face, the smell of leather filling her where the nausea could not. And she understood Ray had *cared,* had wanted her to take the chance offered; but she had come from a world of little white dormitories and Vermont countryside; it was not a real world. *This* was the real world and up there was the God who ruled this world, and she had rejected him, had said no to one of his priests and servitors. *Save me! Don't make me do it!*

She knew she had to call out, to make appeal, to try and win the approbation of that God. *I can't…save me!*

She struggled and made terrible little mewling sounds trying to summon the words to cry out, and suddenly she crossed a line, and screamed up into the echoing courtyard with a voice Leona Ciarelli had never known enough to use.

"Him! Take him! Not me! I'm yours, I love you, I'm yours! Take him, not me, please not me, take him, take him, I'm yours!"

And the black man was suddenly lifted away, wrenched off her, and off the balcony, whirled straight up into the fog-thick air in the courtyard, as Beth sank to her knees on the ruined flower boxes.

She was half-conscious, and could not be sure she saw it just that way, but up he went, end over end, whirling and spinning like a charred leaf.

And the form took firmer shape. Enormous paws with claws and shapes that no animal she had ever seen had ever possessed, and the burglar, black, poor, terrified, whimpering like a whipped dog, was stripped of his flesh. His body was opened with a thin incision, and there was a rush as all the blood poured from him like a sudden cloudburst, and yet he was still alive, twitching with the involuntary horror of a frog's leg shocked with an electric current. Twitched, and twitched again as he was torn piece by piece to shreds. Pieces of flesh and bone and half a face with an eye blinking furiously, cascaded down past Beth, and hit the cement below with sodden thuds. And still he was alive, as his organs were squeezed and musculature and bile and shit and skin were rubbed, sandpapered together and let fall. It went on and on, as the death of Leona Ciarelli had gone on and on, and she understood with the blood-knowledge of survivors *at any cost* that the reason the witnesses to the death of Leona Ciarelli had done nothing was not that they had been frozen with horror, that they didn't want to get involved, or that they were inured to death by years of television slaughter.

They were worshippers at a black mass the city had demanded be staged; not once, but a thousand times a day in this insane asylum of steel and stone.

Now she was on her feet, standing half-naked in her ripped nightgown, her hands tightening on the wrought-iron railing, begging to see more, to drink deeper.

Now she was one of them, as the pieces of the night's sacrifice fell past her, bleeding and screaming.

Tomorrow the police would come again, and they would question her, and she would say how terrible it had been, that burglar, and how she had fought, afraid he would rape her and kill her, and how he had fallen, and she had no idea how he had been so hideously mangled and ripped apart, but a seven-storey fall, after all…

Tomorrow she would not have to worry about walking in the streets, because no harm could come to her. Tomorrow she could even remove the police lock. Nothing in the city could do her any further evil, because she had made the only choice. She was now a dweller in the city, now wholly and richly a part of it. Now she was taken to the bosom of her God.

She felt Ray beside her, standing beside her, holding her, protecting her, his hand on her naked backside, and she watched the fog swirl up and fill the courtyard, fill the city, fill her eyes and her soul and her heart with its power. As Ray's naked body pressed tightly inside her, she drank deeply of the night, knowing whatever voices she heard from this moment forward would be the voices not of whipped dogs, but those of strong, meat-eating beasts.

At last she was unafraid, and it was so good, so very good *not* to be afraid.

When inward life dries up, when feeling decreases and apathy increases, when one cannot affect or even genuinely touch another person, violence flares up as a daimonic necessity for contact, a mad drive forcing touch in the most direct way possible.

—Rollo May, *Love and Will*

THE MONSTER
Joe Haldeman

START AT THE beginning? Which beginning?

Okay, since you be from Outside, I give you the whole thing. Sit over there, be comfort. Smoke 'em if you got 'em.

They talk about these guys that come back from the Nam all fucked up and shit, and say they be like time bombs: they go along okay for years, then get a gun and just go crazy. But it don't go nothing like that for me. Even though there be the gun involved, this time. And an actual murder, this time.

First time I be in prison, after the court martial, I try to tell them what it be and what they get me? Social workers and shrinks. Guy to be a shrink in a prison ain't be no good shrink, what they can make Outside, is the way I figure it, so at first I don't give them shit, but then I always get Discipline, so I figure what the hell and make up a story. You watch any TV you can make up a Nam story too.

So some of them don't fall for it, they go along with it for a while because this is what crazy people do, is make up stories, then they give up and another one comes along and I start over with a different story. And sometime when I know for sure they don't believe, when they start to look at me like you look at an animal in the zoo, that's when I tell them the real true story. And that's when they smile, you know, and nod and the new guy come in next. Because if anybody would make up a story like that one he'd have to be crazy, right? But I swear to God it's true.

Right. The beginning.

I be a lurp in the Nam, which means Long Range Recon Patrol. You look in these magazines about the Nam and they make like the lurps be always heroes, brave boys go out and face Charlie alone, bring down the artillery on them and all, but it was not like that. You didn't want to be no lurp where we be, they make you be a fuckin lurp if they want to get rid of your ass, and that's the God's truth.

Now I can tell you right now that I don't give a flyin fuck for that U.S. Army and I don't like it even more when I be drafted, but I got to admit they be pretty smart, the way they do with us. Because we get off on that lurp shit. I mean we be one bunch of bad ass brothers and good old boys and we did love that rock an roll, and God they give us rock an roll—fuck your M-16, we get real tommy guns with 100-round drum, usually one guy get your automatic grenade launcher, one guy carry that starlite scope, another guy the full demo bag. I mean we could of taken on the whole fuckin North Vietnam Army. We could of killed fuckin Rambo. Now I like to talk strange, though any time I want, I can talk like other people. Even Jamaican like my mama ain't understand me if I try. I be born in New York City, but at that time my mama be only three months there—when she speak her English it be island music, but the guy she live with, bringing me up, he be from Taiwan, so in between them I learn shitty English, same-same shitty Chinese. And live in Cuban neighborhood, *por el español* shitty.

He was one mean mother fuckin Chinese cab driver, slap shit out of me for twelve year, and then I take a kitchen knife and slap him back. He never come back for the ear. I think maybe he go off someplace and die, I don't give a shit anymore, but when I be drafted they find out I speak Chinese, send me to language school in California, and I be so dumb I believe them when they say this means no Nam for the boy: I stay home and translate for them tapes from the radio.

So they send me to the Nam anyhow, and I go a little wild. I hit everybody that outranks me. They put me in the hospital and I hit the doctor. They put me in the stockade and I hit the guards, the guards hit back, some more hospital. I figure sooner or later they got to kill me or let me out. But then one day this strac dude come in and tell me about the lurp shit. It sound all right, even though the dude say if I fuck up they can waste me and it's legal. By now I know they can do that shit right there in LBJ, Long Binh Jail, so what the fuck? In two days I'm in the jungle with three real bad ass dudes with a map and a compass and enough shit we could start our own war.

They give us these maps that never have no words on them, like names of places, just "TOWN POP. 1000" and shit like that. They play it real cute, like we so dumb we don't know there be places outside of Vietnam, where no GIs can go. They keep all our ID in base camp, even the dog tags, and tell us not to be capture. Die first, they say, that shall be more pleasant. We laugh at that later, but I keep to myself the way I do feel. That the grave be one place we all be getting to, long road or short, and maybe the short road be less bumps, less trouble. Now I know from twenty years how true that be.

They don't tell us where the place be we leave from, after the slick drop us in, but we always sure as hell head west. Guy name Duke, mean honky but not dumb, he say all we be doin is harassment, bustin up supply lines comin down the Ho Chi Minh Trail, in Cambodia. It do look like that, long lines of gooks carryin ammo and shit, sometime on bicycles. We would set up some mine and some Claymores and wait till the middle of the line be there, then pop the shit, then maybe waste a few with the grenade launcher and tommy guns, not too long so they ain't regroup and get us. Duke be taking a couple Polaroids and we go four different ways, meet a couple miles away, then sneak back to the LZ and call the slick. We go out maybe six time a month, maybe lose one guy a month. Me and Duke make it through all the way to the last one, that last one.

That time no different from the other times except they tell us try to blow a bridge up, not a big bridge like the movies, but one that hang off a mountain side, be hard to fix afterward. It also be hard to get to.

We lose one guy, new guy name of Winter, just tryin to get to the fuckin bridge. That be bad in a special kind of way. You get used to guys gettin shot or be wasted by frags and like that. But to fall like a hundred feet onto rocks be a different kind of bad. And it just break his back or something. He laying there and crying, tell all the world where we be, until Duke shut him up.

So it be just Duke and Cherry and me, the Chink. I am for goin back, no fuckin way they could blame us for that. But Duke crazy for action, always be crazy for killing, and Cherry would follow Duke anywhere, I think he a fag even then. Later I do know. When the Monster kill them.

This is where I usually feel the need to change. It's natural to adjust one's mode of discourse to a level appropriate to the subject at hand, is it not? To talk about this "Monster" requires addressing such concepts as disassociation and multiple personality, if only to discount them, and it would be awkward to speak of these things directly the way I normally speak, as Chink. This does not mean that there are two or several personalities resident within the sequestered hide of this disabled black veteran. It only means that I can speak in different ways. You could as well, if you grew up switching back and forth among Spanish, Chinese, and two flavors of English: chocolate and vanilla. It might also help if you had learned various Vietnamese dialects, and then spent the past twenty years in a succession of small rooms, mainly reading and writing. There still be the bad mother fucker in here. He simply uses appropriate language. The right tool for the job, or the right weapon.

Let me save us some time by demonstrating the logical weakness of some facile first-order rationalizations that always seem to come up. One: that this whole Monster business is a bizarre lie I concocted and have stubbornly held on to for twenty years—which requires that it never have occurred to me that recanting it would result in much better treatment and, possibly, release. Two: that the Monster is some sort of psychological shield, or barrier, that I have erected between my "self" and the enormity of the crime I committed. That hardly holds up to inspection, since my job and life at that time comprised little more than a succession of premeditated cold-blooded murders. I didn't kill the two men, but if I had, it wouldn't have bothered me enough to require elaborate psychological defenses. Three: that I murdered Duke and Cherry because I was...upset at discovering them engaged in a homosexual act. I am and was indifferent toward that aberration, or hobby. Growing up in the ghetto and going directly from there to an Army prison in Vietnam, I witnessed perversions for which you psychologists don't even have names.

Then of course there is the matter of the supposed eyewitness. It seemed particularly odious to me at the time that my government would prefer the testimony of an erstwhile enemy soldier over one of its own. I see the process more clearly now, and realize that I was convicted before the court-martial was even convened.

The details? You know what a *hoi chan* was? You're too young. Well, *chieu hoi* is Vietnamese for "open arms"; if an enemy soldier came up to the barbed wire with his hands up, shouting *chieu hoi,* then in theory he would be welcomed into our loving, also open, arms and rehabilitated. Unless he was killed before people could figure out what he was saying. The rehabilitated ones were called *hoi chans,* and sometimes were used as translators and so forth.

Anyhow, this Vietnamese deserter's story was that he had been following us all day, staying out of sight, waiting for an opportunity to surrender. I don't believe that for a second. Nobody moves that quietly, that fast, through unfamiliar jungle. Duke had been a professional hunting guide back in the World, and he would have heard any slightest movement.

What do I say happened? You must have read the transcript.... I see. You want to check me for consistency.

I had sustained a small but deep wound in the calf, a fragment from a rifle grenade, I believe. I did elude capture, but the wound slowed me down.

We had blown the bridge at 1310, which was when the guards broke for lunch, and had agreed to rendezvous by 1430 near a large banyan tree about a mile from the base of the cliff. It was after 1500 when I got there, and I was worried. Winter had been carrying our only radio when he fell, and if I wasn't at the LZ with the other two, they would sensibly enough leave without me. I would be stranded, wounded, lost.

I was relieved to find them still waiting. In this sense I may *have* caused their deaths: if they had gone on, the Monster might have killed only me.

This is the only place where my story and that of the *hoi chan* are the same. They were indeed having sex. I waited under cover rather than interrupt them.

Yes, I know, this is where he testified I jumped them and did all those terrible things. Like *he* had been sitting off to one side, waiting for them to finish their business. What a bunch of bullshit.

What actually happened—what *actually* happened—was that I was hiding there behind some bamboo, waiting for them to finish so we could get on with it, when there was this sudden loud crashing in the woods on the other side of them, and bang. There was the Monster. It was bigger than any man, and black—not black like me, but glossy black, like shiny hair—and it just flat smashed into them, bashed them apart. Then it was on Cherry, I could hear bones crack like sticks. It bit him between the legs, and that was enough for me. I was gone. I heard a couple of short bursts from Duke's tommy gun, but I didn't go back to check it out. Just headed for the LZ as fast as my legs would let me.

So I made a big mistake. I lied. Wouldn't you? I'm supposed to tell them sorry, the rest of the squad got eaten by a werewolf? So while I'm waiting for the helicopter I make up this believable account of what happened at the bridge.

The slick comes and takes me back to the fire base, where the medics dress the wound and I debrief to the major there. They send me to Tuy Hoa, nice hospital on the beach, and I debrief again, to a bunch of captains and a bird colonel. They tell me I'm in for a Silver Star.

So I'm resting up there in the ward, reading a magazine, when in comes a couple of MPs and they grab me and haul me off to the stockade. Isn't that just like the Army, to have a stockade in a hospital?

What has happened is that this gook, honorable *hoi chan* Nguyen Van Trong, has come out of the woodwork with his much more believable story. So I get railroaded and wind up in jail.

Come on now, it's all in the transcript. I'm tired of telling it. It upsets me.

Oh, all right. This Nguyen claims he was a guard at the bridge we blew up, and he'd been wanting to escape—they don't say "desert"—ever since they'd left Hanoi a few months before. Walking down the Ho Chi Minh Trail. So in the confusion after the blast, he runs away; he hears Duke and Cherry and follows them. Waiting for the right opportunity to go *chieu hoi*. I've told you how improbable that actually is.

So he's waiting in the woods while they blow each other and up walks me. I get the drop on them with my Thompson. I make Cherry tie Duke to the tree. Then I tie Cherry up, facing him. Then I castrate Cherry—with my *teeth!* You believe that? And then with my teeth and fingernails, I flay Duke, skin him alive, from the neck down, while he's watching Cherry die. Then for dessert, I bite off his cock too. Then I cut them down and stroll away.

You got that? This Nguyen claims to have watched the whole thing, must have taken hours. Like he never had a chance to interrupt my little show. What, did I hang on to my weapon all the time I was nibbling away? Makes a lot of sense.

After I leave, he say he try to help the two men. Duke, he say, be still alive, but not worth much. Say he follow Duke's gestures and get the Polaroid out of his pack.

When those picture show up at the trial, I be a Had Daddy. Forget that his story ain't makin sense. Forget for Chris' sake that he be the fuckin *enemy!* Picture of Duke be still alive and his guts all hangin out, this godawful look on his face, I could of been fuckin Sister Teresa and they wouldn't of listen to me.

[At this point the respondent was silent for more than a minute, apparently controlling rage, perhaps tears. When he continued speaking, it was with the cultured white man's accent again.]

I know you are constrained not to believe me, but in order to understand what happened over the next few years, you must accept as tentatively true the fantastic premises of my delusional system. Mainly, that's the reasonable assertion that I didn't mutilate my friends, and the unreasonable one that the Cambodian jungle hides at least one glossy black humanoid over seven feet tall, with the disposition of a barracuda.

If you accept that this Monster exists, then where does that leave Mr. Nguyen Van Trong? One possibility is that he saw the same thing I did, and lied for the same reason I initially did—because no one in his right mind would believe the truth—but his lie implicated me, I suppose for verisimilitude.

A second possibility is the creepy one that Nguyen was somehow allied with the Monster; in league with him.

The third possibility…is that they were the same.

If the second or the third were true, it would probably be a good policy for me never to cross tracks with Nguyen again, or at least never to meet him unarmed. From that, it followed that it would be a good precaution for me to find out what had happened to him after the trial.

A maximum-security mental institution is far from an ideal place from which to conduct research. But I had several things going for me. The main thing was that I was not, despite all evidence to the contrary, actually crazy. Another was that I could take advantage of people's preconceptions, which is to say prejudices: I can tune my language from a mildly accented Jamaican dialect to the almost impenetrable patois that I hid behind while I was in the Army. Since white people assume that the smarter you are, the more like them you sound, and since most of my keepers were white, I could control their perception of me pretty well. I was a dumb nigger who with their help was getting a little smarter.

Finally I wangled a work detail in the library. Run by a white lady who thought she was hardass but had a heart of purest tapioca. Loved to see us goof off so long as we were reading.

I was gentle and helpful and appreciative of her guidance. She let me read more and more, and of course I could take books back to my cell. There was no record of many of the books I checked out: computer books.

She was a nice woman but fortunately not free of prejudice. It never occurred to her that it might not be a good idea to leave her pet darky alone with the computer terminal.

Once I could handle the library's computer system, my Nguyen project started in earnest. Information networks are wonderful, and computerized ordering and billing is, for a thief, the best tool since the credit card. I could order any book in print—after all, I opened the boxes, shelved the new volumes, and typed up the catalogue card for each book. If I wanted it to be catalogued.

Trying to find out what the Monster was, I read all I could find about extraterrestrials, werewolves, mutations; all that science fiction garbage. I read up on Southeast Asian religions and folk tales. Psychology books, because Occam's razor can cut the person who's using it, and maybe I *was* crazy after all.

Nothing conclusive came out of any of it. I had seen the Monster for only a couple of seconds, but the quick impression was of course branded on my memory. The face was intelligent, perhaps I should say "sentient," but it was not at all human. Two eyes, okay, but no obvious nose or ears. Mouth too big and lots of teeth like a shark's. Long fingers with too many joints, and claws. No mythology or pathology that I read about produced anything like it.

The other part of my Nguyen project was successful. I used the computer to track him down, through my own court records and various documents that had been declassified through the Freedom of Information Act.

Not surprisingly, he had emigrated to the United States just before the fall of Saigon. By 1986 he had his own fish market in San Francisco. Pillar of the community, the bastard.

Eighteen years of exemplary behavior and I worked my way down to minimum security. It was a more comfortable and freer life, but I didn't see any real chance of parole. I probably couldn't even be paroled if I'd been white and had bitten the cocks off two *black* men. I might get a medal, but not a parole.

So I had to escape. It wasn't hard.

I assumed that they would alert Nguyen, and perhaps watch him or even guard him for a while. So for two years I stayed away from San Francisco, burying myself in a dirt-poor black neighborhood in Washington. I saved my pennies and purchased or contrived the tools I would need when I eventually confronted him.

Finally I boarded a Greyhound, crawled to San Francisco, and rested up a couple of days. Then for another couple of days I kept an intermittent watch on the fish market, to satisfy myself that Nguyen wasn't under guard.

He lived in a two-room apartment in the rear of the store. I popped the back-door lock a half hour before closing and hid in the bedroom. When I heard him lock the front door, I walked in and pointed a .44 Magnum at his face.

That was the most tense moment for me. I more than half-expected him to turn into the Monster. I had even gone to the trouble of casting my own bullets of silver, in case that superstition turned out to be true.

He asked me not to shoot and took out his wallet. Then he recognized me and clammed up.

I made him strip to his shorts and tied him down with duct tape to a wooden chair. I turned the television on fairly loud, since my homemade silencer was not perfect, and traded the Magnum for a .22 automatic. It made about as much noise as a flyswatter each time I shot.

CRUCIFIED DREAMS

There are places where you can shoot a person even with a .22 and he will die quickly and without too much pain. There are other sites that are quite the opposite. Of course I concentrated on those, trying to make him talk. Each time I shot him I dressed the wound, so there would be a minimum of blood loss.

I first shot him during the evening news, and he lasted well into Johnny Carson, with a new bullet each half hour. He never said a word, or cried out. Just stared.

After he died, I waited a few hours, and nothing happened. So I walked to the police station and turned myself in. That's it.

So here we be now. I know it be life for me. Maybe it be that rubber room. I ain't care. This be the only place be safe. The Monster, he know. I can feel. [This is the end of the transcript proper. The respondent did not seem agitated when the guards led him away. Consistent with his final words, he seemed relieved to be back in prison, which makes his subsequent suicide mystifying. The circumstances heighten the mystery, as the attached coroner's note indicates.]

State of California
Department of Corrections
Forensic Pathology Division
Glyn Malin, M.D., Ph.D.—Chief of Research

I have read about suicides that were characterized by sudden hysterical strength, including a man who had apparently choked himself to death by throttling (though I seem to recall that it was a heart attack that actually killed him). The case of Royce "Chink" Jackson is one I would not have believed if I had not seen the body myself.

The body is well muscled, but not unusually so; when I'd heard how he died I assumed he was a mesomorphic weight-lifter type. Bones are hard to break.

Also, his fingernails are cut to the quick. It must have taken a burst of superhuman strength, to tear his own flesh without being able to dig in.

My first specialty was thoracic surgery, so I well know how physically difficult it is to get to the heart. It's hard to believe that a person could tear out his own. It's doubly hard to believe that someone could do it after having brutally castrated himself.

I do have to confirm that that is what happened. The corridor leading to his solitary confinement cell is under constant video surveillance. No one came or went from the time the door was shut behind him until breakfast time, when the body was discovered.

He did it to himself, and in total silence.

GM:wr

THE MOJAVE TWO-STEP
Norman Partridge

THE DESERT, JUST past midnight. A lone truck on a scorched black licorice strip, two men—Anshutes and Coker—inside.

Outside it's one hundred and twenty-five degrees under a fat December moon. Frosty weather in the twilight days of global warming...and just in time for the holiday season.

Sure, driving across the desert was a risk, even in such balmy weather. Not many people owned cars anymore, and those who did avoided the wide white lonesome. Even roadcops were smart enough to leave the Mojave alone. It was too hot and too empty, and it could make you as crazy as a scorpion on a sizzling-hot skillet. If you broke down out here, you ended up cooked to a beautiful golden brown—just like Tiny Tim's Christmas goose.

But that wasn't going to happen to Coker. He was going to spend New Year's Eve in Las Vegas. The town that Frank and Dean and Sammy had built all those years ago was still the place he wanted to be. Hell on earth outside, air-conditioned splendor within. If you had the long green, Vegas gave you everything a growing boy could desire. A/C to the max, frosty martinis... maybe even a woman with blue eyes that sparkled like icebergs.

Let the swells fly into town in air-conditioned jets, Coker figured. He'd take the hard road. The dangerous road. The real gambler's road. He'd ride that scorched highway straight down the thermometer into double digits, and the A/C would frost everything but his dreams. A little business, a couple lucky rolls of the dice, and his life would change for good…then *he'd* leave town with a jet of his own. Slice it up like an Eskimo Pie and that was cool, any way you figured it.

It was all part of the gamble called life. Like always, Lady Luck was rolling the dice. Rattling the bones for Coker and for his partner, too, even though Anshutes would never admit to believing in any airy jazz like that.

Coker believed it. Lady Luck was calling him now. Just up the road in Vegas, she waited for him like a queen. God knew he'd dreamed about her long enough, imagining those iceberg eyes that sparkled like diamonds flashing just for him.

All his life, he'd been waiting for the Lady to give him a sign. Coker knew it was coming soon. Maybe with the next blink of his eyes. Or maybe the one after that.

Yeah. That was the way it was. It had to be.

Really, it was the only explanation.

Check it out. Just two days ago Coker and Anshutes had been on foot. Broiling in Bakersfield with maybe a gallon of water between them, seven bucks, and Anshutes' .357 Magnum…which was down to three shells. But with that .357 they'd managed to steal five hundred and seventy-two bucks, a shotgun, and an ice cream truck tanked with enough juice to get them all the way to Vegas. Plus they still had the Magnum…and those three shells.

Now if that wasn't luck, what was?

One-handing the steering wheel, Coker gave the ice cream truck a little juice. Doing seventy on the straightaway, and the electric engine purred quieter than a kitten. The rig wasn't much more than a pick-up with a refrigeration unit mounted on the back, but it did all right. Coker's only complaint was the lack of air-conditioning. Not that many automobiles had A/C anymore… these days, the licensing fees for luxuries which negatively impacted the sorry remains of the ozone layer cost more than the cars. But why anyone who could afford the major bucks for a freon-licensed vehicle would forgo the pleasure of A/C, Coker didn't know.

The only guy who had the answer was the owner of the ice cream truck. *If* he was still alive…and Coker kind of doubted that he was. Because Anshutes had excavated the poor bastard's bridgework with the butt of his .357 Magnum, emptied the guy's wallet, and left him tied to a telephone pole on the outskirts of Bakersfield. By now, the ice cream man was either cooked like the ubiquitous Xmas goose or in a hospital somewhere sucking milkshakes through a straw.

Coker's left hand rested on the sideview mirror, desert air blasting over his knuckles. Best to forget about the ice cream man. His thoughts returned to the Lady. Like always, those thoughts had a way of sliding over his tongue, no matter how dry it was. Like always, they had a way of parting his chapped lips and finding Anshutes's perennially sunburnt ear.

"Know where I'm heading after Vegas?" Coker asked.

"No," Anshutes said. "But I'm sure you're gonna tell me."

Coker smiled. "There's this place called Lake Louise, see? It's up north, in Canada. Fifty years ago it used to be a ski resort. Now the only skiing they do is on the water. They've got palm trees, papayas and mangoes, and girls with skin the color of cocoa butter. Days it's usually about thirty-five Celsius, which is ninety-five degrees American. Some nights it gets as low as sixty."

Anshutes chuckled. "Sounds like you'll have to buy a coat."

"Go ahead and laugh. I'm talking double-digit degrees, partner. Sixty. *Six-oh*. And girls with skin like cocoa butter. If that's not a big slice of paradise, I don't know what is."

"Get real, amigo. A guy with your record isn't exactly a prime candidate for immigration. And our dollar isn't worth shit up north, anyway."

"Drop some luck into that equation."

"Oh, no. Here we go again—"

"Seriously. I can feel it in my bones. Something big is just ahead, waiting for us. I'm gonna take my cut from the ice cream job and hit the tables. I'm not walking away until I have a million bucks in my pocket."

"Even God isn't that lucky." Anshutes snorted. "And luck had nothing to do with this, anyway. Planning did. And hard work. And a little help from a .357 Magnum."

"So what are you gonna do with your money?" Coker asked sarcastically. "Bury it in the ground?"

"Depends on how much we get."

"The way I figure it, we're looking at something large. Forty grand, maybe fifty."

"Well, maybe thirty." Anshutes gnawed on it a minute, doing some quick calculations. "I figure the Push Ups will go for about fifty a pop. We got five cases of those. The Fudgsicles'll be about sixty-five. Figure seventy-five for the Drumsticks. And the Eskimo Pies—"

"A hundred each, easy," Coker said. "Maybe even a hundred and twenty-five. And don't forget—we've got ten cases."

"You sound pretty sure about the whole thing."

"That's because I believe in luck," Coker said. "Like the song says, she's a lady. And she's smiling on us. Right now. Tonight. And she's gonna keep on smiling for a long, long time."

Coker smiled, too. Screw Anshutes if he wanted to be all sour. "You know what we ought to do?" Coker said. "We ought to pull over and celebrate a little. Have us a couple of Eskimo Pies. Toast Lady Luck, enjoy the moment. Live a little—"

"I've lived a lot," Anshutes said. "And I plan to live a lot longer. I'm not going to play the fool with my money. I'm not going to blow it on some pipe dream. I'm going to play it smart."

"Hey, relax. All I'm saying is—"

"No," Anshutes said, and then he really went verbal. "You've said enough. We're in this to make some real money for a change. And we're not gonna make it by pulling over to the side of the road, and we're not gonna make it by toasting Lady Luck with an Eskimo Pie in the middle of the Mojave Desert, and we're not going to make it by blowing our swag in some casino...."

Anshutes went on like that.

Coker swallowed hard.

He'd had just about enough.

"I'm pulling over," he said. "I'm going to have an Eskimo Pie, and you're goddamn well going to have one with me if you know what's good for you."

"The hell I am!" Anshutes yanked his pistol. "You goddamn fool! You take your foot off the brake right now or I'll—"

Suddenly, Anshutes' complaints caught in his throat like a chicken bone. Ahead on the road, Coker saw the cause of his partner's distress. Beneath the ripe moon, knee-deep in heat waves that shimmered up from the asphalt, a big man wearing a ten-gallon cowboy hat walked the yellow center line of the highway. He only had one arm, and he was carrying a woman piggyback—her arms wrapped around his neck, her long slim legs scissored around his waist. But the woman wasn't slowing the big guy down. His pace was brisk, and it was one hundred and twenty-five degrees and the rangy bastard didn't even look like he'd broken a sweat—

Coker honked the horn, but the cowboy didn't seem to notice.

"Don't hit him!" Anshutes yelled. "You'll wreck the truck!"

Anshutes closed his eyes as Coker hit the brakes. Tires screamed as the ice cream truck veered right and bounded along the shoulder of the road. Gravel rattled in the wheel wells and slapped against the undercarriage like gunfire, and Coker downshifted from fourth gear to third, from third to second, ice cream visions dancing in his head, visions of Drumsticks and Push Ups bashing around in the refrigeration unit, visions of broken Fudgsicles and mashed Eskimo Pies...

Visions of Lady Luck turning her back....

The electric engine whined as he shifted from second to first and yanked the emergency brake. The truck seized up like a gutshot horse, and the only thing that prevented Coker from doing a header through the windshield was his seat belt.

Coker unbuckled his belt. Anshutes set his pistol on the seat and fumbled with his seat belt. Coker grabbed the .357 and was out of the cab before his partner could complain.

The hot asphalt was like sponge cake beneath Coker's boots as he hurried after the man in the ten-gallon hat. The cowboy didn't turn. Neither did the woman who rode him. In fact, the woman didn't move at all, and as Coker got closer he noticed a rope around her back. She was tied to the cowboy. Coker figured she was dead.

That was bad news. Two strangers. One alive, one dead. Snake eyes. A jinxed roll if ever he saw one.

Bad enough that the cowboy had nearly killed him. But if he'd put the jinx on Coker's luck—

Coker aimed at the ripe moon and busted a round. "Turn around, cowboy," he yelled. "Unless you want it in the back."

The cowboy turned double-quick, like some marching band marionette. The one-armed man's face was lost under the brim of his ten-gallon hat, but moonlight splashed across his torso and gleamed against his right hand.

Which was wrapped around a pistol.

"Shit!" Coker spit the word fast and fired another shot. The bullet caught the cowboy in the chest, but the big man didn't even stumble. He didn't return fire, either...and Coker wasn't going to give him the chance.

Coker fired again, dead center, and this time the bullet made a sound like a marble rattling around in a tin can.

The cowboy's chest lit up. Neon rattlesnakes slithered across it. Golden broncos bucked over his bulging pecs. Glowing Gila monsters hissed and spread their jaws.

Three broncos galloped into place.

The cowboy's chest sprung open like the batwing doors on an old-fashioned saloon.

Silver dollars rained down on the highway.

And the cowboy kept on coming. Coker couldn't even move now. Couldn't breathe. Oh man, this wasn't a jinx after all. This was the moment he'd been waiting for. This was the omen to end all omens. All of it happening in the blink of an eye.

One more blink and he'd see things clearly. One more blink and the future would turn up like a Blackjack dealt for high stakes.

But Coker couldn't blink. He couldn't even move—

Anshutes could. He stepped past his partner, scooped up a silver dollar as it rolled along the highway's center line. The cowboy kept on coming, heading for Anshutes now, but Anshutes didn't twitch. He waited until the big man was within spitting distance, and then he slipped the coin between the determined line of the advancing cowboy's lips.

Immediately, the cowboy's gunhand swept in an upward arc.

Then he stopped cold.

Anshutes scooped a handful of silver dollars off the road and tossed them at Coker.

"Guess you've never heard of a one-armed bandit," he said.

Coker's jaw dropped. Anshutes sighed. Christ, being partnered up with this starry-eyed fool was something else.

"The cowboy here's a robot," Anshutes explained. "Comes from a casino called Johnny Ringo's, named after the gangster who owns the place. Ringo himself came up with the concept for an ambulating slot machine, hired some ex–Disney Imagineers to design the things. They walk around his joint twenty-four hours a day. You'd be surprised how many idiots feed dollars into them. I guess they all think they're lucky...just like you."

"This thing's a *robot*?" Coker asked.

"That's what I said."

"Why'd it stop moving?"

"'Cause I fed it a dollar, genius." Anshutes pointed at the machine's lone arm, which was raised in the air. "The Cogwheel Kid here can't do anything until I make my play. I have to pull his arm to set him in motion again. Then those neon wheels will spin, and either he'll cough up some dough or start walking, looking for another mark. Unless, of course, your bullets dug a hole in his motherboard, in which case who knows what the hell he'll do."

Coker blinked several times but said nothing. To Anshutes, he looked like some stupid fish that had just figured out it lived in a tank. Blink-blink-blinking, checking out the big bad pet shop world that lurked beyond the glass.

"It's an omen," Coker said finally. "A sign—"

"Uh-uh, buddy. It's called the Mojave Two-Step."

"The Mojave what?"

"The Mojave Two-Step." Anshutes sighed. "Here's what happened. This little lady crossed Johnny Ringo. Who knows what the hell she did, but it was bad enough that he wanted to kill her good and slow. So he tied her to one of his walking slots, and he pointed the damn thing west and turned it loose. It's happened before. Just a couple months ago, one of these things trudged into Barstow with a dead midget tied to its back. Leastways, folks thought it was a midget. A couple weeks under the Mojave sun is liable to shrink anyone down to size."

"Jesus!" Coker said. "How does Ringo get away with it?"

"He's rich, idiot. And that means you don't mess with him, or anything to do with him or he'll kill you the same way he killed this girl—"

Right on cue, the girl groaned. Annoyed, Anshutes grabbed her chin and got a look at her. Blue eyes, cold as glaciers. Surprisingly, she wasn't even sunburned.

Anshutes huffed another sigh. There wasn't any mystery to it, really. They weren't that far from Vegas. Twenty, maybe thirty miles. Could be that Ringo had turned the robot loose after dark, that the girl hadn't even been in the sun yet. Of course, if that was the case it would make sense to assume that the robot had followed the highway, taking the most direct route. Anshutes didn't know what kind of directional devices Ringo had built into his walking slots, but he supposed it was possible. There wasn't anything between Vegas and Barstow. Nobody traveled the desert highway unless they absolutely had to. Even if the robot stuck to the road, it was an odds-on cinch that the girl would wind up dead before she encountered another human being.

The girl glanced at Anshutes, and it was like that one glance told her exactly what kind of guy he was. So she turned her gaze on Coker. "Help me," she whispered.

"This is too weird," Coker said. "A woman riding a slot machine...a slot machine that paid off on the road to Vegas. It *is* an omen. Or a miracle! Like Lady Luck come to life...like Lady Luck *in the flesh*—"

"Like Lady *Luck personified.*" Anshutes dropped a hand on his partner's shoulder. "Now you listen to me, boy—what we've got here is a little Vegas whore riding a walking scrap heap. She doesn't have anything to do with luck, and she isn't our business. *Our* business is over there in that truck. *Our* business is a load of ice cream. *Our* business is getting that ice cream to Vegas before it melts."

Coker's eyes flashed angrily, and Anshutes nearly laughed. Seeing his partner go badass was like watching a goldfish imitate a shark.

"You'd better back down, boy," Anshutes warned.

Coker ignored him. He untied the young woman's wrists and feet. He pulled her off of the Cogwheel Kid's back and cradled her in his arms, and then he started toward the ice cream truck.

Anshutes cleared his throat. "Where do you think you're going?"

"Even if she's not Lady Luck, this lady's hurting," Coker said. "I think she deserves an ice cream. Hell, maybe she deserves two. Maybe I'll let her eat her fill."

Anshutes didn't answer.

Not with words, anyway.

He raised the sawed-off shotgun he'd stolen from the ice cream man, and he cocked both barrels.

Coker said, "You think you're pretty cool, don't you?"

"Cooler than Santa's ass," Anshutes said.

"And you'll shoot me if I give the lady an ice cream?"

"Only way she gets any ice cream is if she pays for it."

Coker turned around. "How about if I pay for it?"

"I don't care who pays. You, the little whore, Lady Luck or Jesus Christ. As long as I get the money."

"That's fine." Coker smiled. "You'll find your money on the road, asshole."

"What?"

"The jackpot. The money I shot out of the slot machine. It's all yours."

"You're crazy."

"Maybe. But I'm gonna buy me a shitload of ice cream, and this little lady's gonna eat it."

Coker set the girl down at the side of the road, peeling off his shirt and rolling it into a pillow for her head. Then he walked over to the truck and opened the refrigerated compartment.

"No Eskimo Pies," Anshutes said. "Let's get that straight."

"I'm getting what I paid for," Coker said.

Anshutes shook his head. What a moron. Ponying up fistfuls of silver dollars, just so some little Vegas whore could lick a Push Up. If that was the way Coker wanted it, that was fine. In the meantime, Anshutes would make himself some money, and Lady Luck wouldn't have jack to do with it. Hell, for once hard work wouldn't have jack to do with it either. For once, all Anshutes had to do to make some money was bend over and pick it up.

Silver dollars gleamed in the moonlight. Anshutes put down the shotgun. Not that he was taking any chances—he made sure that the weapon was within reach as he got down to work, filling his pockets with coins.

Behind him, he heard the sound of the refrigerator compartment door slamming closed. Coker. Jesus, what an idiot. Believing that some Vegas slut was Lady Luck. *Personified.*

Anshutes had told the kid a thousand times that luck was an illusion. Now he realized that he could have explained it a million times, and he still wouldn't have made a dent. The kid might as well be deaf. He just wouldn't listen—

Anshutes listened. He heard everything.

The sound of silver dollars jingling in his pocket, like the sound of happiness.

But wait…there was another sound, too.

A quiet hum, hardly audible.

The sound of an electric engine accelerating.

Anshutes turned around fast, dropping coins on the roadway. The ice cream truck was coming fast. The shotgun was right there on the double yellow line. He made a grab for it.

Before he touched the gun, the ice cream truck's bumper cracked his skull like a hard-boiled egg.

Kim felt better now.

A couple Eskimo Pies could do that for a girl.

"Want another?" the guy asked.

"Sure," Kim said. "I could probably eat a whole box."

"I guess it's like they say: a walk in the desert does wonders for the appetite."

The guy smiled and walked over to the ice cream truck. She watched him. He was kind of cute. Not as cute as Johnny Ringo, of course, but Johnny definitely had his downside.

She sat in the dirt and finished her third pie. You had to eat the suckers fast or else they'd melt right in your hand. It was funny—she'd left Vegas worse than flat broke, owing Johnny twenty grand, and now she had three hundred bucks worth of ice cream in her belly. Things were looking up. She kind of felt like a safe-deposit box on legs. Kind of a funny feeling. Kind of like she didn't know whether she should laugh or cry.

The guy handed her another Eskimo Pie. "Thanks—" she said, and she said it with a blank that he was sure to fill in.

"Coker," he said. "My first name's Dennis, but I don't like it much."

"It's a nice name," Kim said. Which was a lie, but there was no sense hurting the poor guy's feelings. "Thanks, Dennis."

"My pleasure. You've had a hell of a hard time."

She smiled. Yeah. That was one way of putting it.

"So you're heading for Vegas," she said.

Coker nodded. "Me and my buddy…well, we ended up with this truckload of ice cream. We wanted a place where we could sell it without much trouble from the law."

"Vegas is definitely the place."

"You lived there awhile?"

She smiled. She guessed you could call what she'd done in Vegas living. If you were imaginative enough.

"Kim?" he prodded. "You okay?"

"Yeah," she said. Man, it was tough. She should have been happy…because the guy had saved her life. She should have been sad…because Johnny Ringo had tried to kill her. But she couldn't seem to hold on to any one emotion.

She had to get a grip.

"You ever been to Vegas?" she asked.

"No," the guy said. "Going there was my partner's idea."

"It's a tough place."

"I don't care how tough it is." He laughed. "As long as it's the kind of place you can sell an ice cream bar for a hundred bucks, I'm there."

She nodded. Ice cream was worth a lot in Vegas.

But other things came pretty cheap.

"It's a rich town," she said, because saying that was really like saying nothing. "It's full of rich men and women. I read somewhere that the entire budget for law enforcement in the United States is about a third of what it costs to power Vegas' air-conditioners for a month."

"Wow. That's amazing."

"Not really. Vegas is a desert. It's an empty place. Everything that's there, someone put it there. Only the rich can afford a place like that. They come and go as they please, jetting in and out in their fancy planes. Everybody else—they're pretty much stuck there. That's what happened to me. I was a dancer. I made pretty good money that way. But every dime I made was already spent on my apartment, or A/C, or water or food. I kept waiting for my lucky break, but it never came. I just couldn't get ahead. Before I knew it, I got behind. And then I got in trouble with my boss—"

"Johnny Ringo?"

"You know about him?"

Coker nodded at the one-armed bandit. "I've heard of the Mojave Two-Step."

Kim swallowed hard. "You never want to dance that one," she said. "I'm here to tell you."

The guy looked down at the road, kind of embarrassed. Like he wanted to know her story, but was too shy to ask for the details.

"Well, maybe your luck's due to change," he said. "It happened to me. Or it's going to happen. It's like I can see it coming."

"Like a dream?"

"Or an omen."

Kim smiled. "I like that word."

"Me too. It's kind of like a dream, only stronger."

"I used to have this dream," Kim said. "When I first came to Vegas. That I was going to hit it big. That I'd live in a penthouse suite with the A/C set at sixty-eight degrees. That the sun would never touch my skin and I'd be white as a pearl."

The guy didn't say anything. Still shy. Kim had forgotten about that particular emotion. She hadn't run across it much in the last few years. Not with Johnny Ringo, and not with any of his friends. Not even with the two-legged slots that followed her around the casino night after night until she fed them dollars just so they'd leave her alone.

In Vegas, everyone wanted something. At least the walking slots came a lot cheaper than their flesh-and-blood counterparts.

Funny. She didn't feel good about it, but she didn't exactly feel bad, either.

That's just the way it was in Vegas.

It was a rich man's town.

Or a rich woman's.

Kim finished her Eskimo Pie. She liked what the guy (what was his name again?) had said about omens. That they were dreams only stronger.

She stared at the ice cream truck.

She thought: It's not often you get a second chance.

"You want another?" the guy asked.

She laughed. "Just one more?"

Of course, he thought she was talking about an Eskimo Pie, when that really wasn't what she wanted at all.

He went after the ice cream. She watched him go.

Past the dead guy on the highway.

Past the second chance that lay there on the yellow line.

Kim really didn't have a choice.

She had to pick it up.

She heard the freezer door close. Watched the guy (*Dennis,* that was his name) step from behind the truck.

He was all right about it. He kind of smiled when he saw the shotgun in her hands, like he already understood.

"I'm sorry, Dennis," she said. "But dreams die hard. Especially strong ones."

"Yeah," he said. "Yeah."

Coker stood in the middle of the road, eating an Eskimo Pie, listening to "Pop Goes the Weasel."

The ice cream truck was gone from view, but he could still hear its little song. That meant she was up ahead somewhere, playing the tape.

Maybe she was playing it for him. The music drifted through the night like a sweet connection. Coker listened to the song while he finished his Eskimo Pie. Anshutes couldn't stand the music the truck made. He wouldn't let Coker play it at all.

Well, Anshutes didn't have a say in anything anymore. Coker stared at his ex-partner. The big man lay dead on the highway, like roadkill of old, his pockets stuffed with silver dollars.

Coker turned them out, filling his own pockets with the coins. Then he walked over to the one-armed bandit.

The Cogwheel Kid was primed for action—Anshutes's coin between his lips, his lone robotic arm held high in the air. Coker pulled the slot machine's arm. Ribbons of neon danced across the one-armed bandit's chest. Bucking broncos, charging buffaloes, jackalopes that laughed in the desert night.

After a while, the neon locked up.

Two tittering jackalopes with a snorting buffalo between them.

Hardly a jackpot.

Coker smiled as the neon flickered out. Losing wasn't a big surprise, really. After all, Lady Luck was gone. She was up ahead, driving an ice cream truck, heading for the land of dreams.

The Cogwheel Kid started walking. He headed east, toward Vegas, looking for another mark.

Coker jumped on the robot's back and held on tight.

He smiled, remembering the look of her frosty blue eyes. Lady Luck with a shotgun. He should have hated her. But he was surprised to find that he couldn't do that.

She was chasing a dream, the same way he was.

He couldn't help hoping she'd catch it.

The same way he hoped he'd catch her.

If he was lucky.

FRONT MAN
David Morrell

"TELL ME THAT again," I said. "He must have been joking."

"Mort, you know what it's like at the networks these days." My agent sighed. "Cost cutting. Layoffs. Executives so young they think *Seinfeld* is nostalgia. He wasn't joking. He's willing to take a meeting with you, but he's barely seen your work, and he wants a list of your credits."

"All *two hundred and ninety* of them? Steve, I like to think I'm not vain, but how can this guy be in charge of series development and not know what I've written?"

This conversation was on the phone. Mid-week, mid-afternoon. I'd been revising computer printouts of what I'd written in the morning, but frustration at what Steve had told me made me press my pencil down so hard I broke its tip. Rising from my desk, I clutched the phone tighter.

Steve hesitated before he replied. "No argument. You and I know how much you contributed to television. The Golden Age. *Playhouse 90. Kraft Theater. Alcoa Presents.* You and Rod Serling and Paddy Chayefsky practically invented TV drama. But that was then. This executive just started his job three months ago. He's only twenty-eight, for Christ's sake. He's been clawing his way to network power since he graduated from business school. He doesn't actually *watch* television. He's too damned busy to watch it, except for current in-house projects. What he does is program, check the ratings, and read the trades. If you'd won your Emmys for something this season, he might be impressed. But *The Sidewalks of New York*? That's something they show on Nickelodeon cable reruns, a company he doesn't work for, so what does he care?"

I stared out my study window. From my home on top of the Hollywood Hills, I had a view of rushing traffic on smoggy Sunset Boulevard, of Spago, Tower Records, and Chateau Marmont. But at the moment, I saw none of them, indignation blinding me.

"Steve, am I nuts, or are the scripts I sent you good?"

"Don't put yourself down. They're better than good. They don't only grab me. They're fucking smart. I *believe* them, and I can't say that for...." He named a current hit series about a female detective that made him a fortune in commissions but was two-thirds tits and ass and one-third car chases.

"So what's the real problem?" I asked, unable to suppress the stridency in my voice. "Why can't I get any work?"

"The truth?"

"Since when did I tolerate lies?"

"You won't get pissed off?"

"I *will* get pissed off if—"

"All right already. The truth is, it doesn't matter how well you write. The fact is, you're too old. The networks think you're out of touch with their demographics."

"*Out of*—"

"You promised you wouldn't get pissed off."

"But after I shifted from television, I won an Oscar for *The Dead of Noon*."

"Twenty years ago. To the networks, that's like the Dark Ages. You know the axiom—what have you done for us lately? The fact is, Mort, for the past two years, you've been out of town, out of the country, out of the goddamn *industry*."

My tear ducts ached. My hurried breathing made me dizzy. "I had a good reason. The most important reason."

"Absolutely," Steve said. "In your place, I'd have done the same. And your friends respect that reason. But the movers and shakers, the new regime that doesn't give a shit about tradition, *they* think you died or retired, if they give you a moment's thought at all. *Then* isn't *now*. To them, last week's ratings are ancient history. What's next? they want to know. What's new? they keep asking. What they really mean is, What's *young?*"

"That sucks."

"Of course. But young viewers are loose with their dough, my friend, and advertisers pay the bills. So the bottom line is, the networks feel unless you're under thirty-five or better yet under *thirty*, you can't communicate with their target audience. It's an uphill grind for writers like you, of a certain age, no matter your talent."

"Swell." My knuckles ached as I squeezed the phone. "So what do I do? Throw my word processor out the window, and collect on my Writers Guild pension?"

"It's not as bad as that. But bear in mind, your pension is the highest any Guild member ever accumulated."

"But if I retire, I'll die like—"

"No, what I'm saying is be patient with this network kid. He needs a little educating. Politely, you understand. Just pitch your idea, look confident and dependable, show him your credits. He'll come around. It's not as if you haven't been down this path before."

"When I was in my twenties."

"There you go. You identify with this kid already. You're in his mind."

My voice dropped. "When's the meeting?"

"Friday. His office. I pulled in some favors to get you in so soon. Four p.m. I'll be at my house in Malibu. Call me when you're through."

"Steve...."

"Yeah, Mort?"

"Thanks for sticking with me."

"Hey, it's an honor. To me, you're a legend."

"What I need to be is a *working* legend."

"I've done what I can. Now it's up to you."

"Sure." I set down the phone, discovered I still had my broken pencil in one hand, dropped it, and massaged the aching knuckles of my other hand.

The reason I'd left L.A. two years ago, at the age of sixty-eight, was that my dear wife—

—Doris—

—my best friend—

—my cleverest editor—

—my exclusive lover—

—had contracted a rare form of leukemia.

As her strength had waned, as her sacred body had gradually failed to obey her splendid mind, I'd disrupted my workaholic's habit of writing every day and acted as her constant attendant. We'd traveled to every major cancer research center in the United States. We'd gone to specialists in Europe. We'd stayed in Europe because their hospice system is humane about pain-relieving drugs. We'd gotten as far as Sweden.

Where Doris had died.

And now struggling with grief, I'd returned to my career. What other meaning did I have? It was either kill myself or write. So I wrote. And wrote. Even faster than in my prime when I'd contributed every episode in the four-year run of *The Sidewalks of New York*.

And now a network yuppie bastard with the cultural memory of a four-year-old had asked for my credits. Before I gulped a stiff shot of Scotch, I vowed I'd show this town that *this* old fuck still had more juice than when I'd first started.

Century City. Every week, you see those monoliths of power behind the credits on this season's hit lawyer show, but I remembered, bitterly nostalgic, when the land those skyscrapers stood upon had been the back lot for Twentieth Century-Fox.

I parked my leased Audi on the second level of an underground garage and took an elevator to the seventeenth floor of one of the buildings. The network's reception room was wide and lofty, with plentiful leather couches where actors, writers, and producers made hurried phone calls to agents and assistants while they waited to be admitted to the Holy of Holies.

I stopped before a young, attractive woman at a desk. Thin. No bra. Presumably she wanted to be an actress and was biding her time, waiting for the right connections. She finished talking to one of three phones and studied me, her boredom tempered by the fear that, if she wasn't respectful, she might lose a chance to make an important contact.

I'm not bad-looking. Although seventy, I keep in shape. Sure, my hair's receding. I have wrinkles around my eyes. But my family's genes are spectacular. I look ten years younger than I am, especially when I'm tanned, as I was after recent, daily, half-hour laps in my swimming pool.

My voice has the resonance of Ed McMahon. "Mort Davidson to see Arthur Lewis. I've got a four o'clock appointment."

The would-be-actress receptionist scanned a list. "Of course. You're expected. Unfortunately Mr. Lewis has been detained. If you'll please wait over there." She pointed toward a couch and picked up a Judith Krantz novel. Evidently she'd decided that I couldn't promote her career.

So I waited.

And waited.

An hour later, the receptionist gestured for me to come over. Miracle of miracles, Arthur Lewis was ready to see me.

He wore an Armani linen suit, fashionably wrinkled. No tie. Gucci loafers. No socks. His skin was the color of bronze. His thick, curly, black hair had a calculated, wind-blown look. Photographs of his blonde wife and infant daughter stood on his glass-topped desk. His wife seemed even younger and thinner than he was. Posters of various current hit series hung on the wall. A tennis racket was propped in a corner.

"It's an honor to meet you. I'm a fan of everything you've done," he lied.

I made an appropriate humble comment.

His next remark contradicted what he'd just said. "Did you bring a list of your credits?"

I gave him a folder and sat on a leather chair across from him while he flipped through the pages. His expression communicated a mixture of boredom and stoic endurance.

Finally his eyebrows narrowed. "Impressive. I might add, astonishing. Really, it's hard to imagine anyone writing this much."

"Well, I've been in the business quite a while."

"Yes. You certainly have."

I couldn't tell if he referred to my age or my numerous credits. "There used to be a joke," I said.

"Oh?" His eyes were expressionless.

"'How can Mort Davidson be so prolific?' This was back in the early sixties. The answer was, 'He uses an electric typewriter.'"

"Very amusing," he said as if I'd farted.

"These days, of course, I use a word processor."

"Of course." He folded his hands on the desk and sat straighter. "So. Your agent said you had an idea that might appeal to us."

"That's right."

The phone rang.

"Excuse me a moment." He picked up the phone. Obviously, if he'd been genuinely interested in my pitch, he'd have instructed his secretary that he didn't want any calls.

An actor named Sid was important enough for Arthur Lewis to gush with compliments. And by all means, Sid shouldn't worry about the rewrites that would make his character more "with it" in today's generation. The writer in charge of the project was under orders to deliver the changes by Monday morning. If he didn't, that writer would never again work on something called *The Goodtime Guys*. Sid was a helluva talent, Arthur Lewis assured him. Next week's episode would get a 35 ratings share at least. Arthur chuckled at a joke, set down the phone, and narrowed his eyebrows again. "So your idea that you think we might like." He glanced at his Rolex.

"It's about an at-risk youth center, a place where troubled kids can go and get away from their screwed-up families, the gangs, and the drug dealers on the streets. There's a center in the Valley that I see as our model—an old Victorian house that has several additions. Each week, we'd deal with a special problem—teenage pregnancy, substance abuse, runaways—but mostly this would be a series about emotions, about people, the kids, but also the staff, a wide range of interesting, committed professionals, an elderly administrator, a female social worker, an Hispanic who used to be in the gangs, a priest, whatever mix works. I call it—"

The phone rang again.

"Just a second," Arthur Lewis said.

Another grin. A producer this time. A series about a college sorority next to a fraternity, *Crazy 4 U*, had just become this season's new hit. Arthur Lewis was giving its cast and executives a party at Le Dome tomorrow evening. Yes, he guaranteed. Ten cases of Dom Perignon would arrive at the producer's home before the party. And beluga caviar? Enough for an after-party power party? No problem. And yes, Arthur Lewis was having the same frustrations as the producer. It was mighty damned hard to find a preschool for gifted children.

He set down the phone. His face turned to stone. "So that's your idea?"

"Drama, significance, emotion, action, and realism."

"But what's the hook?"

I shook my head in astonishment.

"Why would anyone want to watch it?" Arthur Lewis asked.

"To feel what it's like to help kids in trouble, to *understand* those kids."

"Didn't you have a stroke a while ago?"

"*What?*"

"I believe in honesty, so I'll be direct. You put in your time. You paid your dues. So why don't you back away gracefully?"

"I *didn't* have a stroke."

"Then why did I hear—?"

"My wife had cancer. She died...." I caught my breath. "Six months ago."

"I see. I'm sorry. I mean that sincerely. But television isn't the same as when you created...." He checked my list of credits. "*The Sidewalks of New York*. A definite classic. One of my absolute personal favorites. But times have changed. The industry's a lot more competitive. The pressure's unbelievable. A series creator has to act as one of the producers, to oversee the product, to guarantee consistency. I'm talking thirteen hours a day minimum, and ideally the creator ought to contribute something to every script."

"That's what I did on *The Sidewalks of New York*."

"Oh?" Arthur Lewis looked blank. "I guess I didn't notice that in your credits." He straightened. "But my point's the same. Television's a pressure cooker. A game for people with energy."

"Did I need a wheelchair when I came in here?"

"You've lost me."

"Energy's not my problem. I'm full to bursting with the need to work. What matters is, what do you think of my idea?"

"It's...."

The phone rang.

Arthur Lewis looked relieved. "Let me get back to you."

"Of course. I know you're busy. Thanks for your time."

"Hey, *any*time. I'm always here and ready for new ideas." Again he checked his Rolex.

The phone kept ringing.

"Take care," he said.

"You, too."

I took my list of credits off his desk.

The last thing I heard when I left was, "No, that old fuck's wrong for the part. He's losing his hair. A rug? Get real. The audience can tell the difference. For God's sake, a hairpiece is death in the ratings."

Steve had said to phone him when the meeting was over. But I felt so upset I decided to hell with phoning him and drove up the Pacific Coast Highway toward his place in Malibu. Traffic was terrible—rush hour, Friday evening. For once, though, it had an advantage. After an hour, my anger began to abate enough for me to realize that I wouldn't accomplish much by showing up unexpectedly in a fit at Steve's. He'd been loyal. He didn't need my aggravation. As he'd told me, "I've done what I can. Now it's up to you." But there wasn't much I *could* do if my age and not my talent was how I was judged. Certainly that wasn't Steve's fault.

So I stopped at something called the Pacific Coast Diner and took the advice of a bumper sticker on a car I'd been stuck behind—CHILL OUT. Maybe a few drinks and a meditative dinner would calm me down. The restaurant had umbrella-topped tables on a balcony that looked toward the ocean. I had to wait a half hour, but a Scotch and soda made the time go quickly, and the crimson reflection of the setting sun on the ocean was spectacular.

Or would have been if I'd been paying attention. The truth was, I couldn't stop being upset. I had another Scotch and soda, ordered poached salmon, tried to enjoy my meal, and suddenly couldn't swallow, suddenly felt about as lonely as I'd felt since Doris had died. Maybe the network executives are right, I thought. Maybe I *am* too old. Maybe I *don't* know how to relate to a young audience. Maybe it's time I packed it in.

"Mort Davidson," a voice said.

"Excuse me?" I blinked, distracted from my thoughts.

My waiter was holding the credit card I'd given him. "Mort Davidson." He looked at the name on the card, then at me. "The screenwriter?"

I spared him a bitter "used to be" and nodded with what I hoped was a pleasant manner.

"Wow." He was tall and thin with sandy hair and a glowing tan. His blue eyes glinted. He had the sort of chiseled, handsome face that made me think he was yet another would-be actor. He looked to be about twenty-three. "When I saw your name, I thought, 'No, it couldn't be. Who knows how many Mort Davidsons there are? The odds against this being....' But it *is* you. The screenwriter."

"Guilty," I managed to joke.

"I bet I've seen everything you ever wrote. I must have watched *The Dead of Noon* twenty-five times. I really learned a lot."

"Oh?" I was puzzled. What would my screenplay have taught him about acting?

"About structure. About pace. About not being afraid to let the characters talk. That's what's wrong with movies today. The characters don't have anything important to say."

At once, it hit me. He wasn't a would-be actor.

"I'm a writer," he said. "Or trying to be. I mean, I've still got a lot to learn. That I'm working here proves it." The glint went out of his eyes. "I still haven't sold anything." His enthusiasm was forced. "But hey, nothing important is easy. I'll just keep writing until I crack the market. The boss is...I'd better not keep chattering at you. He doesn't like it. For sure, you've got better things to do than listen to me. I just wanted to say how much I like your work, Mr. Davidson. I'll bring your credit card right back. It's a pleasure to meet you."

As he left, it struck me that the speed with which he talked suggested not only energy but insecurity. For all his good looks, he felt like a loser.

Or maybe I was just transferring my own emotions onto him. This much was definite—getting a compliment was a hell of a lot better than a sharp stick in the eye or the meeting I'd endured.

When he came back with my credit card, I signed the bill and gave him a generous tip.

"Thanks, Mr. Davidson."

"Hang in there. You've got one important thing on your side."

"What's that?"

"You're young. You've got plenty of time to make it."

"Unless...."

I wondered what he meant.

"Unless I don't have what it takes."

"Well, the best advice I can give you is never doubt yourself."

As I left the restaurant and passed beneath hissing arc lamps toward my car, I couldn't ignore the irony. The waiter had youth but doubted his ability. I had confidence in my ability but was penalized because of my age. Despite the roar of traffic on the Pacific Coast Highway, I heard waves on the beach.

And that's when the notion came to me. A practical joke of sorts, like stories you hear about frustrated writers submitting Oscar-winning screenplays, *Casablanca*, for example, but the frustrated writers change the title and the characters' names. The notes they get back from producers as much as say that the screenplays are the lousiest junk the producers ever read. So then the frustrated writers tell the trade papers what they've done, the point being that the writers are trying to prove it doesn't matter *how* good a writer you are if you don't have connections.

Why not? I thought. It would be worth seeing the look on those bastards' faces.

"What's your name?"

"Ric Potter."

"Short for Richard?"

"No. For Eric."

I nodded. Breaking-the-ice conversation. "The reason I came back is I have something I want to discuss with you, a way that might help your career."

His eyes brightened.

At once, they darkened, as if he thought I might be trying to pick him up.

"Strictly business," I said. "Here's my card. If you want to talk about writing and how to make some money, give me a call."

His suspicion persisted, but his curiosity was stronger. "What time?"

"Eleven tomorrow?"

"Fine. That's before my shift starts."

"Come over. Bring some of your scripts."

That was important. I had to find out if he could write or if he was fooling himself. My scheme wouldn't work unless he had a basic feel for the business. So the next morning, when he arrived exactly on time at my home in the hills above West Hollywood, we swapped: I let him see a script I'd just finished while I sat by the pool and read one of his. I finished around one o'clock. "Hungry?"

"Starved. Your script is wonderful," Ric said. "I can't get over the pace. The sense of reality. It didn't feel like a story."

"Thanks." I took some tuna salad and Perrier from the refrigerator. "Whole-wheat bread and kosher dills okay? Or maybe you'd rather go to a restaurant."

"After working in one every night?" Ric laughed.

But I could tell that he was marking time, that he was frustrated and anxious to know what I thought of his script. I remembered how I had felt at his age, the insecurity when someone important was reading my work. I got to the point.

"I like your story," I said.

He exhaled.

"But I don't think it's executed properly."

His cheek muscles tensed.

"Given what they're paying A-list actors these days, you have to get the main character on screen as quickly as possible. *Your* main character doesn't show up until page fifteen."

He sounded embarrassed. "I couldn't figure out a way to...."

"And the romantic element is so familiar it's tiresome. A shower scene comes from a washed-up imagination."

That was tough, I knew, but I waited to see how he'd take it. If he turned out to be the sensitive type, I wasn't going to get anywhere.

"Yeah. Okay. Maybe I did rely on a lot of other movies I'd seen."

His response encouraged me. "The humorous elements don't work. I don't think comedy is your thing."

He squinted.

"The ending has no focus," I continued. "Was your main character right or not? Simply leaving the dilemma up in the air is going to piss off your audience."

He studied me. "You said you liked the story."

"Right. I did."

"Then why do I feel like I'm on the *Titanic*?"

"Because you've got a lot of craft to learn, and it's going to take you quite a while to master it. If you ever do. There aren't any guarantees. The average Guild member earns less than six thousand dollars a year. Writing screenplays is one of the most competitive enterprises in the world. But I think I can help you."

"...Why?"

"Excuse me?"

"We met just last night. I was your waiter, for God's sake. Now suddenly I'm in your house, having lunch with you, and you're saying you want to help me. It can't be because of the force of my personality. You want something."

"Yes, but not what you're thinking. I told you last night—this is strictly business. Sit down and eat while I tell you how we can both make some money."

"This is Ric Potter," I said. We were at a reception in one of those mansions in the hills near the Hollywood Bowl. Sunset. A string quartet. Champagne. Plenty of movers and shakers. "Fox is very hot on one of his scripts. I think it'll go for a million."

The man to whom I'd introduced Ric was an executive at Warners. He couldn't have been over thirty. "Oh?"

"Yeah, it's got a youth angle."

"Oh?" The executive looked Ric up and down, confused, never having heard of him, at the same time worried because he didn't want to be out of the loop, fearing he *ought* to have heard of him.

"If I sound a little proud," I said, "it's because I discovered him. I found him last May when I was giving a talk to a young screenwriters' workshop at the American Film Institute. Ric convinced me to look at some things and...I'm glad I did. My *agent's* glad I did." I chuckled.

The executive tried to look amused, although he hated like hell to pay writers significant money. For his part, Ric tried to look modest but unbelievably talented, young, young, young, and hot, hot, hot.

"Well, don't let Fox tie you up," the executive told Ric. "Have your agent send me something."

"I'll do that, Mr. Ballard. Thanks," Ric said.

"Do I look old enough to be a 'mister'? Call me 'Ed.'"

We made the rounds. While all the executives considered me too old to be relevant to their 16–25 audience, they still had reverence for what they thought of as an institution. Sure, they wouldn't buy anything from me, but they were more than happy to talk to me. After all, it didn't cost them any money, and it made them feel like they were part of a community.

By the time I was through introducing Ric, my rumors about Ric had been accepted as fact. Various executives from various studios considered themselves in competition with executives from other studios for the services of this hot, new, young writer who was getting a million dollars a script.

Ric had driven with me to the reception. On the way back, he kept shaking his head in amazement. "And that's the secret? I just needed the right guy to give me introductions? To be anointed as a successor?"

"Not quite. Don't let their chumminess fool you. They only care if you can deliver."

"Well, tomorrow I'll send them one of my scripts."

"No," I said. "Remember our agreement. Not one of your scripts. One of *mine*. By Eric Potter."

So there it was. The deal Ric and I had made was that I'd give him ten percent of whatever my scripts earned in exchange for his being my front man. For his part, he'd have to take calls and go to meetings and behave as if he'd actually written the scripts. Along the way, we'd inevitably talk about the intent and technique of the scripts, thus providing Ric with writing lessons. All in all, not a bad deal for him.

Except that he had insisted on *fifteen* percent.

"Hey, I can't go to meetings if I'm working three-to-eleven at the restaurant," he'd said. "Fifteen percent. And I'll need an advance. You'll have to pay me what I'm earning at the restaurant so I can be free for the meetings."

I wrote him a check for a thousand dollars.

The phone rang, interrupting the climactic speech of the script I was writing. Instead of picking up the receiver, I let my answering machine take it, but I answered anyhow when I heard my agent talking about Ric.

"What about him, Steve?"

"Ballard over at Warners likes the script you had me send him. He wants a few changes, but basically he's happy enough to offer seven hundred and fifty thousand."

"Ask for a million."

"I'll ask for nothing."

"I don't understand. Is this a new negotiating tactic?"

"You told me not to bother reading the script, just to do the kid a favor and send it over to Warners because Ballard asked for it. As you pointed out, I'm too busy to do any reading anyhow. But I made a copy of the script, and for the hell of it, last night I looked it over. Mort, what are you trying to pull? Ric Potter didn't write that script. *You* did. Under a different title, you showed it to me a year ago."

I didn't respond.

"Mort?"

"I'm making a point. The only thing wrong with my scripts is an industry bias against age. Pretend somebody young wrote them, and all of a sudden they're wonderful."

"Mort, I won't be a part of this."

"Why not?"

"It's misrepresentation. I'd be jeopardizing my credibility as an agent. You know how the clause in the contract reads—the writer guarantees that the script is solely his or her own work. If somebody else was involved, the studio wants to know about it—to protect itself against a plagiarism suit."

"But if you tell Ballard I wrote that script, he won't buy it."

"You're being paranoid, Mort."

"Facing facts and being practical. Don't screw this up."

"I told you, I won't go along with it."

"Then if you won't make the deal, I'll get somebody else who will."

A long pause. "Do you know what you're saying?"

"Ric Potter and I need a new agent."

I'll say this for Steve—even though he was furious about my leaving him, he finally swore, for old time's sake, at my insistence, that he wouldn't tell anybody what I was doing. He was loyal to the end. It broke my heart to leave him. The new agent I selected knew squat about the arrangement I had with Ric.

She believed what I told her—that Ric and I were friends and by coincidence we'd decided simultaneously to get new representation. I could have chosen one of those superhuge agencies like CAA, but I've always been uncomfortable when I'm part of a mob, and in this case especially, it seemed to me that small and intimate were essential. The fewer people who knew my business, the better.

The Linda Carpenter Agency was located in a stone cottage just past the gates to the old Hollywoodland subdivision. Years ago, the "land" part of that subdivision's sign collapsed. The "Hollywood" part remained, and you see that sign all the time in film clips about Los Angeles. It's a distance up past houses in the hills. Nonetheless, from outside Linda Carpenter's stone cottage, you feel that the sign's looming over you.

I parked my Audi and got out with Ric. He was wearing sneakers, jeans, and a blue cotton pullover. At my insistence. I wanted his outfit to be self-consciously informal and youthful in contrast with my own mature, conservative slacks and sport coat. When we entered the office, Linda—who's thirty, with short red hair, and loves to look at gorgeous young men—sat straighter when I introduced Ric. His biceps bulged at the sleeves of his pullover. I was reminded again of how much—with his sandy hair, blue eyes, and glowing tan—he looked like an actor.

Linda took a moment before she reluctantly shifted her attention away from him, as if suddenly realizing that I was in the room. "Good to see you again, Mort. But you didn't have to come all this way. I could have met you for lunch at Le Dome."

"A courtesy visit. I wanted to save you the long drive, not to mention the bill."

I said it as if I was joking. The rule is that agents always pick up the check when they're at a restaurant with clients.

Linda's smile was winning. Her red hair seemed brighter. "Any time. I'm still surprised that you left Steve." She tactfully didn't ask what the problem had been. "I promise I'll work hard for you."

"I know you will," I said. "But I don't think you'll have to work hard for my friend here. Ric already has some interest in a script of his over at Warners."

"Oh?" Linda raised her elegant eyebrows. "Who's the executive?"

"Ballard."

"My, my." She frowned slightly. "And Steve isn't involved in this? Your ties are completely severed?"

"Completely. If you want, call him to make sure."

"That won't be necessary."

But I found out later that Linda did phone Steve, and he backed up what I'd said. Also he refused to discuss why we'd separated.

"I have a hunch the script can go for big dollars," I continued.

"How big is big?"

"A million."

Linda's eyes widened. "That certainly isn't small."

"Ballard heard there's a buzz about Ric. Ballard thinks that Ric might be a young Joe Eszterhas." The reference was to the screenwriter of *Basic Instinct*, who had become a phenomenon for writing sensation-based scripts on speculation and intriguing so many producers that he'd manipulated them into a bidding war and collected megabucks. "I have a suspicion that Ballard would like to make a preemptive bid and shut out the competition."

"Mort, you sound more like an agent than a writer."

"It's just a hunch."

"And Steve doesn't want a piece of this?"

I shook my head no.

Linda frowned harder.

But her frown dissolved the moment she turned again toward Ric and took another look at his perfect chin. "Did you bring a copy of the script?"

"Sure." Ric grinned with becoming modesty, the way I'd taught him. "Right here."

Linda took it and flipped to the end to make sure it wasn't longer than 115 pages—a shootable size. "What's it about?"

Ric gave the pitch that I'd taught him—the high concept first, then the target audience, the type of actor he had in mind, and ways the budget could be kept in check. The same as when we'd clocked it at my house, he took four minutes.

Linda listened with growing fascination. She turned to me. "Have you been coaching him?"

"Not much. Ric's a natural."

"He must be to act this polished."

"And he's young," I said.

"You don't need to remind me."

"And Ballard *certainly* doesn't need reminding," I said.

"Ric," Linda said. "From here on in, whatever you do, don't get writer's block. I'm going to make you the highest paid new kid in town."

Ric beamed.

"And Mort," Linda said, "I think you're awfully generous to help your friend through the ropes like this."

"Well"—I shrugged—"isn't that what friends are for?"

I had joked with Linda that our trip to her office was a courtesy visit—to save her a long drive and the cost of buying us lunch at an expensive restaurant. That was partly true. But I also wanted to see how Ric made his pitch about the script. If he got nerves and screwed up, I didn't want it to be in Le Dome, where producers at neighboring tables might see him get flustered. We were trying out the show on the road, so to speak, before we brought it to town. And I had to agree with Linda—Ric had done just fine.

I told him so, as we drove along Sunset Boulevard. "I won't always be there to back you up. In fact, it'll be rare that I am. We have to keep training you so you give the impression there's very little about writing or the business you don't understand. Most of getting along with studio executives is making them have confidence in you."

"You really think I impressed her?"

"It was obvious."

Ric thought about it, peering out the window, nodding. "Yeah."

So we went back to my home in the hills above West Hollywood, and I ran him through more variations of questions he might get asked—where he'd gotten the idea, what actors would be good in the roles, who he thought could direct the material, that sort of thing. At the start of a project, producers pay a lot of attention to a screenwriter, and they promise to keep consulting him the way they're consulting him now. It's all guff, of course. As soon as a director and a name actor are attached to a project, the producers suddenly get amnesia about the original screenwriter. But at the start, he's king, and I wanted Ric to be ready to answer any kind of question about the screenplay so he could be convincing that he'd actually written it.

Ric was a fast study. At eight, when I couldn't think of any more questions he might have to answer, we took a drive to dinner at a fish place near the Santa Monica pier. Afterward, we strolled to the end of the pier and watched the sunset.

"So this is what it's all about," Ric said.

"I'm not sure what you mean."

"The action. I can feel the action."

"Don't get fooled by Linda's optimism. Nothing might come of this."

Ric shook his head. "I'm close."

"I've got some pages I want to do tomorrow, but if you'll come around at four with your own new pages, I'll go over them for you. I'm curious to see how you're revising that script you showed me."

Ric kept staring out at the sunset and didn't answer for quite a while. "Yeah, my script."

As things turned out, I didn't get much work done the next day. I had just managed to solve a problem in a scene that was running too long when my phone rang. That was around ten o'clock, and rather than be interrupted, I let my answering machine take it. But when I heard Ric's excited voice, I picked up the phone.

"Slow down," I said. "Take it easy. What are you so worked up about?"

"They want the script!"

I wasn't prepared. "Warners?"

"Can you believe that this is happening so fast?"

"Ballard's actually taking it? How did you find this out?"

"Linda just phoned me!"

"Linda?" I frowned. "But why didn't Linda...?" I was about to say "Why didn't Linda phone *me?*" Then I realized my mistake. There wasn't any reason for Linda to phone me, except maybe to tell me the good news about my friend. But she definitely had to phone Ric. After all, he was supposedly the author of the screenplay.

Ric kept talking excitedly. "Linda says Ballard wants to have lunch with me."

"Great." The truth is, I was vaguely jealous. "When?"

"Today."

I was stunned. Any executive with power was always booked several weeks in advance. For Ballard to decide to have lunch with Ric this soon, he would have had to cancel lunch with someone else. It definitely wouldn't have been the other way around. No one cancels lunch with Ballard.

"Amazing," I said.

"Apparently he's got big plans for me. By the way, he likes the script as is. No changes. At least, for now. Linda says when they sign a director, the director always asks for changes."

"Linda's right," I said. "And then the director'll insist that the changes aren't good enough and ask to bring in a friend to do the rewrite."

"No fucking way," Ric said.

"A screenwriter doesn't have any clout against a director. You've still got a lot to learn about industry politics. School isn't finished yet."

"Sure." Ric hurried on. "Linda got Ballard up to a million and a quarter for the script!"

For a moment, I had trouble breathing.

"Great." And this time I meant it.

Ric phoned again in thirty minutes. He was nervous about the meeting and needed reassurance.

Ric phoned thirty minutes after that, saying that he didn't feel comfortable going to a power lunch in the sneakers, jeans, and pullover that I had told him were necessary for the role he was playing.

"You have to," I said. "You've got to look like you don't belong to the Establishment or whatever the hell it is they call it these days. If you look like every other writer trying to make an impression, Ballard will *treat* you like every other writer. We're selling nonconformity. We're selling youth."

"I still say I'd feel more comfortable in a jacket by...." Ric mentioned the name of the latest trendy designer.

"Even assuming that's a good idea, which it isn't, how on earth are you going to pay for it? A jacket by that designer costs fifteen hundred dollars."

"I'll use my credit card," Ric said.

"But a month from now, you'll still have to pay the bill. You know the whopping interest rates those credit card companies charge."

"Hey, I can afford it. I just made a million and a quarter bucks."

"No, Ric. You're getting confused."

"All right, I know Linda has to take her ten percent commission."

"You're still confused. *You* don't get the bulk of that money. *I* do. What *you* get is fifteen percent of it."

"That's still a lot of cash. Almost two hundred thousand dollars."

"But remember, you probably won't get it for at least six months."

"*What?*"

"On a spec script, they don't simply agree to buy it and hand you a check. The fine points on the negotiation have to be completed. Then the contracts have to be drawn up and reviewed and amended. Then their business office drags its feet before issuing the check. I once waited a year to get paid for a spec script."

"But I can't wait that long. I've got...."

"Yes?"

"Responsibilities. Look, Mort, I have to go. I need to get ready for this meeting."

"And I need to get back to my pages."

"With all this excitement, you mean you're actually writing today?"

"*Every* day."

"No shit."

But I was too preoccupied to get much work done.

Ric finally phoned around five. "Lunch was fabulous."

I hadn't expected to feel so relieved. "Ballard didn't ask you any tricky questions? He's still convinced you wrote the script?"

"Not only that. He says I'm just the talent he's been looking for. A fresh imagination. Someone in tune with today's generation. He asked me to do a last-minute rewrite on an action picture he's starting next week."

"*The Warlords?*"

"That's the one."

"I've been hearing bad things about it," I said.

"Well, you won't hear anything bad anymore."

"Wait a.... Are you telling me you accepted the job?"

"Damned right."

"Without talking to me about it first?" I straightened in shock. "What in God's name did you think you were doing?"

"Why would I need to talk to you? You're not my agent. Ballard called Linda from our table at the restaurant. The two of them settled the deal while I was sitting there. Man, when things happen, they happen. All those years of trying, and now, wham, pow, all of a sudden I'm there. And the best part is, since I'm a writer for hire on this job, they have to pay some of the money the minute I sit down to work, even if the contracts aren't ready."

"That's correct," I said. "On work for hire, you have to get paid on a schedule. The Writers Guild insists on that. You're learning fast. But Ric, before you accepted the job, don't you think it would have been smart to read the script first—to see if it *can* be fixed?"

"How bad can it be?" Ric chuckled.

"You'd be surprised."

"It doesn't matter *how* bad. The fee's a hundred thousand dollars. I need the money."

"For *what?* You don't live expensively. You can afford to be patient and take jobs that build a career."

"Hey, I'll tell you what I can afford. Are you using that portable phone in your office?"

"Yes. But I don't see why that matters."

"Take a look out your front window."

Frowning, I left my office, went through the TV room and the living room, and peered past the blossoming rhododendron outside my front window. I scanned the curving driveway, then focused on the gate.

Ric was wearing a designer linen jacket, sitting in a red Ferrari, using a car phone, waving to me when he saw me at the window. "Like it?" he asked over the phone.

"For God's sake." I broke the connection, set down the phone, and stalked out the front door.

"Like it?" Ric repeated when I reached the gate. He gestured toward his jacket and the car.

"You didn't have time to....Where'd you get....?"

"This morning, after Linda phoned about the offer from Ballard, I ordered the car over the phone. Picked it up after my meeting with Ballard. Nifty, huh?"

"But you don't have any assets. You mean they just let you drive the car off the lot?"

"Bought it on credit. I made Linda sign as the guarantor."

"You made Linda...." I couldn't believe what I was hearing. "Damn it, Ric, why don't you let me finish coaching you before you run off and.... After I taught you about screenplay technique and industry politics, I wanted to explain to you how to handle your money."

"Hey, what's to teach? Money's for spending."

"Not in *this* business. You've got to put something away for when you have bad years."

"Well, I'm certainly not having any trouble earning money so far."

"What happened today is a fluke! This is the first script I've sold in longer than I care to think about. There aren't any guarantees."

"Then it's a good thing I came along, huh?" Ric grinned.

"Before you accepted the rewrite job, you should have asked me if I wanted to do it."

"But you're not involved in this. Why should I divide the money with you? *I'm* going to do it."

"In that case, you should have asked yourself another question."

"What?"

"Whether you've got the *ability* to do it."

Ric flushed with anger. "Of course, I've got the ability. You've read my stuff. All I needed was a break."

I didn't hear from Ric for three days. That was fine by me. I'd accomplished what I'd intended. I'd proven that a script with my name on it had less chance of being bought than the same script with a youngster's name on it. And to tell the truth, Ric's lack of discipline was annoying me. But after the third day, I confess I got curious. What was he up to?

He called at nine in the evening. "How's it going?"

"Fine," I said. "I had a good day's work."

"Yeah, that's what I'm calling about. Work."

"Oh?"

"I haven't been in touch lately because of this rewrite on *The Warlords*."

I waited.

"I had a meeting with the director," Ric said. "Then I had a meeting with the star." He mentioned the name of the biggest action hero in the business. He hesitated. "I was wondering. Would you look at the material I've got?"

"You can't be serious. After the way you talked to me about it? You all but told me to get lost."

"I didn't mean to be rude. Honestly. This is all new to me, Mort. Come on, give me a break. As you keep reminding me, I don't have the experience you do. I'm young."

I had to hand it to him. He'd not only apologized. He'd used the right excuse.

"Mort?"

At first I didn't want to be bothered. I had my own work to think about, and *The Warlords* would probably be so bad that it would contaminate my mind.

But then my curiosity got the better of me. I couldn't help wondering what Ric would do to improve junk.

"Mort?"

"When do you want me to look at what you've done?"

"How about right now?"

"Now? It's after nine. It'll take you an hour to get here and—"

"I'm already here."

"What?"

"I'm on my car phone. Outside your gate again."

Ric sat across from me in my living room. I couldn't help noticing that his tan was darker, that he was wearing a different designer jacket, a more expensive one. Then I glanced at the title page on the script he'd handed me.

THE WARLORDS

revisions by Eric Potter

I flipped through the pages. All of them were typed on white paper. That bothered me. Ric's inexperience was showing again. On last-minute rewrites, it's always helpful to submit changed pages on different-colored paper. That way, the producer and director can save time and not have to read the entire script to find the changes.

"These are the notes the director gave me," Ric said. He handed me some crudely typed pages. "And these"—Ric handed me pages with scribbling on them—"are what the star gave me. It's a little hard to decipher them."

"More than a little. Jesus." I squinted at the scribbling and got a headache. "I'd better put on my glasses." They helped a little. I read what the director wanted. I switched to what the star wanted.

"These are the notes the producer gave me," Ric said.

I thanked God that they were neatly typed and studied them as well. Finally I leaned back and took off my glasses.

"Well?"

I sighed. "Typical. As near as I can tell, these three people are each talking about a different movie. The director wants more action and less characterization. The star has decided to be serious—he wants more characterization and less action. The producer wants it funny and less expensive. If they're not careful, this movie will have multiple personalities."

Ric looked at me anxiously.

"Okay," I said, feeling tired. "Get a beer from the refrigerator and watch television or something while I go through this. It would help if I knew where you'd made changes. Next time you're in a situation like this, identify your work with colored paper."

Ric frowned.

"What's the matter?" I asked.

"The changes."

"So? What about them?"

"Well, I haven't started to make them."

"You *haven't*? But on this title page, it says 'revisions by Eric Potter'."

Ric looked sheepish. "The title page is as far as I got."

"Sweet Jesus. When are these revisions due?"

"Ballard gave me a week."

"And for the first three days of that week, you didn't work on the changes? What have you been doing?"

Ric glanced away.

Again I noticed that his tan was darker. "Don't tell me you've just been sitting in the sun?"

"Not exactly."

"Then *what* exactly?"

"I've been thinking about how to improve the script."

I was so agitated I had to stand. "You don't *think* about changes. You *make* changes. How much did you say you were being paid? A hundred thousand dollars?"

Ric nodded, uncomfortable.

"And the Writers Guild insists that on work for hire you get a portion of the money as soon as you start."

"Fifty thousand." Ric squirmed. "Linda got the check by messenger the day after I made the deal with Ballard."

"What a mess."

Ric lowered his head, more uncomfortable.

"If you don't hand in new pages four days from now, Ballard will want his money back."

"I know," Ric said, then added, "But I can't."

"What?"

"I already spent the money. A deposit on a condo in Malibu."

I was stunned.

"And the money isn't the worst of it," I said. "Your reputation. *That's* worse. Ballard gave you an incredible break. He decided to take a chance on the bright new kid in town. He allowed you to jump over all the shit. But if you don't deliver, he'll be furious. He'll spread the word all over town that you're not dependable. You won't be hot anymore. We won't be able to sell another script as easily as we did this one."

"Look, I'm sorry, Mort. I know I bragged to you that I could do the job on my own. I was wrong. I don't have the experience. I admit it. I'm out of my depth."

"Even on a piece of shit like this."

Ric glanced down, then up. "I was wondering.... Could you give me a hand?"

My mouth hung open in astonishment.

Before I could tell him *no damned way*, Ric quickly added, "It would really help both of us."

"How do you figure that?"

"You just said it yourself. If I don't deliver, Ballard will spread the word. No producer will trust me. You won't be able to sell another script through me."

My head began to throb. He was right, of course. If I wanted to keep selling my scripts, if I wanted to see them produced, I needed him. There was no doubt in my mind that as old as I was, I would never be able to sell another script with my name on it. I finally had to admit that all along, secretly, I had never intended the deception with Ric to be a one-time-only arrangement.

I swallowed and finally said, "All right."

"Thank you."

"But I won't clean up your messes for nothing."

"Of course not. The same arrangement as before. All I get out of this is fifteen percent."

"By rights, you shouldn't get anything."

"Hey, without me, Ballard wouldn't have offered the job."

"Since you already spent the first half of the payment, how do I get that money?"

Ric made an effort to think of a solution. "We'll have to wait until the money comes through on the spec script we sold. I'll give you the money out of the two hundred thousand that's owed to me."

"But you owe the Ferrari dealer a bundle. Otherwise Linda's responsible for your debt."

"I'll take care of it." Ric gestured impatiently. "I'll take care of all of it. What's important now is that you make the changes on *The Warlords*. Ballard has to pay the remaining fifty thousand dollars when I hand in the pages. That money's yours."

"Fine."

It wasn't until later that I realized how Ric had set a precedent for restructuring our deal. Regardless of his promise to pay me what I was owed, the reality was that he had pocketed half the fee. Instead of getting fifteen percent, he was now getting *fifty* percent.

The script for *The Warlords* was even worse than I'd feared. How do you change bad junk into good junk? In the process, how do you please a director, a star, and a producer who ask for widely different things? One of the rules I've learned over the years is that what people say they want isn't always what they mean. Sometimes it's a matter of interpretation. And after I endured reading the script for *The Warlords*, I thought I had that interpretation.

The director said he wanted more action and less characterization. In my opinion, the script already had more than enough action. The trouble was that some of the action sequences were redundant, and others weren't paced effectively. The biggest stunts occurred two-thirds of the way into the story. The last third had stunts that suffered by comparison. So the trick here was to do some pruning and restructuring—to take the good stunts from the end and put them in the middle, to build on them and put the great stunts at the end, all the while struggling to retain the already feeble logic of the story.

The star said he wanted less action and more characterization. As far as I could tell, what he really wanted was to be sympathetic, to make the audience like the character he was playing. So I softened him a little, threw in some jokes, had him wait for an old lady to cross a street before he blew away the bad guys, basic things like that. Since his character was more like a robot than a human being, any vaguely human thing he did would make him sympathetic.

The producer said he wanted more humor and a less expensive budget. Well, by making the hero sympathetic, I added the jokes the producer wanted. By restructuring the sequence of stunts, I managed to eliminate some of the weaker ones, thus giving the star his request for less action and the producer his request for holding down the budget since the preponderance of action scenes had been what inflated the budget in the first place.

I explained this to Ric as I made notes. "They'll all be happy."

"Amazing," Ric said.

"Thanks."

"No, what I mean is, the ideas you came up with, *I* could have thought of them."

"Oh?" My voice hardened. "Then why didn't you?"

"Because, well, they seem so obvious."

"*After* I thought of them. Good ideas always seem obvious in retrospect. The real job is putting them on paper. I'm going to have to work like crazy to get this job done in four days. And then there's a further problem. I have to teach you how to pitch these changes to Ballard, so he'll be convinced you're the one who wrote them."

"You can count on me," Ric said.

"I want you to...." Suddenly I found myself yawning and looked at my watch. "Three a.m.? I'm not used to staying up this late. I'd better get some sleep if I'm going to get this rewrite done in four days."

"I'm a night person myself," Ric said.

"Well, come back tomorrow at four in the afternoon. I'll take a break and start teaching you what to say to Ballard."

Ric didn't show up, of course. When I phoned his apartment, I got his answering machine. I couldn't get in touch with him the next day, or the day after that.

But the day the changes were due, he certainly showed up. He phoned again from his car outside the gate, and when I let him in, he was so eager to see the pages that he barely said hello to me.

"Where the hell have you been?"

"Mexico."

"*What?*"

"With all this stress, I needed to get away."

"What have you done to put you under stress? *I'm* the one who's been doing all the work."

Instead of responding, Ric sat on my living-room sofa and quickly leafed through the pages. I noticed he was wearing yet another designer jacket. His tan was even darker.

"Yeah," he said. "This is good." He quickly came to his feet. "I'd better get to the studio."

"But I haven't coached you about what to say to Ballard."

Ric stopped at the door. "Mort, I've been thinking. If this partnership is going to work, we need to give each other more space. You take care of the writing. Let me worry about what to say in meetings. Ballard likes me. I know how to handle him. Trust me."

And Ric was gone.

I waited to hear about what happened at the meeting. No phone call. When I finally broke down and phoned *him*, an electronic-sounding voice told me that his number was no longer in service. It took me a moment to figure out that he must have moved to the condo in Malibu. So I phoned Linda to get the new number, and she awkwardly told me that Ric had ordered her to keep it a secret.

"Even from me?"

"Especially from you. Did you guys have an argument or something?"

"No."

"Well, he made it sound as if you had. He kept complaining about how you were always telling him what to do."

"Of all the...." I almost told Linda the truth—that Ric hadn't written the script she had sold but rather *I* had. Then I realized that she'd be conscience-bound to tell the studio. The deception would make the studio feel chilly about the script. After all, as far as they were concerned, an old guy couldn't possibly write a script that appealed to a young generation. They would reread the script with a new perspective, prejudiced by knowing the true identity of the author. The deal would fall through. I'd lose the biggest fee I'd ever been promised.

So I mumbled something about intending to talk with him and straighten out the problem. Then I hung up and cursed.

After I didn't hear from Ric for a week, it became obvious that Linda would long ago have forwarded to him the check for the rewrite on *The Warlords*. He'd had ample time to send me my money. He didn't intend to pay me.

That made me furious, partly because he'd betrayed me, partly because I didn't like being made to feel naive, and partly because I'm a professional. To me, it's a matter of honor that I get paid for what I write. Ric had violated one of my most basic rules.

My arrangement with him was finished. When I read about him in *Daily Variety* and *Hollywood Reporter*—about how Ballard was delighted with the rewrite and predicting that the script he had bought from Ric would be next year's smash hit, not to mention that Ric would win an Oscar for it—I was apoplectic. Ric was compared to Robert Towne and William Goldman, with the advantage that he was young and had a powerful understanding of today's generation. Ric had been hired for a half-million dollars to do another rewrite. Ric had promised that he would soon deliver another original script, for which he hinted that his agent would demand an enormous price. "Quality is always worth the cost," Ballard said.

I wanted to vomit.

As I knew he would have to, Ric eventually came to see me. Again the car phone at the gate. Three weeks later. After dark. A night person, after all.

I made a pretense of reluctance, feigned being moved by his whining, and let him in. Even in the muted lights of my living room, he had the most perfect tan I had ever seen. His clothes were even more expensive and trendy. I hated him.

"You didn't send me my money for the rewrite on *The Warlords*."

"I'm sorry about that," Ric said. "That's part of the reason I'm here."

"To pay me?"

"To explain. My condo at Malibu. The owners demanded more money as a down payment. I couldn't give up the place. It's too fabulous. So I had to.... Well, I knew you'd understand."

"But I don't."

"Mort, listen to me. I promise—as soon as the money comes through on the script we sold, I'll pay you everything I owe."

"You went to fifteen percent of the fee, to fifty percent, to one hundred percent. Do you think I work for nothing?"

"Mort, I can appreciate your feelings. But I was in a bind."

"You *still* are. I've been reading about you in the trade papers. You're getting a half-million for a rewrite on another script, and you're also promising a new original script. How are you going to manage all that?"

"Well, I tried to do it on my own. I handed Ballard the script I showed you when we first met."

"Jesus, no."

"He didn't like it."

"What a surprise."

"I had to cover my tracks and tell him it was something I'd been fooling with but that I realized it needed a lot of work. I told him I agreed with his opinion. From now on, I intended to stick to the tried and true—the sort of thing I'd sold him."

I shook my head.

"I guess you were right," Ric said. "Good ideas seem obvious after somebody's thought of them. But maybe I don't have what it takes to come up with them. I've been acting like a jerk."

"I couldn't agree more."

"So what do you say?" Ric offered his hand. "Let's let bygones be bygones. I screwed up, but I've learned from my mistake. I'm willing to give our partnership another try if you are."

I stared at his hand.

Suddenly beads of sweat burst out onto his brow. He lifted his hand and wiped the sweat.

"What's the matter?" I asked.

"Hot in here."

"Not really. Actually, I thought it was getting chilly."

"Feels stuffy."

"The beer I gave you. Maybe you drank it too fast."

"Maybe."

"You know, *I've* been thinking," I said.

The beer was drugged, of course. After the nausea wore off, giddiness set in, as it was supposed to. The drug, which I'd learned about years ago when I was working on a TV crime series, left its victim open to suggestion. It took me only ten minutes to convince him it was a great idea to do what I wanted. As I instructed, Ric giddily phoned Linda and told her that he was feeling stressed out and intended to go back down to Mexico. He told her he suddenly felt trapped by materialism. He needed a spiritual retreat. He might be away for as long as six months.

Linda was shocked. Listening to the speaker phone, I heard her demand to know how Ric intended to fulfill the contracts he'd signed. She said his voice was slurred and accused him of being drunk or high on something.

I picked up the phone, switched off the speaker, and interrupted to tell Linda that Ric was calling from my house and that we'd made up our differences, that he'd been pouring out his soul to me. He was drunk, yes, but what he had told her was no different than what he had told *me* when he was sober. He was leaving for Mexico tonight and might not be back for quite a while. How was he going to fulfill his contracts? No problem. Just because he was going on a retreat in Mexico, that didn't mean he wouldn't be writing. Honest work was what he thrived on. It was food for his soul.

By then, Ric was almost asleep. After I hung up, I roused him, made him sign two documents that I'd prepared, then made him tell me where he was living in Malibu. I put him in his car, drove over to his place, packed a couple of his suitcases, crammed them into the car, and set out for Mexico.

We got there shortly after dawn. He was somewhat conscious when we crossed the border at Tijuana, enough to be able to answer a few questions and to keep the Mexican immigration officer from becoming suspicious. After that, I drugged him again.

I drove until mid-afternoon, took a back road into the desert, gave him a final lethal amount of the drug, and dumped his body into a sinkhole. I drove back to Tijuana, left Ric's suitcases minus identification in an alley, left his Ferrari minus identification in another alley, the key in the ignition, and caught a bus back to Los Angeles. I was confident that neither the suitcases nor the car would ever be reported. I was also confident that by the time Ric's body was discovered, if ever, it would be in such bad shape that the Mexican authorities, with limited resources, wouldn't be able to identify it. Ric had once told me that he hadn't spoken to his parents in five years, so I knew *they* wouldn't wonder why he wasn't in touch with them. As far as his friends went, well, he didn't have any. He'd ditched them when he came into money. They wouldn't miss him.

For an old guy, I'm resilient. I'd kept up my energy, driven all night and most of the day. I finally got some sleep on the bus. Not shabby, although toward the end I felt as if something had broken in me and I doubt I'll ever be able to put in that much effort again. But I had to, you see. Ric was going to keep hounding me, enticing me, using me. And I was going to be too desperate to tell him to get lost. Because I knew that no matter how well I wrote, I would never be able to sell a script under my own name again.

When I first started as a writer, the money and the ego didn't matter to me as much as the need to work, to tell stories, to teach and delight, as the Latin poet Horace said. But when the money started coming in, I began to depend on it. And I grew to love the action of being with powerful people, of having a reputation for being able to deliver quality work with amazing speed. Ego. That's why I hated Ric the most. Because producers stroked his ego over scripts that I had written.

But not anymore. Ric was gone, and his agent had heard him say that he'd be in Mexico, and I had a document, with his signature on it, saying that he was going to mail in his scripts through me, that I was his mentor and that he wanted me to go to script meetings on his behalf. The document also gave me his power of attorney, with permission to oversee his income while he was away.

And that should have been the end of it. Linda was puzzled but went along. After all, she'd heard Ric on the phone. Ballard was even more puzzled, but he was also enormously pleased with the spec script that I pulled out of a drawer and sent in with Ric's name on it. As far as Ballard was concerned, if Ric wanted to be eccentric, that was fine as long as Ric kept delivering. Really, his speed and the quality of his work were amazing.

So in a way I got what I wanted—the action and the pleasure of selling my work. But there's a problem. When I sit down to do rewrites, when I type "revisions by Eric Potter," I suddenly find myself gazing out the window, wanting to sit in the sun. At the same time, I find that I can't sleep. Like Ric, I've become a night person.

I've sold the spec scripts that I wrote over the years and kept in a drawer. All I had to do was change the titles. Nobody remembered reading the original stories. But I couldn't seem to do the rewrites, and now that I've run out of old scripts, now that I'm faced with writing something new....

For the first time in my life, I've got writer's block. All I have to do is think of the title page and the words "by Eric Potter," and my imagination freezes. It's agony. All my life, every day, I've been a writer. For thirty-five years of married life, except for the last two when Doris got sick, I wrote every day. I sacrificed everything to my craft. I didn't have children because I thought it would interfere with my schedule. Nothing was more important than putting words on a page. Now I sit at my desk, stare at my word processor, and....

Mary had a little....

CRUCIFIED DREAMS

I can't bear this anymore.
I need rest.
The quick brown fox jumped over....
I need to forget about Ric.
Now is the time for all good men to....

INTERROGATION B
Charlie Huston

THE BITCH CAN'T stand her.

Well, that's a given. Her sitting on that side of the desk, she's not going to like anyone on this side. But The Bitch does have a special hate on for her.

—Date of birth?

—Fuck am I gonna tell you that?

Second question. Second question on the damn form and The Bitch is already giving her shit. This after she already gave an obvious alias on the first question.

Betty Crocker my ass.

It's like this already with this shit, what's it going to be like when she asks The Bitch about her priors?

—Just met you, gonna tell you my fucking birthday? Next you be asking my weight, some other shit. Fuck that. Fuck you.

—How's it going, Borden?

She looks at Daws.

Why are so many male cops such clothes horses? Not just the dicks either. See them on the beat. Uniforms take their stuff and have it tailored. Not just hem the pants, bring up the cuff. Beat cops having their blues custom made. Daws, when he was a cadet, no doubt he was taking his grays to some chink tailor, having pleats put in, a break in the cuff if you please.

Lady cop tried to get away with that, wearing something even looks designer on The Job, she'd get the treatment for a year. Pictures from fashion magazines taped to her locker. Stories about cheek implants emailed to her. Name put on contact lists for fucking modeling schools. Assholes in the bullpen pointing at the Victoria's Secret catalog and asking why she didn't make the cut.

Guy like Daws hits the Barneys sale every six months and brags about the deal he got on his Versace and boys are treating him like he caught fucking Son of Sam.

She pictures him naked. Decides it's a bad idea. Way he always keeps his jacket buttoned, he's hiding something in there. Gut like an ape no doubt.

—What's up, Daws?

—Game tonight?

—I'll be there.

The Bitch clears her throat.

—What, motherfucker, come over here, invite to a game, got no invite for me?

He points at The Bitch.

—This her?

Borden nods.

Daws folds his arms.

—She throwing attitude?

The Bitch raises her eyebrow.

—Don't be talking 'bout me like I ain't here. Show you *attitude,* motherfucker.

She hawks up a ball of pack-a-day phlegm, rolls her tongue into a tube and scores a bull's eye on the square toe of his left shoe. Borden taps the space bar on her keyboard a couple times.

Daws looks at the thick brown gob on his toe. He slides his foot under Borden's desk and scrapes it clean on the bottom of one of her drawers, leaving a shiny streak down the middle of his shoe.

—How 'bout you let me take her off your hands, Borden?

Borden hits the backspace key, deleting the empty spaces on her monitor.

—I got it.

—Hey, I'm not saying I want the collar, just let me finish processing the bitch for you.

—*Bitch?* Who you callin' *bitch,* motherfucker? Show you *bitch.*

She coughs up another winner and nails the crotch of his slacks.

—Bitch! Fucking bitch!

He sweeps his open palm across her face, ready to bring it back across and rake her with his knuckles.

Borden snags the sleeve of his jacket.

—Cool it, Daws. Don't fuck up my collar.

The Bitch covers her face with the hand not cuffed to her chair.

Daws jerks his hand free.

—Fucking bitch!

Borden takes the box of Kleenex from the top of her desk and offers it to him.

—Clean that stuff off.

He snatches three tissues and wipes at the dripping brown wad on the pale gray wool.

—Goddamn. Goddamnit! Gonna stain. Fucking bitch!

The Bitch is rubbing her cheek.

—Looks like a shit stain. Looks like you been shittin' out your dick.

Daws points at the stain.

—C'mon, Borden, give her to me. Look at this shit. Slacks cost me two bills. Give me five minutes with her.

Borden leans back in her chair.

—Go to the john, Daws, put some cold water on that.

He balls the Kleenex and throws it in The Bitch's face.

—Stain doesn't come out, I'm gonna find you in holding, bitch.

—Your mama's a cum stain, motherfucker.

Daws nods.

—Uh-huh. OK. OK. I'm gonna deal with your AIDS-infected spit, then I'm going to holding and tell the matron about you. Gonna make an announcement to all the mamas in there about what we got your ass in for, bitch. See how fucking amusing you are when they get done with you.

—Your mama's a cum stain and your daddy's a shit smear.

But Daws is already out the door. The Bitch's smile disappears with him.

Borden rocks her chair back and forth. Detectives, uniforms, and city employees in the bullpen getting back to work now that the show looks to be over.

The Bitch probes the inside of her cheek with her tongue.

—Dick.

Borden nods.

—You got that right.

The Bitch grunts.

Borden leans in.

—Only reason he stops by my desk, I lost a button from my blouse one day, he saw some tit. Now, every day, he stops by. Doesn't even work homicide. Works upstairs. Fucking narc. Comes by because he thinks I lost that button special for him. Comes by like it's a titty bar here waiting to happen. Worst part?

—Hn?

—Worst part is, dick doesn't even bring around a few singles to stick in my g-string.

The Bitch looks her over, nods.

—Yeah. Alright. You OK. Twelve. Ten. Eighty-one.

Borden taps a couple keys.

—Date of birth. December ten in nineteen and eighty-one. Got it.

She looks at the door. Looks at The Bitch. Nods to herself and stands up.

—Let's get out of here.

She takes a key out of her jacket pocket.

—Hold up your hand.

The Bitch offers her cuffed wrist and Borden leans over and frees it; unlocks the other bracelet from the steel chair and drops the cuffs and key in her pocket.

—Come on. Before he realizes that shit's not coming out and comes back to give you a dry cleaning bill and look at my tits some more.

The Bitch stands and stretches.

—Fine on me.

Borden takes an old paper form from her desk and leads The Bitch to Interrogation B. The Bitch sits and Borden takes the cuffs from her pocket, looks at them, weighs them on her palm, and sits, placing the cuffs on the table.

—So. Name: Betty Crocker. DOB: twelve, ten, eighty-one. How about place of residence?

—Shit, you should know, you picked me up there.

—Uh-huh, so you're saying that was your place?

—Not my place, my sister's place. But that's where I was keeping my ass.

—Uh-huh. And, so, not to get ahead of myself, but that was your sister in the tub with the hair dryer?

—Shit. *Not to get ahead of yourself.* Bitch, yes that was her. Always hogging the fucking bathroom. One fucking bathroom in the place. Bitch always soaking in that damn tub. Meanwhile, I'm the one got her moneymaker out on the street earning the rent.

Borden twirls her pen, ignores the form in front of her.

—Had a roommate like that once.

—A roommate.

—Yeah.

—College, I bet. A fucking roommate. Uh-huh.

—No. Army.

—Army? No shit. You in the Army?

—Straight out of high school.

—No shit. I served.

—No shit?

—Two years. Be in now, they didn't kick my ass to the curb.

—What for?

—Hustling. Sold a piece to a second looey. Ask me is he still in.

—Is he still in?

—Fuck, you know he is. Not a fucking mark on his record. Probably a major now. Hope his ass in Iraq.

—No surprise if it is.

—You a MP, I bet.

—No surprise. Here I am.

—Yeah. Sure. But I'd know anyway. That shit about having a roommate. MPs got them a dorm, rooms to share. Grunts in the barracks.

—Hell, why you think I went after the MPs? Got me out of the barracks. Twenty, thirty chicks all living together. After the first couple months, all hitting the rag the same week. Had to get away from that madness.

The Bitch leans back and uncrosses her arms.

—Can't blame a bitch for wanting out of that shit.

Borden drops her pen and leans forward, resting her elbows on the table.

—Almost as bad with my roommate. Never thought someone could get away with being a slob in the service. Chick threw her shit everywhere. Inspections, I got dinged right along with her. *Disordered quarters.*

—I hear that shit. Fucking sister, bitch was the same way. Her and the fucking kid.

—The kid hers?

—No, he mine. But he a pain in the ass. Cryin'. Whinin' all the time. Boy could have kept his mouth shut, I never lay much of a hand on him.

—But he was a whiner.

—Got that right. Boy a crybaby. *Auntie, auntie! Get out the tub, Auntie! Mama! Help auntie out the tub!*

—He freaked out, huh?

—Freaked like the pussy he was.

—That when you pushed him in the tub with your sister?

—Fuck yes.

Borden loops the fingers of her right hand in the closed bracelet of the cuffs and whips the open hook of the other bracelet across The Bitch's face.

The Bitch falls out of her chair, hands covering the eyebrow half ripped from her forehead.

Borden goes around the table, snapping the open bracelet closed and fitting the twin hoops of steel around her fist. She grabs The Bitch's hair and pulls her head back and punches her in the face four times. She lets The Bitch flop to the floor, opens the cuffs and snaps them around The Bitch's wrists, bangs her own forehead against the edge of the table twice and walks out of Interrogation B.

Daws tosses a twenty in the pot.

—Saw that bitch's face when they rolled her out on the gurney.

Borden watches the other police at the table as they fold out of the hand.

—Uh-huh.

She calls Daws and raises another twenty.

He looks at his cards.

—Twenty, huh?

She doesn't look at her cards.

—Yep.

He points at the scabby lump on her forehead and the eight stitches running across it.

—Hurt much?

—Itches like hell.

He looks at his cards again.

—Twenty, huh?

She doesn't move.

He tosses a twenty on the table.

—Call.

She lays down the winning hand and rakes the pot.

The other guys grunt and shake their heads, get up and wander to the deli tray and booze bottles.

Daws fingers her cards.

—Didn't figure that.

She stacks the cash.

—No, you didn't.

He shakes his head.

—Poker face like yours, Borden, you should go pro.

She pulls the cards together.

He gets up and comes around to the seat on her left.

—Good lookin' out on that bitch. Fucking kid killer. Probably doesn't know that's as easy as it's gonna get for her. She goes inside, they're gonna cut slices off her just so there's enough to go around.

Borden knocks the edge of the deck against the edge of the table.

Daws taps the green felt table top with his index finger.

—Still gonna be looking to get a shot at her myself. Kids of my own. Show her a thing or two about abuse.

Borden shuffles the cards.

Kid killer. Like killing a kid is worse somehow than killing anyone else. Like a five-year-old getting pushed in a tub full of water with his dead aunt and a plugged-in hair dryer is worse than some dealer putting a bullet in his rival's back. Like she gives a shit who kills who. Like how old the corpse is or how it's related to the killer makes any fucking difference to how the job gets done or how you get paid. Fucking killing like this, no cash coming from any angle. Dealers start pulling triggers, there's always some scratch to be made.

Kid killer. Waste of fucking time. And time is money.

And The Bitch did worse than waste her time. Bitch fucked with the police. Bitch spat on police.

In her precinct. No one gets away with that shit. No bitch, no cocksucker. No one makes police look bad in her house.

The other guys are coming back to the table, plates full of sandwiches, hands full of highballs.

Daws moves back to his seat and winks at her.

Fucking asshole.

She thinks about setting the deck. Giving him a winner, letting him get cocky before she cleans him out. But no, it'll be better doing it cold. Watching him get angry as he picks up loser after loser, always thinking he's due a winner. Going heavy in the pot, trying to get even. Losing straight through.

See how many $200 pairs of slacks the motherfucking titty peeper buys when she's done with him.

She places the deck in front of the cop on her right, watches him cut, takes the deck and looks at the loser across the table.

—Yeah, well, The Bitch shouldn't have done what she did.

THE QUICKENING
Michael Bishop

I

LAWSON CAME OUT of his sleep feeling drugged and disoriented. Instead of the susurrus of traffic on Rivermont and the early-morning barking of dogs, he heard running feet and an unsettling orchestration of moans and cries. No curtains screened or softened the sun that beat down on his face, and an incandescent blueness had replaced their ceiling. "Marlena," Lawson said doubtfully. He wondered if one of the children was sick and told himself that he ought to get up to help.

But when he tried to rise, scraping the back of his hand on a stone set firmly in mortar, he found that his bed had become a parapet beside a river flowing through an unfamiliar city. He was wearing, instead of the green Chinese-peasant pajamas that Marlena had given him for Christmas, a suit of khaki 1505s from his days in the Air Force and a pair of ragged Converse sneakers. Clumsily, as if deserting a mortuary slab, Lawson leapt away from the wall. In his sleep, the world had turned over. The forms of a bewildered anarchy had begun to assert themselves.

The city—and Lawson knew that it sure as hell wasn't Lynchburg, that the river running through it wasn't the James—was full of people. A few, their expressions terrified and their postures defensive, were padding past Lawson on the boulevard beside the parapet. Many shrieked or babbled as they ran. Other human shapes, dressed not even remotely alike, were lifting themselves bemusedly from paving stones, or riverside benches, or the gutter beyond the sidewalk. Their grogginess and their swiftly congealing fear, Lawson realized, mirrored his own: like him, these people were awakening to nightmare.

Because the terrible fact of his displacement seemed more important than the myriad physical details confronting him, it was hard to take in everything at once—but Lawson tried to balance and integrate what he saw.

The city was foreign. Its architecture was a clash of the Gothic and the sterile, pseudoadobe Modern, one style to each side of the river. On this side, palm trees waved their dreamy fronds at precise intervals along the boulevard, and toward the city's interior an intricate cathedral tower defined by its great height nearly everything beneath it. Already the sun crackled off the rose-colored tower with an arid fierceness that struck Lawson, who had never been abroad, as Mediterranean.... Off to his left was a bridge leading into a more modern quarter of the city, where beige and brick-red high-rises clustered like tombstones. On both sides of the bridge buses, taxicabs, and other sorts of motorized vehicles were stalled or abandoned in the thoroughfares.

Unfamiliar, Lawson reflected, but not unearthly—he recognized things, saw the imprint of a culture somewhat akin to his own. And, for a moment, he let the inanimate bulk of the city and the languor of its palms and bougainvillea crowd out of his vision the human horror show taking place in the streets.

A dark woman in a sari hurried past. Lawson lifted his hand to her. Dredging up a remnant of a high-school language course, he shouted, *"¿Habla Español?"* The woman quickened her pace, crossed the street, recrossed it, crossed it again; her movements were random, motivated, it seemed, by panic and the complicated need to *do* something.

At a black man in loincloth farther down the parapet, Lawson shouted, "This is Spain! We're somewhere in Spain! That's all I know! Do you speak English? Spanish? Do you know what's happened to us?"

The black man, grimacing so that his skin went taut across his cheekbones, flattened himself atop the wall like a lizard. His elbows jutted, his eyes narrowed to slits. Watching him, Lawson perceived that the man was listening intently to a sound that had been steadily rising in volume ever since Lawson had opened his eyes: the city was wailing. From courtyards, apartment buildings, taverns, and plazas, an eerie and discordant wail was rising into the bland blue indifference of the day. It consisted of many strains. The Negro in the loincloth seemed determined to separate these and pick out the ones that spoke most directly to him. He tilted his head.

"Spain!" Lawson yelled against this uproar. *"¡España!"*

The black man looked at Lawson, but the hieroglyph of recognition was not among those that glinted in his eyes. As if to dislodge the wailing of the city, he shook his head. Then, still crouching lizard-fashion on the wall, he began methodically banging his head against its stones. Lawson, helplessly aghast, watched him until he had knocked himself insensible in a sickening, repetitive spattering of blood.

But Lawson was the only one who watched. When he approached the man to see if he had killed himself, Lawson's eyes were seduced away from the African by a movement in the river. A bundle of some sort was floating in the greasy waters below the wall—an infant, clad only in a shirt. The tie-strings on the shirt trailed out behind the child like the severed, wavering legs of a water-walker. Lawson wondered if, in Spain, they even had water-walkers....

Meanwhile, still growing in volume, there crooned above the highrises and Moorish gardens the important air-raid siren of four hundred thousand human voices. Lawson cursed the sound. Then he covered his face and wept.

II

The city was Seville. The river was the Guadalquivir. Lynchburg and the James River, around which Lawson had grown up as the eldest child of an itinerant fundamentalist preacher, were several thousand miles and one helluva big ocean away. You couldn't get there by swimming, and if you imagined that your loved ones would be waiting for you when you got back, you were probably fantasizing the nature of the world's changed reality. No one was where he or she belonged anymore, and Lawson knew himself lucky even to realize where he was. Most of the dispossessed, displaced people inhabiting Seville today *didn't* know that much; all they knew was the intolerable cruelty of their uprooting, the pain of separation from husbands, wives, children, lovers, friends. These things, and fear.

The bodies of infants floated in the Guadalquivir; and Lawson, from his early reconnoiterings of the city on a motor scooter that he had found near the Jardines de Cristina park, knew that thousands of adults already lay dead on streets and in apartment buildings—victims of panic-inspired beatings or their own traumatized hearts. Who knew exactly what was going on in the morning's chaos? Babel had come again and with it, as part of the package, the utter dissolution of all family and societal ties. You couldn't go around a corner without encountering a child of some exotic ethnic caste, her face snot-glazed, sobbing loudly or maybe running through a crush of bodies calling out names in an alien tongue.

What were you supposed to do? Wheeling by on his motor scooter, Lawson either ignored these children or searched their faces to see how much they resembled his daughters.

Where was Marlena now? Where were Karen and Hannah? Just as he played deaf to the cries of the children in the boulevards, Lawson had to harden himself against the implications of these questions. As dialects of German, Chinese, Bantu, Russian, Celtic, and a hundred other languages rattled in his ears, his scooter rattled past a host of cars and buses with un-certain-seeming drivers at their wheels. Probably he too should have chosen an enclosed vehicle. If these frustrated and angry drivers, raging in polyglot defiance, decided to run over him, they could do so with impunity. Who would stop them?

Maybe—in Istanbul, or La Paz, or Mangalore, or Jönköping, or Boise City, or Kaesŏng—his own wife and children had already lost their lives to people made murderous by fear or the absence of helmeted men with pistols and billy sticks. Maybe Marlena and his children were dead....

I'm in Seville, Lawson told himself, cruising. He had determined the name of the city soon after mounting the motor scooter and going by a sign that said *Plaza de Toros de Sevilla*. A circular stadium of considerable size near the river. The bullring. Lawson's Spanish was just good enough to decipher the signs and posters plastered on its walls. *Corrida a las cinco de la tarde.* (García Lorca, he thought, unsure of where the name had come from.) *Sombra y sol*. That morn-ing, then, he took the scooter around the stadium three or four times and then shot off toward the center of the city.

Lawson wanted nothing to do with the nondescript high-rises across the Gaudalquivir but had no real idea what he was going to do on the Moorish and Gothic side of the river, either. All he knew was that the empty bullring, with its dormant potential for death, frightened him. On the other hand, how did you go about establishing order in a city whose population had not willingly chosen to be there?

Seville's population, Lawson felt sure, had been redistributed across the face of the globe, like chess pieces flung from a height. The population of every other human community on Earth had undergone similar displacements. The result, as if by malevolent design, was chaos and suffering. Your ears eventually tried to shut out the audible manifestations of this pain, but your eyes held you accountable and you hated yourself for ignoring the wailing Arab child, the assaulted Polynesian woman, the blue-eyed old man bleeding from the palms as he prayed in the shadow of a department-store awning. Very nearly, you hated yourself for surviving.

Early in the afternoon, at the entrance to the Calle de Sierpes, Lawson got off his scooter and propped it against a wall. Then he waded into the crowd and lifted his right arm above his head.

"I speak English!" he called. *"¡Y hablo un poco Español!* Any who speak English or Spanish please come to me!"

A man who might have been Vietnamese or Kampuchean, or even Malaysian, stole Lawson's motor scooter and rode it in a wobbling zigzag down the Street of the Serpents. A heavyset blonde woman with red cheeks glared at Lawson from a doorway, and a twelve- or thirteen-year-old boy who appeared to be Italian clutched hungrily at Lawson's belt, seeking purchase on an adult, hoping for commiseration. Although he did not try to brush the boy's hand away, Lawson avoided his eyes.

"English! English here! *¡Un poco Español también!"*

Farther down Sierpes, Lawson saw another man with his hand in the air; he was calling aloud in a crisp but melodic Slavic dialect, and already he had succeeded in attracting two or three other people to him. In fact, pockets of like-speaking people seemed to be forming in the crowded commercial avenue, causing Lawson to fear that he had put up his hand too late to end his own isolation. What if those who spoke either English or Spanish had already gathered into survival-conscious groups? What if they had already made their way into the countryside, where the competition for food and drink might be a little less predatory? If they had, he would be a lost, solitary Virginian in this Babel. Reduced to sign language and guttural noises to make his wants known, he would die a cipher….

"Signore," the boy hanging on his belt cried. *"Signore."*

Lawson let his eyes drift to the boy's face. *"Ciao,"* he said. It was the only word of Italian he knew, or the only word that came immediately to mind, and he spoke it much louder than he meant.

The boy shook his head vehemently, pulled harder on Lawson's belt. His words tumbled out like the contents of an unburdened closet into a darkened room, not a single one of them distinct or recognizable.

"English!" Lawson shouted. "English here!"

"English here, too, man!" a voice responded from the milling crush of people at the mouth of Sierpes. "Hang on a minute, I'm coming to you!"

A small muscular man with a large head and not much chin stepped daintily through an opening in the crowd and put out his hand to Lawson. His grip was firm. As he shook hands, he placed his left arm over the shoulder of the Italian boy hanging on to Lawson's belt. The boy stopped talking and gaped at the newcomer.

"Dai Secombe," the man said. "I went to bed in Aberystwyth, where I teach philosophy, and I wake up in Spain. Pleased to meet you, Mr.—"

"Lawson," Lawson said.

The boy began babbling again, his hand shifting from Lawson's belt to the Welshman's flannel shirt facing. Secombe took the boy's hands in his own. "I've got you, lad. There's a ragged crew of your compatriots in a pool-hall pub right down this lane. Come on, then, I'll take you." He glanced at Lawson. "Wait for me, sir. I'll be right back."

Secombe and the boy disappeared, but in less than five minutes the Welshman had returned. He introduced himself all over again. "To go to bed in Aberystwyth and to wake up in Seville," he said, "is pretty damn harrowing. I'm glad to be alive, sir."

"Do you have a family?"

"Only my father. He's eighty-four."

"You're lucky. Not to have anyone else to worry about, I mean."

"Perhaps," Dai Secombe said, a sudden trace of sharpness in his voice. "Yesterday I would not've thought so."

The two men stared at each other as the wail of the city modulated into a less hysterical but still inhuman drone. People surged around them, scrutinized them from foyers and balconies, took their measure. Out of the corner of his eye Lawson was aware of a moonfaced woman in summer deerskins slumping abruptly and probably painfully to the street. An Eskimo woman—the conceit was almost comic, but the woman herself was dying and a child with a Swedish-steel switchblade was already freeing a necklace of teeth and shells from her throat.

Lawson turned away from Secombe to watch the plundering of the Eskimo woman's body. Enraged, he took off his wristwatch and threw it at the boy's head, scoring a glancing sort of hit on his ear.

"You little jackal, get away from there!"

The red-cheeked woman who had been glaring at Lawson applied her foot to the rump of the boy with the switchblade and pushed him over. Then she retrieved the thrown watch, hoisted her skirts, and retreated into the dim interior of the café whose door she had been haunting.

"In this climate, in this environment," Dai Secombe told Lawson, "an Eskimo is doomed. It's as much psychological and emotional as it is physical. There may be a few others who've already died for similar reasons. Not much we can do, sir."

Lawson turned back to the Welshman with a mixture of awe and disdain. How had this curly-haired lump of a man, in the space of no more than three or four hours, come to respond so lackadaisically to the deaths of his fellows? Was it merely because the sky was still blue and the edifices of another age still stood?

Pointedly, Secombe said, "That was a needless forfeiture of your watch, Lawson."

"How the hell did that poor woman get here?" Lawson demanded, his gesture taking in the entire city. "How the hell did any of us get here?" The stench of open wounds and the first sweet hints of decomposition mocked the luxury of his ardor.

"Good questions," the Welshman responded, taking Lawson's arm and leading him out of the Calle de Sierpes. "It's a pity I can't answer 'em."

III

That night they ate fried fish and drank beer together in a dirty little apartment over a shop whose glass display cases were filled with a variety of latex contraceptives. They had obtained the fish from a *pescadería* voluntarily tended by men and women of Greek and Yugoslavian citizenship, people who had run similar shops in their own countries. The beer they had taken from one of the classier bars on the Street of the Serpents. Both the fish and the beer were at room temperature, but tasted none the worse for that.

With the fall of evening, however, the wail that during the day had subsided into a whine began to reverberate again with its first full burden of grief. If the noise was not quite so loud as it had been that morning, Lawson thought, it was probably because the city contained fewer people. Many had died, and a great many more, unmindful of the distances involved, had set out to return to their homelands.

Lawson chewed a piece of *adobo* and washed this down with a swig of the vaguely bitter *Cruz del Campo* beer.

"Isn't this fine?" Secombe said, his butt on the tiles of the room's one windowsill. "Dinner over a Durex shop. And this a Catholic country, too."

"I was raised a Baptist," Lawson said, realizing at once that his confession was a non sequitur.

"Oh," Secombe put in immediately. "Then I imagine you could get all the condoms you wanted."

"Sure. For a quarter. In almost any gas-station restroom."

"Sorry," Secombe said.

They ate for a while in silence. Lawson's back was to a cool plaster wall; he leaned his head against it, too, and released a sharp moan from his chest. Then, sustaining the sound, he moaned again, adding his own strand of grief to the cacophonous harmonies already afloat over the city. He was no different from all the bereaved others who shared his pain by concentrating on their own.

"What did you do in...in Lynchburg?" Secombe suddenly asked.

"Campus liaison for the Veterans Administration. I traveled to four different colleges in the area straightening out people's problems with the GI Bill. I tried to see to it that—Sweet Jesus, Secombe, who cares? I miss my wife. I'm afraid my girls are dead."

"Karen and Hannah?"

"They're three and five. I've taught them to play chess. Karen's good enough to beat me occasionally if I spot her my queen. Hannah knows the moves, but she hasn't got her sister's patience—she's only three, you know. Yeah. Sometimes she sweeps the pieces off the board and folds her arms, and we play hell trying to find them all. There'll be pawns under the sofa, horsemen upside down in the shag—" Lawson stopped.

"She levels them," Secombe said. "As we've all been leveled. The knight's no more than the pawn, the king no more than the bishop."

Lawson could tell that the Welshman was trying to turn aside the ruinous thrust of his grief. But he brushed the metaphor aside: "I don't think we've been 'leveled,' Secombe."

"Certainly we have. Guess who I saw this morning near the cathedral when I first woke up."

"God only knows."

"God and Dai Secombe, sir. I saw the Marxist dictator of...oh, you know, that little African country where there's just been a coup. I recognized the bastard from the telly broadcasts during the purge trials there. There he was, though, in white ducks and a ribbed T-shirt—terrified, Lawson, and as powerless as you and I. He'd been quite decidedly leveled; you'd better believe he had."

"I'll bet he's alive tonight, Secombe."

The Welshman's eyes flickered with a sudden insight. He extended the greasy cone of newspaper from the *pescadería*. "Another piece of fish, Lawson? Come on, then, there's only one more."

"To be leveled, Secombe, is to be put on a par with everyone else. Your dictator, even deprived of office, is a grown man. What about infant children? Toddlers and preadolescents? And what about people like that Eskimo woman who haven't got a chance in an unfamiliar environment, even if its inhabitants don't happen to be hostile?… I saw a man knock his brains out on a stone wall this morning because he took a look around and knew he couldn't make it here. Maybe he thought he was in Hell, Secombe. I don't know. But his chance certainly wasn't ours."

"He knew he couldn't adjust."

"Of course he couldn't adjust. Don't give me that bullshit about leveling!"

Secombe turned the cone of newspaper around and withdrew the last piece of fish. "I'm going to eat this myself, if you don't mind." He ate. As he was chewing, he said, "I didn't think that Virginia Baptists were so free with their tongues, Lawson. Tsk, tsk. Undercuts my preconceptions."

"I've fallen away."

"Haven't we all."

Lawson took a final swig of warm beer. Then he hurled the bottle across the room. Fragments of amber glass went everywhere. "God!" he cried. "God, God, God!" Weeping, he was no different from three-quarters of Seville's new citizens-by-chance. Why, then, as he sobbed, did he shoot such guilty and threatening glances at the Welshman?

"Go ahead," Secombe advised him, waving the empty cone of newspaper. "I feel a little that way myself."

IV

In the morning an oddly blithe woman of forty-five or so accosted them in the alley outside the contraceptive shop. A military pistol in a patent-leather holster was strapped about her skirt. Her seeming airiness, Lawson quickly realized, was a function of her appearance and her movements; her eyes were as grim and frightened as everyone else's. But, as soon as they came out of the shop onto the cobblestones, she approached them fearlessly, hailing Secombe almost as if he were an old friend.

"You left us yesterday, Mr. Secombe. Why?"

"I saw everything dissolving into cliques."

"Dissolving? Coming together, don't you mean?"

Secombe smiled noncommittally, then introduced the woman to Lawson as Mrs. Alexander. "She's one of your own, Lawson. She's from Wyoming or some such place. I met her outside the cathedral yesterday morning when the first self-appointed muezzins started calling their language-mates together. She didn't have a pistol then."

"I got it from one of the Guardia Civil stations," Mrs. Alexander said. "And I feel lots better just having it, let me tell you." She looked at Lawson. "Are you in the Air Force?"

"Not anymore. These are the clothes I woke up in."

"My husband's in the Air Force. Or was. We were stationed at Warren in Cheyenne. I'm originally from upstate New York. And these are the clothes *I* woke up in." A riding skirt, a blouse, low-cut rubber-soled shoes. "I think they tried to give us the most serviceable clothes we had in our wardrobes—but they succeeded better in some cases than others."

"'They'?" Secombe asked.

"Whoever's done this. It's just a manner of speaking."

"What do you want?" Secombe asked Mrs. Alexander. His brusqueness of tone surprised Lawson.

Smiling, she replied, "The word for today is Exportadora. We're trying to get as many English-speaking people as we can to Exportadora. That's where the commercial center for American servicemen and their families in Seville is located, and it's just off one of the major boulevards to the south of here."

On a piece of paper sack Mrs. Alexander drew them a crude map and explained that her husband had once been stationed in Zaragoza in the north of Spain. Yesterday she had recalled that Seville was one of the four Spanish cities supporting the American military presence, and with persistence and a little luck a pair of carefully briefed English-speaking DPs (the abbreviation was Mrs. Alexander's) had discovered the site of the American PX and commissary just before nightfall. Looting the place when they arrived had been an impossibly mixed crew of foreigners, busily hauling American merchandise out of the ancient buildings. But Mrs. Alexander's DPs had run off the looters by the simple expedient of revving the engine of their commandeered taxicab and blowing its horn as if to announce Armageddon. In ten minutes the little American enclave had emptied of all human beings but the two men in the cab. After that, as English-speaking DPs all over the city learned of Exportadora's existence and sought to reach it, the place had begun to fill up again.

"Is there an air base in Seville?" Lawson asked the woman.

"No, not really. The base itself is near Morón de la Frontera, about thirty miles away, but Seville is where the real action is." After a brief pause, lifting her eyebrows, she corrected herself: "Was."

She thrust her map into Secombe's hands. "Here. Go on out to Exportadora. I'm going to look around for more of us. You're the first people I've found this morning. Others are looking, too, though. Maybe things'll soon start making some sense."

Secombe shook his head. "Us. Them. There isn't anybody now who isn't a 'DP,' you know. This regrouping on the basis of tired cultural affiliations is probably a mistake. I don't like it."

"You took up with Mr. Lawson, didn't you?"

"Out of pity only, I assure you. He looked lost. Moreover, you've got to have companionship of *some* sort—especially when you're in a strange place."

"Sure. That's why the word for today is Exportadora."

"It's a mistake, Mrs. Alexander."

"Why?"

"For the same reason your mysterious 'they' saw fit to displace us to begin with, I'd venture. It's a feeling I have."

"Old cultural affiliations are a source of stability," Mrs. Alexander said earnestly. As she talked, Lawson took the rumpled map out of Secombe's fingers. "This chaos around us won't go away until people have settled themselves into units—it's a natural process, it's beginning already. Why, walking along the river this morning, I saw several groups of like-speaking people burying yesterday's dead. The city's churches and chapels have begun to fill up, too. You can still hear the frightened and the heartbroken keening in solitary rooms, of course—but it can't go on forever. They'll either make connection or die. I'm not one of those who wish to die, Mr. Secombe."

"Who wishes that?" Lawson put in, annoyed by the shallow metaphysical drift of this exchange and by Secombe's irrationality. Although Mrs. Alexander was right, she didn't have to defend her position at such length. The map was her most important contribution to the return of order in their lives, and Lawson wanted her to let them use that map.

"Come on, Secombe," he said. "Let's get out to this Exportadora. It's probably the only chance we have of making it home."

"I don't think there's any chance of our making it home again, Lawson. Ever."

Perceiving that Mrs. Alexander was about to ask the Welshman why, Lawson turned on his heel and took several steps down the alley. "Come on, Secombe. We have to try. What the hell are you going to do in this flip-flopped city all by yourself?"

"Look for somebody else to talk to, I suppose."

But in a moment Secombe was at Lawson's side helping him decipher the smudged geometries of Mrs. Alexander's map, and the woman herself, before heading back to Sierpes to look for more of her own kind, called out, "It'll only take you twenty or so minutes, on foot. Good luck. See you later."

Walking, they passed a white-skinned child lying in an alley doorway opening onto a courtyard festooned with two-day-old washing and populated by a pack of orphaned dogs. The child's head was covered by a coat, but she did appear to be breathing. Lawson was not even tempted to examine her more closely, however. He kept his eyes resolutely on the map.

V

The newsstand in the small American enclave had not been looted. On Lawson's second day at Exportadora it still contained quality paperbacks, the most recent American news and entertainment magazines, and a variety of tabloids, including the military paper *The Stars and Stripes*. No one knew how old these publications were because no one knew over what length of time the redistribution of the world's population had taken place. How long had everyone slept? And what about the discrepancies among time zones and the differences among people's waking hours within the same time zones? These questions were academic now, it seemed to Lawson, because the agency of transfer had apparently encompassed every single human being alive on Earth.

Thumbing desultorily through a copy of *Stars and Stripes*, he encountered an article on the problems of military hospitals and wondered how many of the world's sick had awakened in the open, doomed to immediate death because the care they required was nowhere at hand. The smell of spilled tobacco and melted Life Savers made the newsstand a pleasant place to contemplate these horrors; and, even as his conscience nagged and a contingent of impatient DPs awaited him, Lawson perversely continued to flip through the newspaper.

Secombe's squat form appeared in the doorway. "I thought you were looking for a local roadmap."

"Found it already, just skimmin' the news."

"Come on, if you would. The folks're ready to be off."

Reluctantly, Lawson followed Secombe outside, where the raw Andalusian sunlight broke like invisible surf against the pavement and the fragile-seeming shell of the Air Force bus. It was of the Bluebird shuttle variety, and Lawson remembered summer camp at Eglin Air Force Base in Florida and bus rides from his squadron's minimum-maintenance ROTC barracks to the survival-training camps near the swamp. That had been a long time ago, but this

Bluebird might have hailed from an even more distant era. It was as boxy and sheepish-looking as if it had come off a 1954 assembly line, and it appeared to be made out of warped tin rather than steel. The people inside the bus had opened all its windows, and many of those on the driver's side were watching Secombe and Lawson approach.

"Move your asses!" a man shouted at them. "Let's get some wind blowing through this thing before we all suffo-damn-cate."

"Just keep talking," Secombe advised him. "That should do fine."

Aboard the bus was a motley lot of Americans, Britishers, and Australians, with two or three English-speaking Europeans and an Oxford-educated native of India to lend the group ballast. Lawson took up a window seat over the hump of one of the bus's rear tires, and Secombe squeezed in beside him. A few people introduced themselves; others, lost in fitful reveries, ignored them altogether. The most unsettling thing about the contingent to Lawson was the absence of children. Although about equally divided between men and women, the group contained no boys or girls any younger than their early teens.

Lawson opened the map of southern Spain he had found in the newsstand and traced his finger along a highway route leading out of Seville to two small American enclaves outside the city, Santa Clara and San Pablo. Farther to the south were Jerez and the port city of Cádiz. Lawson's heart misgave him; the names were all so foreign, so formidable in what they evoked, and he felt this entire enterprise to be hopeless....

About midway along the right-hand side of the bus a black woman was sobbing into the hem of her blouse, and a man perched on the Bluebird's long rear seat had his hands clasped to his ears and his head canted forward to touch his knees. Lawson folded up the map and stuck it into the crevice between the seat and the side of the bus.

"The bottom-line common denominator here isn't our all speaking English," Secombe whispered. "It's what we're suffering."

Driven by one of Mrs. Alexander's original explorers, a doctor from Ivanhoe, New South Wales, the Bluebird shuddered and lurched forward. In a moment it had left Exportadora and begun banging along one of the wide avenues that would lead it out of town.

"And our suffering," Secombe went on, still whispering, "unites us with all those poor souls raving in the streets and sleeping face-down in their own vomit. You felt that the other night above the condom shop, Lawson. I know you did, talking of your daughters. So why are you so quick to go looking for what you aren't likely to find? Why are you so ready to unite yourself with this artificial family born out of catastrophe? Do you really think you're going to catch a flight home to Lynchburg? Do you really think the bird driving this sardine can—who ought to be out in the streets plying his trade instead of running a shuttle service—d'you really think he's ever going to get back to Australia?"

"Secombe —"

"Do you, Lawson?"

Lawson clapped a hand over the Welshman's knee and wobbled it back and forth. "You wouldn't be badgering me like this if you had a family of your own. What the hell do you want us to do? Stay here forever?"

"I don't know, exactly." He removed Lawson's hand from his knee. "But I do have a father, sir, and I happen to be fond of him.... All I know for certain is that things are *supposed* to be different now. We shouldn't be rushing to restore what we already had."

"Shit," Lawson murmured. He leaned his head against the bottom edge of the open window beside him.

From deep within the city came the brittle noise of gunshots. The Bluebird's driver, in response to this sound and to the vegetable carts and automobiles that had been moved into the streets as obstacles, began wheeling and cornering like a stock-car jockey. The bus clanked and stuttered alarmingly. It growled through an intersection below a stone bridge, leapt over that bridge like something living, and roared down into a semi-industrial suburb of Seville where a Coca-Cola bottling factory and a local brewery lifted huge competing signs.

On top of one of these buildings Lawson saw a man with a rifle taking unhurried potshots at anyone who came into his sights. Several people already lay dead.

And a moment later the Bluebird's front window shattered, another bullet ricocheted off its flank, and everyone in the bus was either shouting or weeping. The next time Lawson looked, the bus's front window appeared to have woven inside it a large and exceedingly intricate spider's web.

The Bluebird careened madly, but the doctor from Ivanhoe kept it upright and turned it with considerable skill onto the highway to San Pablo. Here the bus eased into a quiet and rhythmic cruising that made this final incident in Seville—except for the evidence of the front window—seem only the cottony aftertaste of nightmare. At last they were on their way. Maybe.

"Another good reason for trying to get home," Lawson said.

"What makes you think it's going to be different there?"

Irritably Lawson turned on the Welshman. "I thought your idea was that this change was some kind of *improvement.*"

"Perhaps it will be. Eventually."

Lawson made a dismissive noise and looked at the olive orchard spinning by on his left. Who would harvest the crop? Who would set the aircraft factories, the distilleries, the chemical and textile plants running again? Who would see to it that seed was sown in the empty fields?

Maybe Secombe had something. Maybe, when you ran for home, you ran from the new reality at hand. The effects of this new reality's advent were not going to go away very soon, no matter what you did—but seeking to reestablish yesterday's order would probably create an even nastier entropic pattern than would accepting the present chaos and working to rein it in. How, though, did you best rein it in? Maybe by trying to get back home....

Lawson shook his head and thought of Marlena, Karen, Hannah; of the distant mist-softened cradle of the Blue Ridge. Lord. That was country much easier to get in tune with than the harsh white-sky bleakness of this Andalusian valley. If you stay here, Lawson told himself, the pain will *never* go away.

They passed Santa Clara, which was a housing area for the officers and senior NCOs who had been stationed at Morón. With its neatly trimmed hedgerows, tall aluminum streetlamps, and low-roofed houses with carports and picture windows, Santa Clara resembled a middle-class exurbia in New Jersey or Ohio. Black smoke was curling over the area, however, and the people on the streets and lawns were definitely not Americans—they were transplanted Dutch South Africans, Amazonian tribesmen, Poles, Ethiopians, God-only-knew-what. All Lawson could accurately deduce was that a few of these people had moved into the vacant houses—maybe they had awakened in them—and that others had aimlessly set bonfires about the area's neighborhoods. These fires, because there was no wind, burned with a maddening slowness and lack of urgency.

"Little America," Secombe said aloud.

"That's in Antarctica," Lawson responded sarcastically.

"Right. No matter where it happens to be."

"Up yours."

Their destination was now San Pablo, where the Americans had hospital facilities, a library, a movie theater, a snackbar, a commissary, and, in conjunction with the Spaniards, a small commercial and military airfield. San Pablo lay only a few more miles down the road, and Lawson contemplated the idea of a flight to Portugal. What would be the chances, supposing you actually reached Lisbon, of crossing the Atlantic, either by sea or air, and reaching one of the United States' coastal cities? One in a hundred? One in a thousand? Less than that?

A couple of seats behind the driver, an Englishman with a crisp-looking moustache and an American woman with a distinct Southwestern accent were arguing the merits of bypassing San Pablo and heading on to Gibraltar, a British possession. The Englishman seemed to feel that Gibraltar would have escaped the upheaval to which the remainder of the world had fallen victim, whereas the American woman thought he was crazy. A shouting match involving five or six other passengers ensued. Finally, his patience at an end, the Bluebird's driver put his elbow on the horn and held it there until everyone had shut up.

"It's San Pablo," he announced. "Not Gibraltar or anywhere else. There'll be a plane waitin' for us when we get there."

VI

Two aircraft were waiting, a pair of patched-up DC-7s that had once belonged to the Spanish airline known as Iberia. Mrs. Alexander had recruited one of her pilots from the DPs who had shown up at Exportadora; the other, a retired TWA veteran from Riverside, California, had made it by himself to the airfield by virtue of a prior acquaintance with Seville and its American military installations. Both men were eager to carry passengers home, one via a stopover in Lisbon and the other by using Madrid as a steppingstone to the British Isles. The hope was that they could transfer their passengers to jet aircraft at these cities' more cosmopolitan airports, but no one spoke very much about the real obstacles to success that had already begun stalking them: civil chaos, delay, inadequate communications, fuel shortages, mechanical hangups, doubt and ignorance, a thousand other things.

At twilight, then, Lawson stood next to Dai Secombe at the chain link fence fronting San Pablo's pothole-riven runway and watched the evening light glimmer off the wings of the DC-7s. Bathed in a muted dazzle, the two old airplanes were almost beautiful. Even though Mrs. Alexander had informed the DPs that they must spend the night in the installation's movie theater, so that the Bluebird could make several more shuttle runs to Exportadora, Lawson truly believed that he was bound for home.

"Goodbye," Secombe told him.

"Goodbye…? Oh, because you'll be on the other flight?"

"No, I'm telling you goodbye, Lawson, because I'm leaving. Right now, you see. This very minute."

"Where are you going?"

"Back into the city."

"How? What for?"

"I'll walk, I suppose. As for why, it has something to do with wanting to appease Mrs. Alexander's 'they,' also with finding out what's to become of us all. Seville's the place for that, I think."

"Then why'd you even come out here?"

"To say goodbye, you bloody imbecile." Secombe laughed, grabbed Lawson's hand, shook it heartily. "Since I couldn't manage to change your mind."

With that, he turned and walked along the chain link fence until he had found the roadway past the installation's commissary. Lawson watched him disappear behind the building's complicated system of loading ramps. After a time the Welshman reappeared on the other side, but, against the vast Spanish sky, his compact striding form rapidly dwindled to an imperceptible smudge. A smudge on the darkness.

"Goodbye," Lawson said.

That night, slumped in a lumpy theater chair, he slept with nearly sixty other people in San Pablo's movie house. A teenage boy, over only a few objections, insisted on showing all the old movies still in tins in the projection room. As a result, Lawson awoke once in the middle of *Apocalypse Now* and another time near the end of Kubrick's *Left Hand of Darkness*. The ice on the screen, dunelike *sastrugi* ranged from horizon to horizon, chilled him, touching a sensitive spot in his memory. "Little America," he murmured. Then he went back to sleep.

VII

With the passengers bound for Lisbon, Lawson stood at the fence where he had stood with Secombe, and watched the silver pin-wheeling of propellers as the aircraft's engines engaged. The DC-7 flying to Madrid would not leave until much later that day, primarily because it still had several vacant seats and Mrs. Alexander felt sure that more English-speaking DPs could still be found in the city.

The people at the gate with Lawson shifted uneasily and whispered among themselves. The engines of their savior airplane whined deafeningly, and the runway seemed to tremble. What woebegone eyes the women had, Lawson thought, and the men were as scraggly as railroad hoboes. Feeling his jaw, he understood that he was no more handsome or well-groomed than any of those he waited with. And, like them, he was impatient for the signal to board, for the thumbs-up sign indicating that their airplane had passed its latest rudimentary ground tests.

At least, he consoled himself, you're not eating potato chips at ten-thirty in the morning. Disgustedly, he turned aside from a jut-eared man who was doing just that.

"There's more people here than our plane's supposed to carry," the potato-chip cruncher said. "That could be dangerous."

"But it isn't really that far to Lisbon, is it?" a woman replied. "And none of us has any luggage."

"Yeah, but—" The man gagged on a chip, coughed, tried to speak again. Facing deliberately away, Lawson felt the man's words would acquire eloquence only if he suddenly volunteered to ride in the DC-7's unpressurized baggage compartment.

As it was, the signal came to board and the jut-eared man had no chance to finish his remarks. He threw his cellophane sack to the ground, and Lawson heard it crackling underfoot as people crowded through the gate onto the grassy verge of the runway.

In order to fix the anomaly of San Pablo in his memory, Lawson turned around and walked backward across the field. He saw that bringing up the rear were four men with automatic weapons—weapons procured, most likely, from the installation's Air Police station. These men, like Lawson, were walking backward, but with their guns as well as their eyes trained on the weirdly constituted band of people who had just appeared, seemingly out of nowhere, along the airfield's fence.

One of these people wore nothing but a ragged pair of shorts, another an ankle-length burnoose, another a pair of trousers belted with a rope. One of their number was a doe-eyed young woman with an exposed torso and a circlet of bright coral on her wrist. But there were others, too, and they all seemed to have been drawn to the runway by the airplane's engine whine; they moved along the fence like desperate ghosts. As the first members of Lawson's group mounted into the plane, even more of these people appeared—an assembly of nomads, hunters, hodcarriers, fishers, herdspeople. Apparently they all understood what an airplane was for, and one of the swarthiest men among them ventured out onto the runway with his arms thrown out imploringly.

"Where you go?" he shouted. "Where you go?"

"There's no more room!" responded a blue-jean-clad man with a machine gun. "Get back! You'll have to wait for another flight!"

Oh, sure, Lawson thought, the one to Madrid. He was at the base of the airplane's mobile stairway. The jut-eared man who had been eating potato chips nodded brusquely at him.

"You'd better get on up there," he shouted over the robust hiccoughing of the airplane's engines, "before we have unwanted company breathing down our necks!"

"After you." Lawson stepped aside.

Behind the swarthy man importuning the armed guards for a seat on the airplane, there clamored thirty or more insistent people, their only real resemblance to one another their longing for a way out. "Where you go? Where you go?" the bravest and most desperate among them yelled, but they all wanted to board the airplane that Mrs. Alexander's charges had already laid claim to; and most of them could see that it was too late to accomplish their purpose without some kind of risk-taking. The man who had been shouting in English, along with four or five others, broke into an assertive dogtrot toward the plane. Although their cries continued to be modestly beseeching, Lawson could tell that the passengers' guards now believed themselves under direct attack.

A burst of machine-gun fire sounded above the field and echoed away like rain drumming on a tin roof. The man who had been asking, "Where you go?" pitched forward on his face. Others fell beside him, including the woman with the coral bracelet. Panicked or prodded by this evidence of their assailants' mortality, one of the guards raked the chain link fence with his weapon, bringing down some of those who had already begun to retreat and summoning forth both screams and the distressingly incongruous sound of popping wire. Then, eerily, it was quiet again.

"Get on that airplane!" a guard shouted to Lawson. He was the only passenger still left on the ground, and everyone wanted him inside the plane so that the mobile stairway could be rolled away.

"I don't think so," Lawson said to himself.

Hunching forward like a man under fire, he ran toward the gate and the crude mandala of bodies partially blocking it. The slaughter he had just witnessed struck him as abysmally repetitive of a great deal of recent history, and he did not wish to belong to that history anymore. Further, the airplane behind him was a gross iron-plated emblem of the burden he no longer cared to bear—even if it also seemed to represent the promise of passage home.

"Hey, where the hell you think you're goin'?"

Lawson did not answer. He stepped gingerly through the corpses on the runway's margin, halted on the other side of the fence, and, his eyes misted with glare and poignant bewilderment, turned to watch the DC-7 taxi down the scrub-lined length of concrete to the very end of the field. There the airplane negotiated a turn and started back the way it had come. Soon it was hurtling along like a colossal metal dragonfly, building speed. When it lifted from the ground, its tires screaming shrilly with the last series of bumps before takeoff, Lawson held his breath.

Then the airplane's right wing dipped, dipped again, struck the ground, and broke off like a piece of balsa wood, splintering brilliantly. After that, the airplane went flipping, cartwheeling, across the end of the tarmac and into the desolate open field beyond, where its shell and remaining wing were suddenly engulfed in flames. You could hear people frying in that inferno; you could smell gasoline and burnt flesh.

"Jesus," Lawson said.

He loped away from the airfield's fence, hurried through the short grass behind the San Pablo library, and joined a group of those who had just fled the English-speaking guards' automatic-weapon fire. He met them on the highway going back to Seville and walked among them as merely another of their number. Although several people viewed his 1505 trousers with suspicion, no one argued that he did not belong, and no one threatened to cut his throat for him.

As hangdog and exotically nondescript as most of his companions, Lawson watched his tennis shoes track the pavement like the feet of a mechanical toy. He wondered what he was going to do back in Seville. Successfully dodge bullets and eat fried fish, if he was lucky. Talk with Secombe again, if he could find the man. And, if he had any sense, try to organize his life around some purpose other than the insane and hopeless one of returning to Lynchburg. What purpose, though? What purpose beyond the basic animal purpose of staying alive?

"Are any of you hungry?" Lawson asked.

He was regarded with suspicious curiosity.

"Hungry," he repeated. *"¿Tiene hambre?"*

English? Spanish? Neither worked. What languages did they have, these refugees from an enigma? It looked as if they had all tried to speak together before and found the task impossible—because, moving along the asphalt under the hot Andalusian sun, they now relied on gestures and easily interpretable noises to express themselves.

Perceiving this, Lawson brought the fingers of his right hand to his mouth and clacked his teeth to indicate chewing.

He was understood. A thin barefoot man in a capacious linen shirt and trousers led Lawson off the highway into an orchard of orange trees. The fruit was not yet completely ripe, and was sour because of its greenness, but all twelve or thirteen of Lawson's crew ate, letting the juice run down their arms. When they again took up the trek to Seville, Lawson's mind was almost absolutely blank with satiety. The only thing rattling about in it now was the fear that he would not know what to do once they arrived. He never did find out if the day's other scheduled flight, the one to Madrid, made it safely to its destination, but the matter struck him now as of little import. He wiped his sticky mouth and trudged along numbly.

VIII

He lived above the contraceptive shop. In the mornings he walked through the alley to a bakery that a woman with calm Mongolian features had taken over. In return for a daily allotment of bread and a percentage of the goods brought in for barter, Lawson swept the bakery's floor, washed the utensils that were dirtied each day, and kept the shop's front counter. His most rewarding skill, in fact, was communicating with those who entered to buy something. He had an uncanny grasp of several varieties of sign language, and, on occasion, he found himself speaking a monosyllabic patois whose derivation was a complete mystery to him. Sometimes he thought that he had invented it himself; sometimes he believed that he had learned it from the transplanted Sevillanos among whom he now lived.

English, on the other hand, seemed to leak slowly out of his mind, a thick, unrecoverable fluid.

The first three or four weeks of chaos following The Change had, by this time, run their course, a circumstance that surprised Lawson. Still, it was true. Now you could lie down at night on your pallet without hearing pistol reports or fearing that some benighted freak was going to set fire to your staircase. Most of the city's essential services—electricity, water, and sewerage—were working again, albeit uncertainly, and agricultural goods were coming in from the countryside. People had gone back to doing what they knew best, while those whose previous jobs had had little to do with the basics of day-to-day survival were now apprenticing as bricklayers, carpenters, bakers, fishers, water and power technicians. That men and women chose to live separately and that children were as rare as sapphires, no one seemed to find disturbing or unnatural. A new pattern was evolving. You lived among your fellows without tension or quarrel, and you formed no dangerously intimate relationships.

One night, while standing at his window, Lawson struck a loose tile below the casement. He removed the tile and set it on the floor. Every night for nearly two months he pried away at least one tile and, careful not to chip or break it, stacked it near an inner wall with those he had already removed.

After completing this task, as he lay on his pallet, he would often hear a man or a woman somewhere in the city singing a high, sweet song whose words had no significance for him. Sometimes a pair of voices would answer each other, always in different languages. Then, near the end of the summer, as Lawson stood staring at the lathing and the wall beams he had methodically exposed, he was moved to sing a melancholy song of his own. And he sang it without knowing what it meant.

The days grew cooler. Lawson took to leaving the bakery during its midafternoon closing and proceeding by way of the Calle de Sierpes to a *bodega* across from the bullring. A crew of silent laborers, who worked very purposively in spite of their seeming to have no single boss, was dismantling the Plaza de Toros, and Lawson liked to watch as he drank his wine and ate the breadsticks he had brought with him.

Other crews about the city were carefully taking down the government buildings, banks, and *barrio* chapels that no one frequented anymore, preserving the bricks, tiles, and beams as if in the hope of some still unspecified future construction. By this time Lawson himself had knocked out the rear wall of his room over the contraceptive shop, and he felt a strong sense of identification with the laborers craftily gutting the bullring of its railings and barricades. Eventually, of course, everything would have to come down. Everything.

The rainy season began. The wind and the cold. Lawson continued to visit the sidewalk café near the ruins of the stadium; and because the bullring's destruction went forward even in wet weather, he wore an overcoat he had recently acquired and staked out a nicely sheltered table under the *bodega*'s awning. This was where he customarily sat.

One particularly gusty day, rain pouring down, he shook out his umbrella and sat down at this table only to find another man sitting across from him. Upon the table was a wooden game board of some kind, divided into squares.

"Hello, Lawson," the interloper said.

Lawson blinked and licked his lips thoughtfully. Although he had not called his family to mind in some time, and wondered now if he had ever really married and fathered children, Dai Secombe's face had occasionally floated up before him in the dark of his room. But now Lawson could not remember the Welshman's name, or his nationality, and he had no notion of what to say to him. The first words he spoke, therefore, came out sounding like dream babble, or a voice played backward on the phonograph. In order to say hello he was forced to the indignity, almost comic, of making a childlike motion with his hand.

Secombe, pointing to the game board, indicated that they should play. From a carved wooden box with a velvet lining he emptied the pieces onto the table, then arranged them on both sides of the board. Chess, Lawson thought vaguely, but he really did not recognize the pieces—they seemed changed from what he believed they should look like. And when it came his turn to move, Secombe had to demonstrate the capabilities of all the major pieces before he, Lawson, could essay even the most timid advance. The piece that most reminded him of a knight had to be moved according to two distinct sets of criteria, depending on whether it started from a black square or a white one; the "rooks," on the other hand, were able, at certain times, to *jump* an opponent's intervening pieces. The game boggled Lawson's understanding. After ten or twelve moves he pushed his chair back and took a long bittersweet taste of wine. The rain continued to pour down like an endless curtain of deliquescent beads.

"That's all right," Secombe said. "I haven't got it all down yet myself, quite. A Bhutanese fellow near where I live made the pieces, you see, and just recently taught me how to play."

With difficulty Lawson managed to frame a question: "What work have you been doing?"

"I'm in demolition. As we all will be soon. It's the only really constructive occupation going." The Welshman chuckled mildly, finished his own wine, and rose. Lifting his umbrella, he bid Lawson farewell with a word that, when Lawson later tried to repeat and intellectually encompass it, had no meaning at all.

Every afternoon of that dismal, rainy winter Lawson came back to the same table, but Secombe never showed up there again. Nor did Lawson miss him terribly. He had grown accustomed to the strange richness of his own company. Besides, if he wanted people to talk to, all he needed to do was remain behind the counter at the bakery.

IX

Spring came again. All of his room's interior walls were down, and it amused him to be able to see the porcelain chalice of the commode as he came up the stairs from the contraceptive shop.

The plaster that he had sledgehammered down would never be of use to anybody again, of course, but he had saved from the debris whatever was worth the salvage. With the return of good weather, men driving oxcarts were coming through the city's backstreets and alleys to collect these items. You never saw anyone trying to drive a motorized vehicle nowadays, probably because, over the winter, most of them had been hauled away. The scarcity of gasoline and replacement parts might well have been a factor, too—but, in truth, people seemed no longer to want to mess with internal-combustion engines. Ending pollution and noise had nothing to do with it, either. A person with dung on his shoes or front stoop was not very likely to be convinced of a vast improvement in the environment, and the clattering of wooden carts—the ringing of metal-rimmed wheels on cobblestone—could be as ear-wrenching as the hum and blare of motorized traffic. Still, Lawson liked to hear the oxcarts turn into his alley. More than once, called out by the noise, he had helped their drivers load them with masonry, doors, window sashes, even ornate carven mantels.

At the bakery the Mongolian woman with whom Lawson worked, and had worked for almost a year, caught the handle of his broom one day and told him her name. Speaking the odd quicksilver monosyllables of the dialect that nearly everyone in Seville had by now mastered, she asked him to call her Tij. Lawson did not know whether this was her name from before The Change or one she had recently invented for herself. Pleased in either case, he responded by telling her his own Christian name. He stumbled saying it, and when Tij also had trouble pronouncing the name, they laughed together about its uncommon awkwardness on their tongues.

A week later he had moved into the tenement building where Tij lived. They slept in the same "room" three flights up from a courtyard filled with clambering wisteria. Because all but the supporting walls on this floor had been knocked out, Lawson often felt that he was living in an open-bay barracks. People stepped over his pallet to get to the stairwell and dressed in front of him as if he were not even there. Always a quick study, he emulated their casual behavior.

And when the ice in his loins finally began to thaw, he turned in the darkness to Tij—without in the least worrying about propriety. Their coupling was invariably silent, and the release Lawson experienced was always a serene rather than a shuddering one. Afterwards, in the wisteria fragrance pervading their building, Tij and he lay beside each other like a pair of larval bumblebees as the moon rolled shadows over their naked sweat-gleaming bodies.

Each day after they had finished making and trading away their bread, Tij and Lawson closed the bakery and took long walks. Often they strolled among the hedge-enclosed pathways and the small wrought-iron fences at the base of the city's cathedral. From these paths, so overwhelmed were they by buttresses of stones and arcaded balconies, they could not even see the bronze weather vane of Faith atop the Giralda. But, evening after evening, Lawson insisted on returning to that place, and at last his persistence and his sense of expectation were rewarded by the sound of jackhammers biting into marble in each one of the cathedral's five tremendous naves. He and Tij, holding hands, entered.

Inside, men and women were at work removing the altar screens, the metalwork grilles, the oil paintings, sections of stained-glass windows, religious relics. Twelve or more oxcarts were parked beneath the vault of the cathedral, and the noise of the jackhammers echoed shatteringly from nave to nave, from floor to cavernous ceiling. The oxen stood so complacently in their traces that Lawson wondered if the drivers of the carts had somehow contrived to deafen the animals. Tij released Lawson's hand to cover her ears. He covered his own ears. It did no good. You could remain in the cathedral only if you accepted the noise and resolved to be a participant in the building's destruction. Many people had already made that decision. They were swarming through its chambered stone belly like a spectacularly efficient variety of stone-eating termite.

An albino man of indeterminate race—a man as pale as a termite—thrust his pickax at Lawson. Lawson uncovered his ears and took the pickax by its handle. Tij, a moment later, found a crowbar hanging precariously from the side of one of the oxcarts. With these tools the pair of them crossed the nave they had entered and halted in front of an imposing mausoleum. Straining against the cathedral's poor light and the strange linguistic static in his head, Lawson painstakingly deciphered the plaque near the tomb.

"Christopher Columbus is buried here," he said.

Tij did not hear him. He made a motion indicating that this was the place where they should start. Tij nodded her understanding. Together, Lawson thought, they would dismantle the mausoleum of the discoverer of the New World and bring his corrupt remains out into the street. After all these centuries they would free the man.

Then the bronze statue of Faith atop the bell tower would come down, followed by the lovely bell tower itself. After that, the flying buttresses, the balconies, the walls; every beautiful, tainted stone.

It would hurt like hell to destroy the cathedral, and it would take a long, long time—but, considering everything, it was the only meaningful option they had. Lawson raised his pickax.

THE EVENING AND THE MORNING AND THE NIGHT
Octavia E. Butler

WHEN I WAS fifteen and trying to show my independence by getting careless with my diet, my parents took me to a Duryea-Gode disease ward. They wanted me to see, they said, where I was headed if I wasn't careful. In fact, it was where I was headed no matter what. It was only a matter of when: now or later. My parents were putting in their vote for later.

I won't describe the ward. It's enough to say that when they brought me home, I cut my wrists. I did a thorough job of it, old Roman style in a bathtub of warm water. Almost made it. My father dislocated his shoulder breaking down the bathroom door. He and I never forgave each other for that day.

The disease got him almost three years later—just before I went off to college. It was sudden. It doesn't happen that way often. Most people notice themselves beginning to drift—or their relatives notice—and they make arrangements with their chosen institution. People who are noticed and who resist going in can be locked up for a week's observation. I don't doubt that that observation period breaks up a few families. Sending someone away for what turns out to be a false alarm.... Well, it isn't the sort of thing the victim is likely to forgive or forget. On the other hand, not sending someone away in time—missing the signs or having a person go off suddenly without signs—is inevitably dangerous for the victim. I've never heard of it going as badly, though, as it did in my family. People normally injure only themselves when their time comes—unless someone is stupid enough to try to handle them without the necessary drugs or restraints.

My father had killed my mother, then killed himself. I wasn't home when it happened. I had stayed at school later than usual, rehearsing graduation exercises. By the time I got home, there were cops everywhere. There was an ambulance, and two attendants were wheeling someone out on a stretcher—someone covered. More than covered. Almost…bagged.

The cops wouldn't let me in. I didn't find out until later exactly what had happened. I wish I'd never found out. Dad had killed Mom, then skinned her completely. At least that's how I hope it happened. I mean I hope he killed her first. He broke some of her ribs, damaged her heart. Digging.

Then he began tearing at himself, through skin and bone, digging. He had managed to reach his own heart before he died. It was an especially bad example of the kind of thing that makes people afraid of us. It gets some of us into trouble for picking at a pimple or even for daydreaming. It has inspired restrictive laws, created problems with jobs, housing, schools…. The Duryea-Gode Disease Foundation has spent millions telling the world that people like my father don't exist.

A long time later, when I had gotten myself together as best I could, I went to college—to the University of Southern California—on a Dilg scholarship. Dilg is the retreat you try to send your out-of-control DGD relatives to. It's run by controlled DGDs like me, like my parents while they lived. God knows how any controlled DGD stands it. Anyway, the place has a waiting list miles long. My parents put me on it after my suicide attempt, but chances were, I'd be dead by the time my name came up.

I can't say why I went to college—except that I had been going to school all my life and didn't know what else to do. I didn't go with any particular hope. Hell, I knew what I was in for eventually. I was just marking time. Whatever I did was just marking time. If people were willing to pay me to go to school and mark time, why not do it?

The weird part was, I worked hard, got top grades. If you work hard enough at something that doesn't matter, you can forget for a while about the things that do.

Sometimes I thought about trying suicide again. How was it I'd had the courage when I was fifteen but didn't have it now? Two DGD parents both religious, both as opposed to abortion as they were to suicide. So they had trusted God and the promises of modern medicine and had a child. But how could I look at what had happened to them and trust anything?

I majored in biology. Non-DGDs say something about our disease makes us good at the sciences—genetics, molecular biology, biochemistry.... That something was terror. Terror and a kind of driving hopelessness. Some of us went bad and became destructive before we had to—yes, we did produce more than our share of criminals. And some of us went good—spectacularly—and made scientific and medical history. These last kept the doors at least partly open for the rest of us. They made discoveries in genetics, found cures for a couple of rare diseases, made advances against other diseases that weren't so rare—including, ironically, some forms of cancer. But they'd found nothing to help themselves. There had been nothing since the latest improvements in the diet, and those came just before I was born. They, like the original diet, gave more DGDs the courage to have children. They were supposed to do for DGDs what insulin had done for diabetics—give us a normal or nearly normal life span. Maybe they had worked for someone somewhere. They hadn't worked for anyone I knew.

Biology school was a pain in the usual ways. I didn't eat in public anymore, didn't like the way people stared at my biscuits—cleverly dubbed "dog biscuits" in every school I'd ever attended. You'd think university students would be more creative. I didn't like the way people edged away from me when they caught sight of my emblem. I'd begun wearing it on a chain around my neck and putting it down inside my blouse, but people managed to notice it anyway. People who don't eat in public, who drink nothing more interesting than water, who smoke nothing at all—people like that are suspicious. Or rather, they make others suspicious. Sooner or later, one of those others, finding my fingers and wrists bare, would fake an interest in my chain. That would be that. I couldn't hide the emblem in my purse. If anything happened to me, medical people had to see it in time to avoid giving me the medications they might use on a normal person. It isn't just ordinary food we have to avoid, but about a quarter of a *Physicians' Desk Reference* of widely used drugs. Every now and then there are news stories about people who stopped carrying their emblems—probably trying to pass as normal. Then they have an accident. By the time anyone realizes there is anything wrong, it's too late. So I wore my emblem. And one way or another, people got a look at it or got the word from someone who had. "She *is!*" Yeah.

At the beginning of my third year, four other DGDs and I decided to rent a house together. We'd all had enough of being lepers twenty-four hours a day. There was an English major. He wanted to be a writer and tell our story from the inside—which had only been done thirty or forty times before. There was a special-education major who hoped the handicapped would accept her more readily than the able-bodied, a premed who planned to go into research, and a chemistry major who didn't really know what she wanted to do.

Two men and three women. All we had in common was our disease, plus a weird combination of stubborn intensity about whatever we happened to be doing and hopeless cynicism about everything else. Healthy people say no one can concentrate like a DGD. Healthy people have all the time in the world for stupid generalizations and short attention spans.

We did our work, came up for air now and then, ate our biscuits, and attended classes. Our only problem was housecleaning. We worked out a schedule of who would clean what when, who would deal with the yard, whatever. We all agreed on it; then, except for me, everyone seemed to forget about it. I found myself going around reminding people to vacuum, clean the bathroom, mow the lawn.... I figured they'd all hate me in no time, but I wasn't going to be their maid, and I wasn't going to live in filth. Nobody complained. Nobody even seemed annoyed. They just came up out of their academic daze, cleaned, mopped, mowed, and went back to it. I got into the habit of running around in the evening reminding people. It didn't bother me if it didn't bother them.

"How'd you get to be housemother?" a visiting DGD asked.

I shrugged. "Who cares? The house works." It did. It worked so well that this new guy wanted to move in. He was a friend of one of the others, and another premed. Not bad looking.

"So do I get in or don't I?" he asked.

"As far as I'm concerned, you do," I said. I did what his friend should have done—introduced him around, then, after he left, talked to the others to make sure nobody had any real objections. He seemed to fit right in. He forgot to clean the toilet or mow the lawn, just like the others. His name was Alan Chi. I thought Chi was a Chinese name, and I wondered. But he told me his father was Nigerian and that in Ibo the word meant a kind of guardian angel or personal God. He said his own personal God hadn't been looking out for him very well to let him be born to two DGD parents. Him too.

I don't think it was much more than that similarity that drew us together at first. Sure, I liked the way he looked, but I was used to liking someone's looks and having him run like hell when he found out what I was. It took me a while to get used to the fact that Alan wasn't going anywhere.

I told him about my visit to the DGD ward when I was fifteen—and my suicide attempt afterward. I had never told anyone else. I was surprised at how relieved it made me feel to tell him. And somehow his reaction didn't surprise me.

"Why didn't you try again?" he asked. We were alone in the living room.

"At first, because of my parents," I said. "My father in particular. I couldn't do that to him again."

"And after him?"

"Fear. Inertia."

He nodded. "When I do it, there'll be no half measures. No being rescued, no waking up in a hospital later."

"You mean to do it?"

"The day I realize I've started to drift. Thank God we get some warning."

"Not necessarily."

"Yes, we do. I've done a lot of reading. Even talked to a couple of doctors. Don't believe the rumors non-DGDs invent."

I looked away, stared into the scarred, empty fireplace. I told him exactly how my father had died—something else I'd never voluntarily told anyone.

He sighed. "Jesus!"

We looked at each other.

"What are you going to do?" he asked.

"I don't know."

He extended a dark, square hand, and I took it and moved closer to him. He was a dark, square man my height, half again my weight, and none of it fat. He was so bitter sometimes, he scared me.

"My mother started to drift when I was three," he said. "My father only lasted a few months longer. I heard he died a couple of years after he went into the hospital. If the two of them had had any sense, they would have had me aborted the minute my mother realized she was pregnant. But she wanted a kid no matter what. And she was Catholic." He shook his head. "Hell, they should pass a law to sterilize the lot of us."

"They?" I said.

"You want kids?"

"No, but—"

"More like us to wind up chewing their fingers off in some DGD ward."

"I don't want kids, but I don't want someone else telling me I can't have any."

He stared at me until I began to feel stupid and defensive. I moved away from him.

"Do you want someone else telling you what to do with your body?" I asked.

"No need," he said. "I had that taken care of as soon as I was old enough."

This left me staring. I'd thought about sterilization. What DGD hasn't? But I didn't know anyone else our age who had actually gone through with it. That would be like killing part of yourself—even though it wasn't a part you intended to use. Killing part of yourself when so much of you was already dead.

"The damned disease could be wiped out in one generation," he said, "but people are still animals when it comes to breeding. Still following mindless urges, like dogs and cats."

My impulse was to get up and go away, leave him to wallow in his bitterness and depression alone. But I stayed. He seemed to want to live even less than I did. I wondered how he'd made it this far.

"Are you looking forward to doing research?" I probed. "Do you believe you'll be able to—"

"No."

I blinked. The word was as cold and dead a sound as I'd ever heard.

"I don't believe in anything," he said.

I took him to bed. He was the only other double DGD I had ever met, and if nobody did anything for him, he wouldn't last much longer. I couldn't just let him slip away. For a while, maybe we could be each other's reasons for staying alive.

He was a good student—for the same reason I was. And he seemed to shed some of his bitterness as time passed. Being around him helped me understand why, against all sanity, two DGDs would lock in on each other and start talking about marriage. Who else would have us?

We probably wouldn't last very long, anyway. These days, most DGDs make it to forty, at least. But then, most of them don't have two DGD parents. As bright as Alan was, he might not get into medical school because of his double inheritance. No one would tell him his bad genes were keeping him out, of course, but we both knew what his chances were. Better to train doctors who were likely to live long enough to put their training to use.

Alan's mother had been sent to Dilg. He hadn't seen her or been able to get any information about her from his grandparents while he was at home. By the time he left for college, he'd stopped asking questions. Maybe it was hearing about my parents that made him start again. I was with him when he called Dilg. Until that moment, he hadn't even known whether his mother was still alive. Surprisingly, she was.

"Dilg must be good," I said when he hung up. "People don't usually.... I mean...."

"Yeah, I know," he said. "People don't usually live long once they're out of control. Dilg is different." We had gone to my room, where he turned a chair backward and sat down. "Dilg is what the others ought to be, if you can believe the literature."

"Dilg is a giant DGD ward," I said. "It's richer—probably better at sucking in the donations—and it's run by people who can expect to become patients eventually. Apart from that, what's different?"

"I've read about it," he said. "So should you. They've got some new treatment. They don't just shut people away to die the way the others do."

"What else is there to do with them? With us."

"I don't know. It sounded like they have some kind of…sheltered workshop. They've got patients doing things."

"A new drug to control the self-destructiveness?"

"I don't think so. We would have heard about that."

"What else could it be?"

"I'm going up to find out. Will you come with me?"

"You're going up to see your mother."

He took a ragged breath. "Yeah. Will you come with me?"

I went to one of my windows and stared out at the weeds. We let them thrive in the backyard. In the front we mowed them, along with the few patches of grass.

"I told you my DGD-ward experience."

"You're not fifteen now. And Dilg isn't some zoo of a ward."

"It's got to be, no matter what they tell the public. And I'm not sure I can stand it."

He got up, came to stand next to me. "Will you try?"

I didn't say anything. I focused on our reflections in the window glass—the two of us together. It looked right, felt right. He put his arm around me, and I leaned back against him. Our being together had been as good for me as it seemed to have been for him. It had given me something to go on besides inertia and fear. I knew I would go with him. It felt like the right thing to do.

"I can't say how I'll act when we get there," I said.

"I can't say how I'll act, either," he admitted. "Especially…when I see her."

He made the appointment for the next Saturday afternoon. You make appointments to go to Dilg unless you're a government inspector of some kind. That is the custom, and Dilg gets away with it.

We left L.A. in the rain early Saturday morning. Rain followed us off and on up the coast as far as Santa Barbara. Dilg was hidden away in the hills not far from San Jose. We could have reached it faster by driving up I-5, but neither of us were in the mood for all that bleakness. As it was, we arrived at one P.M. to be met by two armed gate guards. One of these phoned the main building and verified our appointment. Then the other took the wheel from Alan.

"Sorry," he said. "But no one is permitted inside without an escort. We'll meet your guide at the garage."

None of this surprised me. Dilg is a place where not only the patients but much of the staff has DGD. A maximum security prison wouldn't have been as potentially dangerous. On the other hand, I'd never heard of anyone getting chewed up here. Hospitals and rest homes had accidents. Dilg didn't. It was beautiful—an old estate. One that didn't make sense in these days of high taxes. It had been owned by the Dilg family. Oil, chemicals, pharmaceuticals. Ironically, they had even owned part of the late, unlamented Hedeon Laboratories. They'd had a briefly profitable interest in Hedeonco: the magic bullet, the cure for a large percentage of the world's cancer and a number of serious viral diseases—and the cause of Duryea-Gode disease. If one of your parents was treated with Hedeonco and you were conceived after the treatments, you had DGD. If you had kids, you passed it on to them. Not everyone was equally affected. They didn't all commit suicide or murder, but they all mutilated themselves to some degree if they could. And they all drifted—went off into a world of their own and stopped responding to their surroundings.

Anyway, the only Dilg son of his generation had had his life saved by Hedeonco. Then he had watched four of his children die before Doctors Kenneth Duryea and Jan Gode came up with a decent understanding of the problem and a partial solution: the diet. They gave Richard Dilg a way of keeping his next two children alive. He gave the big, cumbersome estate over to the care of DGD patients.

So the main building was an elaborate old mansion. There were other, newer buildings, more like guest houses than institutional buildings. And there were wooded hills all around. Nice country. Green. The ocean wasn't far away. There was an old garage and a small parking lot. Waiting in the lot was a tall, old woman. Our guard pulled up near her, let us out, then parked the car in the half-empty garage.

"Hello," the woman said, extending her hand. "I'm Beatrice Alcantara." The hand was cool and dry and startlingly strong. I thought the woman was DGD, but her age threw me. She appeared to be about sixty, and I had never seen a DGD that old. I wasn't sure why I thought she was DGD. If she was, she must have been an experimental model—one of the first to survive.

"Is it Doctor or Ms.?" Alan asked.

"It's Beatrice," she said. "I am a doctor, but we don't use titles much here."

I glanced at Alan, was surprised to see him smiling at her. He tended to go a long time between smiles. I looked at Beatrice and couldn't see anything to smile about. As we introduced ourselves, I realized I didn't like her. I couldn't see any reason for that either, but my feelings were my feelings. I didn't like her.

"I assume neither of you have been here before," she said, smiling down at us. She was at least six feet tall, and straight.

We shook our heads. "Let's go in the front way, then. I want to prepare you for what we do here. I don't want you to believe you've come to a hospital."

I frowned at her, wondering what else there was to believe. Dilg was called a retreat, but what difference did names make?

The house close up looked like one of the old-style public buildings— massive, baroque front with a single domed tower reaching three stories above the three-story house. Wings of the house stretched for some distance to the right and left of the tower, then cornered and stretched back twice as far. The front doors were huge—one set of wrought iron and one of heavy wood. Neither appeared to be locked. Beatrice pulled open the iron door, pushed the wooden one, and gestured us in.

Inside, the house was an art museum—huge, high ceilinged, tile floored. There were marble columns and niches in which sculptures stood or paintings hung. There were other sculptures displayed around the rooms. At one end of the rooms there was a broad staircase leading up to a gallery that went around the rooms. There more art was displayed. "All this was made here," Beatrice said. "Some of it is even sold from here. Most goes to galleries in the Bay Area or down around L.A. Our only problem is turning out too much of it."

"You mean the patients do this?" I asked.

The old woman nodded. "This and much more. Our people work instead of tearing at themselves or staring into space. One of them invented the p.v. locks that protect this place. Though I almost wish he hadn't. It's gotten us more government attention than we like."

"What kind of locks?" I asked.

"Sorry. Palmprint-voiceprint. The first and the best. We have the patent." She looked at Alan. "Would you like to see what your mother does?"

"Wait a minute," he said. "You're telling us out-of-control DGDs create art and invent things?"

"And that lock," I said. "I've never heard of anything like that. I didn't even see a lock."

"The lock is new," she said. "There have been a few news stories about it. It's not the kind of thing most people would buy for their homes. Too expensive. So it's of limited interest. People tend to look at what's done at Dilg in the way they look at the efforts of idiot savants. Interesting, incomprehensible, but not really important. Those likely to be interested in the lock and able to afford it know about it." She took a deep breath, faced Alan again. "Oh, yes, DGDs create things. At least they do here."

"Out-of-control DGDs."

"Yes."

"I expected to find them weaving baskets or something—at best. I know what DGD wards are like."

"So do I," she said. "I know what they're like in hospitals, and I know what it's like here." She waved a hand toward an abstract painting that looked like a photo I had once seen of the Orion Nebula. Darkness broken by a great cloud of light and color. "Here we can help them channel their energies. They can create something beautiful, useful, even something worthless. But they create. They don't destroy."

"Why?" Alan demanded. "It can't be some drug. We would have heard."

"It's not a drug."

"Then what is it? Why haven't other hospitals—?"

"Alan," she said. "Wait."

He stood frowning at her.

"Do you want to see your mother?"

"Of course I want to see her!"

"Good. Come with me. Things will sort themselves out."

She led us to a corridor past offices where people talked to one another, waved to Beatrice, worked with computers.... They could have been anywhere. I wondered how many of them were controlled DGDs. I also wondered what kind of game the old woman was playing with her secrets. We passed through rooms so beautiful and perfectly kept it was obvious they were rarely used. Then at a broad, heavy door, she stopped us.

"Look at anything you like as we go on," she said. "But don't touch anything or anyone. And remember that some of the people you'll see injured themselves before they came to us. They still bear the scars of those injuries. Some of those scars may be difficult to look at, but you'll be in no danger. Keep that in mind. No one here will harm you." She pushed the door open and gestured us in.

Scars didn't bother me much. Disability didn't bother me. It was the act of self-mutilation that scared me. It was someone attacking her own arm as though it were a wild animal. It was someone who had torn at himself and been restrained or drugged off and on for so long that he barely had a recognizable human feature left, but he was still trying with what he did have to dig into his own flesh. Those are a couple of the things I saw at the DGD ward when I was fifteen. Even then I could have stood it better if I hadn't felt I was looking into a kind of temporal mirror.

I wasn't aware of walking through that doorway. I wouldn't have thought I could do it. The old woman said something, though, and I found myself on the other side of the door with the door closing behind me. I turned to stare at her.

She put her hand on my arm. "It's all right," she said quietly. "That door looks like a wall to a great many people."

I backed away from her, out of her reach, repelled by her touch. Shaking hands had been enough, for God's sake.

Something in her seemed to come to attention as she watched me. It made her even straighter. Deliberately, but for no apparent reason, she stepped toward Alan, touched him the way people do sometimes when they brush past—a kind of tactile "Excuse me." In that wide, empty corridor, it was totally unnecessary. For some reason, she wanted to touch him and wanted me to see. What did she think she was doing? Flirting at her age? I glared at her, found myself suppressing an irrational urge to shove her away from him. The violence of the urge amazed me.

Beatrice smiled and turned away. "This way," she said. Alan put his arm around me and tried to lead me after her.

"Wait a minute," I said, not moving.

Beatrice glanced around.

"What just happened?" I asked. I was ready for her to lie—to say nothing happened, pretend not to know what I was talking about.

"Are you planning to study medicine?" she asked.

"What? What does that have to do—?"

"Study medicine. You may be able to do a great deal of good." She strode away, taking long steps so that we had to hurry to keep up. She led us through a room in which some people worked at computer terminals and others with pencils and paper. It would have been an ordinary scene except that some people had half their faces ruined or had only one hand or leg or had other obvious scars. But they were all in control now. They were working. They were intent but not intent on self-destruction. Not one was digging into or tearing away flesh. When we had passed through this room and into a small, ornate sitting room, Alan grasped Beatrice's arm.

"What is it?" he demanded. "What do you do for them?"

She patted his hand, setting my teeth on edge. "I will tell you," she said. "I want you to know. But I want you to see your mother first." To my surprise, he nodded, let it go at that.

"Sit a moment," she said to us.

We sat in comfortable, matching upholstered chairs—Alan looking reasonably relaxed. What was it about the old lady that relaxed him but put me on edge? Maybe she reminded him of his grandmother or something. She didn't remind me of anyone. And what was that nonsense about studying medicine?

"I wanted you to pass through at least one workroom before we talked about your mother—and about the two of you." She turned to face me. "You've had a bad experience at a hospital or a rest home?"

I looked away from her, not wanting to think about it. Hadn't the people in that mock office been enough of a reminder? Horror film office. Nightmare office.

"It's all right," she said. "You don't have to go into detail. Just outline it for me."

I obeyed slowly, against my will, all the while wondering why I was doing it.

She nodded, unsurprised. "Harsh, loving people, your parents. Are they alive?"

"No."

"Were they both DGD?"

"Yes, but...yes."

"Of course, aside from the obvious ugliness of your hospital experience and its implications for the future, what impressed you about the people in the ward?"

I didn't know what to answer. What did she want? Why did she want anything from me? She should have been concerned with Alan and his mother.

"Did you see people unrestrained?"

"Yes," I whispered. "One woman. I don't know how it happened that she was free. She ran up to us and slammed into my father without moving him. He was a big man. She bounced off, fell, and...began tearing at herself. She bit her own arm and...swallowed the flesh she'd bitten away. She tore at the wound she'd made with the nails of her other hand. She...I screamed at her to stop." I hugged myself, remembering the young woman, bloody, cannibalizing herself as she lay at our feet, digging into her own flesh. Digging. "They try so hard, fight so hard to get out."

"Out of what?" Alan demanded.

I looked at him, hardly seeing him.

"Lynn," he said gently. "Out of what?"

I shook my head. "Their restraints, their disease, the ward, their bodies...."

He glanced at Beatrice, then spoke to me again. "Did the girl talk?"

"No. She screamed."

He turned away from me uncomfortably. "Is this important?" he asked Beatrice.

"Very," she said.

"Well...can we talk about it after I see my mother?"

"Then and now." She spoke to me. "Did the girl stop what she was doing when you told her to?"

"The nurses had her a moment later. It didn't matter."

"It mattered. Did she stop?"

"Yes."

"According to the literature, they rarely respond to anyone," Alan said.

"True." Beatrice gave him a sad smile. "Your mother will probably respond to you, though."

"Is she...?" He glanced back at the nightmare office. "Is she as controlled as those people?"

"Yes, though she hasn't always been. Your mother works with clay now. She loves shapes and textures and—"

"She's blind," Alan said, voicing the suspicion as though it were fact. Beatrice's words had sent my thoughts in the same direction. Beatrice hesitated. "Yes," she said finally. "And for...the usual reason. I had intended to prepare you slowly."

"I've done a lot of reading."

I hadn't done much reading, but I knew what the usual reason was. The woman had gouged, ripped, or otherwise destroyed her eyes. She would be badly scarred. I got up, went over to sit on the arm of Alan's chair. I rested my hand on his shoulder, and he reached up and held it there.

"Can we see her now?" he asked.

Beatrice got up. "This way," she said.

We passed through more workrooms. People painted; assembled machinery; sculpted in wood, stone; even composed and played music. Almost no one noticed us. The patients were true to their disease in that respect. They weren't ignoring us. They clearly didn't know we existed. Only the few controlled-DGD guards gave themselves away by waving or speaking to Beatrice. I watched a woman work quickly, knowledgeably, with a power saw. She obviously understood the perimeters of her body, was not so dissociated as to perceive herself as trapped in something she needed to dig her way out of. What had Dilg done for these people that other hospitals did not do? And how could Dilg withhold its treatment from the others?

"Over there we make our own diet foods," Beatrice said, pointing through a window toward one of the guest houses. "We permit more variety and make fewer mistakes than the commercial preparers. No ordinary person can concentrate on work the way our people can."

I turned to face her. "What are you saying? That the bigots are right? That we have some special gift?"

"Yes," she said. "It's hardly a bad characteristic, is it?"

"It's what people say whenever one of us does well at something. It's their way of denying us credit for our work."

"Yes. But people occasionally come to the right conclusions for the wrong reasons." I shrugged, not interested in arguing with her about it.

"Alan?" she said. He looked at her.

"Your mother is in the next room."

He swallowed, nodded. We both followed her into the room.

Naomi Chi was a small woman, hair still dark, fingers long and thin, graceful as they shaped the clay. Her face was a ruin. Not only her eyes but most of her nose and one ear were gone. What was left was badly scarred. "Her parents were poor," Beatrice said. "I don't know how much they told you, Alan, but they went through all the money they had, trying to keep her at a decent place. Her mother felt so guilty, you know. She was the one who had cancer and took the drug…. Eventually, they had to put Naomi in one of those state-approved, custodial-care places. You know the kind. For a while, it was all the government would pay for. Places like that…well, sometimes if patients were really troublesome—especially the ones who kept breaking free—they'd put them in a bare room and let them finish themselves. The only things those places took good care of were the maggots, the cockroaches, and the rats."

I shuddered. "I've heard there are still places like that."

"There are," Beatrice said, "kept open by greed and indifference." She looked at Alan. "Your mother survived for three months in one of those places. I took her from it myself. Later I was instrumental in having that particular place closed."

"You took her?" I asked.

"Dilg didn't exist then, but I was working with a group of controlled DGDs in L.A. Naomi's parents heard about us and asked us to take her. A lot of people didn't trust us then. Only a few of us were medically trained. All of us were young, idealistic, and ignorant. We began in an old frame house with a leaky roof. Naomi's parents were grabbing at straws. So were we. And by pure luck, we grabbed a good one. We were able to prove ourselves to the Dilg family and take over these quarters."

"Prove what?" I asked.

She turned to look at Alan and his mother. Alan was staring at Naomi's ruined face, at the ropy, discolored scar tissue. Naomi was shaping the image of an old woman and two children. The gaunt, lined face of the old woman was remarkably vivid—detailed in a way that seemed impossible for a blind sculptress.

Naomi seemed unaware of us. Her total attention remained on her work. Alan forgot about what Beatrice had told us and reached out to touch the scarred face.

Beatrice let it happen. Naomi did not seem to notice. "If I get her attention for you," Beatrice said, "we'll be breaking her routine. We'll have to stay with her until she gets back into it without hurting herself. About half an hour."

"You can get her attention?" he asked.

"Yes."

"Can she...?" Alan swallowed. "I've never heard of anything like this. Can she talk?"

"Yes. She may not choose to, though. And if she does, she'll do it very slowly."

"Do it. Get her attention."

"She'll want to touch you."

"That's all right. Do it."

Beatrice took Naomi's hands and held them still, away from the wet clay. For several seconds Naomi tugged at her captive hands, as though unable to understand why they did not move as she wished.

Beatrice stepped closer and spoke quietly. "Stop, Naomi." And Naomi was still, blind face turned toward Beatrice in an attitude of attentive waiting. Totally focused waiting.

"Company, Naomi."

After a few seconds, Naomi made a wordless sound.

Beatrice gestured Alan to her side, gave Naomi one of his hands. It didn't bother me this time when she touched him. I was too interested in what was happening. Naomi examined Alan's hand minutely, then followed the arm up to the shoulder, the neck, the face. Holding his face between her hands, she made a sound. It may have been a word, but I couldn't understand it. All I could think of was the danger of those hands. I thought of my father's hands.

"His name is Alan Chi, Naomi. He's your son." Several seconds passed.

"Son?" she said. This time the word was quite distinct, though her lips had split in many places and had healed badly. "Son?" she repeated anxiously. "Here?"

"He's all right, Naomi. He's come to visit."

"Mother?" he said.

She reexamined his face. He had been three when she started to drift. It didn't seem possible that she could find anything in his face that she would remember. I wondered whether she remembered she had a son.

"Alan?" she said. She found his tears and paused at them. She touched her own face where there should have been an eye, then she reached back toward his eyes. An instant before I would have grabbed her hand, Beatrice did it.

"No!" Beatrice said firmly.

The hand fell limply to Naomi's side. Her face turned toward Beatrice like an antique weather vane swinging around. Beatrice stroked her hair, and Naomi said something I almost understood. Beatrice looked at Alan, who was frowning and wiping away tears.

"Hug your son," Beatrice said softly.

Naomi turned, groping, and Alan seized her in a tight, long hug. Her arms went around him slowly. She spoke words blurred by her ruined mouth but just understandable.

"Parents?" she said. "Did my parents…care for you?" Alan looked at her, clearly not understanding.

"She wants to know whether her parents took care of you," I said.

He glanced at me doubtfully, then looked at Beatrice.

"Yes," Beatrice said. "She just wants to know that they cared for you."

"They did," he said. "They kept their promise to you, Mother."

Several seconds passed. Naomi made sounds that even Alan took to be weeping, and he tried to comfort her.

"Who else is here?" she said finally.

This time Alan looked at me. I repeated what she had said.

"Her name is Lynn Mortimer," he said. "I'm…." He paused awkwardly. "She and I are going to be married."

After a time, she moved back from him and said my name. My first impulse was to go to her. I wasn't afraid or repelled by her now, but for no reason I could explain, I looked at Beatrice.

"Go," she said. "But you and I will have to talk later."

I went to Naomi, took her hand.

"Bea?" she said.

"I'm Lynn," I said softly.

She drew a quick breath. "No," she said. "No, you're...."

"I'm Lynn. Do you want Bea? She's here."

She said nothing. She put her hand to my face, explored it slowly. I let her do it, confident that I could stop her if she turned violent. But first one hand, then both, went over me very gently.

"You'll marry my son?" she said finally.

"Yes."

"Good. You'll keep him safe."

As much as possible, we'll keep each other safe. "Yes," I said.

"Good. No one will close him away from himself. No one will tie him or cage him." Her hand wandered to her own face again, nails biting in slightly.

"No," I said softly, catching the hand. "I want you to be safe, too."

The mouth moved. I think it smiled. "Son?" she said.

He understood her, took her hand.

"Clay," she said. Lynn and Alan in clay. "Bea?"

Of course," Beatrice said. "Do you have an impression?"

"No!" It was the fastest that Naomi had answered anything. Then, almost childlike, she whispered. "Yes."

Beatrice laughed. "Touch them again if you like, Naomi. They don't mind."

We didn't. Alan closed his eyes, trusting her gentleness in a way I could not. I had no trouble accepting her touch, even so near my eyes, but I did not delude myself about her. Her gentleness could turn in an instant. Naomi's fingers twitched near Alan's eyes, and I spoke up at once, out of fear for him.

"Just touch him, Naomi. Only touch."

She froze, made an interrogative sound.

"She's all right," Alan said.

"I know," I said, not believing it. He would be all right, though, as long as someone watched her very carefully, nipped any dangerous impulses in the bud.

"Son!" she said, happily possessive. When she let him go, she demanded clay, wouldn't touch her old-woman sculpture again. Beatrice got new clay for her, leaving us to soothe her and ease her impatience. Alan began to recognize signs of impending destructive behavior. Twice he caught her hands and said no. She struggled against him until I spoke to her. As Beatrice returned, it happened again, and Beatrice said, "No, Naomi." Obediently Naomi let her hands fall to her sides.

"What is it?" Alan demanded later when we had left Naomi safely, totally focused on her new work—clay sculptures of us. "Does she only listen to women or something?"

Beatrice took us back to the sitting room, sat us both down, but did not sit down herself. She went to a window and stared out. "Naomi only obeys certain women," she said. "And she's sometimes slow to obey. She's worse than most—probably because of the damage she managed to do to herself before I got her." Beatrice faced us, stood biting her lip and frowning. "I haven't had to give this particular speech for a while," she said. "Most DGDs have the sense not to marry each other and produce children. I hope you two aren't planning to have any—in spite of our need." She took a deep breath. "It's a pheromone. A scent. And it's sex-linked. Men who inherit the disease from their fathers have no trace of the scent. They also tend to have an easier time with the disease. But they're useless to use as staff here. Men who inherit from their mothers have as much of the scent as men get. They can be useful here because the DGDs can at least be made to notice them. The same for women who inherit from their mothers but not their fathers. It's only when two irresponsible DGDs get together and produce girl children like me or Lynn that you get someone who can really do some good in a place like this." She looked at me. "We are very rare commodities, you and I. When you finish school you'll have a very well-paying job waiting for you."

"Here?" I asked.

"For training, perhaps. Beyond that, I don't know. You'll probably help start a retreat in some other part of the country. Others are badly needed." She smiled humorlessly. "People like us don't get along well together. You must realize that I don't like you any more than you like me."

I swallowed, saw her through a kind of haze for a moment. Hated her mindlessly—just for a moment.

"Sit back," she said. "Relax your body. It helps."

I obeyed, not really wanting to obey her but unable to think of anything else to do. Unable to think at all. "We seem," she said, "to be very territorial. Dilg is a haven for me when I'm the only one of my kind here. When I'm not, it's a prison."

"All it looks like to me is an unbelievable amount of work," Alan said.

She nodded. "Almost too much." She smiled to herself. "I was one of the first double DGDs to be born. When I was old enough to understand, I thought I didn't have much time. First I tried to kill myself. Failing that, I tried to cram all the living I could into the small amount of time I assumed I had. When I got into this project, I worked as hard as I could to get it into shape before I started to drift. By now I wouldn't know what to do with myself if I weren't working."

"Why haven't you…drifted?" I asked.

"I don't know. There aren't enough of our kind to know what's normal for us."

"Drifting is normal for every DGD sooner or later."

"Later, then."

"Why hasn't the scent been synthesized?" Alan asked. "Why are there still concentration-camp rest homes and hospital wards?"

"There have been people trying to synthesize it since I proved what I could do with it. No one has succeeded so far. All we've been able to do is keep our eyes open for people like Lynn." She looked at me. "Dilg scholarship, right?"

"Yeah. Offered out of the blue."

"My people do a good job keeping track. You would have been contacted just before you graduated or if you dropped out."

"Is it possible," Alan said, staring at me, "that she's already doing it? Already using the scent to…influence people?"

"You?" Beatrice asked.

"All of us. A group of DGDs. We all live together. We're all controlled, of course, but…." Beatrice smiled. "It's probably the quietest house full of kids that anyone's ever seen."

I looked at Alan, and he looked away. "I'm not doing anything to them," I said. "I remind them of work they've already promised to do. That's all."

"You put them at ease," Beatrice said. "You're there. You…well, you leave your scent around the house. You speak to them individually. Without knowing why, they no doubt find that very comforting. Don't you, Alan?"

"I don't know," he said. "I suppose I must have. From my first visit to the house, I knew I wanted to move in. And when I first saw Lynn, I…." He shook his head. "Funny, I thought all that was my idea."

"Will you work with us, Alan?"

"Me? You want Lynn."

"I want you both. You have no idea how many people take one look at one workroom here and turn and run. You may be the kind of young people who ought to eventually take charge of a place like Dilg."

"Whether we want to or not, eh?" he said.

Frightened, I tried to take his hand, but he moved it away. "Alan, this works," I said. "It's only a stopgap, I know. Genetic engineering will probably give us the final answers, but for God's sake, this is something we can do now!"

"It's something *you* can do. Play queen bee in a retreat full of workers. I've never had any ambition to be a drone."

"A physician isn't likely to be a drone," Beatrice said.

"Would you marry one of your patients?" he demanded. "That's what Lynn would be doing if she married me—whether I become a doctor or not."

She looked away from him, stared across the room. "My husband is here," she said softly. "He's been a patient here for almost a decade. What better place for him...when his time came?"

"Shit!" Alan muttered. He glanced at me. "Let's get out of here!" He got up and strode across the room to the door, pulled at it, then realized it was locked. He turned to face Beatrice, his body language demanding she let him out. She went to him, took him by the shoulder, and turned him to face the door. "Try it once more," she said quietly. "You can't break it. Try."

Surprisingly, some of the hostility seemed to go out of him. "This is one of those p.v. locks?" he asked.

"Yes."

I set my teeth and looked away. Let her work. She knew how to use this thing she and I both had. And for the moment, she was on my side.

I heard him make some effort with the door. The door didn't even rattle. Beatrice took his hand from it, and with her own hand flat against what appeared to be a large brass knob, she pushed the door open.

"The man who created that lock is nobody in particular," she said. "He doesn't have an unusually high I.Q., didn't even finish college. But sometime in his life he read a science-fiction story in which palmprint locks were a given. He went that story one better by creating one that responded to voice or palm. It took him years, but we were able to give him those years. The people of Dilg are problem solvers, Alan. Think of the problems you could solve!"

He looked as though he were beginning to think, beginning to understand. "I don't see how biological research can be done that way," he said. "Not with everyone acting on his own, not even aware of other researchers and their work."

"It *is* being done," she said, "and not in isolation. Our retreat in Colorado specializes in it and has—just barely—enough trained, controlled DGDs to see that no one really works in isolation. Our patients can still read and write—those who haven't damaged themselves too badly. They can take each other's work into account if reports are made available to them. And they can read material that comes in from the outside. They're working, Alan. The disease hasn't stopped them, *won't* stop them." He stared at her, seemed to be caught by her intensity—or her scent. He spoke as though his words were a strain, as though they hurt his throat. "I won't be a puppet. I won't be controlled...by a goddamn smell!"

"Alan—"

"I won't be what my mother is. I'd rather be dead!"

"There's no reason for you to become what your mother is."

He drew back in obvious disbelief.

"Your mother is brain damaged—thanks to the three months she spent in that custodial-care toilet. She had no speech at all when I met her. She's improved more than you can imagine. None of that has to happen to you. Work with us, and we'll see that none of it happens to you."

He hesitated, seemed less sure of himself. Even that much flexibility in him was surprising. "I'll be under your control or Lynn's," he said.

She shook her head. "Not even your mother is under my control. She's aware of me. She's able to take direction from me. She trusts me the way any blind person would trust her guide."

"There's more to it than that."

"Not here. Not at any of our retreats."

"I don't believe you."

"Then you don't understand how much individuality our people retain. They know they need help, but they have minds of their own. If you want to see the abuse of power you're worried about, go to a DGD ward."

"You're better than that, I admit. Hell is probably better than that. But...."

"But you don't trust us."

He shrugged.

"You do, you know." She smiled. "You don't want to, but you do. That's what worries you, and it leaves you with work to do. Look into what I've said. See for yourself. We offer DGDs a chance to live and do whatever they decide is important to them. What do you have, what can you realistically hope for that's better than that?"

Silence. "I don't know what to think," he said finally.

"Go home," she said. "Decide what to think. It's the most important decision you'll ever make."

He looked at me. I went to him, not sure how he'd react, not sure he'd want me no matter what he decided.

"What are you going to do?" he asked.

The question startled me. "You have a choice," I said. "I don't. If she's right...how could I not wind up running a retreat?"

"Do you want to?"

I swallowed. I hadn't really faced that question yet. Did I want to spend my life in something that was basically a refined DGD ward? "No!"

"But you will."

"...Yes." I thought for a moment, hunted for the right words. "You'd do it."

"What?"

"If the pheromone were something only men had, you would do it."

That silence again. After a time he took my hand, and we followed Beatrice out to the car. Before I could get in with him and our guard-escort, she caught my arm. I jerked away reflexively. By the time I caught myself, I had swung around as though I meant to hit her. Hell, I did mean to hit her, but I stopped myself in time. "Sorry," I said with no attempt at sincerity.

She held out a card until I took it. "My private number," she said. "Before seven or after nine, usually. You and I will communicate best by phone."

I resisted the impulse to throw the card away. God, she brought out the child in me.

Inside the car, Alan said something to the guard. I couldn't hear what it was, but the sound of his voice reminded me of him arguing with her—her logic and her scent. She had all but won him for me, and I couldn't manage even token gratitude. I spoke to her, low voiced.

"He never really had a chance, did he?"

She looked surprised. "That's up to you. You can keep him or drive him away. I assure you, you *can* drive him away."

"How?"

"By imagining that he doesn't have a chance." She smiled faintly. "Phone me from your territory. We have a great deal to say to each other, and I'd rather we didn't say it as enemies."

She had lived with meeting people like me for decades. She had good control. I, on the other hand, was at the end of my control. All I could do was scramble into the car and floor my own phantom accelerator as the guard drove us to the gate. I couldn't look back at her. Until we were well away from the house, until we'd left the guard at the gate and gone off the property, I couldn't make myself look back. For long, irrational minutes, I was convinced that somehow if I turned, I would see myself standing there, gray and old, growing small in the distance, vanishing.

"The Evening and the Morning and the Night" grew from my ongoing fascinations with biology, medicine, and personal responsibility.

In particular, I began the story wondering how much of what we do is encouraged, discouraged, or otherwise guided by what we are genetically. This is one of my favorite questions, parent to several of my novels. It can be a dangerous question. All too often, when people ask it, they mean who has the biggest or the best or the most of whatever they see as desirable, or who has the smallest and the least of what is undesirable. Genetics as a board game, or worse, as an excuse for the social Darwinism that swings into popularity every few years. Nasty habit.

And yet the question itself is fascinating. And disease, grim as it is, is one way to explore answers. Genetic disorders in particular may teach us much about who and what we are.

I built Duryea-Gode disease from elements of three genetic disorders. The first is Huntington's disease—hereditary, dominant, and thus an inevitability if one has the gene for it. And it is caused by only one abnormal gene. Also Huntington's does not usually show itself until its sufferers are middle-aged.

In addition to Huntington's, I used phenylketonuria (PKU), a recessive genetic disorder that causes severe mental impairment unless the infant who has it is put on a special diet.

Finally, I used Lesch-Nyhan disease, which causes both mental impairment and self-mutilation.

To elements of these disorders, I added my own particular twists: a sensitivity to pheromones and the sufferers' persistent delusion that they are trapped, imprisoned within their own flesh, and that that flesh is somehow not truly part of them. In that last, I took an idea familiar to us all—present in many religions and philosophies—and carried it to a terrible extreme.

We carry as many as 50,000 different genes in each of the nuclei of our billions of cells. If one gene among the 50,000, the Huntington's gene, for instance, can so greatly change our lives—what we can do, what we can become—then what are we?

What, indeed?

For readers who find this question as fascinating as I do, I offer a brief, unconventional reading list: *The Chimpanzees of Gombe: Patterns of Behavior* by Jane Goodall, *The Boy Who Couldn't Stop Washing: The Experience and Treatment of Obsessive-Compulsive Disorder* by Judith L. Rapoport, *Medical*

Detectives by Berton Roueché, and *An Anthropologist on Mars: Seven Paradoxical Tales* and *The Man Who Mistook His Wife for a Hat and Other Clinical Tales* by Oliver Sacks.

Enjoy!

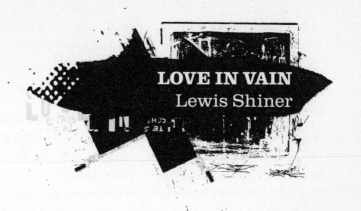

LOVE IN VAIN
Lewis Shiner

THE ROOM HAD whitewashed walls, no windows, and a map of the U.S. on my left as I came in. There must have been a hundred pins with little colored heads stuck along the interstates. By the other door was a wooden table, the top full of scratches and coffee rings. Charlie was already sitting on the far side of it.

They called it Charlie's "office" and a Texas Ranger named Gonzales had brought me back there to meet him. "Charlie?" Gonzales said. "This here's Dave McKenna. He's an Assistant DA up in Dallas?"

"Morning," Charlie said. His left eye, the glass one, drooped a little, and his teeth were brown and ragged. He had on jeans and a plaid short-sleeved shirt and he was shaved clean. His hair was damp and combed straight back. His sideburns had gray in them and came to the bottom of his ears.

I had files and a notebook in my right hand so I wouldn't have to shake with him. He didn't offer. "You looking to close you up some cases?" he said.

I had to clear my throat. "Well, we thought we might give it a try." I sat down in the other chair.

He nodded and looked at Gonzales. "Ernie? You don't suppose I could have a little more coffee?"

Gonzales had been leaning against the wall by the map, but he straightened right up and said, "Sure thing, Charlie." He brought in a full pot from the other room and set it on the table. Charlie had a Styrofoam cup that held about a quart. He filled it up and then added three packets of sugar and some powdered creamer.

"How about you?" Charlie said.

"No," I said. "Thanks."

"You don't need to be nervous," Charlie said. His breath smelled of coffee and cigarettes. When he wasn't talking his mouth relaxed into an easy smile. You didn't have to see anything menacing in it. It was the kind of smile you could see from any highway in Texas, looking out at you from a porch or behind a gas pump, waiting for you to drive on through.

I took out a little pocket-sized cassette recorder. "Would it be okay if I taped this?"

"Sure, go ahead."

I pushed the little orange button on top. "March 27, Williamson County Jail. Present are Sergeant Ernesto Gonzales and Charles Dean Harris."

"Charlie," he said.

"Pardon?"

"Nobody ever calls me Charles."

"Right," I said. "Okay."

"I guess maybe my mother did sometimes. Always sounded wrong somehow." He tilted his chair back against the wall. "You don't suppose you could back that up and do it over?"

"Yeah, okay, fine." I rewound the tape and went through the introduction again. This time I called him Charlie.

Twenty-five years ago he'd stabbed his mother to death. She'd been his first.

It had taken me three hours to drive from Dallas to the Williamson County Jail in Georgetown, a straight shot down Interstate 35. I'd left a little before eight that morning. Alice was already at work and I had to get Jeffrey off to school. The hardest part was getting him away from the television.

He was watching MTV. They were playing the Heart video where the blonde guitar player wears the low-cut golden prom dress. Every time she moved, her magnificent breasts seemed to hesitate before they went along, like they were proud, willful animals, just barely under her control.

I turned the TV off and swung Jeffrey around a couple of times and sent him out for the bus. I got together the files I needed and went into the bedroom to make the bed. The covers were turned back on both sides, but the middle was undisturbed. Alice and I hadn't made love in six weeks. And counting.

I walked through the house, picking up Jeffrey's Masters of the Universe toys. I saw that Alice had loaded up the mantel again with framed pictures of her brothers and parents and the dog she'd had as a little girl. For a second it seemed like the entire house was buried in objects that had nothing to do with me—dolls and vases and doilies and candles and baskets on every inch of every flat surface she could reach. You couldn't walk from one end of a room to the other without running into a Victorian chair or secretary or umbrella stand, couldn't see the floors for the flowered rugs.

I locked up and got in the car and took the LBJ loop all the way around town. The idea was to avoid traffic. I was kidding myself. Driving in Dallas is a matter of manly pride: if somebody manages to pull in front of you he's clearly got a bigger dick than you do. Rather than let this happen, it's better that one of you die.

I was in traffic the whole way down, through a hundred and seventy miles of Charlie Dean Harris country: flat, desolate grasslands with an occasional bridge or culvert where you could dump a body. Charlie had wandered and murdered all over the south, but once he found I-35 he was home to stay.

I opened one of the folders and rested it against the edge of the table so Charlie wouldn't see my hand tremble. "I've got a case here from 1974. A Dallas girl on her way home from Austin for spring break. Her name was Carol, uh, Fairchild. Black hair, blue eyes. Eighteen years old."

Charlie was nodding. "She had braces on her teeth. Would have been real pretty without 'em."

I looked at the sheet of paper in the folder. Braces, it said. The plain white walls seemed to wobble a little. "Then you remember her."

"Yessir, I suppose I do. I killed her." He smiled. It looked like a reflex, something he didn't even know he was doing. "I killed her to have sex with her."

"Can you remember anything else?"

He shrugged. "It was just to have sex, that's all. I remember when she got in the car. She was wearing a T-shirt, one of them man's T-shirts, with the straps and all." He dropped the chair back down and put his elbows on the table. "You could see her titties," he explained.

I wanted to pull away but I didn't. "Where was this?"

He thought for a minute. "Between here and Round Rock, right there off the Interstate."

I looked down at my folder again. Last seen wearing navy tank top, blue jeans. "What color was the T-shirt?"

"Red," he said. "She would have been strangled. With a piece of electrical wire I had there in the car. I had supposed she was a prostitute, dressed the way she was and all. I asked her to have sex and she said she would, so I got off the highway and then she didn't want to. So I killed her and I had sex with her."

Nobody said anything for what must have been at least a minute. I could hear a little scratching noise as the tape moved inside the recorder. Charlie was looking straight at me with his good eye. "I wasn't satisfied," he said.

"What?"

"I wasn't satisfied. I had sex with her but I wasn't satisfied."

"Listen, you don't have to tell me...."

"I got to tell it all," he said.

"I don't want to hear it," I said. My voice came out too high, too loud. But Charlie kept staring at me.

"It don't matter," he said. "I still got to tell it. I got to tell it all. I can't live with the terrible things I did. Jesus says that if I tell everything I can be with Betsy when this is all over." Betsy was his common-law wife. He'd killed her too, after living with her since she was nine. The words sounded like he'd practiced them, over and over.

"I'll take you to her if you want," he said.

"Betsy...?"

"No, your girl there. Carol Fairchild. I'll take you where I buried her." He wasn't smiling any more. He had the sad, earnest look of a laundromat bum telling you how he'd lost his oil fortune up in Oklahoma.

I looked at Gonzales. "We can set it up for you if you want," he said. "Sheriff'll have to okay it and all, but we could prob'ly do it first thing tomorrow."

"Okay," I said. "That'd be good."

Charlie nodded, drank some coffee, lit a cigarette. "Well, fine," he said. "You want to try another?"

"No," I said. "Not just yet."

"Whatever," Charlie said. "You just let me know."

Later, walking me out, Gonzales said, "Don't let Charlie get to you. He wants people to like him, you know? So he figures out what you want him to be, and he tries to be that for you."

I knew he was trying to cheer me up. I thanked him and told him I'd be back in the morning.

I called Alice from my friend Jack's office in Austin, thirty miles farther down I-35. "It's me," I said.

"Oh," she said. She sounded tired. "How's it going?"

I didn't know what to tell her. "Fine," I said. "I need to stay over another day or so."

"Okay," she said.

"Are you okay?"

"Fine," she said.

"Jeffrey?"

"He's fine."

I watched thirty seconds tick by on Jack's wall clock. "Anything else?" she said.

"I guess not." My eyes stung and I reflexively shaded them with my free hand. "I'll be at Jack's if you need me."

"Okay," she said. I waited a while longer and then put the phone back on the hook.

Jack had just come out of his office. "Oh oh," he said.

It took a couple of breaths to get my throat to unclench. "Yeah," I said.

"Bad?"

"Bad as it could be, I guess. It's over, probably. I mean, I think it's over, but how do you know?"

"You don't," Jack said. His secretary, a good-looking Chicana named Liz, typed away on her word processor and tried to act like she wasn't having to listen to us. "You just after a while get fed up and you say fuck it. You want to get a burger or what?"

Jack and I went to UT law school together. He'd lost a lot of hair and put on some weight but he wouldn't do anything about it. Jogging was for assholes. He would rather die fat and keep his self-respect.

He'd been divorced two years now and was always glad to fold out the couch for me. It had been a while. After Jeffrey was born Alice and I had somehow lost touch with everything except work and TV. "I've missed this," I said.

"Missed what?"

"Friends," I said. We were in a big prairie-style house north of campus that had been fixed up with a kitchen and bar and hanging plants. I was full, but still working on the last of the batter-dipped French fries.

"Not my fault, you prick. You're the one dropped down to Christmas cards."

"Yeah, well...."

"Forget it. How'd it go with Charlie Dean?"

"Unbelievable," I said. "I mean, really. He confessed to everything. Had details. Even had a couple wrong, enough to look good. But the major stuff was right on."

"So that's great. Isn't it?"

"It was a set up. The name I gave him was a fake. No such person, no such case."

"I don't get it."

"Jack, the son of a bitch has confessed to something like three thousand murders. It ain't possible. So they wanted to catch him lying."

"With his pants down, so to speak."

"Same old Jack."

"You said he had details."

"That's the creepy part. He knew she was supposed to have braces. I had it in the phony case file, but he brought it up before I did."

"Lucky guess."

"No. It was too creepy. And there's all this shit he keeps telling you. Things you wish you'd never heard, you know what I mean?"

"I know exactly what you mean," Jack said. "When I was in junior high I saw a bum go in the men's room at the bus station with a loaf of bread. I told this friend of mine about it and he says the bum was going in there to wipe all the dried piss off the toilets with the bread and then eat it. For the protein. Said it happens all the time."

"Jesus Christ, Jack."

"See? I know what you're talking about. There's things you don't want in your head. Once they get in there, you're not the same any more. I can't eat white bread to this day. Twenty years, and I still can't touch it."

"You asshole." I pushed my plate away and finished my Corona. "Christ, now the beer tastes like piss."

Jack pointed his index finger at me. "You will never be the same," he said.

You could never tell how much Jack had been drinking. He said it was because he was careful not to let on if he was ever sober. I always thought it was because there was something in him that was meaner than the booze and together they left him just about even.

It was a lot of beers later that Jack said, "What was the name of that bimbo in high school you used to talk about? Your first great love or some shit? Except she never put out for you?"

"Kristi," I said. "Kristi Spector."

"Right!" Jack got up and started to walk around the apartment. It wasn't too long of a walk. "A name like that, how could I forget? I got her off a soliciting rap two months ago."

"Soliciting?"

"There's a law in Texas against selling your pussy. Maybe you didn't know that."

"Kristi Spector, my god. Tell me about it."

"She's a stripper, son. Works over at the Yellow Rose. This guy figured if she'd show her tits in public he could have the rest in his car. She didn't, he called the pigs. Said she made lewd advances. Crock of shit, got thrown out of court."

"How's she look?"

"Not too goddamn bad. I wouldn't have minded taking my fee in trade, but she didn't seem to get the hint." He stopped. "I got a better idea. Let's go have a look for ourselves."

"Oh no," I said.

"Oh yes. She remembers you, man. She says you were 'sweet.' Come on, get up. We're going to go look at some tits."

The place was bigger inside than I expected, the ceilings higher. There were two stages and a runway behind the second one. There were stools right up by the stages for the guys that wanted to stick dollar bills in the dancers' G-strings and four-top tables everywhere else.

I should have felt guilty but I wasn't thinking about Alice at all. The issue here was sex, and Alice had written herself out of that part of my life. Instead I was thinking about the last time I'd seen Kristi.

It was senior year in high school. The director of the drama club, who was from New York, had invited some of us to a "wild" party. It was the first time I'd seen men in dresses. I'd locked myself in the bathroom with Kristi to help her take her bra off. I hadn't seen her in six months. She'd just had an abortion; the father could have been one of a couple of guys. Not me. She didn't want to spoil what we had. It was starting to look to me like there wasn't much left to spoil. That had been eighteen years ago.

The DJ played something by Pat Benatar. The music was loud enough to give you a kind of mental privacy. You didn't really have to pay attention to anything but the dancers. At the moment it seemed like just the thing. It had been an ugly day and there was something in me that was comforted by the sight of young, good-looking women with their clothes off.

"College town," Jack said, leaning toward me so I could hear him. "Lots of local talent."

A tall blonde on the north stage unbuttoned her long-sleeved white shirt and let it hang open. Her breasts were smooth and firm and pale. Like the others she had something on the point of her nipples that made a small, golden flash every time one caught the light.

"See anybody you know?"

"Give me a break," I shouted over the music. "You saw her a couple months ago. It's been almost twenty years for me. I may not even recognize her." A waitress came by, wearing black leather jeans and a red tank top. For a second I could hear Charlie's voice telling me about her titties. I rubbed the sides of my head and the voice went away. We ordered beers, but when they came my stomach was wrapped around itself and I had to let mine sit.

"It's got to be weird to do this for a living," I said in Jack's ear.

"Bullshit," Jack said. "You think they're not getting off on it?"

He pointed to the south stage. A brunette in high heels had let an overweight man in sideburns and a Western shirt tuck a dollar into the side of her bikini bottoms. He talked earnestly to her with just the start of an embarrassed smile. She had to keep leaning closer to hear him. Finally she nodded and turned around. She bent over and grabbed her ankles. His face was about the height of the backs of her knees. She was smiling like she'd just seen somebody else's baby do something cute. After a few seconds she stood up again and the man went back to his table.

"What was that about?" I asked Jack.

"Power, man," he said. "God, I love women. I just love 'em."

"Your problem is you don't know the difference between love and sex."

"Yeah? What is it? Come on, I want to know." The music was too loud to argue with him. I shook my head. "See? You don't know either."

The brunette pushed her hair back with both hands, chin up, fingers spread wide, and it reminded me of Kristi. The theatricality of it. She'd played one of Tennessee Williams's affected Southern bitches once and it had been almost too painful to watch. Almost.

"Come on," I said, grabbing Jack's sleeve. "It's been swell, but let's get out of here. I don't need to see her. I'm better off with the fantasy."

Jack didn't say anything. He just pointed with his chin to the stage behind me.

She had on a leopard skin leotard. She had been a dark blonde in high school but now her hair was brown and short. She'd put on a little weight, not much. She stretched in front of the mirrored wall and the DJ played the Pretenders.

I felt this weird, possessive kind of pride, watching her. That and lust. I'd been married for eight years and the worst thing I'd ever done was kiss an old girlfriend on New Year's Eve and stare longingly at the pictures in *Playboy*. But this was real, this was happening.

The song finished and another one started and she pulled one strap down on the leotard. I remembered the first time I'd seen her breasts. I was fifteen. I'd joined a youth club at the Unitarian Church because she went there Sunday afternoons. Sometimes we would skip the program and sneak off into the deserted Sunday school classrooms and there, in the twilight, surrounded by crayon drawings on manila paper, she would stretch out on the linoleum and let me lie on top of her and feel the maddening pressure of her pelvis and smell the faint, clinically erotic odor of peroxide in her hair.

She showed me her breasts on the golf course next door. We had jumped the fence and we lay in a sandtrap so no one would see us. There was a little light from the street, but not enough for real color. It was like a black and white movie when I played it back in my mind.

They were fuller now, hung a little lower and flatter, but I remembered the small, pale nipples. She pulled the other strap down, turned her back, rotating her hips as she stripped down to a red G-string. Somebody held a dollar out to her. I wanted to go over there and tell him that I knew her.

Jack kept poking me in the ribs. "Well? Well?"

"Be cool," I said. I had been watching the traffic pattern and I knew that after the song she would take a break and then get up on the other stage. It took a long time, but I wasn't tense about it. I'm just going to say hi, I thought. And that's it.

The song was over and she walked down the stairs at the end of the stage, throwing the leotard around her shoulders. I got up, having a little trouble with the chair, and walked over to her.

"Kristi," I said. "It's Dave McKenna."

"Oh my *God!*" She was in my arms. Her skin was hot from the lights and I could smell her deodorant. I was suddenly dizzy, aware of every square inch where our bodies touched. "Do you still hate me?" she said as she pulled away.

"What?" There was so much I'd forgotten. The twang in her voice. The milk chocolate color of her eyes. The beauty mark over her right cheekbone. The flirtatious look up through the lashes that now had a desperate edge to it.

"The last time I saw you, you called me a bitch. It was after that party at your teacher's house."

"No, I…believe me, it wasn't like.…"

"Listen, I'm on again," she said. "Where are you?"

"We're right over there."

"Oh Christ, you didn't bring your wife with you? I heard you were married."

"No, it's.…"

"I got to run, sugar, wait for me."

I went back to the table.

"You rascal," Jack said. "Why didn't you just slip it to her on the spot?"

"Shut up, Jack, will you?"

"Ooooh, touchy."

I watched her dance. She was no movie star. Her face was a little hard and even the heavy makeup didn't hide all the lines. But none of that mattered. What mattered was the way she moved, the kind of puckered smile that said yes, I want it too.

She sat down with us when she was finished. She seemed to be all hands, touching me on the arm, biting on a fingernail, gesturing in front of her face.

She was dancing three times a week, which was all they would schedule her for any more. The money was good and she didn't mind the work, especially here where it wasn't too rowdy. Jack raised his eyebrows at me to say, see? She got by with some modeling and some "scuffling" which I assumed meant turning tricks. Her mother was still in Dallas and had sent Kristi clippings the couple of times I got my name in the paper.

"She always liked me," I said.

"She liked you the best of all of them. You were a gentleman."

"Maybe too much of one."

"It was why I loved you." She was wearing the leotard again but she might as well have been naked. I was beginning to be afraid of her so I reminded myself that nothing had happened yet, nothing *had* to happen, that I wasn't committed to anything. I pushed my beer over to her and she drank about half of it. "It gets hot up there," she said. "You wouldn't believe. Sometimes you think you're going to pass out, but you got to keep smiling."

"Are you married?" I asked her. "Were you ever?"

"Once. It lasted two whole months. The shitheel knocked me up and then split."

"What happened?"

"I kept the kid. He's four now."

"What's his name?"

"Stoney. He's a cute little bastard. I got a neighbor watches him when I'm out, and I do the same for hers. He keeps me going sometimes." She drank the rest of the beer. "What about you?"

"I got a little boy too. Jeffrey. He's seven."

"Just the one?"

"I don't think the marriage could handle more than one kid," I said.

"It's an old story," Jack said. "If your wife puts you through law school, the marriage breaks up. It just took Dave a little longer than most."

"You're getting divorced?" she asked.

"I don't know. Maybe." She nodded. I guess she didn't need to ask for details. Marriages come apart every day.

"I'm on again in a little," she said. "Will you still be here when I get back?" She did what she could to make it sound casual.

"I got an early day tomorrow," I said.

"Sure. It was good to see you. Real good."

The easiest thing seemed to be to get out a pen and an old business card. "Give me your phone number. Maybe I can get loose another night."

She took the pen but she kept looking at me. "Sure," she said.

"You're an idiot," Jack said. "Why didn't you go home with her?"

I watched the streetlights. My jacket smelled like cigarettes and my head had started to hurt.

"That gorgeous piece of ass says to you, 'Ecstasy?' and Dave says, 'No thanks.' What the hell's the matter with you? Alice make you leave your dick in the safe-deposit box?"

"Jack," I said, "will you shut the fuck up?" The card with her number on it was in the inside pocket of the jacket. I could feel it there, like a cool fingernail against my flesh.

Jack went back to his room to crash a little after midnight. I couldn't sleep. I put on the headphones and listened to Robert Johnson, *King of the Delta Blues Singers*. There was something about his voice. He had this deadpan tone that sat down and told you what was wrong like it was no big deal. Then the voice would crack and you could tell it was a hell of a lot worse than he was letting on.

They said the devil himself had tuned Johnson's guitar. He died in 1938, poisoned by a jealous husband. He'd made his first recordings in a hotel room in San Antonio, just another seventy miles on down I-35.

Charlie and Gonzales and I took my car out to what Gonzales called the "site." The sheriff and a deputy were in a brown county station wagon behind us. Charlie sat on the passenger side and Gonzales was in the back. Charlie could have opened the door at a stoplight and been gone. He wasn't even in handcuffs. Nobody said anything about it.

We got on I-35 and Charlie said, "Go on south to the second exit after the caves." The Inner Space Caverns were just south of Georgetown, basically a single long, unspectacular tunnel that ran for miles under the highway. "I killed a girl there once. When they turned off the lights."

I nodded but I didn't say anything. That morning, before I went in to the "office," Gonzales had told me that it made Charlie angry if you let on that you didn't believe him. I was tired, and hung over from watching Jack drink, and I didn't really give a damn about Charlie's feelings.

I got off at the exit and followed the access road for a while. Charlie had his eyes closed and seemed to be thinking hard.

"Having trouble?" I asked him.

"Nah," he said. "Just didn't want to take you to the wrong one." I looked at him and he started laughing. It was a joke. Gonzales chuckled in the back seat and there was this cheerful kind of feeling in the car that made me want to pull over and run away.

"Nosir," Charlie said, "I sure don't suppose I'd want to do that." He grinned at me and he knew what I was thinking, he could see the horror right there on my face. He just kept smiling. Come on, I could hear him say. Loosen up. Be one of the guys.

I wiped the sweat from my hands onto my pant legs. Finally he said, "There's a dirt road a ways ahead. Turn off on it. It'll go over a hill and then across a cattle grating. After the grating is a stand of trees to the left. You'll want to park up under 'em."

How can he do this? I thought. He's got to know there's nothing there. Or does he? When we don't turn anything up, what's he going to do? Are they going to wish they'd cuffed him after all? The sheriff knew what I was up to, but none of the others did. Would Gonzales turn on me for betraying Charlie?

The road did just what Charlie said it would. We parked the cars under the trees and the deputy and I got shovels out of the sheriff's trunk. The trees were oaks and their leaves were tiny and very pale green.

"It would be over here," Charlie said. He stood on a patch of low ground, covered with clumps of Johnson grass. "Not too deep."

He was right. She was only about six or eight inches down. The deputy had a body bag and he tried to move her into it, but she kept coming apart. There wasn't much left but a skeleton and a few rags.

And the braces. Still shining, clinging to the teeth of the skull like a metal smile.

On the way back to Georgetown we passed a woman on the side of the road. She was staring into the hood of her car. She looked like she was about to cry. Charlie turned all the way around in his seat to watch her as we drove by.

"There's just victims ever'where," Charlie said. There was a sadness in his voice I didn't believe. "The highway's full of 'em. Kids, hitchhikers, waitresses.... You ever pick one up?"

"No," I said, but it wasn't true. It was in Dallas, I was home for spring break. It was the end of the sixties. She had on a green dress. Nothing happened. But she had smiled at me and put one arm up on the back of the seat. I was on the way to my girlfriend's house and I let her off a few blocks away. And that night, when I was inside her, I imagined my girlfriend with the hitchhiker's face, with her blonde hair and freckles, her slightly coarse features, the dots of sweat on her upper lip.

"But you thought about it," Charlie said. "Didn't you?"

"Listen," I said. "I've got a job to do. I just want to do it and get out of here, okay?"

"I know what you're saying," Charlie said. "Jesus forgives me, but I can't ask that of nobody else. I was just trying to get along, that's all. That's all any of us is ever trying to do."

I called Dallas collect from the sheriff's phone. He gave me a private room where I could shout if I had to. The switchboard put me through to Ricky Slatkin, Senior Assistant DA for Homicide.

"Dave, will you for Chrissake calm down. It's a coincidence. That's all. Forensics will figure out who this girl is and we'll put another seventy or eighty years on Charlie's sentence. Maybe give him another death penalty. What the hell, right? Meanwhile we'll give him another ringer."

"You give him one. I want out of this. I am fucking terrified."

"I, uh, understand you're under some stress at home these days."

"I am not at home. I'm in Georgetown, in the Williamson County Jail, and I am under some fucking stress right here. Don't you understand? He *thought* this dead girl into existence."

"What, Charlie Dean Harris is God now, is that it? Come on, Dave. Go out and have a few beers and by tomorrow it'll all make sense to you."

"He's evil, Jack," I said. We were back at his place after a pizza at Conan's. Jack had ordered a pitcher of beer and drunk it all himself. "I didn't use to believe in it, but that was before I met Charlie."

He had a women's basketball game on TV, the sound turned down to a low hum. "That's horseshit," he said. His voice was too loud. "Horseshit, Christian horseshit. They want you to believe that Evil has got a capital E and it's sitting over there in the corner, see it? Horseshit. Evil isn't a thing. It's something that's *not* there. It's an absence. The lack of the thing that stops you from doing whatever you damn well please."

He chugged half a beer. "Your pal Charlie ain't evil. He's just damaged goods. He's just like you or me but something died in him. You know what I'm talking about. You've felt it. First it goes to sleep and then it dies. Like when you stand up in court and try to get a rapist off when you know he did it. You tell yourself that it's part of the game, you try to give the asshole the benefit of the doubt, hell, somebody's got to do it, right? You try to believe the girl is just some slut that changed her mind, but you can smell it. Something inside you starting to rot."

He finished the beer and threw it at a paper sack in the corner. It hit another bottle inside the sack and shattered. "Then you go home and your wife's got a goddamn headache or her period or she's asleep in front of the TV or she's not in the goddamn mood and you just want to beat the...." His right fist was clenched up so tight the knuckles were a shiny yellow. His eyes looked like open sores. He got up for another beer and he was in the kitchen for a long time.

When he came back I said, "I'm going out." I said it without giving myself a chance to think about it.

"Kristi," Jack said. He had a fresh beer and was all right again.

"Yeah."

"You bastard! Can I smell your fingers when you get back?"

"Fuck you, Jack."

"Oh no, save it for her. She's going to use you up, you lucky bastard."

✠   ✠   ✠

I called her from a pay phone and she gave me directions. She was at the Royal Palms Trailer Park, near Bergstrom Air Force Base on the south end of town. It wasn't hard to find. They even had a few palm trees. There were rural-type galvanized mailboxes on posts by the gravel driveways. I found the one that said Spector and parked behind a white Dodge with six-figure mileage.

The temperature was in the sixties but I was shaking. My shoulders kept trying to crawl up around my neck. I got out of the car. I couldn't feel my feet. Asshole, I told myself. I don't want to hear about your personal problems. You better enjoy this or I'll fucking kill you.

I knocked on the door and it made a kind of mute rattling sound. Kristi opened it. She was wearing a plaid bathrobe, so old I couldn't tell what the colors used to be. She stood back to let me in and said, "I didn't think you'd call."

"But I did," I said. The trailer was tiny—a living room with a green sofa and a thirteen-inch color TV, a kitchen the size of a short hall, a single bedroom behind it, the door open, the bed unmade. A blond-haired boy was asleep on the sofa, wrapped in an army blanket. The shelf above him was full of plays— Albee, Ionesco, Tennessee Williams. The walls were covered with photographs in dime-store frames.

A couple of them were from the drama club; one even had me in it. I was sixteen and looked maybe nine. My hair was too long in front, my chest was sucked in, and I had a stupid smirk on my face. I was looking at Kristi. Who would want to look at anything else? She had on cutoffs that had frayed up past the crease of her thighs. Her shirt was unbuttoned and tied under her breasts. Her head was back and she was laughing. I'd always been able to make her laugh.

"You want a drink?" she whispered.

"No," I said. I turned to look at her. We weren't either of us laughing now. I reached for her and she glanced over at the boy and shook her head. She grabbed the cuff of my shirt and pulled me gently back toward the bedroom.

It smelled of perfume and hand lotion and a little of mildew. The only light trickled in through heavy, old-fashioned Venetian blinds. She untied the bathrobe and let it fall. I kissed her and her arms went around my neck. I touched her shoulder blades and her hair and her buttocks and then I got out of my clothes and left them in a pile on the floor. She ran on tiptoes back to the front of the trailer and locked and chained the door. Then she came back and shut the bedroom door and lay down on the bed.

I lay down next to her. The smell and feel of her was wonderful, and at the same time it was not quite real. There were too many unfamiliar things and it was hard to connect to the rest of my life.

Then I was on my knees between her legs, gently touching her. Her arms were spread out beside her, tangled in the sheets, her hips moving with pleasure. Only once, in high school, had she let me touch her there, in the back seat of a friend's car, her skirt up around her hips, panties to her knees, and before I had recovered from the wonder of it she had pulled away.

But that was eighteen years ago and this was now. A lot of men had touched her since then. But that was all right. She took a condom out of the nightstand and I put it on and she guided me inside her. She tried to say something, maybe it was only my name, but I put my mouth over hers to shut her up. I put both my arms around her and closed my eyes and let the heat and pleasure run up through me.

When I finished and we rolled apart she lay on top of me, pinning me to the bed. "That was real sweet," she said.

I kissed her and hugged her because I couldn't say what I was thinking. I was thinking about Charlie, remembering the earnest look on his face when he said, "It was just to have sex, that's all."

She was wide awake and I was exhausted. She complained about the state cutting back on aid to single parents. She told me about the tiny pieces of tape she had to wear on the ends of her nipples when she danced, a weird Health Department regulation. I remembered the tiny golden flashes and fell asleep to the memory of her dancing.

Screaming woke me up. Kristi was already out of bed and headed for the living room. "It's just Stoney," she said, and I lay back down.

I woke up again a little before dawn. There was an arm around my waist but it seemed much too small. I rolled over and saw that the little boy had crawled into bed between us.

I got up without moving him and went to the bathroom. There was no water in the toilet; when I pushed the handle a trap opened in the bottom of the bowl and a fine spray washed the sides. I got dressed, trying not to bump into anything. Kristi was asleep on the side of the bed closest to the door, her mouth open a little. Stoney had burrowed into the middle of her back.

I was going to turn around and go when a voyeuristic impulse made me open the drawer of her nightstand. Or maybe I subconsciously knew what I'd find. There was a Beeline book called *Molly's Sexual Follies*, a tube of KY, a box of Ramses lubricated condoms, a few used Kleenex. An emery board, a finger puppet, one hoop earring. A short-barreled Colt .32 revolver.

I got to the jail at nine in the morning. The woman at the visitor's window recognized me and buzzed me back. Gonzales was at his desk. He looked up when I walked in and said, "I didn't know you was coming in today."

"I just had a couple of quick questions for Charlie," I said. "Only take a second."

"Did you want to use the office...?"

"No, no point. If I could just talk to him in his cell for a couple of minutes, that would be great."

Gonzales got the keys. Charlie had a cell to himself, five by ten feet, white-painted bars on the long wall facing the corridor. There were Bibles and religious tracts on his cot, a few paintings hanging on the wall. "Maybe you can get Charlie to show you his pictures," Gonzales said. A stool in the corner had brushes and tubes of paint on the top.

"You painted these?" I asked Charlie. My voice sounded fairly normal, all things considered.

"Yessir, I did."

"They're pretty good." They were landscapes with trees and horses, but no people.

"Thank you kindly."

"You can just call for me when you're ready," Gonzales said. He went out and locked the door.

"I thought you'd be back," Charlie said. "Was there something else you wanted to ask me?" He sat on the edge of the cot, forearms on his knees.

I didn't say anything. I took the Colt out of the waistband of my pants and pointed it at him. I'd already looked it over on the drive up and there were bullets in all six cylinders. My hand was shaking so I steadied it with my left and fired all six rounds into his head and chest.

I hadn't noticed all the background noises until they stopped, the typewriters and the birds and somebody singing upstairs. Charlie stood up and walked over to where I was standing. The revolver clicked on an empty shell.

"You can't kill me," Charlie said with his droopy-eyed smile. "You can't never kill me." The door banged open at the end of the hall. "You can't kill me because I'm inside you."

I dropped the gun and locked my hands behind my head. Gonzales stuck his head around the corner. He was squinting. He had his gun out and he looked terrified. Charlie and I stared back at him calmly.

"It's okay, Ernie," Charlie said. "No harm done. Mr. McKenna was just having him a little joke."

Charlie told Gonzales the gun was loaded with blanks. They had to believe him because there weren't any bulletholes in the cell. I told them I'd bought the gun off a defendant years ago, that I'd had it in the car.

They called Dallas and Ricky asked to talk to me. "There's going to be an inquiry," he said. "No way around it."

"Sure there is," I said. "I quit. I'll send it to you in writing. I'll put it in the mail today. Express."

"You need some help, Dave. You understand what I'm saying to you here? *Professional* help. Think about it. Just tell me you'll think about it."

Gonzales was scared and angry and wanted me charged with smuggling weapons into the jail. The sheriff knew it wasn't worth the headlines and by suppertime I was out.

Jack had already heard about it through some kind of legal grapevine. He thought it was funny. We skipped dinner and went down to the bars on Sixth Street. I couldn't drink anything. I was afraid of going numb, or letting down my guard. But Jack made up for me. As usual.

"Kristi called me today," Jack said. "I told her I didn't know but that you might be going back to Dallas today. Just a kind of feeling I had."

"I'm not going back," I said. "But it was the right thing to tell her."

"Not what it was cracked up to be, huh?"

"Oh yeah," I said. "That and much, much more."

For once he let it go. "You mean you're not going back tonight or not going back period?"

"Period," I said. "My job's gone, I pissed that away this morning. I'll get something down here. I don't care what. I'll pump gas. I'll fucking wait tables. You can draw up the divorce papers and I'll sign them."

"Just like that?"

"Just like that."

"What's Alice going to say?"

"I don't know if she'll even notice. She can have the goddamn house and her car and the savings. All of it. All I want is some time with Jeffrey. As much as I can get. Every week if I can."

"Good luck."

"I've got to have it. I don't want him growing up screwed up like the rest of us. I've got stuff I've got to tell him. He's going to need help. All of us are. Jack, goddamn it, are you listening to me?"

He wasn't. He was staring at the Heart video on the bar's big screen TV, at the blonde guitarist. "Look at that," Jack said. "Sweet suffering Jesus. Couldn't you just fuck that to death?"

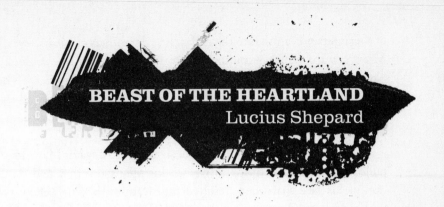

BEAST OF THE HEARTLAND
Lucius Shepard

MEARS HAS A dream the night after he fought the Alligator Man. The dream begins with words: "In the beginning was a dark little god with glowing red eyes...." And then, there it stands, hovering in the blackness of Mears's hotel room, a twisted mandrake root of a god, evil and African, with ember eyes and limbs like twists of leaf tobacco. Even after it vanishes, waking Mears, he can feel those eyes burning inside his head, merged into a single red pain that seems as if it will go on throbbing forever. He wonders if he should tell Leon about the pain—maybe he could give Mears something to ease it—but he figures this might be a bad idea. Leon might cut and run, not wanting to be held responsible should Mears keel over, and there Mears would be: without a trainer, without anyone to coach him for the eye exams, without an accomplice in his blindness. It's not a priority, he decides.

To distract himself, he lies back and thinks about the fight. He'd been doing pretty well until the ninth. Staying right on the Cuban's chest, mauling him in the corners, working the body. The Cuban didn't like it to the body. He was a honey-colored kid a couple of shades lighter than Mears and he punched like a kid, punches that stung but that didn't take your heart like the punches of a man. Fast, though. Jesus, he was fast! As the fight passed into the middle rounds, as Mears tired, the Cuban began to slip away, to circle out of the haze of ring light and vanish into the darkness at the corners of Mears's eyes, so that Mears saw the punches coming only at the last second, the wet-looking red blobs of the gloves looping in over his guard. Then, in the ninth, a left he never saw drove him into the turnbuckle, a flurry of shots under the ribs popped his mouthpiece halfway out and another left to the temple made him clinch, pinning the Cuban's gloves against his sides.

In the clinch, that's when he caught sight of the Alligator Man. The Cuban pulled back his head, trying to wrench his right glove free, and the blurred oval of his face sharpened, resolved into features: blazing yellow eyes and pebbly skin, and slit nostrils at the end of a long snout. Although used to such visions, hallucinations, whatever this was, Mears reacted in terror. He jolted the Alligator Man with an uppercut, he spun him, landed a clubbing right high on the head, another right, and as if those punches were magic, as if their force and number were removing a curse, breaking a spell, the Alligator Man's face melted away, becoming a blurred brown oval once again. Mears's terror also grew blurred, his attack less furious, and the Cuban came back at him, throwing shots from every angle. Mears tried to slide off along the ropes but his legs were gone, so he ducked his head and put his gloves up to block the shots. But they got through, anyway.

Somebody's arms went around him, hemming him in against the ropes, and he smelled flowery cologne and heard a smooth baritone saying, "Take it easy, man! It's over." Mears wanted to tell the ref he could have stood up through ten, the Cuban couldn't punch for shit. But he was too weak to say anything and he just rested his head on the ref's shoulder, strings of drool hanging off his mouthpiece, cooling on his chin. And for the first time in a long while, he heard the crowd screaming for the Cuban, the women's voices bright and crazy, piercing up from the male roar. Then Leon was there, Leon's astringent smell of Avitene and Vaseline and Gelfoam, and somebody shoved Mears down onto a stool and Leon pressed the ice-cold bar of the Enswell against the lump over his eye, and the Cuban elbowed his way through the commission officials and nobodies in the corner and said, "Man, you one tough motherfucker. You almos' kill me with them right hands." And Mears had the urge to tell him, "You think I'm tough, wait'll you see what's coming," but instead, moved by the sudden, heady love that possesses you after you have pounded on a man for nine rounds and he has not fallen, Mears told him that one day soon he would be champion of the world.

Mears wonders if the bestial faces that materialize in the midst of his fights are related to the pain in his head. In his heart he believes they are something else. It could be that he has been granted the magical power to see beneath the surface of things. Or they may be something his mind has created to compensate for his blindness, a kind of spiritual adrenaline that inspires him to fiercer effort, often to victory. Since his retinas became detached, he has slipped from the status of fringe contender to trial horse for young fighters on the way up, and his style has changed from one of grace and elusiveness to that of a brawler, of someone who must keep in constant physical contact with his opponent. Nevertheless, he has won twelve of seventeen fights with his handicap, and he owes much of his success to this symptom or gift or delusion.

He knows most people would consider him a fool for continuing to fight, and he accepts this. But he does not consider himself a greater fool than most people; his is only a more dramatic kind of foolishness than the foolishness of loving a bad woman or stealing a car or speculating on gold futures or smoking cigarettes or taking steroids or eating wrong or involving yourself with the trillion other things that lead to damage and death.

As he lies in that darkened room, in the pall of his own darkness, he imagines attending a benefit held to raise his medical expenses after his secret has been disclosed. All the legends are there. Ali, Frazier, and Foreman are there, men who walk with the pride of a nation. Duran is there, Duran of the demonic fury, who TKO'd him in 1979, back when Mears was a welterweight. The Hitman is there, Thomas Hearns, sinister and rangy, with a cobra-like jab that had once cut him so badly the flesh hung down into his eyes. Sugar Ray Leonard is there, talking about his own detached retina and how he could have gone the same way as Mears. And Hagler, who knocked Mears out in his only title shot, Hagler the tigerish southpaw, he is there, too. Mears ascends to the podium to offer thanks, and a reporter catches his arm and asks him, "What the hell went wrong, Bobby? What happened to you?" He thinks of all the things he could say in response. Bad managers, crooked promoters. Alimony. I forgot to duck. The classic answers. But there is one answer they've never heard, one that he's nourished for almost two years.

"I traveled into the heartland," he tells the reporter, "and when I got done fighting the animals there, I came out blind."

The reporter looks puzzled, but Ali and Foreman, Frazier and Hagler, Duran and Hearns, they nod sagely, they understand. They realize Mears's answer is partly a pride thing, partly intuitive, a summation of punches absorbed, hands lifted in victory, months of painful healing, hours of punishment in the gym. But mainly it is the recasting into a vow of a decision made years before. They would not argue that their sport is brutally stupid, run by uncaring bastards to whom it is a business of dollars and blood, and that tragedies occur, that fighters are swindled and outright robbed. Yet there is something about it they have needed, something they have chosen, and so in the end, unlike the asbestos worker who bitterly decries the management that has lied to him and led him down a fatal path, the fighter feels no core bitterness, not even at himself for being a fool, for making such a choice in the folly of youth, because he has forsworn the illusion of wisdom.

Mears is not without regrets. Sometimes, indeed, he regrets almost everything. He regrets his blindness, his taste in women, his rotten luck at having been a middleweight during the age of Marvin Hagler. But he has never regretted boxing. He loves what he does, loves the gym rats, the old dozers with their half-remembered tales of Beau Jack and Henry Armstrong, the crafty trainers, the quiet cut men with their satchels full of swabs and chemicals. He loves how he has been in the ring, honorable and determined and brave. And now, nodding off in a cheap hotel room, he feels love from the legends of the game returned in applause that has the sound of rushing water, a pure stream of affirmation that bears him away into the company of heroes and a restless sleep.

Three mornings later, as Mears waits for Leon in the gym, he listens happily to the slapping of jump ropes, the grunt and thud of someone working the heavy bag, the jabber and pop of speed bags, fighters shouting encouragement, the sandpapery whisk of shoes on canvas, the meaty thump of fourteen-ounce sparring gloves. Pale winter light chutes through the high windows like a Bethlehem star to Mears's eyes. The smell is a harsh perfume of antiseptic, resin, and sweat. Now and then somebody passes by, says, "Yo, Bobby, what's happenin'?" or "Look good the other night, man!" and he will hold out his hand to be slapped without glancing up, pretending that his diffidence is an expression of cool, not a pose designed to disguise his impaired vision. His body still aches from the Cuban's fast hands, but in a few weeks, a few days if necessary, he'll be ready to fight again.

He hears Leon rasping at someone, smells his cigar, then spots a dark interruption in the light. Not having to see Leon, he thinks, is one of the few virtues of being legally blind. He is unsightly, a chocolate-colored blob of a man with jowls and yellow teeth and a belly that hangs over his belt. The waist of Mears's boxing trunks would not fit over one of Leon's thighs. He is especially unsightly when he lies, which is often—weakness comes into his face, his popped eyes dart, the pink tip of the tongue slimes the gristly upper lip. He looks much better as a blur in an onion-colored shirt and dark trousers.

"Got a fight for us, my man." Leon drops onto a folding chair beside him, and the chair yields a metallic creak. "Mexican name Nazario. We gon' kick his fuckin' ass!"

This is the same thing Leon said about the Cuban, the same thing he said about every opponent. But this time he may actually be sincere. "Guy's made for us," he continues. "Comes straight ahead. Good hook, but a nothin' right. No fancy bullshit." He claps Bobby on the leg. "We need a W bad, man. We whup this guy in style, I can get us a main event on ESPN next month in Wichita."

Mears is dubious. "Fighting who?"

"Vederotta," says Leon, hurrying past the name to say the Nazario fight is in two weeks. "We can be ready by then, can't we, sure, we be ready, we gon' kill that motherfucker."

"That guy calls himself the Heat? Guy everybody's been duckin'?"

"Wasn't for everybody duckin' him, I couldn't get us the fight. He's tough, I ain't gon' tell you no lie. He busts people up. But check it out, man. Our end's twenty grand. Like that, Bobby? Tuh-wenty thousand dollars."

"You shittin' me?"

"They fuckin' desperate. They can't get nobody to fight the son of a bitch. They need a tune-up for a title shot." Leon sucks on his cigar, trying to puff it alight. "It's your ass out there, man. I'll do what you tell me. But we get past Nazario, we show good against Vederotta—I mean give him a few strong rounds, don't just fold in one—guy swears he'll book us three more fights on ESPN cards. Maybe not the main event, but TV bouts. That'd make our year, man. Your end could work out to forty, forty-five."

"You get that in writin' 'bout the three more fights?"

"Pretty sure. Man's so damn desperate for somebody with a decent chin, he'll throw in a weekend with his wife."

"I don't want his damn wife, I want it in writin' 'bout the fights."

"You ain't seen his wife! That bitch got a wiggle take the kinks outta a couch spring." Delighted by his wit, Leon laughs; the laugh turns into a wet, racking cough.

"I'm gon' need you on this one," says Mears after the coughing has subsided. "None of this bullshit 'bout you runnin' round all over after dope and pussy while I'm bustin' my balls in the gym, and then showin' up when the bell rings. I'm gon' need you really working. You hear that, Leon?"

Leon's breath comes hard. "I hear you."

"Square business, man. You gotta write me a book on that Vederotta dude."

"I'll do my thing," says Leon, wheezing. "You just take care of old Señor Nazario."

The deal concluded, Mears feels exposed, as if a vast, luminous eye—God's, perhaps—is shining on him, revealing all his frailties. He sits up straight, holds his head very still, rubs his palms along the tops of his thighs, certain that everyone is watching. Leon's breathing is hoarse and labored, like last breaths. The light is beginning to tighten up around that sound, to congeal into something cold and gray, like a piece of dirty ice in which they are all embedded.

Mears thinks of Vederotta, the things he's heard. The one-round knockouts, the vicious beatings. He knows he's just booked himself a world of hurt. As if in resonance with that thought, his vision ripples and there is a twinge inside his head, a little flash of red. He grips the seat of the chair, prepares for worse. But worse does not come, and after a minute or so, he begins to relax, thinking about the money, slipping back into the peace of morning in the gym, with the starred light shining from on high and the enthusiastic shouts of the young fighters and the slap of leather making a rhythm like a river slapping against a bank and the fat man who is not his friend beginning to breathe easier now beside him.

When Mears phones his ex-wife, Amandla, the next night, he sits on the edge of the bed and closes his eyes so he can see her clearly. She's wearing her blue robe, slim-hipped and light-skinned, almost like a Latin girl, but her features are fine and eloquently African and her hair is kept short in the way of a girl from Brazzaville or Conakry. He remembers how good she looks in big gold hoop earrings. He remembers so much sweetness, so much consolation and love. She simply had not been able to bear his pain, coming home with butterfly patches over his stitched eyes, pissing blood at midnight, having to heave himself up from a chair like an old man. It was a weakness in her, he thinks, yet he knows it was an equivalent weakness in him, that fighting is his crack, his heroin—he would not give it up for her.

She picks up on the fourth ring, and he says, "How you been, baby?"

She hesitates a moment before saying, "Aw, Bobby, what you want?" But she says it softly, plaintively, so he'll know that though it's not a good thing to call, she's glad to hear his voice, anyway.

"Nothin', baby," he says. "I don't want nothin'. I just called to tell you I'll be sendin' money soon. Few weeks, maybe."

"You don't have to. I'm makin' it all right."

"Don't tell me you can't use a little extra. You got responsibilities."

A faded laugh. "I hear that."

There is silence for a few beats, then Mears says, "How's your mama holdin' up?"

"Not so good. Half the time I don't think she knows who I am. She goes to wanderin' off sometimes, and I got to—" She breaks off, lets air hiss out between her teeth. "I'm sorry, Bobby. This ain't your trouble."

That stings him, but he does not respond directly to it. "Well, maybe I send you a little somethin', you can ease back from it."

"I don't want to short you."

"You ain't gon' be shortin' me, baby." He tells her about Nazario, the twenty thousand dollars, but not about Vederotta.

"Twenty thousand!" she says. "They givin' you twenty thousand for fightin' a man you say's easy? That don't make any sense."

"Ain't like I'm just off the farm. I still got a name."

"Yeah, but you—"

"Don't worry about it," he says angrily, knowing that she's about to remind him he's on the downside. "I got it under control."

Another silence. He imagines that he can hear her irritation in the static on the line.

"But I do worry," she says. "God help me, I still worry about you after all this time."

"Ain't been that long. Three years."

She does not seem to have heard. "I still think about you under them lights gettin' pounded on. And now you offerin' me money you gon' earn for gettin' pounded on some more."

"Look here—" he begins.

"Blood money. That's what it is. It's blood money."

"Stop it," he says. "You stop that shit. It ain't no more blood money than any other wage. Money gets paid out, somebody always gettin' fucked over at the end of it. That's just what money is. But this here money, it ain't comin' 'cause of nothin' like that, not even 'cause some damn judge said I got to give it. It's coming from me to you 'cause you need it and I got it."

He steers the conversation away from the topic of fighting, gets her talking about some of their old friends, even manages to get her laughing when he tells her how the cops caught Sidney Bodden and some woman doing the creature in Sidney's car in the parking lot of the A&P. The way she laughs, she tips her head and tucks her chin down onto her shoulder and never opens her mouth, just makes these pleased, musical noises like a shy little girl, and when she lifts her head, she looks so innocent and pretty he wants to kiss her, grazes the receiver with his lips, wishes it would open and let him pour through to her end of the line. The power behind the wish hits his heart like a mainlined drug, and he knows she still loves him, he still loves her, this is all wrong, this long-distance shit, and he can't stop himself from saying, "Baby, I want to see you again."

"No," she says.

It is such a terminal, door-slamming no, he can't come back with anything. His face is hot and numb, his arms and chest heavy as concrete, he feels the same bewildered, mule-stupid helplessness as he did when she told him she was leaving. He wonders if she's seeing somebody, but he promises himself he won't ask.

"I just can't, Bobby," she says.

"It's all right, baby," he says, his voice reduced to a whisper. "It's all right. I got to be goin'."

"I'm sorry, I really am sorry. But I just can't."

"I'll be sending you somethin' real soon. You take care now."

"Bobby?"

He hangs up, an effort, and sits there turning to stone. Brooding thoughts glide through his head like slow black sails. After a while he lifts his arms as if in an embrace. He feels Amandla begin to take on shape and solidity within the circle of his arms. He puts his left hand between her shoulder blades and smoothes the other along her flanks, following the arch of her back, the tight rounds of her ass, the columned thighs, and he presses his face against her belly, smelling her warmth, letting all the trouble and ache of the fight with the Cuban go out of him. All the weight of loss and sadness. His chest seems to fill with something clear and buoyant. Peace, he thinks, we are at peace.

But then some sly, peripheral sense alerts him to the fact that he is a fool to rely on this sentimental illusion, and he drops his arms, feeling her fading away like steam. He sits straight, hands on knees, and turns his head to the side, his expression rigid and contemptuous as it might be during a stare-down at the center of a boxing ring. Since the onset of his blindness, he has never been able to escape the fear that people are spying on him, but lately he has begun to worry that they are not.

For once Leon has not lied. The fight with Nazario is a simple contest of wills and left hooks, and though the two men's hooks are comparable, Mears's will is by far the stronger. Only in the fourth round does he feel his control slipping, and then the face of a hooded serpent materializes where Nazario's face should be, and he pounds the serpent image with right leads until it vanishes. Early in the fifth round, he bulls Nazario into a corner, and following a sequence of twelve unanswered punches, the ref steps in and stops it.

Two hours after the fight, Mears is sitting in the dimly lit bar on the bottom floor of his hotel, having a draft beer and a shot of Gentleman Jack, listening to Mariah Carey on the jukebox. The mirror is a black, rippling distance flocked by points of actinic light, a mysterious lake full of stars and no sign of his reflection. The hooker beside him is wearing a dark something sewn all over with spangles that move over breasts and hips and thighs like the scattering of moonlight on choppy water. The bartender, when he's visible at all, is a cryptic shadow. Mears is banged up some, a small but nasty cut at his hairline from a head butt and a knot on his left cheekbone, which the hooker is making much of, touching it, saying, "That's terrible-lookin', honey, just terrible. You inna accident or somepin'?" Mears tells her to mind her own damn business, and she says, "Who you think you is, you ain't my business? You better quit yo' dissin' 'cause I ain't takin' that kinda shit from nobody!"

He buys her another drink to mollify her and goes back to his interior concerns. Although the pain from the fight is minimal, his eyes are acting up and there is a feeling of dread imminence inside his head, an apprehension of a slight wrongness that can bloom into a fiery red presence. He is trying, by maintaining a certain poise, to resist it.

The hooker leans against him. Her breasts are big and sloppy soft and her perfume smells cheap like flowered Listerine, but her waist is slender and firm, and despite her apparent toughness, he senses that she is very young, new to the life. This barely hardened innocence makes him think of Amandla.

"Don't you wan' go upstairs, baby?" she says as her hand traces loops and circles along the inside of his thigh.

"We be there soon enough," he says gruffly. "We got all night."

"Whoo!" She pulls back from him. "I never seen a young man act so stern! 'Mind me of my daddy!" From her stagy tone, he realizes she is playing to the other patrons of the place, whom he cannot see, invisible as gods on their bar stools. Then she is rubbing against him again, saying, "You gon' treat me like my daddy, honey? You gon' be hard on me?"

"Listen up," he says quietly, putting a hand on her arm. "Don't you be playin' these games. I'm payin' you good, so you just sit still and we'll have a couple drinks and talk a little bit. When the time comes, we'll go upstairs. Can you deal with that?"

He feels resentment in the tension of her arm. "OK, baby," she says with casual falsity. "What you wan' talk about?"

Mariah Carey is having a vision of love, her sinewy falsetto going high into a gospel frequency, and Mears asks the hooker if she likes the song.

She shrugs. "It's all right."

"You know the words?"

"Uh-huh."

"Sing it with me?"

"Say what?"

He starts to sing, and after a couple of seconds the hooker joins in. Her voice is slight and sugary but blends well with Mears's tenor. As they sing, her enthusiasm grows and Mears feels a frail connection forming between them. When the record ends, she giggles, embarrassed, and says, "That was def, baby. You sing real good. You a musician?"

"Naw, just church stuff, you know."

"Bobby Mears!" A man's voice brays out behind him, a hand falls heavily onto his shoulder. "Goddamn, it is you! My fren', he saying, 'Ain't that Bobby Mears over there?' and I said, 'Shit, what he be doin' in here?'"

The man is huge, dark as a coal sack against the lesser darkness, and Mears has no clue to his identity.

"Yes, sir! Bobby 'the Magician' Mears! I'm your biggest fan, no shit! I seen you fight a dozen times. And I ain't talkin' TV. I mean in person. Man, this is great! Can I get you a drink? Lemme buy you one. Hey, buddy! Give us another round over here, OK?"

"'Nother draft, 'nother shot of the Gentleman," says the bartender in a singsong delivery as he pours. He picks up the hooker's glass and says with less flair, "Vodka and coke."

"Sister," the man says to the hooker, "I don't know what Bobby's been tellin' you, but you settin' next to one of the greatest fighters ever lived."

The hooker says, "You a fighter, baby?" and Mears, who has been seething at this interruption, starts to say it's time to leave, but the man talks through him.

"The boy was slick! I'm tellin' you. Slickest thing you ever seen with that jab of his. Like to kill Marvin Hagler. That old baldhead was one lucky nigger that night. Ain't it the truth, man?"

"Bullshit," Mears says.

"Man's jus' bein' modest."

"I ain't bein' modest. Hagler was hurtin' me from round one, and all I's doin' was tryin' to survive." Mears digs a roll of bills from his pocket, peels a twenty from the top—the twenties are always on top; then the tens, then the fives. "Anybody saw that fight and thinks Hagler was lucky don't know jack shit. Hagler was the best, and it don't make me feel no better 'bout not bein' the best, you comin' round and bullshittin' me."

"Be cool, Bobby! All right, man? Be cool."

The hooker caresses Mears's shoulders, his neck, and he feels the knots of muscle, like hard tumors. It would take a thousand left hooks to work out that tension, a thousand solid impacts to drain off the poisons of fear lodged there, and he experiences a powerful welling up of despair that seems connected to no memory or incident, no stimulus whatsoever, a kind of bottom emotion, one you would never notice unless the light and the temperature and the noise level, all the conditions, were just right. But it's there all the time, the tarry stuff that floors your soul. He tells the man he's sorry for having lashed out at him. He's tired, he says, got shit on his mind.

"Hey," says the man, "hey, it's not a problem, OK?"

There follows a prickly silence that ends when Aaron Neville comes on the jukebox. Mears goes away with the tune, with the singer's liquid shifts and drops, like the voice of a saxophone, and is annoyed once again when the man says, "Who you fightin' next, Bobby? You got somethin' lined up?"

"Vederotta," Mears says.

"The Heat, man? You fightin' the Heat? No shit! Hey, you better watch your ass with that white boy! I seen him fight Reggie Williams couple months back. Hit that man so hard, two his teeth come away stuck in the mouthpiece."

Mears slides the twenty across the bar and says, "Keep it" to the bartender.

"That's right," says the man with apparent relish. "That white boy ain't normal, you ax me. He jus' be livin' to fuck you up, know what I mean? He got somethin' wrong in his head."

"Thanks for the drink," Mears says, standing.

"Any time, Bobby, any time," the man says as Mears lets the hooker lead him toward the stairs. "You take my advice, man. Watch yourself with that Vederotta. That boy he gon' come hard, and you ain't no way slick as you used to be."

Cold blue neon winks on and off in the window of Mears's room, a vague nebular shine that might be radiating from a polar beacon or a ghostly police car, and as the hooker undresses, he lies on the bed in his shorts and watches the light. It's the only thing he sees, just that chilly blue in a black field, spreading across the surface of the glass like some undersea thing, shrinking and expanding like the contractions of an icy blue heart. He has always been afraid before a fight, yet now he's afraid in a different way. Or maybe it's not the fear that's different, maybe it's his resistance to it that has changed. Maybe he's weaker, wearier. He is so accustomed to suppressing fear, however, that when he tries to examine it, it slithers away into the cracks of his soul and hides there, lurking, eyes aglow, waiting for its time. Vederotta. The man's name even sounds strong, like a foreign sin, an age-old curse.

"Ain't you wan' the lights on, honey?" asks the hooker. "I wan' you be able see what you doin'."

"I see you just fine," he says. "You come on lie down."

A siren curls into the distance; two car horns start to blow in an impatient rhythm like brass animals angry at each other; smells of barbecue and gasoline drift in to overwhelm the odor of industrial cleaner.

Training, he thinks. Once he starts to train, he'll handle the fear. He'll pave it over with thousands of sit-ups, miles of running, countless combinations, and by fight night there'll be just enough left to motivate him.

The hooker settles onto the bed, lies on her side, leaning over him, her breasts spilling onto his chest and arm. He lifts one in his palm, squeezing its heft, and she makes a soft, pleased noise.

"Why you didn't tell me you famous?" she asks.

"I ain't famous."

"Yeah, but you was."

"What difference it make? Bein' famous ain't about nothin'."

She moves her shoulders, making her breasts roll against him, and her hot, sweet scent seems to thicken. "Jus' nice to know is all." She runs a hand along his chest, his corded belly. "Ain't you somepin'," she says, and then, "How old're you, baby?"

"Thirty-two."

He expects her to say, "Thirty-two! Damn, baby. I thought you was twenty-five, you lookin' good." But all she does is give a little *mmm* sound as if she's filing the fact away and goes on caressing him. By this he knows that the connection they were starting to make in the bar has held and she's going to be herself with him, which is what he wants, not some play-acting bitch who will let him turn her into Amandla, because he is sick and tired of having that happen.

She helps him off with his shorts and brings him all the way hard with her hand, then touches his cock to her breasts, lets it butt and slide against her cheek, takes it in her mouth for just seconds, like into warm syrup, her tongue

CRUCIFIED DREAMS

swirling, getting his hips to bridge up from the mattress, wise and playful in her moves, and finally she comes astride him and says, "I believe I'm ready for some of this, baby," her voice burred, and she reaches for him, puts him where she needs it, and then her whole dark, sweet weight swings down slick and hot around him, and his neck arches, his mouth strains open and his head pushes back into the pillow, feeling as if he's dipped the back of his brain into a dark green pool, this ancient place with mossy-stone temples beneath the water and strange carvings and spirits gliding in and out the columns. When that moment passes, he finds she's riding him slow and deep and easy, not talking hooker trash, but fucking him like a young girl, her breath shaky and musical, hands braced on the pillow by his head, and he slides his hands around to cup her ass, to her back, pressing down so that her breasts graze and nudge his chest, and it's all going so right he forgets to think how good it is and gives himself over to the arc of his feelings and the steady, sinuous beat of her heart-filled body.

Afterward there is something shy and delicate between them, something he knows won't survive for long, maybe not even until morning, and maybe it's all false, maybe they have only played a deeper game, but if so, it's deep enough that the truth doesn't matter, and they are for now in that small room somewhere dark and green, the edge of that pool he dipped into for a second, a wood, sacred, with the calls of those strange metal beasts sounding in the distance from the desolate town. A shadow is circling beneath the surface of the pool, it's old, wrinkled, hard with evil, like a pale crocodile that's never been up into the light, but it's not an animal, not even a thought, it's just a name: Vederotta. He holds her tight, keeps two fingers pushed between her legs touching the heated damp of her, feeling her pulse there, still rapid and trilling, and he wants to know a little more about her, anything, just one thing, and when he whispers the only question he can think to ask, she wriggles around, holding his two fingers in place, turns her face to his chest, and says her name is Arlene.

Training is like religion to Mears, the litanies of sparring, the penances of one-arm push-ups, the long retreats of his morning runs, the monastic breakfasts at four A.M., the vigils in the steam room during which he visualizes with the intensity of prayer what will happen in the ring, and as with a religion, he feels it simplifying him, paring him down, reducing his focus to a single consuming pursuit. On this occasion, however, he allows himself to be distracted and twice sleeps with Arlene. At first she tries to act flighty and brittle as she did in the bar, but when they go upstairs, that mask falls away and it is good for them again. The next night she displays no pretense whatsoever. They fuck wildly like lovers who have been long separated, and just before dawn they wind up lying on their sides, still joined, hips still moving sporadically. Mears's head is jangled and full of anxious incoherencies. He's worried about how he will suffer for this later in the gym and concerned by what is happening with Arlene. It seems he is being given a last sweetness, a young girl not yet hardened beyond repair, a girl who has some honest affection for him, who perhaps sees him as a means of salvation. This makes him think he is being prepared for something bad by God or whomever. Although he's been prepared for the worst for quite a while, now he wonders if the Vederotta fight will somehow prove to be worse than the worst, and frightened by this, he tells Arlene he can't see her again until after the fight. Being with her, he says, saps his strength and he needs all his strength for Vederotta. If she is the kind of woman who has hurt him in the past, he knows she will react badly, she will accuse him of trying to dump her, she will rave and screech and demand his attentions. And she does become angry, but when he explains that he is risking serious injury by losing his focus, her defensiveness—that's what has provoked her anger—subsides, and she pulls him atop her, draws up her knees and takes him deep, gluing him to her sticky thighs, and as the sky turns the color of tin and delivery traffic grumbles in the streets, and a great clanking and screech of metal comes from the docks, and garbage trucks groan and whine as they tip Dumpsters into their maws like iron gods draining their goblets, she and Mears rock and thrust and grind, tightening their hold on each other as the city seems to tighten around them, winching up its loose ends, notch by notch, in order to withstand the fierce pressures of the waking world.

That afternoon at the gym, Leon takes Mears into the locker room and sits him on a bench. He paces back and forth, emitting an exhaust of cigar smoke, and tells Mears that the boxing commission will be no problem, the physical exam—like most commission physicals—is going to be a joke, no eye charts, nothing, just blood pressure and heart and basic shit like that. He paces some more, then says he's finished watching films of Vederotta's last four fights.

"Ain't but one way to fight him," he says. "Smother his punches, grab him, hold him, frustrate the son of a bitch. Then when he get wild and come bullin' in, we start to throw uppercuts. Uppercuts all night long. That's our only shot. Understand?"

"I hear you."

"Man's strong." Leon sighs as he takes a seat on the bench opposite Mears. "Heavyweight strong. He gon' come at us from the bell and try to hurt us. He use his head, his elbows, whatever he gots. We can't let him back us up. We back up on this motherfucker, we goin' to sleep."

There is more, Mears can feel it, and he waits patiently, picking at the wrappings on his hands while he listens to the slap and babble from the gym.

"'Member that kid Tony Ayala?" Leon asks. "Junior middleweight 'bout ten years ago. Mean fuckin' kid, wound up rapin' some schoolteacher in Jersey. Big puncher. This Vederotta 'mind me of him. He knock Jeff Toney down and then he kick him. He hold up Reggie Williams 'gainst the ropes when the man out on his feet so he kin hit him five, six times more." Leon pauses. "Maybe he's too strong. Maybe we should pull out of this deal. What you think?"

Mears realizes that Leon is mainly afraid Vederotta will knock him into retirement, that his cut of the twenty thousand dollars will not compensate for a permanent loss of income. But the fact that Leon has asked what he thinks, that's new, that's a real surprise. He suspects that deep within that gross bulk, the pilot light of Leon's moral self, long extinguished, has been relit and he is experiencing a flicker of concern for Mears's well-being. Recognizing this, Mears is, for reasons he cannot fathom, less afraid.

"Ain't you listenin', man? I axed what you think."

"Got to have that money," Mears says.

Leon sucks on his cigar, spits. "I don't know 'bout this," he says, real doubt in his voice, real worry. "I just don't know."

Mears thinks about Leon, all the years, the lies, the petty betrayals and pragmatic loyalty, the confusion that Leon must be experiencing to be troubled by emotion at this stage of the relationship. He tries to picture who Leon is and conjures the image of something bloated and mottled washed up on a beach—something that would have been content to float and dream in the deep blue-green light, chewing on kelp, but would now have to heave itself erect and lumber unsightly through the bright, terrible days without solace or satisfaction. He puts a hand on the man's soft, sweaty back, feels the sick throb of his heart. "I know you don't," he says. "But it's all right."

The first time he meets Vederotta, it's the morning of the fight, at the weigh-in. Just as he's stepping off the scale, he is startled to spot him standing a few feet away, a pale, vaguely human shape cut in the middle by a wide band of black, the trunks. And a face. That's the startling thing, the thing that causes Mears to shift quickly away. It's the sort of face that appears when a fight is going badly, when he needs more fear in order to keep going, but it's never happened so early, before the fight even begins. And this one is different from the rest.

Not a comic-book image slapped onto a human mold, it seems fitted just below the surface of the skin, below the false human face, rippling like something seen through a thin film of water. It's coal black, with sculpted cheeks and a flattened bump of a nose and a slit mouth and hooded eyes, an inner mask of black lusterless metal. From its eyes and mouth leaks a crumbling red glow so radiant it blurs the definition of the features. Mears recognizes it for the face of his secret pain, and he can only stare at it. Then Vederotta smiles, the slit opening wider to show the furnace glow within, and says in a dull, stuporous voice, a voice like ashes, "You don't look so hot, man. Try and stay alive till tonight, will ya?" His handlers laugh and Leon curses them, but Mears, suddenly spiked with terror, can find no words, no solidity within himself on which to base a casual response. He lashes out at that evil, glowing face with a right hand, which Vederotta slips, and then everyone—handlers, officials, the press—is surging back and forth, pulling the two fighters apart, and as Leon hustles Mears away, saying, "Fuck's wrong with you, man? You crazy?" he hears Vederotta shouting at him, more bellowing than shouting, no words, nothing intelligible, just the raving of the black beast.

Half an hour before the fight is scheduled to start, Mears is lying on a training table in the dressing room, alone, his wrapped hands folded on his belly. From the arena come intermittent announcements over the PA, the crowd booing one of the preliminary bouts, and some men are talking loudly outside his door. Mears scarcely registers any of this. He's trying to purge himself of fear but is not having much success. He believes his peculiar visual trick has revealed one of God's great killers, and that tonight the red seed of pain in his head will bloom and he will die, and nothing—no determined avowal, no life-affirming hope—will diminish that belief. He could back out of the fight, he could fake an injury of some sort, and he considers this possibility, but something—and it's not just pride—is pulling him onward. No matter whether or not that face he saw is real, there's something inhuman about Vederotta. Something evil and implacable. And stupid. Some slowness natural to sharks and demons. Maybe he's not a fate, a supernatural creature; maybe he's only malformed, twisted in spirit. Whatever, Mears senses his wrongness the way he would a change in the weather, not merely because of the mask but from a wealth of subtle yet undeniable clues. All these months of imagining beasts in the ring and now he's finally come up against a real one. Maybe the only real one there is. The one he always knew was waiting. Could be, he thinks, it's just his time. It's his time and he has to confront it. Then it strikes him that there may be another reason. It's as if he's been in training, sparring with the lesser beasts, Alligator Man, the Fang, Snakeman, and the rest, in order to prepare for this bout. And what if there's some purpose to his sacrifice? What if he's supposed to do something out there tonight aside from dying?

Lying there, he realizes he's already positioned for the coffin, posed for eternity, and that recognition makes him roll up to his feet and begin his shadowboxing, working up a sweat. His sweat stinks of anxiety, but the effort tempers the morbidity of his thoughts.

A tremendous billow of applause issues from the arena, and not long thereafter, Leon pops in the door and says, "Quick knockout, man. We on in five." Then it goes very fast. The shuffling, bobbing walk along the aisle through the Wichita crowd, hearing shouted curses, focusing on that vast, dim tent of white light that hangs down over the ring. Climbing through the ropes, stepping into the resin box, getting his gloves checked a final time. It's all happening too quickly. He's being torn away from important details. Strands of tactics, sustaining memories, are being burned off him. He does not feel prepared. His belly knots and he wants to puke. He needs to see where he is, exactly where, not just this stretch of blue canvas that ripples like shallow water and the warped circles of lights suspended in blackness like an oddly geometric grouping of suns seen from outer space. The heat of those lights, along with the violent, murmurous heat of the crowd, it's sapping—it should be as bright as day in the ring, like noon on a tropic beach, and not this murky twilight reeking of Vaseline and concession food and fear. He keeps working, shaking his shoulders, testing the canvas with gliding footwork, jabbing and hooking. Yet all the while he's hoping the ring will collapse or Vederotta will sprain something, a power failure, anything to spare him. But when the announcer brays his weight, his record, and name over the mike, he grows calm as if by reflex and submits to fate and listens to the boos and desultory clapping that follows.

"His opponent," the announcer continues, "in the black trunks with a red stripe, weighs in tonight at a lean and mean one hundred fifty-nine and one-half pounds. He's undefeated and is currently ranked number one by both the WBC and WBA, with twenty-four wins, twenty-three by knockout! Let's have a great big prairie welcome for Wichita's favorite son, Toneee! The Heat! Ve-de-rot-taaaaa! Vederotta!"

Vederotta dances forward into the roar that celebrates him, arms lifted above his head, his back to Mears; then he turns, and as Leon and the cut man escort Mears to the center of the ring for the instructions, Mears sees that menacing face again. Those glowing eyes.

"When I say 'break,'" the ref is saying, "I want you to break clean. Case of a knockdown, go to a neutral corner and stay there till I tell ya to come out. Any questions?"

One of Vederotta's handlers puts in his mouthpiece, a piece of opaque plastic that mutes the fiery glow, makes it look liquid and obscene; gassy red light steams from beneath the black metal hulls that shade his eyes.

"OK," says the ref. "Let's get it on."

Vederotta holds out his gloves and says something through his mouthpiece. Mears won't touch gloves with him, frightened of what this acquiescence might imply. Instead, he shoves him hard, and once again the handlers have to intervene. Screams from the crowd lacerate the air, and the ref admonishes him, saying, "Gimme a clean fight, Bobby, or I'll disqualify ya." But Mears is listening to Vederotta shouting fierce, garbled noises such as a lion might make with its mouth full of meat.

Leon hustles him back to the corner, puts in his mouthpiece, and slips out through the ropes, saying, "Uppercuts, man! Keep throwin' them uppercuts!" Then he's alone, that strangely attenuated moment between the instructions and the bell, longer than usual tonight because the TV cameraman standing on the ring apron is having problems. Mears rolls his head, working out the kinks, shaking his arms to get them loose, and pictures himself as he must look from the cheap seats, a tiny dark figure buried inside a white pyramid. The image of Amandla comes into his head. She, too, is tiny. A doll in a blue robe, like a Madonna, she has that kind of power, a sweet, gentle idea, nothing more. And there's Arlene, whom he has never seen, of whom he knows next to nothing, African and voluptuous and mysterious like those big-breasted ebony statues they sell in the import stores. And Leon hunkered down at the corner of the ring, sweaty already, breath thick and quavery, peering with his pop eyes. Mears feels steadier and less afraid, triangulated by them: the only three people who have any force in his life. When he glances across the ring and finds that black death's head glaring at him, he is struck by something—he can see Vederotta. Since his eyes went bad, he's been unable to see his opponent until the man closes on him, and for that reason he circles tentatively at the beginning of each round, waiting for the figure to materialize from the murk, backing, letting his opponent come to him. Vederotta must know this, must have seen that tendency on film, and Mears thinks it may be possible to trick him, to start out circling and then surprise him with a quick attack. He turns, wanting to consult Leon, not sure this would be wise, but the bell sounds, clear and shocking, sending him forward as inexorably as a toy set in motion by a spark.

Less than ten seconds into the fight, goaded in equal measure by fear and hope, Mears feints a sidestep, plants his back foot, and lunges forward behind a right that catches Vederotta solidly above the left eye, driving him into the ropes. Mears follows with a jab and two more rights before Vederotta backs him up with a wild flurry, and he sees that Vederotta has been cut. The cut is on the top of the eyelid, not big but in a bad place, difficult to treat. It shows as a fuming red slit in that black mask, like molten lava cracking open the side of a scorched hill. Vederotta rubs at the eye, holds up his glove to check for blood, then hurls himself at Mears, taking another right on the way in but managing to land two stunning shots under the ribs that nearly cave him in. From then on it's all downhill for Mears. Nobody, not Hagler or Hearns or Duran, has ever hit him with such terrible punches. His face is numb from Vederotta's battering jab and he thinks one of his back teeth may have been cracked. But the body shots are the worst. Their impact is the sort you receive in a car crash when the steering wheel or the dash slams into you. They sound like football tackles, they dredge up harsh groans as they sink deep into his sides, and he thinks he can feel Vederotta's fingers, his talons, groping inside the gloves, probing for his organs. With less than a minute to go in the round, a right hand to the heart drops him onto one knee. It takes him until the count of five to regain his breath, and he's up at seven, wobbly, dazed by the ache spreading across his chest. As Vederotta comes in, Mears wraps his arms about his waist and they go lurching about the ring, faces inches apart, Vederotta's arm barred under his throat, trying to push him off. Vederotta spews words in a goblin language, wet, gnashing sounds. He sprays fiery brimstone breath into Mears's face, acid spittle, the crack on his eyelid leaking a thin track of red phosphorus down a black cheek. When the ref finally manages to separate them, he tells Mears he's going to deduct a point if he keeps holding. Mears nods, grateful for the extra few seconds' rest, more grateful when he hears the bell.

Leon squirts water into Mears's mouth, tells him to rinse and spit. "You cut him," he says excitedly. "You cut the motherfucker!"

"I know," Mears says. "I can see him."

Leon, busy with the Enswell, refrains from comment, restrained by the presence of the cut man. "Left eye," he says, ignoring what Mears has told him. "Throw that right. Rights and uppercuts. All night long. That's a bad cut, huh, Eddie?"

"Could be a winner," the cut man says, "we keep chippin' on it."

Leon smears Vaseline on Mears's face. "How you holdin' up?"

"He's hurtin' me. Everything he throws, he's hurtin' me."

Leon tells him to go ahead and grab, let the ref deduct the fucking points, just hang in there and work the right. The crowd is buzzing, rumorous, and from this, Mears suspects that he may really have Vederotta in some trouble, but he's still afraid, more afraid than ever now that he has felt Vederotta's power. And as the second round begins, he realizes he's the one in trouble. The cut has turned Vederotta cautious. Instead of brawling, he circles Mears, keeping his distance, popping his jab, throwing an occasional combination, wearing down his opponent inch by inch, a pale, indefinite monster, his face sheathed in black metal, eyes burning like red suns at midnight. Each time Mears gets inside to throw his shots or grab, the price is high—hooks to the liver and heart, rights to the side of the neck, the hinge of the jaw. His face is lumping up. Near the end of the round, a ferocious straight right to the temple blinds him utterly in the left eye for several seconds. When the bell rings, he sinks onto the stool, legs trembling, heartbeat ragged. Exotic eye trash floats in front of him. His head's full of hot poison, aching and unclear. But oddly enough, that little special pain of his has dissipated, chased away by the same straight right that caused his temporary blackout.

The doctor pokes his head into the desperate bustle of the corner and asks him where he is, how he's doing. Mears says, "Wichita" and "OK." When the ref asks him if he wants to continue, he's surprised to hear himself say, "Yeah," because he's been doing little other than wondering if it would be all right to quit. Must be some good reason, he thinks, or else you're one dumb son of a bitch. That makes him laugh.

"Fuck you doin' laughin'?" Leon says. "We ain't havin' that much fun out there. Work on that cut! You ain't done diddly to that cut!"

Mears just shakes his head, too drained to respond.

The first minute of the third round is one of the most agonizing times of Mears's life. Vederotta continues his cautious approach, but he's throwing heavier shots now, head-hunting, and Mears can do nothing other than walk forward and absorb them. He is rocked a dozen times, sent reeling. An uppercut jams the mouthpiece edge-on into his gums and his mouth fills with blood. A hook to the ear leaves him rubber-legged. Two rights send spears of white light into his left eye and the tissue around the eye swells, reducing his vision to a slit. A low blow smashes the edge of his cup, drives it sideways against his testicles, causing a pain that brings bile into his throat. But Vederotta does not follow up. After each assault he steps back to admire his work. It's clear he's prolonging things, trying to inflict maximum damage before the finish. Mears peers between his gloves at the beast stalking him and wonders when that other little red-eyed beast inside his head will start to twitch and burn. He's surprised it hasn't already, he's taken so many shots.

When the ref steps in after a series of jabs, Mears thinks he's stopping the fight, but it's only a matter of tape unraveling from his left glove. The ref leads him into the corner to let Leon retape it. He's so unsteady, he has to grip the ropes for balance, and glancing over his shoulder, he sees Vederotta spit his mouthpiece into his glove, which he holds up like a huge red paw. He expects Vederotta to say something, but all Vederotta does is let out a maniacal shout. Then he reinserts the mouthpiece into that glowing red maw and stares at Mears, shaking his black and crimson head the way a bear does before it charges, telling him—Mears realizes—that this is it, there's not going to be a fourth round. But Mears is too wasted to be further intimidated, his fear has bottomed out, and as Leon fumbles with the tape, giving him a little more rest, his pride is called forth, and he senses again just how stupid Vederotta is, bone stupid, dog stupid, maybe just stupid and overconfident enough to fall into the simplest of traps. No matter what happens to him, Mears thinks, maybe he can do something to make Vederotta remember this night.

The ref waves them together, and Mears sucks it up, banishes his pain into a place where he can forget about it for a while and shuffles forward, presenting a picture of reluctance and tentativeness. When Vederotta connects with a jab, then a right that Mears halfway picks off with his glove, Mears pretends to be sorely afflicted and staggers back against the ropes. Vederotta's in no hurry. He ambles toward him, dipping his left shoulder, so sure of himself he's not even trying to disguise his punches, he's going to come with the left hook under, he's going to hurt Mears some more before he whacks him out. Mears peeks between his gloves, elbows tight to his sides, knowing he's got this one moment, waiting, the crowd's roar like a jet engine around him, the vicious, smirking beast planting himself, his shoulder dipping lower yet, his head dropping down and forward as he cocks the left, and it's then, right at that precise instant, when Vederotta is completely exposed, that Mears explodes from his defensive posture and throws the uppercut, aiming not at the chin or the nose, but at that red slit on the black eyelid. He lands the shot clean, feels the impact, and above the crowd noise he hears Vederotta shriek like a woman, sees him stumble into the corner, his head lowered, glove held to the damaged eye. Mears follows, spins him about and throws another shot that knocks Vederotta's glove aside, rips at the eye. The slit, it's torn open now, has become an inch-long gash, and that steaming, luminous red shit is flowing into the eye, over the dull black cheek and jaw, dripping onto his belly and trunks. Mears pops a jab, a right, then another jab, not hard punches—they don't have to be hard, just accurate—splitting Vederotta's guard, each landing on the gash, slicing the eyelid almost its entire length. Then the ref's arms wrap around him from behind and haul him back, throwing him into ring center, where he stands, confused by this sudden cessation of violence, by this solitude imposed on him after all that brutal intimacy, as the doctor is called in to look at Vederotta's eye. He feels light and unreal, as if he's been shunted into a place where gravity is weaker and thought has no emotional value. The crowd has gone quiet and he hears the voice of Vederotta's manager above the babbling in the corner. Then a second voice shouting the manager down, saying, "I can see the bone, Mick! I can see the goddamn bone!" And then—this is the most confusing thing of all—the ref is lifting his arm and the announcer is declaring, without enthusiasm, to a response of mostly silence and some scattered boos, that "the referee stops the contest at a minute fifty-six seconds of the third round. Your winner by TKO: Bobby! The Magician! Mears!"

Mears's pain has returned, the TV people want to drag him off for an interview, Leon is there hugging him, saying, "We kicked his ass, man! We fuckin' kicked his ass!" and there are others, the promoter, the nobodies, trying to congratulate him, but he pushes them aside, shoulders his way to Vederotta's corner. He has to see him, because this is not how things were supposed to play. Vederotta is sitting on his stool, someone smearing his cut with Avitene. His face is still visible, still that of the beast. Those glowing red eyes stare up at Mears, connect with the eye of pain in his head, and he wants there to be a transfer of knowledge, to learn that one day soon that pain will open wide and he will fall the way a fighter falls after one punch too many, disjointed, graceless, gone from the body. But no such transfer occurs, and he begins to suspect that something is not wrong, or rather that what's wrong is not what he suspected.

There's one thing he thinks he knows, however, looking at Vederotta, and while the handlers stand respectfully by, acknowledging his place in this ritual, Mears says, "I was lucky, man. You a hell of a fighter. But that eye's never gon' be the same. Every fight they gon' be whacking at it, splittin' it open. You ain't gon' be fuckin' over nobody no more. You might as well hang 'em up now."

As he walks away, as the TV people surround him, saying, "Here's the winner, Bobby Mears"—and he wonders what exactly it is he's won—it's at that instant he hears a sound behind him, a gush of raw noise in which frustration and rage are commingled, both dirge and challenge, denial and lament, the final roar of the beast.

Two weeks after the fight he's sitting in the hotel bar with Arlene, staring into that infinite dark mirror, feeling lost, undefined, sickly, like there's a cloud between him and the light that shines him into being, because he's not sure when he's going to fight again, maybe never, he's so busted up from Vederotta. His eyes especially seem worse, prone to dazzling white spots and blackouts, though the pain deep in his head has subsided, and he thinks that the pain may have had something to do only with his eyes, and now that they're fading, it's fading, too, and what will he do if that's the case? Leon has been working with this new lightweight, a real prospect, and he hasn't been returning Mears's calls, and when the bartender switches on the TV and a rapper's voice begins blurting out his simple, aggressive rhymes, Mears gets angry, thoughts like gnats swarming around that old reeking nightmare shape in his head, that thing that may never have existed, and he pictures a talking skull on the TV shelf, with a stuffed raven and a coiled snake beside it. He drops a twenty on the counter and tells Arlene he wants to take a walk, a disruption of their usual routine of a few drinks, then upstairs. It bewilders her, but she says, "OK, baby," and off they go into the streets, where the Christmas lights are gleaming against the black velour illusion of night like green and red galaxies, as if he's just stepped into an incredible distance hung here and there with plastic angels filled with radiance. And people, lots of people brushing past, dark and shiny as beetles, scuttling along in this holy immensity, chattering their bright gibberish, all hustling toward mysterious crossroads where they stop and freeze into silhouettes against the streams of light, and Mears, who is walking very fast because walking is dragging something out of him, some old weight of emotion, is dismayed by their stopping, it goes contrary to the flow he wants to become part of, and he bursts through a group of shadows assembled like pilgrims by a burning river, and steps out, out and down—he's forgotten the curb—and staggers forward into the traffic, into squealing brakes and shouts, where he waits for a collision he envisions as swift and ultimately stunning, luscious in its finality, like the fatal punch Vederotta should have known. Yet it never comes. Then Arlene, who has clattered up, unsteady in her high heels, hauls him back onto the sidewalk, saying, "You tryin' to kill yo'self, fool?" And Mears, truly lost now, truly bereft of understanding, either of what he has done or why he's done it, stands mute and tries to find her face, wishes he could put a face on her, not a mask, just a face that would be her, but she's nowhere to be found, she's only perfume, a sense of presence. He knows she's looking at him, though.

"You sick, Bobby?" she asks. "Ain't you gon' tell me what's wrong?"

How can he tell her that what's wrong is he's afraid he's not dying, that he'll live and go blind? How can that make sense? And what does it say about how great a fool he's been? He's clear on nothing apart from that, the size of his folly.

"C'mon," Arlene says with exasperation, taking his arm. "I'm gon' cook you some dinner. Then you can tell me what's been bitin' yo' ass."

He lets her steer him along. He's too dazed to make decisions. Too worried. It's funny, he thinks, or maybe funny's not the word, maybe it's sad that what's beginning to worry him is exactly the opposite of what was troubling him a few seconds before. What if she proves to be someone who'll stand by him no matter how bad things get, what if the pain in his head hasn't gone away, it's just dormant, and instead of viewing death as a solution, one he feared but came to rely on, he now comes to view it as something miserable and dread? The darkness ahead will be tricky to negotiate, and the simple trials of what he's already starting to characterize as his old life seem, despite blood and attrition, unattainably desirable. But no good thing can arise from such futile longing, he realizes. Loving Amandla has taught him that.

Between two department stores, two great, diffuse masses of white light, there's an alley, a doorway, a dark interval of some sort, and as they pass, Mears draws Arlene into it and pulls her tightly to him, needing a moment to get his bearings. The blackness of street and sky is so uniform, it looks as if you could walk a black curve up among the blinking red and green lights, and as Arlene's breasts flatten against him, he feels like he is going high, like it feels when the man in the tuxedo tells you that you've won and the pain is washed away by perfect exhilaration and sweet relief. Then, as if jolted forward by the sound of a bell, he steps out into the crowds, becoming part of them, just another fool with short money and bad health and God knows what kind of woman trouble, who in another time might have been champion of the world.

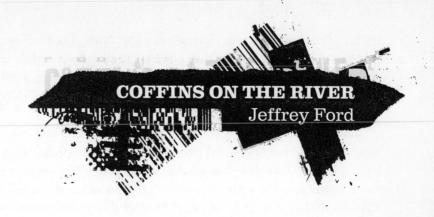

COFFINS ON THE RIVER
Jeffrey Ford

BARNEY AND I are getting long in the tooth. We've got bad knees, bad backs, bad eyes, and bad breath. We've got wives and kids and mortgages and car loans, and if that isn't enough to elicit your sympathy, we're both artists of a sort.

Barney's a painter, self-taught over decades. He turns out some very fine landscapes of his local area in deep South Jersey along the Delaware River, where the neighbors still eat muskrat and late June brings so many green flies that yawning becomes a repast, itself. He makes most of his income on scenes of meadows and giant oaks, white heron skimming along the estuaries in violet twilight, but his heart is really in his more expressionistic work—for instance, his series, *Coffins on the River*.

The theme plays itself out in a hundred canvases that show super heroes laid to rest in pine boxes. The viewer sees them from above as they glide in the flow—dark, turbulent waters churning to either side, occasionally a fish breaking the surface in an arc, a bit of the bank, a beer bottle on its way to the ocean. The coffins are missing their lids, and the fallen heroes are sometimes wrapped in colorful capes like winding sheets, or donned in spandex uniforms displaying chest emblems of, say, an hourglass, a vibrator, a thimble....

They are no super heroes you might know, but ones solely from the planets of his imagination, with powers never tested as they were created to lie in state.

He has a little notebook with their names—Qua Num, The Ineffable, Biscuit Boy, Six Figures—a brief list of their powers, and how they met their respective ends. One carries a little doll by the neck, one, a ray gun, one, a cell phone, and all of their faces are like beautiful landscapes of frozen anguish or melted wonder.

Most people didn't grok *Coffins,* but nothing could stop him from making more of them. When he couldn't afford canvas, he used the sides of refrigerator boxes, pieces of discarded plywood, half a ping-pong table, panes of glass. At times, he was jazzed on them, at times he was depressed by them, and when he had done the last of them he told me, "They are their own worst enemies."

Whereas Barney might measure his life in brush strokes, I had pecked mine away at a keyboard, writing fiction of a speculative nature. My most recent novel, which you might have seen last year, was called *Deluge*, wherein the Earth is struck by a cosmic gamma ray from a relatively nearby exploding star, and pieces of reality are changed through a partial disturbance of the inherent nature of matter.

A great deluge sweeps the Earth, and a particular hundred-year-old apartment building made of wood cracks off its foundation in the onslaught of catastrophic flooding and is swept away containing its inhabitants. They sail the newly made world in the bobbing structure, searching for dry land and other survivors. Perno Shell, a previously quiet, bookish man, becomes the captain of the odd vessel and takes upon himself the task of bringing all of his neighbors to safety. The seas teem with mutated monsters, barges of blind pirates returned from the dead, sentient islands, as the unlikely adventurers search for the secret of how, through the manipulation of Time, to remake the world in its previous image.

It tanked like a lead doughnut. For all my hard work and sterling reviews, only two hundred people bought copies, and I got notice from my agent and publisher that I was on thin ice. That same day, at the bookstore, I found a tall stack of *Deluge* on the three-dollar bargain table—a Babel that reached to the bottom of my chin. For a moment, I rested my head atop it while standing upright.

Rough times for true artists, but Barney and I, we had a little ace in the hole. As old and cranky and screwed up as we were, we still puffed the weed from time to time whenever we needed to get the back legs of that creative beast twitching again. We were old potheads, warhorses from way back, who had thoroughly traversed the highways and byways of the world of weed. We were as familiar with the filthy, light headache engendered by a bolus toke of Coney

Island Green as we were with the subtle, slowly dawning revelations of Thai Stick, the souped-up crap chronic of the latter years of the twentieth century, the illusive but hallucinatory magic of high altitude, Northern California Red Hair. We'd smoked it out of bongs, pipes, cored apples, beer cans, power hitters, skins, and one-toke smokeless spy jobs.

Now, save your lectures about bad health and moral turpitude. Save your religion for the faint of heart and your jurisprudence for hardened criminals. You'll get no argument from us that a steady diet of rope is going to brutally eat your brain and turn your soul to mist. We know guys who are zombified from decades of waking and baking—the blank stare, the sighs, the drool. We've been through it, gone in one end of that joint, come out the other as nothing but smoke, and then had to reconstitute the corporeality of our lives.

On the other hand, when you're a true artist, there's nothing that will goose the muse like a strategic hit or two. All it takes sometimes is half a bone to crack the alabaster vault, and then the treasure comes spilling out—handfuls of vision, truckloads of inspiration. Do I wish it didn't have to be that way? Sure. I want to be wealthy and good looking too, but when the reservoir has gone dry, you'll do anything to get back in Athena's good graces. Why do you think so many artists cash in early, taking the gas pipe or swinging from the end of a rope?

Anyway, once every couple of months I'd drive south to Barney's home and visit with him in the studio out back, past the magnolia that hides the outhouse and just before that wall of cattails throughout which runs a swampy maze of a path that eventually leads to the estuary. We sit out there at night, in the glow of a storm lantern, amidst the thick, hair-raising scent of turpentine and oil paint, have a few beers, smoke a number, and bullshit for a while. We've known each other since college days, so there's always a lot to talk over—old times, how brilliant and ball-busting our kids are, how fed up our wives are with us, who's in the hospital, and who's in the ground. Not until we'd smoke up would we talk about the work, the glimmers of notions. Then the conversation would increase in speed and intensity and the ideas would fly like bats at sundown, like phone calls from our creditors.

We worked that pot jump-start for years, throughout our thirties and well into our forties, and it always served its purpose. Then, last November, after Barney had capped the paint on *Coffins on the River* and was searching around unsuccessfully for a new direction, and I had to come up with a blockbuster to follow *Deluge* and save my ass from the midlist chopping block, we met and puffed the weed. We were both empty as dried gourds and were hoping to bust things open and get back to work as quickly as possible, but when we left the studio that night, we were the same blank slates as when we had entered. We lit up, we smoked, and then we just sat there with nothing to say. My head was filled with fog, and Barney said, "Christ, if I strain any harder for an idea, I'm likely to crap myself."

So there it was. I went home and stewed for another week, smoking butts and staring at an empty computer screen. Then I called Barney. The phone was busy, because as it turns out, he was calling me. When we finally connected, we decided not to wait another month, but this time to get the good stuff and give it another go. Back I drove to South Jersey, over an hour trip. When I arrived, we hung out in his kitchen for a while, talking to his wife and little girl, but with the first lull in the conversation, we excused ourselves and repaired to the studio.

We couldn't light up right away, because we had to wait for Stick, our connection. He was also a painter, a young guy, incredibly talented *and* prolific. He did these brightly colored portraits—the hues of the flesh the most outlandish shades of violet and green and yellow, awe inspiring, two-hair brush, minute detail, and three-dimensional to boot. At his art shows, he laid out a dozen pairs of these spectacles, and when you put them on and turned to the work, those leering party heads looked like they were floating in midair with all the weight and mass of holiday hams. The kid had more talent than both of us ever had, and when we'd mention being stuck or burnt out, he'd laugh at us and call us old men.

His contempt was mitigated, though, by the fact that Barney and I knew a lot of stuff and didn't mind talking about it. If anything, over the years, we had become consummate gasbags. We had read widely and had eclectic tastes. Like my wife often said, "You've read all of Jules Verne, but you can't fix the fucking sink." And it was true. But Stick liked the conversation, so sometimes he hung out with us and just listened.

In addition to this kid being a great painter, he was also a can-do kind of guy. He could fix the sink, score the best weed in three states, work on a car, and play a mean bass. Somebody stole the stereo system out of his truck. He went to the local police, but when he could see they didn't care and told him to forget it, he bought a handgun and hunted the guy down. By canvassing local bars, buying a few drinks for seedy characters, he got a line on who the culprit might be. He traced the guy to an abandoned factory out in Shell Pile, found his stereo components and the thief, made a citizen's arrest, and turned the guy over to the police.

Out in the studio, Barney moved a couple of *Coffins on the River* so we could get to our chairs. I set the beer down between us and lit a cigarette. There was no heat in the studio and the autumn wind came in through a hole in the window, keeping the room cool, and whining as it squeezed through the jagged opening. From outside we could hear the fallen leaves rolling across the field next to his house. We sat there surrounded by dead heroes and he told me that: his cat had cat AIDS, a bar in town had become a meeting place for the Klan, his porch roof was in danger of collapsing, a young girl who went to his daughter's school had been abducted, his wife needed expensive dental work, a guy down the street had lit his own house on fire, he hadn't sold a painting in weeks. I let him vent, knowing that when the work wasn't flowing, the world in general was a uniquely frightening place.

Stick popped his shaved head in the door just when I'd had about enough of Barney's list of grievances. As always, the kid had the weed. Barney handed over his half of the cash and I did the same. A minute didn't pass before my old friend was rolling a fat number. He licked it, sealed it, and then held that blunt, white mummy up for inspection. I made like the Pope and shot a two-fingered sign of the cross at it. Stick found a chair and I handed him a beer while Barney fired up.

Barney had a weak right eye, and whenever he smoked, that eye would close and he'd squint on one side like Popeye. He tapped the ashes onto his jeans and rubbed them in a circle, exhaled, took another deep one, and then passed it on. The weed made the rounds, we drank, and I told Stick his portraits reminded me of the portrait of beef that Soutine had painted.

"Who's Soutine?" he asked.

"French painter, originally from Lithuania, early twentieth century, Paris. He did this painting, I guess it would be a still life, of a side of beef. He went out to the stockyard, bought a side of beef, and hung it up in his apartment."

"I like the sound of that," said Stick.

Barney took another hit and jumped in, "Soutine had a friend who worked for the department of health, and the guy would come around to his place every few days and inject the meat with something, probably formaldehyde, to keep it from rotting. It took him weeks to paint that beef."

"Must've stunk like hell by the time he was done," I said.

"I saw that painting somewhere," said Barney, "and all I remember is translucent pink and blue."

Stick put his beer down and took a pad and pen from the inside pocket of his leather jacket. "I gotta give that a try," he said, writing.

"Sure," said Barney, "you don't need a whole side of beef. Just get yourself like a London broil or something and string it up with fishing line."

"I was thinking along the lines of poultry. Maybe a twenty-pound butterball," said Stick.

"Absolutely," I said.

"In 3-D," said Stick.

"Why the fuck not?" I said.

"Make it a series," said Barney. *"Meat on the River."*

By the time the night had drawn to a close, Stick had three pages of ideas, and Barney and I were sitting there holding our own, still uninspired.

"What's next, trepanning?" said Barney.

"I had a couple of ideas that crawled out of the muck and fainted from embarrassment," I said.

"Well," said Stick, "you guys are dicking around with this pot. You need something more cosmic. You need to get in touch with your totem spirits and so forth."

"What are you talking?" asked Barney. "Meth, ecstasy, acid?"

"Last time I did LSD," I said, "about twenty years ago, an ambulance pulled up outside of my apartment, Saint Francis of Assisi got out, knocked on the front door, and handed me a slip of paper. On it was written the word *OVERDOSE.*"

"Yeah," said Barney, "we've got kids, we can't be tripping."

"No, no, no," said Stick, shaking his head. "Have you ever heard of ayahuasca? I'm telling you, one session with this stuff and you'll be good to go for a couple of years."

"Tell me more," said Barney.

"You see the quality and output I have?" he asked. "Pot's okay for watching television with the sound off and the stereo on or talking to you guys, but if you want to get in touch with the cosmic energy, you gotta have the Amazon jungle juice."

"Dangerous?" I asked.

"Don't worry, I'll watch out for you guys."

"What are the side effects?" asked Barney.

"A little dizziness, maybe some nausea, diarrhea."

"Sounds like a normal day," said Barney.

We asked for more details, but Stick said he had to be going. He jotted down the titles of a couple of books on a piece of notepad paper and then copied them again. He handed each of us a list and said, "Read these books, especially the first one, and then let me know if you want to take a shot at it. I swear, you'll see a story in every fallen leaf. Images'll tap your back and give you a phone number."

The next morning at home, sitting at the computer was like a restaurant with bad service. I looked out the window and watched those last few autumn leaves fall. Stick's promise came back to me: *a story in every fallen leaf.* Life was no longer whispering its secrets to me, and I was turning my back on it. My wife wanted to visit some friends, but I couldn't possibly get up the energy to be social. My sons wanted me to throw the football, take them to a movie, but I dared not stray from the office in case some trifle flitted across the desert of my imagination. I was a prisoner in that bleak November.

I drove to the local bookstore in search of the books on the scrap of notepad paper, still in my pocket from the night before. What were the chances Barnes & Noble would be carrying Stick's greatest hits of screwball drug writing? To my amazement they had one of the two volumes. The book he pointed to as being the most important, *The Cosmic Serpent*, by one Jeremy Narby, I was able to purchase. The second was by a fellow named Terrence McKenna.

When I got home, I made a pot of coffee, and then taking a cup, sat in my corner of the living room couch with *The Cosmic Serpent*. Just from the cover, it looked like some kind of New Age dither—*Cosmic, dude.* Nothing ventured, nothing gained, though, so I cracked the back and started reading. From the very first page, I was into it. My concentration had been like a leaf on the wind for the past few months, but even when the kids came in, played Eminem at top volume, and wrestled with the dog, I didn't look up.

Narby's book tells about his experiences in the Peruvian Amazon region of Quirishari, in the Pichis Valley, among the Ashaninca people. While doing field work for his dissertation on the distribution of plant species—an attempt to stave off corporate developers and their desire to clear cut and "manage" the treasures of the jungle—he met local shamans, *ayahuasqueros* as they are called, who had an incredible grasp of the biochemistry of the local plant life and how it could be used in creating effective medicines. Narby was astonished at the knowledge these adepts had garnered about the abundant and diverse species of plants indigenous to the region.

When Narby asked one how the Ashaninca had learned so much from the jungle, the shaman answered that the knowledge was revealed from the plants themselves. In other words, Nature itself had told them. He dismissed this at first, thinking it was mere mythology, but the ayahuasqueros insisted that they were not speaking metaphorically. They offered to show him, but he would have to ingest ayahuasca.

In taking the drug, his hallucinations showed him images of entwined snakes and other odd creatures and designs that he later realized were very reminiscent of the figures found in biochemistry. One image that often repeated was the double helix of DNA—the substance responsible for all life on Earth. It came to him later that perhaps the drug was able to unlock the information stored in DNA.

Usually I am fascinated with ideas like this because they make interesting fodder for my fictions, but I didn't fall off the turnip truck yesterday and have developed a healthy skepticism about outlandish claims. Narby's argument for the Ashaninca shamans learning cures directly from the forest spirit convinced me, though, when he detailed the biochemical properties of ayahuasca itself. The drug is formed from two different plants, one a vine, the other a bush. Only one carries a hallucinogenic substance, a chemical that is also secreted under certain circumstances by the brain. It has no effect when ingested because existing chemicals in the stomach neutralize it. The other plant contains no hallucinogen but merely an enzyme that blocks the chemical in the stomach from rendering the hallucinogen ineffective. The odds that someone would be able to stumble upon this particular chemical reaction, out of 80,000 possible species of plants, is nearly impossible, not to mention all the hundreds of other intricate chemical combinations and cures the shamans were privy to. In short, ayahuasca put you in touch with, essentially, the *mind* of life.

"Crazy shit," said Barney when I spoke to him on the phone the next day. He'd read *The Cosmic Serpent* as well.

"Are we going to tap that DNA?" I asked.

"I'm going for it," he said. "After I finished reading the book the other day, I was heading out to the studio to sit there like a wooden Indian for an hour or so, and what did I see over by the outhouse but a snake. This long, multicolored job, winding through the leaves. What's the chances of seeing a snake in November?"

"It's your Lady of Fatima," I told him.

He'd already set up a date with Stick to take the ayahuasca. "Stick said eat a lot of bananas to keep your serotonin level up and no heavy stuff like meat or sweets for a couple days before. No sex for the same amount of time."

"Sounds doable," I said.

"You're a damn shaman," said Barney.

A week later, we were in Stick's truck, sitting three across in the cab. We headed out toward Money Island, a spit of land that juts into the Delaware at the farthest southern point on the west side of Jersey. Sometimes it's a peninsula and sometimes an island, but there's a little bridge that keeps it connected to the mainland. All the houses there are on stilts.

"No Ugly American stuff," said Stick. "This guy's a real ayahuasquero."

"We're PC," said Barney.

"But what's he doing in Jersey?" I asked.

"He's on the run," said Stick.

"From?"

"He did some rabble-rousing against a couple of the companies raping the jungle down there."

We pulled up in front of a weathered gray shack on legs just as the sun was going down. The place had a boarded window and was listing forward slightly. It was at the end of a dirt road, all by itself. Behind it was a wall of reeds, and behind that the river. The temperature had dropped and it was really cold, but not enough to subdue the smell of low tide.

Stick led the way up the rickety steps and knocked on the door. As we waited for the shaman to answer, I started to have misgivings about this enterprise. I thought of my wife, Lynn, and my kids and got the urge to bolt back to the car. Barney, who was behind me on the steps, leaned in and whispered, "Did you really eat the bananas?" Just then the door opened.

The next thing I knew, we were inside and Stick was introducing us in Spanish to this little brown fellow, Rosario. He had a lot of wild black hair and a big smile—perfectly white teeth. I put out my hand and he shook it, and although he had a small frame I could feel real power in his grip. He was dressed in a blue-and-red-striped dress shirt with the sleeves cut off and a pair of green polyester bell-bottoms, with sandals on his feet.

Barney shook hands with Rosario, and he and I stood there smiling and nodding, bowing as if we were meeting the emperor of Japan. We moved away from the front door to a living room with doctor's waiting-room furniture, a lot of mod vinyl. Barney and I took the couch, Stick sat in a chair, and Rosario fell, playfully, into a big, pink beanbag thing on the floor. He cocked his head to the side, a look of seriousness set in, and he started talking, making gestures with his hands.

Stick wasn't exactly Ricardo Montalban, but he translated as best he could. Still, he was able to relay that Rosario was welcoming us, that he was pleased to meet two artists, a painter and a writer, from the U.S. We did some more nodding and smiling and thanked him. The détente and pleasantries continued for a while, and then he told us that the *maninkari,* the spirits, had told him we would be coming. He said he had been instructed to administer the ayahuasca to us.

I asked him why, and when Stick translated, Rosario laughed and responded, "We'll see," in perfect English. When I looked over at him, he was lighting what looked like a big fat joint. It and the lighter seemed to have materialized out of thin air. He took a hit and launched into a monologue in Spanish.

Stick said, "This is real tobacco, not the poison of American cigarettes. Jungle tobacco. It will draw the spirits close to us, so that when we take the ayahuasca, they'll be present. Spirits feast on tobacco. Once they've gathered, the drug will focus your senses so that you might see and talk with them."

The jungle cigarette made the rounds, and it was strong. Barney, who didn't smoke cigarettes coughed like an old man. I wasn't unhappy when it was finally stubbed out in an ashtray on the table next to Stick's chair. The shaman then rose, and asking our friend to accompany him, left the room.

"If a cigarette smoked cigarettes, *that's* the cigarette it would smoke," said Barney.

"I'm on the verge of puking," I whispered.

"Are the spirits around us now?" he said, glancing briefly over his shoulder.

"You didn't eat the bananas."

"Fuck the bananas," he said. "I ate McDonald's only about two hours ago."

"I'm ready to bag this whole thing," I said.

I heard the floorboards creak then and knew Rosario and Stick were returning. The shaman was carrying a two-liter Pepsi bottle half-filled with a reddish brown liquid, and in his other hand what looked like a dried out sweet potato with holes in it. Stick carried three gas station giveaway glasses with scenes from *Star Wars* on them. He had promised that he wouldn't take the drug so he could keep an eye on us. Barney was specifically afraid of getting up on the roof and jumping off, trying to fly. He had mentioned it about a dozen times in the truck on the way over.

Rosario carefully poured juice into each of the glasses. He lifted his off the table and brought it up near his mouth. "May the force be with you," he said.

I held my breath and chugged the ayahuasca. It was horrible. Before I could even reach over and put the glass on the table, I could hear my stomach saying, *Wrong.*

Barney gagged once and then managed to get the rest down. Rosario drank his like it was chocolate milk. We didn't have time to say anything stupid, because Rosario started singing. His song sounded like gibberish, but his lone voice and the honesty with which he sang was immediately fascinating to me. I sat back, closed my eyes, and followed the permutations of the tune.

After a short time I became aware of a rush of images presenting themselves behind my eyes, like a slide show on fast forward: my vision of the character, Perno Shell, from *Deluge*, standing on the roof of the floating apartment building, staring through a spyglass at the horizon; my older son, shooting baskets; the computer in my empty office; a small, dilapidated ranch house, the color pink of Rosario's beanbag chair, nestled like a cottage out of *Hansel and Gretel* at the edge of a forest; Soutine's side of beef; my father teaching me to drive; my dog, Shadow, laying in a sunspot on the living room floor; my wife, fixing the kitchen sink.

Rosario's song turned into musical notes, and I opened my eyes to see how he was accomplishing this. He was blowing into one end of that crusty sweet potato and fingering the holes as if it was a recorder. Tracks of bright colors shot across my field of vision, and then a golden rain fell out of the ceiling. The song he was playing somehow turned into the flute solo from Eric Burden's "Spill the Wine."

"I know that one," I said, and laughed. Then I asked, "Where's the bathroom?" I knew I was going to puke. It's not that I felt particularly bad. In fact, I was buzzing throughout my body, but I just knew I had to puke.

Rosario said, "Follow the butterfly," and opened his hand to release a phosphorescent specimen as big as a small bird. The creature languidly flapped its wings, heading down the hallway to our left. I followed it. As I passed Stick, I saw that his face had taken on the characteristics of one of his paintings, super detailed with a complexion of violet and yellow.

I found the bathroom and puked; no big deal—the easiest puke I ever did. When I stood up, though, I got a rush, and the distant notes of Rosario's music started to sound like birdcalls. I stepped out of the bathroom into what had been the hallway only to discover that I was now in the jungle. I found this amusing instead of frightening. It was dark green (even the light) and extremely warm, trees everywhere and resplendent undergrowth of ferns and vines. Above, in the canopy, birds called out and monkeys screeched.

I started walking, heading in the direction I thought the living room was in. Before going too far, I came upon a tattered object hanging by a string from the branch of a small tree. Oddly enough, the tree was a dogwood, like the one I have in my backyard. The object was a kind of talisman I remembered having read about: a god's-eye. It is made of woven yarn and sticks, often having concentric color patterns in the form of rural hex signs, meant to ward off evil. I thought of taking this one down and carrying it off, but something told me not to touch it.

I realized I was on a path, and that path came to a turn that led into a small clearing where the jungle floor had been swept clean. There was a desk and chair and a lab table with test tubes, beakers, and a microscope on it. In the blink of an eye, there suddenly appeared, standing next to the desk, a luminous being with the head of a crow and whose arms were writhing snakes. It had a woman's body that wore a simple black dress, white sneakers, and a lab coat.

"You are the spirit of the forest," I said. I could feel myself start to sweat, her sudden appearance worrying me, as if she could see through to my empty center and might kill me for it.

The beak of the glistening crow head opened and a smooth, quiet voice said, "Do you know why you are here?"

"I took the ayahuasca," I said.

"But why are you here?" it said.

"For a story," I said.

"Well," said the creature, "I have a cure for you." She walked over and removed a beaker from the lab table. I could see that the glass cylinder held a jumble of words. Not words on paper, but just the words, as if type in black ink had been lifted off the paper of a book.

"Why don't you come and take the medicine?" she asked.

"I'm afraid," I said.

"Of course," she said. She let loose a deafening bird screech, and with that sound her features melted and reformed and she was a young woman with long brown hair and beautiful brown eyes. "Come now," she said.

I approached her and she handed me the beaker. I put it to my lips and poured the words into my mouth, chewing them and swallowing until the beaker was empty. They were brittle but sharp and tasted bitter.

When I was finished, I said, "And this will help me to write?"

"No," she said, and laughed. "These are your instructions."

"Instructions for what?" I asked as I handed her the beaker.

"To help you see in the dark," she said.

"Why did I think this experience would help me write?" I asked.

"Because your eyes are closed," she said, and her eyes grew wide. She dropped the beaker on the ground where it shattered. "He's coming," she said. With this, she evaporated into mist, her clothes dropping to the ground.

Off in the distance, I heard something moving through the jungle. When it roared, I started running. I ran and ran for what seemed like an hour. The path disappeared and I scrabbled frantically through the undergrowth. When I was out of breath, sweating profusely, my heart pounding, I stopped and slumped down against a fallen log. I coughed, cleared my eyes, and tried to listen for the approach of my pursuer. That's when I saw it, off to my right, the dogwood with the god's-eye hanging from its bare, lowest branch. I had gone in a complete circle.

Someone elbowed me in the ribs. I looked up and found I was in the cab of Stick's truck. Rosario was at the window. He put his hand in through the open window, past Stick, and I shook it. Barney leaned over and also shook his hand. We thanked him and then Stick drove off. All traces of the nausea had passed and I still felt a little high. I had some coffee at Barney's to wake up and then drove home. There was a full moon. I left the window open for a while to get some fresh air. Passing the fields and forests, I thought I heard them murmuring.

After the night out on Money, Barney and I had decided not to talk about the ayahuasca experience for a while. We didn't last a week, though. I called him a few days later on Friday afternoon.

"It was a coffin on the river for me," he said. "Two really little guys, imperious sons of bitches, with heads like blue jays sat perched at either end. I watched the clouds passing overhead as one of them told me, 'The knowledge that is about to be revealed to you is reserved for the dead or dying.' How do you think that made me feel?"

"Did you get sick?" I asked.

"The McDonald's wasn't a winning strategy."

"What was the knowledge?" I asked.

"We wound up on some island and I sat on a stone bench, really uncomfortable. Across from me was a big fat snake on a concrete throne, partially coiled and sitting upright, wearing a crown. It lectured me for a half-hour and then said I could go. I woke up out in the back of the house by the reeds."

"What'd the snake tell you?"

"I couldn't understand what the hell it was saying. It was actually talking English, but it hissed every word. I made out one or two, but...."

"Since then," I said, "every time I go near the plants Lynn brought in from the yard for the winter, I hear a vague whispering sound, and I get this recurring image."

He started laughing.

"No shit," I said. "I swear."

"There's a field," he said. "About a hundred yards in is the edge of a forest."

"A house," I said.

"Ranch style, pink," he said. "It's right at the tree line and two huge oaks kind of arch above it."

"Yeah," I said.

"Kind of disappointing after all that rigmarole with the ayahuasca."

"I haven't written a damn word. And I can't for the life of me figure out why I ever thought tapping into my DNA was going to help that."

"Well, I'm going to paint that pink house. I figure, I see it enough, I might as well paint it. You should write a story called 'The Pink House.'"

"Who do you think lives there?"

"Richard Burton and Liz Taylor."

I got as far as, *The Taylors lived at the edge of the forest in a pink house*, and then turned the computer off. I left my office with no desire to return. In the next two days, I walked both in the morning and at night, long wanderings with Shadow. As I went along, the pine trees put thoughts in my head that I heard as words. They told me to shave and lose weight. They ridiculed my attire. I paid the bills. I helped my younger son memorize the state capitals. I made a meatloaf. I sat with Lynn on the couch; we drank coffee and talked. When no one was home, I played the Ink Spots on the stereo, "The Trees Don't Need to Know," as I stood by the front window where the plants were gathered and daydreamed that place across the field. I had achieved a certain peace with my blankness.

Thanksgiving came and went, and I was surprised I enjoyed it so much. The weather turned bitter cold and it snowed lightly one night at the end of the month. Life was but a dream, all domestic harmony, the promise of Christmas, soft music, and fires in the fireplace. The hours came and went and I thought nothing of them. Then, one night I was in the kitchen, cooking dinner, and the phone rang.

"I found the pink house," said Barney.

"Bull," I said.

"I was sitting in the studio today, and I decided to get up and go out. So I hopped in the car and just started driving around, not really thinking about anything. I let myself get lost on a road out by the State Forest. The road was empty, the sun was shining, I was easing along. Then I saw the field out of the corner of my eye. I turned and there was the house, right at the edge of the tree line."

"Pink?" I asked.

"Pinker than the pink I remembered. You've got to come down and check it out."

"What for?"

"If it's the same one, I'll go up and knock on the door."

"Who do you think's in there?"

"Man, I hope it's not that snake." He proceeded to give me directions and told me to meet him there the next day at noon.

When people who don't know Jersey think of it, they usually envision the refineries in Elisabeth or the casinos in Atlantic City, maybe beleaguered Camden, but if you go far enough south, you get a clear sense as to why it is called the Garden State. Cumberland County is like something out of the Midwest—forests and swamps and acres and acres of farmland. There are long stretches of plenty of nothing in certain areas. The place that Barney led me to was one of them.

The day was clear and cold. He was sitting in his car, pulled over to the side of the road, at the edge of a wide field that had been cut out of the surrounding forest. The minute I laid eyes on the house, I knew it was the one. He got out of his car and stood staring toward the tree line. I got out.

"That's it," he said, smiling, pointing toward the house.

"Too strange," I said.

There was no question we were going to go to the door, so I put my trepidation aside and followed him across the field. A dirt driveway, leading in from the road, ended about fifteen yards from the house, but there was no car in sight. As we approached the structure, I could see it more clearly, no bigger than an oversized trailer, and because of its dilapidated appearance—missing roof shingles, peeling paint, crumbling concrete steps leading to a chipped front door—I said, "There might not be anybody living here now."

"Maybe," said Barney. The place was silent like a possum playing dead, though; like a snake coiled. I knew he could feel it too. Wind moved through the trees that arched above it and their barren branches clicked together.

"It's a tidy little ship," I whispered as he took the three steps to the door.

He knocked loud five times, took a precautionary step back, and then we waited.

Nothing. Just the sound of the wind in the nearby forest. I looked off to the side, in amidst the shadowed trees at the ground covered with oak leaves, the pines swaying. Barney knocked again. We waited. Then he turned his head to the side and said, "I thought I heard something."

"It's just the wind," I said. "The place is empty."

"Come on," he said, and jumped down off the steps. I followed him around the right side of the house. Just off the corner there was an oil tank sitting flush against the wall, like a small, galvanized submarine in port, and beyond that, a window. Barney stepped up to the glass and, cupping his hands around his eyes, peered inside.

"See anything?" I asked, and stepped up next to him.

"No," he said, "it's just a kid's room...."

It happened so suddenly, we both jumped back and Barney gave a short yelp. A face had popped up suddenly from beneath the inside sill—a young girl, with large, dark eyes and long hair, no more than six or seven years old. She stared at us, unmoving.

"We're busted," I said. "Let's get out of here."

"No," he said, stepping closer to the face. He leaned toward the window and squinted his bad eye to see better. Turning to me, he said, "That's the kid who got snatched."

"What are you talking about?"

"She's the one who was abducted from her yard."

We looked back at the girl and she had her hands on the glass.

Her lips moved. "Help me," she said, and we could very faintly hear her.

I felt the fear start to rise in me.

"We've got to get her out of there," said Barney, who was visibly shaken.

"Are you absolutely certain it's her?"

He started moving around to the back of the house. "Yeah," he said. "She's in Alice's class at school. I know her."

When I caught up to him he was on the back steps, fidgeting with the doorknob, which was obviously locked.

"We've got to do this fast," I said. I took my sweatshirt off and wrapped it around my left hand. "What if whoever kidnapped her is in the house?"

Barney shook his head. "They would have answered the front door, right?"

"Not necessarily," I said, and punched in the pane. Glass shattered onto the kitchen floor. Reaching my arm carefully through the hole I'd made, I undid a deadbolt and chain lock. Seconds later, I had the door open and we were inside. The kitchen was dim with no light but that coming in from the outside where the woods cast the back of the house in shadow. Stained and peeling pink wallpaper with a design of cookie cutters and sinister gingerbread men made the small room absolutely claustrophobic. It stunk like old garbage. There were unwashed plates in the sink, pizza boxes on the table, and what looked like week-old creamed corn in a pot on the stove. I tried to ignore the god's-eye made from yarn and sticks hanging from a nail, beneath a clock with a different type of bird at each hour.

"What's the girl's name?" I asked him as we made our way down a short, dark hallway to the door of the room. There was a deadbolt with a key lock that fit through a hole in the center of the bolt, so whoever had taken her could be assured she wasn't going anywhere.

"Kara, something like that," he said. "Karen or...no, Carly."

I stood thinking what to do. I shook my sweatshirt out and put it back on.

"Any second, I'm expecting some *Deliverance* motherfucker to jump out of the woodwork and brain me with a hammer," whispered Barney.

"Tell her we're gonna kick it in," I said.

"Carly, this is Alice's father. You know Alice from your class? We're here to take you home, but we have to kick this door in, so stand back. Don't be afraid. A little noise and then we'll have you out."

"Okay," said a small voice from the other side of the door.

We put our backs against the opposite wall and counted to three in unison. On the first kick, I hurt my knee. On the second, we heard some wood crack. Five kicks later and the frame and molding of the jamb splintered free. The door swung back, and there was the girl, standing by the window, facing us.

Barney entered the room and approached her very calmly. He got down on his haunches in front of her and said, "Do you want us to take you home to your mom and dad?"

"Take me home," she said, putting her arms around his shoulders. She started to cry.

"It's gonna be okay, babe," I said.

"Everything's good now," said Barney, patting her shoulder.

She let go of him and moved back, drying her eyes.

"Ready to go?" he asked her.

She reached up to take his hand, and as their fingers touched, I heard, from out in front, the sound of a car door slamming shut.

She looked up at me, her eyes wide with terror. "He's coming," she said.

Barney lifted her and flung her over his shoulder. I gave him just a second to get by me, and then we were running—across the broken glass of the kitchen, out the back door. Neither of us bothered with the porch steps. We hit the ground and made for the path that led into the woods.

Adrenaline might be more amazing than ayahuasca. It carried my load at top speed about two hundred yards in beneath the trees on the first burst. Gray trunks, brown leaves, leafless bushes whipped by, and the intermittent light cutting through the tangle of bare branches above was dizzying. We finally ducked in behind a huge old tree just off the path. My beloved Marlboro ultra-lights had a tight grip on my lungs, and I was heaving like a hooked tuna. My Achilles tendons were ready to snap and both knees hurt. Barney, who was in somewhat better shape, gasped less but had to put the girl down and arch his back until it made a sound like knuckles popping. We were too scared to talk, but waited, listening.

The girl pulled on my shirt and I looked down at her. "He's got a gun," she whispered.

An insane bellow rose up from the head of the path. "Marta," cried the kidnapper. "Marta."

"Who's Marta?" I asked.

"That's what he calls me," she said.

Barney leaned out around the side of the tree. There came the report of a pistol from very close by followed by a voice. "Come back, please!" he yelled.

If we didn't start running again, I would have pissed my pants right there I was so scared. Barney had the girl by the hand, and we were dashing off the path through fallen leaves, over logs and sticks, around bushes. Stumbling in ruts, branches slapping our faces, we lurched frantically forward. I heard two more gunshots and expected any minute to feel a slug dig into my back.

We stopped again after a good ten minutes of flight, in behind a blind of tangled sticker bushes. Kneeling down, I tried to control my breathing so as not to give us away. Barney and the girl crouched beside me. Only inches from where my hands leaned against the ground was a broken branch, three feet long and the width of a baseball bat. I grabbed hold of it, more to keep myself anchored to reality than anything else.

"Here he comes," whispered Barney.

I looked up through the bush and saw him approaching about sixty yards away, walking slowly, looking side to side. Every so often he'd stop for a moment or two, turn, and then continue directly for us. I tracked him as he passed behind trees, and even at that distance, I could see he was a big guy. He wore a red plaid hunting jacket and a black wool cap. What struck me most was that his face was too large, overly prominent cheekbones and a shelf of a forehead.

"When he gets close enough, I'm going to rush him with the stick and see if I can catch him off guard," I said. "Don't start running until I hit him. Then take off, stay low, and zigzag."

"No, we've gotta keep going" said Barney. "He'll blow your friggin' head off."

"I have a better chance of staying alive against that guy. If I run five more steps, I'm gonna drop over."

"Okay," he said, shaking his head and looking doubtful.

The girl patted my back. I turned, smiled, and put my finger to my lips. She did the same.

I got quietly to my feet, making sure to stay hunched down beneath the top of the blind. Grasping the stick tightly with both hands, I lifted it back over my shoulder.

"Break his fucking skull," whispered Barney, and then we could say no more because the kidnapper was right in front of us, less than ten yards away. That big, ugly face was twisted with a look of anguish, and I noticed tears in his eyes. He stepped closer. *"Marta!"* he screamed. When he turned to look behind him, I bolted out from behind the bushes with nothing on my mind but swinging for the fence. As I moved, I heard Barney and the girl take off. I could smell the cigarettes and whiskey on the guy and brought the stick around. I had his head directly in my sights when I slipped on the leaves and went down like a 280-pound sack of shit at his feet. I lost my wind and the stick fell out of my hands.

I laid there, eyes closed, working to get my breath back, waiting for the gun to go off. Seconds passed, and then a minute, then two, and there was nothing, just the sound of the wind in the trees. When I finally got up enough courage to open my eyes, there was Barney and the girl looking down at me.

"Where's the guy?" said Barney.

"His name is Gerry," said the girl.

I staggered to my feet and looked around in a daze. "I took a fall on the leaves. I thought I was a dead man," I said.

"I didn't hear a gunshot, so we came back."

"Let's get out of here," I said. "If he didn't shoot me by now, he's not going to...I hope."

We saw no trace of Gerry on the way back to the house, but we were jumpy as hell, turning with every falling twig, always ready to bolt. Barney asked Carly what more she knew about him, so we could tell the police. She told us he drove a black van and also provided part of the license plate number. "The policeman in school told us to remember the numbers," she said.

The instant our cars came into view up by the road, we took off toward them. There was no sign of the black van. Barney and the girl ran and I hobbled as best I could. He opened the back door of his car and she climbed in on the seat.

"Put the belt on," said Barney.

She did as she was told and then said to us, "I'm tired," and lay down on the seat, closed her eyes. My heart went out to the poor kid; she was brave as hell.

He closed the door. "Follow me," he said. "I'm going to head into town to the police station."

I agreed, got into my car, and we drove off. Finally at rest behind the wheel, I began to feel every ache and pain from our adventure in the woods. The sky had, at some point, grown overcast. It seemed later than it should have been. I didn't think the whole ordeal at the pink house could have taken more than an hour and a half at the most, but from the look of things it seemed night was now only an hour or so away.

The fact that we had rescued the girl had begun to sink in, and I felt good about it. With all my bruises, my creaking knees, instead of feeling my age, I felt like I was sixteen again and had just finished high school football practice. Then, on Bascomb Road, heading east toward town, I saw Barney turn into the lot of a closed farm market/gas station and park next to a pay phone. I pulled in behind him.

I thought he was going to get out, but he stayed seated in the car. I got out of mine and walked up next to his window.

He rolled the window down but didn't turn to look at me.

"What's the deal?" I said.

"Look in the back seat," he said.

I stepped back and peered in the window. She was gone. I opened the door and leaned down to touch the seat where she had been.

Barney got out of the car as I slammed the back door. He dropped some money into the pay phone and put through an anonymous call to the police. While I stood there listening as he told them what we thought we knew about the girl's abduction, snow started to fall. By the time he hung up it was really coming down.

I lit up and he bummed a cigarette off me. "We've been played," he said.

"What'd the cop say?" I asked.

"He warned me of the penalty of interfering in a police investigation. 'Get a life, buddy,' he said just before he hung up on me."

Three days later, the news reported that, due to the efforts of law enforcement and a nationwide Amber alert, Gerry Gilfoil had been arrested and the girl he had abducted had been rescued. The black van, the plate number, all of it was on the money. The cops caught up with them in Ohio. The girl, Carly, was fine. He hadn't hurt her. He said he was taking her to Disneyland. The reason he'd grabbed her was because his wife had left him and taken their daughter. She was about the same age as Carly and he missed her terribly. It seems he had grown despondent and depressed of late, uncommunicative, and his wife couldn't take it anymore.

Along with the story, there was a photo of the girl being reunited with her family, and beneath that a photo of poor Gerry, his eyes as empty as Carly's were luminous. I carried that image of her abductor around in my mind for weeks, and every morning, in the bathroom mirror, I'd compare my own to it and contemplate his loss. Sometime soon after that story ran, the kitchen sink busted again, and I can't readily describe what a pleasure it actually was to fix it.

The next time I saw Barney was about two months later, the night before New Year's Eve. We sat out in the frozen studio, dressed in coats and gloves, sipping from a bottle of Four Roses. Because of the bitter cold in recent weeks, the paint on some of the *Coffins on the River* series had cracked and fallen off onto the floor in big, bright chips.

"That's a shame," I said, eyeing Biscuit Boy's leprosy.

"What are we gonna do?" he said.

"I know what you mean," I told him. "I found out the other day that my publisher doesn't want to take a chance on another *Deluge*. They're dropping me." I took a taste from the bottle and passed it to him.

"Jeez," was all he could muster. He shook his head and then drank until he grimaced.

I hadn't mentioned our adventure at the pink house since we had parted in the snow that day, but there were a lot of times I had almost called him. "So," I said, "what did you make of that rescue?"

He reached down and lifted a large paint chip off the floor that held Qua Num's chest emblem: a beautifully rendered alarm clock. Spinning it slowly in his hands, he studied it while he spoke. "Life and Art," he said, "are the same thing; one illusion standing in for the other and vice versa. Even if no one is watching, the only happiness is to try to do your best." He dropped the chip and it broke in two.

"Maybe something's always watching," I said.

"Maybe not," he said. Then he pulled a fat joint out of his coat pocket, lit up, took a drag, and passed it over. "Hold those hits," he said, and I did, my head soon growing light. In the silence that followed the last toke, I heard the boards of the studio creak in the cold, and the wind coming in through the window was like the sound of water rushing by. I pictured that old, tired year, climbing into its coffin and pushing off into the flow, leaving the two of us behind to manage as best we could.

GAME NIGHT AT THE FOX AND GOOSE
Karen Joy Fowler

The reader will discover that my
reputation, wherever I have lived, is
endorsed as that of a true and pure woman.
—Laura D. Fair

ALISON CALLED ALL over the city trying to find a restaurant that served blowfish, but there wasn't one. She settled for Chinese. She would court an MSG attack. And if none came, then she'd been craving red bean sauce anyway. On the way to the restaurant, Alison chose not to wear her seat belt.

Alison had been abandoned by her lover, who was so quick about it she hadn't even known she was pregnant yet. She couldn't ever tell him now. She sat pitifully alone, near the kitchen, at a table for four.

YOU'VE REALLY SCREWED UP THIS TIME, her fortune cookie told her. GIVE UP. And, in small print: CHIN'S ORIENTAL PALACE.

The door from the kitchen swung open, so the air around her was hot for a moment, then cold when the door closed. Alison drank her tea and looked at the tea leaves in the bottom of her cup. They were easy to read. He doesn't love you, they said. She tipped them out onto the napkin and tried to rearrange them. YOU FOOL. She covered the message with the one remaining wonton, left the cookie for the kitchen god, and decided to walk all by herself in the dark, three blocks up Hillside Drive, past two alleyways, to have a drink at the Fox and Goose. No one stopped her.

Alison had forgotten it was Monday night. Sometimes there was music in the Fox and Goose. Sometimes you could sit in a corner by yourself listening to someone with an acoustic guitar singing "Killing Me Softly." On Monday nights the television was on and the bar was rather crowded. Mostly men. Alison swung one leg over the only empty bar stool and slid forward. The bar was made of wood, very upscale.

"What can I get the pretty lady?" the bartender asked, without taking his eyes off the television screen. He wore glasses, low on his nose.

Alison was not a pretty lady and didn't feel like pretending she was. "I've been used and discarded," she told the bartender. "And I'm pregnant. I'd like a glass of wine."

"You really shouldn't drink if you're pregnant," the man sitting to Alison's left said. "Two more downs and they're already in field goal range again."

The bartender set the wine in front of Alison. He was shaking his head. "Pregnant women aren't supposed to drink much," he warned her.

"How?" the man on her left asked.

"How do you think?" said Alison.

"Face mask," said the bartender.

"Turn it up."

Alison heard the amplified *thwock* of football helmets hitting together. "Good coverage," the bartender said. "No protection," said the man on Alison's right.

Alison turned to look at him. He was dressed in a blue sweater with the sleeves pushed up. He had dark eyes and was drinking a dark beer. "I asked him to wear a condom," she said quietly. "I even brought one. He couldn't."

"He couldn't?"

"I really don't want to discuss it." Alison sipped her wine. It had the flat, bitter taste of house white. She realized the bartender hadn't asked her what she wanted. But then, if he had, house white was what she would have requested. "It just doesn't seem fair." She spoke over her glass, unsure that anyone was listening, not really caring if they weren't. "All I did was fall in love. All I did was believe someone who said he loved me. He was the liar. But nothing happens to him."

"Unfair is the way things are," the man on her right told her. Three months ago Alison would have been trying to decide if she were attracted to him. Not that she would necessarily have wanted to do anything about it. It was

CRUCIFIED DREAMS

just a question she'd always asked herself, dealing with men, interested in the answer, interested in those times when the answer changed abruptly, one way or another. But it was no longer an issue. Alison was a dead woman these days. Alison was attracted to no one.

Two men at the end of the bar began to clap suddenly. "He hasn't missed from thirty-six yards yet this season," the bartender said.

Alison watched the kickoff and the return. Nothing. No room at all. "Men handle this stuff so much better than women. You don't know what heartbreak is," she said confrontationally. No one responded. She backed off anyway. "Well, that's how it looks." She drank and watched an advertisement for trucks. A man bought his wife the truck she'd always wanted. Alison was afraid she might cry. "What would you do," she asked the man on her right, "if you were me?"

"Drink, I guess. Unless I was pregnant."

"Watch the game," said the man on her left.

"Focus on your work," said the bartender.

"Join the Foreign Legion." The voice came from behind Alison. She swiveled around to locate it. At a table near a shuttered window a very tall woman sat by herself. Her face was shadowed by an Indiana Jones–type hat, but the candle on the table lit up the area below her neck. She was wearing a black T-shirt with a picture on it that Alison couldn't make out. She spoke again. "Make new friends. See distant places." She gestured for Alison to join her. "Save two galaxies from the destruction of the alien armada."

Alison stood up on the little ledge that ran beneath the bar, reached over the counter, and took an olive, sucking the pimiento out first, then eating the rest. She picked up her drink, stepped down, and walked over to the woman's table. Elvis. That was Elvis's face on the T-shirt right between the woman's breasts. ARE YOU LONESOME TONIGHT? the T-shirt asked.

"That sounds good." Alison sat down across from the woman. She could see her face better now; her skin was pale and a bit rough. Her hair was long, straight, and brown. "I'd rather time travel, though. Back just two months. Maybe three months. Practically walking distance."

"You could get rid of the baby."

"Yes," said Alison. "I could."

The woman's glass sat on the table in front of her. She had finished whatever she had been drinking; the maraschino cherry was all that remained. The woman picked it up and ate it, dropping the stem onto the napkin under her glass. "Maybe he'll come back to you. You trusted him. You must have seen something decent in him."

Alison's throat closed so that she couldn't talk. She picked up her drink, but she couldn't swallow either. She set it down again, shaking her head. Some of the wine splashed over the lip and onto her hand.

"He's already married," the woman said.

Alison nodded, wiping her hand on her pant leg. "God."

She searched in her pockets for a Kleenex. The woman handed her the napkin from beneath the empty glass. Alison wiped her nose with it and the cherry stem fell out. She did not dare look up. She kept her eyes focused on the napkin in her hand, which she folded into four small squares.

"When I was growing up," she said, "I lived on a block with lots of boys. Sometimes I'd come home and my knees were all scraped up because I'd fallen or I'd taken a ball in the face or I'd gotten kicked or punched, and I'd be crying and my mother would always say the same thing. 'You play with the big boys and you're going to get hurt,' she'd say. Exasperated." Alison unfolded the napkin, folded it diagonally instead. Her voice shrank. "I've been so stupid."

"The universe is shaped by the struggle between two great forces," the woman told her. It was not really responsive. It was not particularly supportive. Alison felt just a little bit angry at this woman who now knew so much about her.

"Good and evil?" Alison asked, slightly nastily. She wouldn't meet the woman's eyes. "The Elvis and the anti-Elvis?"

"Male and female. Minute by minute, the balance tips one way or the other. Not just here. In every universe. There are places"—the woman leaned forward—"where men are not allowed to gather and drink. Places where football is absolutely illegal."

"England?" Alison suggested and then didn't want to hear the woman's answer. "I like football," she added quickly. "I like games with rules. You can be stupid playing football and it can cost you the game, but there are penalties for fouls, too. I like games with rules."

"You're playing one now, aren't you?" the woman said. "You haven't hurt this man, even though you could. Even though he's hurt you. He's not playing by the rules. So why are you?"

"It doesn't have anything to do with rules," Alison said. "It only has to do with me, with the kind of person I think I am. Which is not the kind of person he is." She thought for a moment. "It doesn't mean I wouldn't like to see him get hurt," she added. "Something karmic. Justice."

"'We must storm and hold Cape Turk before we talk of social justice.'" The woman folded her arms under her breasts and leaned back in her chair. "Did Sylvia Townsend Warner say that?"

"Not to me."

Alison heard more clapping at the bar behind her. She looked over her shoulder. The man in the blue sweater slapped his hand on the wooden bar. "Good call. Excellent call. They won't get another play in before the half."

"Where I come from she did." Alison turned back as the woman spoke. "And she was talking about women. No one gets justice just by deserving it. No one ever has."

Alison finished off her wine. "No." She wondered if she should go home now. She knew when she got there that the apartment would be unbearably lonely and that the phone wouldn't ring and that she would need immediately to be somewhere else. No activity in the world could be more awful than listening to a phone not ring. But she didn't really want to stay here and have a conversation that was at worst too strange and at best too late. Women usually supported you more when they talked to you. They didn't usually make you defensive or act as if they had something to teach you, the way this woman did. And anyhow, justice was a little peripheral now, wasn't it? What good would it really do her? What would it change?

She might have gone back and joined the men at the bar during the half. They were talking quietly among themselves. They were ordering fresh drinks and eating beer nuts. But she didn't want to risk seeing cheerleaders. She didn't want to risk the ads with the party dog and all his women, even though she'd read in a magazine that the dog was a bitch. Anywhere she went, there she'd be. Just like she was. Heartbroken.

The woman was watching her closely. Alison could feel this, though the woman's face remained shadowed and she couldn't quite bring herself to look back at her directly. She looked at Elvis instead and the way his eyes wavered through her lens of candlelight and tears. Lonesome tonight? "You really have it bad, don't you?" the woman said. Her tone was sympathetic. Alison softened again. She decided to tell this perceptive woman everything. How much she'd loved him. How she'd never loved anyone else. How she felt it every time she took a breath, and had for weeks now.

"I don't think I'll ever feel better," she said. "No matter what I do."

"I hear it takes a year to recover from a serious loss. Unless you find someone else."

A year. Alison could be a mother by then. How would she find someone else, pregnant like she was or with a small child? Could she spend a year hurting like this? Would she have a choice?

"Have you ever heard of Laura D. Fair?" the woman asked.

Alison shook her head. She picked up the empty wineglass and tipped it to see if any drops remained. None did. She set it back down and picked up the napkin, wiping her eyes. She wasn't crying. She just wasn't exactly not crying.

"Mrs. Fair killed her lover," the woman told her. Alison looked at her own fingernails. One of them had a ragged end. She bit it off shorter while she listened. "He was a lawyer. A. P. Crittenden. She shot him on the ferry to Oakland in November of 1870 in front of his whole family because she saw him kiss his wife. He'd promised to leave her and marry Mrs. Fair instead, and then he didn't, of course. She pleaded a transient insanity known at that time as emotional insanity. She said she was incapable of killing Mr. Crittenden, who had been the only friend she'd had in the world." Alison examined her nail. She had only succeeded in making it more ragged. She bit it again, too close to the skin this time. It hurt and she put it back in her mouth. "Mrs. Fair said she had no memory of the murder, which many people, not all of them related to the deceased, witnessed. She was the first woman sentenced to hang in California."

Loud clapping and catcalls at the bar. The third quarter had started with a return all the way to the fifty-yard line. Alison heard it. She did not turn around, but she took her finger out of her mouth and picked up the napkin. She folded it again. Four small squares. "Rules are rules," Alison said.

"But then she didn't hang. Certain objections were made on behalf of the defense and sustained, and a new trial was held. This time she was acquitted. By now she was the most famous and the most hated woman in the country."

Alison unfolded the napkin and tried to smooth out the creases with the side of her palm. "I never heard of her."

"Laura D. Fair was not some little innocent." The woman's hat brim dipped decisively. "Mrs. Fair had been married four times, and each had been a profitable venture. One of her husbands killed himself. She was not pretty, but she was passionate. She was not smart, but she was clever. And she saw, in her celebrity, a new way to make money. She announced a new career as a public speaker. She traveled the country with her lectures. And what was her message? She told women to murder the men who seduced and betrayed them."

"I never heard of her," said Alison.

"Mrs. Fair was a compelling speaker. She'd had some acting and elocution experience. Her performance in court showed training. On the stage she was even better. 'The act will strike a terror to the hearts of sensualists and libertines.'" The woman stabbed dramatically at her own breast with her fist, hitting Elvis right in the eye. Behind her hand, Elvis winked at Alison in the candlelight. "Mrs. Fair said that women throughout the world would glory in the revenge exacted by American womanhood. Overdue. Long overdue. Thousands of women heard her. Men, too, and not all of them entirely unsympathetic. Fanny Hyde and Kate Stoddart were released in Brooklyn. Stoddart never even stood trial. But then there was a backlash. The martyred Marys were hanged in Philadelphia. And then...."

The woman's voice dropped suddenly in volume and gained in intensity. Alison looked up at her quickly. The woman was staring back. Alison looked away.

"And then a group of women hunted down and dispatched Charles S. Smith in an alley near his home. Mr. Smith was a married man and his victim, Edith Wilson, was pregnant, an invalid, and eleven years old. But this time the women wore sheets and could not be identified. Edith Wilson was perhaps the only female in Otsego County, New York, who could not have taken part." Alison folded her napkin along the diagonal.

"So no one could be tried. It was an inspiring and purging operation. It was copied in many little towns across the country. God knows, the women had access to sheets."

Alison laughed, but the woman was not expecting it, had not paused to allow for laughter. "And then Annie Oakley shot Frank Butler in a challenge match in Cincinnati."

"Excuse me," said Alison. "I didn't quite hear you." But she really had and the woman continued anyway, without pausing or repeating.

"She said it was an accident, but she was too good a shot. They hanged her for it. And then Grover Cleveland was killed by twelve sheeted women on the White House lawn. At teatime," the woman said.

"Wait a minute." Alison stopped her. "Grover Cleveland served out two terms. Nonconsecutively. I'm sure."

The woman leaned into the candlelight, resting her chin on a bridge she made of her hands. "You're right, of course," she said. "That's what happened here. But in another universe where the feminine force was just a little stronger in 1872, Grover Cleveland died in office. With a scone in his mouth and a child in New York."

"All right," said Alison accommodatingly. Accommodation was one of Alison's strengths. "But what difference does that make to us?"

"I could take you there." The woman pushed her hat back so that Alison could have seen her eyes if she wanted to. "The universe right next door. Practically walking distance."

The candle flame was casting shadows which reached and withdrew and reached at Alison over the table. In the unsteady light, the woman's face flickered like a silent film star's. Then she pulled back in her chair and sank into the darkness beyond the candle. The ball was on the ten-yard line and the bar was quiet. "I knew you were going to say that," Alison said finally. "How did I know you were going to say that? Who would say that?"

"Some lunatic?" the woman suggested.

"Yes."

"Don't you want to hear about it anyway? About my universe?" The woman smiled at her. An unperturbed smile. Nice even teeth. And a kind of confidence that was rare among the women Alison knew. Alison had noticed it immediately without realizing she was noticing. The way the woman sat back in her chair and didn't pick at herself. Didn't play with her hair. Didn't look at her hands. The way she lectured Alison.

"All right," Alison said. She put the napkin down and fit her hands together, forcing herself to sit as still. "But first tell me about Laura Fair. My Laura Fair."

"Up until 1872 the two histories are identical," the woman said. "Mrs. Fair married four times and shot her lover and was convicted and the conviction was overturned. She just never lectured. She planned to. She was scheduled to speak at Platt's Hotel in San Francisco on November 11, 1872, but a mob of some two thousand men gathered outside the hotel and another two thousand surrounded the apartment building she lived in. She asked for police protection, but it was refused and she was too frightened to leave her home. Even staying where she was proved dangerous. A few men tried to force their way inside. She spent a terrifying night and never attempted to lecture again. She died in poverty and obscurity.

"Fanny Hyde and Kate Stoddart were released anyway. I can't find out what happened to the Marys. Edith Wilson was condemned by respectable people everywhere and cast out of her family."

"The eleven-year-old child?" Alison said.

"In your universe," the woman reminded her. "Not in mine. You don't know much of your own history, do you? Name a great American woman."

The men at the bar were in an uproar. Alison turned to look. "Interception," the man in the blue sweater shouted to her exultantly. "Did you see it?"

"Name a great American woman," Alison called back to him.

"Goddamn interception with goal to go," he said. "Eleanor Roosevelt?"

"Marilyn Monroe," said a man at the end of the bar.

"The senator from California?" the woman asked. "Now that's a good choice."

Alison laughed again. "Funny," she said, turning back to the woman. "Very good."

"We have football, too," the woman told her. "Invented in 1873. Outlawed in 1950. No one ever got paid to play it."

"And you have Elvis."

"No, we don't. Not like yours. Of course not. I got this here."

"Interception," the man in the blue sweater said. He was standing beside Alison, shaking his head with the wonder of it. "Let me buy you ladies a drink." Alison opened her mouth and he waved his hand. "Something nonalcoholic for you," he said. "Please. I really want to."

"Ginger ale, then," she agreed. "No ice."

"Nothing for me," said the woman. They watched the man walk back to the bar, and then, when he was far enough away not to hear, she leaned forward toward Alison. "You like men, don't you?"

"Yes," said Alison. "I always have. Are they different where you come from? Have they learned to be honest and careful with women, since you kill them when they're not?" Alison's voice was sharper than she intended, so she softened the effect with a sadder question. "Is it better there?"

"Better for whom?" The woman did not take her eyes off Alison. "Where I come from the men and women hardly speak to each other. First of all, they don't speak the same language. They don't here, either, but you don't recognize that as clearly. Where I come from there's men's English and there's women's English."

"Say something in men's English."

"'I love you.' Shall I translate?"

"No," said Alison. "I know the translation for that one." The heaviness closed over her heart again. Not that it had ever gone away. Nothing made Alison feel better, but many things made her feel worse. The bartender brought her ginger ale. With ice. Alison was angry, suddenly, that she couldn't even get a drink with no ice. She looked for the man in the blue sweater, raised the glass at him, and rattled it. Of course he was too far away to hear even if he was listening, and there was no reason to believe he was.

"Two-minute warning," he called back. "I'll be with you in two minutes."

Men were always promising to be with you soon. Men could never be with you now. Alison had only cared about this once, and she never would again. "Football has the longest two minutes in the world," she told the woman. "So don't hold your breath. What else is different where you come from?" She sipped at her ginger ale. She'd been grinding her teeth recently—stress, the dentist said—and so the cold liquid made her mouth hurt.

"Everything is different. Didn't you ask for no ice? Don't drink that," the woman said. She called to the bartender. "She didn't want ice. You gave her ice."

"Sorry." The bartender brought another bottle and another glass. "Nobody told me no ice."

"Thank you," Alison said. He took the other glass away. Alison thought he was annoyed. The woman didn't seem to notice.

"Imagine your world without a hundred years of adulterers," she said. "The level of technology is considerably depressed. Lots of books never written because the authors didn't live. Lots of men who didn't get to be president. Lots of passing. Although it's illegal. Men dressing as women. Women dressing as men. And the dress is more sexually differentiated. Codpieces are fashionable again. But you don't have to believe me," the woman said. "Come and see for yourself. I can take you there in a minute. What would it cost you to just come and see? What do you have here that you'd be losing?"

The woman gave her time to think. Alison sat and drank her ginger ale and repeated to herself the things her lover had said the last time she had seen him. She remembered them all, some of them surprisingly careless, some of them surprisingly cruel, all of them surprising. She repeated them again, one by one, like a rosary. The man who had left was not the man she had loved. The man she had loved would never have said such things to her. The man she had loved did not exist. She had made him up. Or he had. "Why would you want me to go?" Alison asked.

"The universe is shaped by the struggle between two great forces. Sometimes a small thing can tip the balance. One more woman. Who knows?" The woman tilted her hat back with her hand. "Save a galaxy. Make new friends. Or stay here where your heart is. Broken."

"Can I come back if I don't like it?"

"Yes. Do you like it here?"

She drank her ginger ale and then set the glass down, still half full. She glanced at the man in the blue sweater, then past him to the bartender. She let herself feel just for a moment what it might be like to know that she could finish this drink and then go home to the one person in the world who loved her.

Never in this world. "I'm going out for a minute. Two minutes," she called to the bartender. One minute to get back. "Don't take my drink."

She stood and the other woman stood too, even taller than Alison had thought. "I'll follow you. Which way?" Alison asked.

"It's not hard," the woman said. "In fact, I'll follow you. Go to the back. Find the door that says WOMEN and go on through it. I'm just going to pay for my drink and then I'll be right along."

VIXENS was what the door actually said, across the way from the one marked GANDERS. Alison paused and then pushed through. She felt more than a little silly, standing in the small bathroom that apparently fronted two universes. One toilet, one sink, one mirror. Two universes. She went into the stall and closed the door. Before she had finished she heard the outer door open and shut again. "I'll be right out," she said. The toilet paper was small and unusually rough. The toilet wouldn't flush. It embarrassed her. She tried three times before giving up.

The bathroom was larger than it had been, less clean, and a row of urinals lined one wall. The woman stood at the sink, looking into the mirror, which was smaller. "Are you ready?" she asked and removed her breasts from behind Elvis, tossing them into a wire wastebasket. She turned. "Ready or not."

"No," said Alison, seeing the face under the hat clearly for the first time. "Please, no." She began to cry again, looking up at his face, looking down at his chest. ARE YOU LONESOME TONIGHT?

"You lied to me," she said dully.

"I never lied," he answered. "Think back. You just translated wrong. Because you're that kind of woman. We don't have women like you here now. And anyway, what does it matter whose side you play on? All that matters is that no one wins. Aren't I right? Aren't I?" He tipped his hat to her.

COPPING SQUID
Michael Shea

RICKY DEUCE, TWENTY-EIGHT and three years sober, was the night clerk at Mahmoud's Mom and Pop Market. He was a small, leanly muscled guy, and as he sat there, the darkness outside deepening toward midnight, his tight little Irish face looked pleased with where he was. Behind Ricky on his stool, the whole wall was bottles of every kind of Hard known to man.

This job was easy money—a sit-down after his day forklifting at the warehouse. He already owned an awesomely restored sixty-four Mustang, and had near ten K saved, and by rights he ought to be casting around for where he might take off to next. But the fact was, he got a kick out of clerking here till two a.m. each night.

A kick that was not powder nor pill nor smoke nor booze, that was not needing any of them, especially not booze, which could shine and glint in its bottles and surround him all night long, and he not give a shit. He never got tired of sitting here immune, savoring the unadorned adventure of being alive.

Not that the job lacked irritants. There were obnoxious clientele, and these preponderated toward the deep of night.

Ricky thought he heard one even now.

Single cars shushed past outside, long silences falling between, and a scuffy tread advanced along the sidewalk. A purposeful tread that nonetheless staggered now and then. It reminded Ricky that he was It, the only island of comfort and light for a half a mile in all directions, in a big city, in the dead of night.

Then, there in Mahmoud's Mom and Pop Market's entryway, stood a big gaunt black guy. Youngish, but with a strange, outdated look, his hair growing weedily out towards a 'fro. His torso and half his legs were engulfed in an oversize nylon athletic jacket that looked like it might have slept in an alley or two, and which revealed the chest of a dark T-shirt that said something indecipherable RULES. The man had a drugged look, but he also had wide-arched, inquiring brows. His glossy black eyes checked you out, as if maybe the real him was somewhere back in there, smarter than he looked.

But then, as he lurched inside the store, and into the light, he just looked drunk.

"Evening," Ricky said smiling. He always opened by giving all his clientele the benefit of the doubt.

The man came and planted his hands on the counter, not aggressively, it seemed, but in the manner of someone tipsily presenting a formal proposition.

"Hi. I'm Andre. I need your money, man."

Ricky couldn't help laughing. "What a coincidence! So do I!"

"OK, Bro," Andre said calmly, agreeably. As if he was shaping a counter-proposal, he straightened and stepped back from the counter. "Then Ima cut your fuckin ass to *ribbons* till you *give* me your fuckin money!"

The odd picture this plan of action presented almost made Ricky laugh again, but then the guy whipped out and flipped open—with great expertise—a very large gravity knife, which he then swept around by way of threat, though still out of striking range. Ricky was so startled that he half fell off his stool.

Getting his legs under him, furious at having been galvanized like that, Ricky shrieked, "A knife? You're gonna rob me with a fucking *knife? I've* got a fucking knife!"

And he unpocketed his lock-back Buck knife, and snapped it open. All this while he found himself once again trying to decipher the big, uncouthly lettered word on the guy's T-shirt above the word RULES.

Andre didn't seem drunk at all now. He swept a slash over the counter at Ricky's head, which Ricky had to recoil from right smartly.

"You shit! You do that again and I'm gonna slice your—"

Here came the gravity knife again, as quick as a shark, and, snapping his head back out of the way, Ricky counter-slashed at the sweeping arm, and felt the rubbery tug of flesh unzipped by the tip of his Buck's steel.

Andre abruptly stepped back and relaxed. He put his knife away, and held up his arm. It had a nice bloody slash across the inner forearm. He stood there letting it bleed for Ricky. Ricky had seen himself and others bleed, but not a black man. On black skin, he found, blood looked more opulent, a richer red, and so did the meat underneath the skin. That cut would take at least a dozen stitches. They both watched the blood soak the elastic cuff of Andre's jacket.

"So here's what it is," said Andre, and dipped his free hand in the jacket and pulled out a teensy, elegant little silver cellphone. "Ima call the oinkers, and say I need an ambulance because this mad whacked white shrimp—that's you—slashed me when I just axed him for some spare change, and then Ima ditch the shit outta this knife before they show up, and it won't matter if they believe me or not, when they see me bleedin like this they gonna take us both down for questioning and statements. How's your rap sheet, Chief, hey? So look. Just give me a little money and I'm totally outta your face. It don't have to be much. Ten dollars would do it!"

This took Ricky aback. "Ten dollars? You make me cut you for ten dollars?"

"You wanna give me a hundred, give me a hundred! Ten's all you gotta give me—and a ride. A short ride, over to the Hood."

"You want money and a ride! You think I'm outta my mind? You wanna ride to your connection to score, and when we get there, you're gonna try an get more money out of me. And that's the *best* case scenario." Ricky was dismayed to hear a hint of negotiation in his own words. It was true, he'd had a number of contacts with the San Francisco Police Department, as the result of alcohol-enhanced conflicts here and there. But also, he felt intrigued by the guy. Something fascinating burned in this Andre whack. Intensity came off him in waves, along with his faint scent of street-funk. The man was consumed by a passion. In the deformed letters on his T-shirt, Ricky thought he could make out a T _ H _ U.

"What could I be coppin for ten bucks?" crowed Andre. "I'm not out to harm you! This just has to do with *me*. See, it's *required*. I have to get these two things from someone else, the money and the ride."

"Explain that. Explain why you *have* to get these two things from someone else."

Andre didn't answer for a moment. He stared and stared, not exactly at Ricky, but at something he seemed to see in Ricky. He seemed to be weighing this thing he detected. He had eyes like black opals, and strange slow thoughts seemed to move within their shiny hemispheres....

"The reason is," he said at last, "that's the *procedure*. There are these particular rules for seeing the one I want to see."

"And who is that?"

"I can't tell you. I'm not allowed."

It was almost time to close up anyway. Ricky became aware of a powerful tug of curiosity, and aware of the fact that Andre saw it in his eyes. This put Ricky's back up.

"No. You gotta give me something. You gotta tell me at least—"

"Thassit! Fuck you!" And Andre flipped open the cellphone. His big spatulate fingertips made quick dainty movements on the minute keys. Ricky heard the bleep, minuscule but crystal clear, of the digits, and then a micro-voice saying, "Nine One One Emergency."

"I been stabbed by a punk in a liquor store! I been stabbed!"

Ricky violently shook his head, and held up his hands in surrender. With a bleep, Andre clicked off. "Believe me! You're not makin a mistake. It's something I can't talk about, but you can *see* it. You can see it yourself. But the thing is, it's got to be now. We can't hem an haw. And Ima tell you now, now that you're in, that there's something *in* it for you, something good as gold. Trust me, you'll see. Help me with this knot," he said, pulling a surprisingly clean-looking handkerchief from his jacket pocket. He folded it—rather expertly, Ricky thought—into a bandage. Ricky wrapped it round the wound, and tied the ends in a neat, tight squareknot, feeling as his fingers pressed against flesh that he was forming a bond with this whack by stanching his blood. He was accepting a dangerous complicity with his whack aims, whatever they might be....

Bandaged, Andre held out his hand. Ricky put a ten in it.

"Thanks," said Andre. "So. Where's your ride?"

The blue Mustang boomed down Sixteenth through the Mission. All the signals were on blink. Here and there under the streetlights, there was a wino or two, or someone walking fast, shoulders hunched against the emptiness, but mostly the Mustang rolled through pure naked City, a vacant concrete stage.

Ricky liked driving around at this hour, and often did it on his own for fun. When he was a kid, he'd always felt sorcery in the midnight streets, in the mosaic of their lights, and he'd never lost the sense of unearthly shapes stirring beneath their web, stirring till they almost cohered, as the stars did for the ancients into constellations. Tonight, with mad, bleeding Andre riding shotgun, the lights glittered wilder possibilities, and a sinister grandeur seemed to lurk in them.

They passed under the freeway, and down to the Bayside, hanging south on Third. After long blocks of big blank buildings, Third took a snaky turn, and they were rolling through the Hood.

Pawn shops and thrift stores and liquor stores. A whiff of Mad Dog hung over it, Mad Dog with every other drug laced through it. The Hood was lit, was like a long jewel. The signals were working here.

The signals stretched out of sight ahead, like a python with scales of red and green, their radiance haloed in a light fog that was drifting in off the Bay. And people were out, little knots of them near the corners. They formed isolated clots of gaudy life, like tidepools, all of them dressed in baggy clothes of bright-colored nylon, panelled and logo'd with surreal pastels under the emerald-and-ruby signal glare. And as they stood and talked together, they moved in a way both fitful and languid, like sealife bannering in a restless sea.

The signals changed in pattern to a slow tidal rhythm. It seemed a rhythm meant to accommodate rush-hour traffic. You got a green for two blocks max, and then you got a red. A long, long red. Ricky's blue Mustang was almost the only car on the road in this phantom rush-hour, creeping down the long bright python two blocks at a time, and then idling, idling interminably, while the sealife on the corners seemed astir with interest and attention.

Ricky had no qualms about running red lights on deserted streets, but here it seemed dangerous, a declaration of unease.

"Fuck this!" he said at their fourth red light, and slipped the brake, and rolled forward. At a stroll though, under twenty. The Mustang lounged along, taking green and red alike, as if upon a scenic country road. The bright languid people on the corners threw laughter at them now, a shout or two, and it seemed as if the whole great submarine python stirred to quicker currents. Ricky felt a ripple of hallucination, and saw here, for just a moment, a vast inked mural, the ink not dry, themselves and all around them still half-liquid entities billowing in an aqueous universe....

Out of nowhere, for the first time in three years, Ricky had the thought that he would like a drink. He was amazed at this thought. He was frightened. Then he was angry.

"I'm not drivin much farther, Andre. Spit out where we're going, and it better be nearby, or you can call 911 and I'll take my chances. I'll bet you got a longer past with the SFPD than I do."

"*Damn* you! Whip in here, then."

This cross street was mostly houses—some abandoned—with a liquor store on the next corner, and a lot of sealife lounging out in front of it. "Pull up into some light where you can *see* this."

They idled at the curb. The people on the main drag were two-thirds of a block behind them, the liquor store tidepool much closer ahead of them. Andre leaned his fanatic's face close to Ricky. The intensity of the man was an almost tactile experience; Ricky seemed to feel the muffled crackling of his will through the inches of air that separated them. "Here," hissed Andre. "I'm gonna give you *this,* just to drive me another coupla miles up into these hills. Look at it. Count it. Take it." He shoved a thick roll of bills into Ricky's ribs.

It was in twenties and fifties and hundreds.... It was over five thousand dollars.

"You're...you're batshit, Andre! You make me cut you to get ten bucks, and now you—"

"Just listen." Some people from the liquor store tidepool were drifting their way, and Ricky saw similar movement from Third Street in his rearview mirror. "What I needed," said Andre, "was money that blood was spilt for—it didn't matter how much blood, it didn't matter how much money. Your ten-spot? It's worth that much to me there in your hand. Your ten-spot and another couple miles in your car."

The locals were flowing closer to the Mustang at both ends. Ricky fingered the money. The gist of it was, he decided, that if he didn't follow this waking dream to its end, he would never forgive himself. "Ok," he said.

"Another couple miles in your car," said Andre, "an one more thing. You gotta come in."

"You fuck! You shit! Where does it *end* with you? You just keep—"

"You come in, you watch me connect, and you go out again, scott-free, no harm, no strings attached! I gotta bring blood money, and I gotta bring a *witness.* I lied to you. It wasn't the ride I needed. It was a *witness.*"

A huge shape in lavender running-sweats, and a gaunt one wearing a lime-green jumpsuit, stood beside the Mustang, smiling and making roll-down-the-window gestures. Behind the car, shapes from the main drag were moving laterally out into the street to come up to the driver's side....

But in that poised moment what Ricky saw most vividly was Andre's face, his taut narrow face within its weedy 'fro. This man was in the visionary's trance. His eyes, his soul were locked upon something that filled him with awe. What he pursued had nothing to do with Ricky, nor with anything Ricky could imagine, and Ricky wanted to know what that thing was.

Andre said, "Ima show you—what's your name again?"

"Ricky."

"Ima show you, Richie, the power and the glory. They are right here *among* you, man, an you don't even see it! Hell, even these fools out here can *see* it!"

The Mustang was surrounded now. From behind it sprouted shapes in crimson hoods, with fists bulging inside gold velvet jacket pockets. Up to Ricky's door (its window already open, his elbow thrust out, and five K in cash on his lap) stepped two men with thundercloud hair, wearing shades, their cheeks and brows all whorled with Maori tattooing like ink-black flames. A trio of gaudy nylon scarecrows leaned on his hood, conferring, the side-thrust bills of their caps switching like blades. But Ricky also noted that all this audience, every one of them, had eyes strictly for Andre sitting there at his side. Ricky was free to scan all those exotic, piratical faces as though he were invisible....

All their eyes were grave. They showed awe, and they showed loathing too, as if they abhorred something Andre had done, but just as piercingly, longed for his nerve to do it. Ricky realized he had embarked on a longer journey than he'd thought.

Andre scanned all these buccaneer faces, his fellow mariners of the Hood. A remote little grin was hanging slantwise across his jaw. "Check this out, Rocky," he growled, "an learn from these fools. Learn their *awe,* man, cause what Ima show you, up in those hills, is *awe.*"

He shouldered his door open, and thrust himself up onto the sidewalk. He towered just as tall as the giant in lavender sweats, but he was narrow as a reed. Yet his voice fairly boomed:

"Yo! Alla you! Listen up! Looka here! Looka me! You all wanna see something? Wanna see something *about* something besides *shit!?* See something *real,* just for a *change?* See the ice-cold, spine-crawlin, hair-stirrin *truth?* Looka here! Looka here, at the power! Looka here! Looka here, at the glory!"

Ricky scanned all the dark faces that ringed them round, and every eye was locked upon that wild gaunt man in his rapture, who now, with a powerful shrug, shouldered off his nylon jacket. It flopped down on the sidewalk with a slither and a sigh, and lay there on the concrete like a sloughed cocoon. He stretched the fabric of his T-shirt, displaying it to every locked-on eye.

Rickey's angle was still too acute to let him decipher exactly who it was who "ruled." But all these encircling faces, *they* seemed to know. They shared a vision of awe and terror and...something like hope. A frosty hope, endlessly remote...but hope. Ricky realized that there prevailed on these mean streets a consensus of vision. He clearly saw that all these eyes had seen, and understood, a catastrophic spectacle beyond his own imagining.

Andre barked, hoarse and brutish as a sea-lion, "Jus *look* at me here! I have gone up to see Him, and I have looked through His eyes, and I have *been* where He *is,* time without end! An I'm here to tell you, all you dearly beloved mongrel dogs of mine, I'm here to tell you that it's *consumed* me! My flesh, and my time, have been blown off my bones, by the searing winds of His breath! I'm not far off now from eternity! Not far off from infinity now!"

The raving seer then hiked up his T-shirt to his chest. What Ricky, from behind, saw there, was like a blow to his own chest, an impact of terror and dizziness, for Andre's thorax on its left side was normal, gauntly fleshed and sinewed, but along its right side, his spine was denuded bone, and midriff was there none, and just below his hoisted shirt-hem, a lathed bracket looped down: a fleshless rib, as clean and bare as sculpture....

His rapt audience recoiled like a single person, some lifting their arms convulsively, as in a reflex of self-protection, or acclaim....

Ricky dropped the Mustang into gear, and launched it from the curb, but in that selfsame instant Andre dropped into his seat again, and slammed his door, and so he was snatched deftly away, as if he were a prize that Ricky treasured, and not a horror that Ricky had been trying to flee.

Moonsilvered, lightless blocks floated past, yet Ricky never took his eyes from the gaunt shape whose T-shirt he could now, uncomprehending, read: CTHULHU RULES.

Somehow he drove, and, shortly, pulled again to a more deserted curb, and killed the engine. On this block, a sole dim streetlight shone. Half the houses were doorless, windowless....

He sat with only silence between himself and a man who had, at the least, submitted to a grave surgical mutilation in the service of his deity. Ricky looked into Andre's eyes.

That was the first challenge, to establish that he dared to look into Andre's eyes—and he found that he did dare.

"For all you've lost," Ricky said, queasily referencing the gruesome marvel, "...you seem very...alive."

"I'm more alive than you will ever be, and when I'm all consumed, I'll be far *more* alive, and I will live forever!"

Ricky fingered the little bale of cash in his hand. "If you want me to go on, you have to tell me this. *Why* do you have to have a witness?"

"Because the One I'm gonna see wants someone new to see Him. He doesn't wanna know you. He wants *you* to know *Him.*" In the darkness, Andre's polished eyes seemed to burn with this thing that he knew, and Ricky did not.

"He wants me to know him. And then?"

"And then it's up to you. To walk away, or to see him like I do."

"And how is that? How do you see him?"

"All the way."

Ricky's hand absently stroked the gearshift knob. "The choice is absolutely mine?"

"Your will is your own! Only your knowledge will be changed!"

Ricky slipped the Mustang into gear, and once more the blue beast growled onward. "Take a right here," purred Andre. "We going up to the top of the hills."

It was the longest "couple miles" that Ricky had ever driven. The road poured down past the Mustang like time itself, a slow stream of old, and older houses, on steepening blocks gapped by vacant lots, or by derelict cottages whose windows and doors were coffined in graffitied plywood.

They began to wind, and a rising sense of peril woke in Ricky. He was charging up into the sinister unknown! There was just too much missing from this man's body! You couldn't lose all that and still walk around, still fight with knives....could you?

But you could. Just look at him.

The houses thinned out even more, big old trees half-shrouding them. Dead cars slept under drifts of leaves, and dim bedroom lights showed life just barely hanging on, here in the hungry heights.

As they mounted this shoulder of the hills, Ricky saw glimpses of other ridges to the right and left, rooftop-and-tree-encrusted like this one. All these crestlines converged toward the same summit, and when Ricky looked behind, it seemed that these ridges poured down like a spill of titanic tentacles. They plunged far below into a thick, surprisingly deep fog that drowned and dimmed the jewelled python of the Hood.

Near the summit, their road entered a deepening gully. At the apex stood a municipal water tank, the dull gloss of its squat cylinder half-sunk in trees and houses.

"We goin to that house there right upside the tank. See that big gray roof pokin from the trees? The driveway goes down through the trees, it's steep an dark. Just roll down slow and easy, kill the engine, an let me get out first an talk to her."

"Her?"

Andre didn't answer. The road briefly crested before plunging, and Ricky had a last glimpse below of the tentacular hills rooted in the fogbank—and rooted beyond that, he imagined, more deeply still into the black floor of the Bay, as if the tentacles rummaged there for their deep-sunk food....

"Right there," said Andre, pointing ahead. "See the gap in the bushes?"

The Mustang crept muttering down the dark leafy tunnel, just as a wind rose, rattling dry oak foliage all around them.

A dim grotto of grassy ground opened below. There was a squat house on it, so dark it was almost a shadow-house. It showed one dim yellow light on the floor of its porch. A lantern, it looked like. A large dark shape loomed on one side of this lantern, and a smaller dark shape lay on the other.

Ricky cut his engine. Andre drew a long, slow breath, and got out. Leaves whispered in the silence. Andre's feet crackled across the yard. Ricky could hear the creak of his weight on the porch-steps as he climbed them, halfway up to the two dark shapes and their dim shared light. And Ricky could also hear...a growly breathing, wasn't it? Yes.... A slow, phlegmy purr of big lungs.

Andre's voice was a new one to Ricky: low and implacable. "I'm back again, Mamma Hagg. I got the toll. I got the witness." Then he looked back and said, "Stand on out here...what's your name again?"

Ricky got out. How dangerous it suddenly seemed to declare himself in this silence, this place! Well, shit. He was here. He might as well say who he was. Loudly: "Ricky Deuce."

When he'd said it, he found his eyes could suddenly decipher the smaller dark shape by the lantern: it was a seated black dog, a big one, with the hint of aging frost on his lower jaw, and with his red tongue hanging and gently pulsing by that frosted jaw. The dog was looking steadily back at him, its tongue a bright spoon of greedy tissue scooping up the taste of the night....

It was not the brute's breathing Ricky had heard. It was Momma Hagg's, her voice deep now from the vault of her cave-like lungs:

"Then show the toll, fool."

Andre bent slightly to hold something towards the hound. And above his bent back, the woman in her turn became visible to Ricky. Within a briar-patch of dreads as pale as mushrooms, her monolithic black face melted in its age, her eyes two tarpools in this terrain of gnarled ebony. The shadowy bulk of her body eclipsed the mighty chair she sat in, though its armrests jutted into view, dark wood intricately carven into the coils and claws and thews of two heraldic monsters. Ricky couldn't make out what they were, but they seemed to snarl beneath the fingers of Momma Hagg's immense hands.

The dog's tongue was licking what Andre held up to it—Ricky's ten-spot. The mastiff sniffed and sniffed, then snorted, and licked the bill again, and licked his chops.

"Come on up," said Momma. "The two of you." The big woman's voice had a strange kind of pull to it. Like surf at your legs, its growl dragged you towards her. Ricky approached. Andre mounted to the porch, and Ricky climbed after him. He had the sensation with each step up that he entered a bigger and emptier kind of space. When he stood on the porch, Momma Hagg seemed farther off than he had expected. From her distance wafted the smell of her— an ashen scent like the drenched coals of a bonfire that had included flesh and bones in its fuel. The dog rose.

The porch took too long to cross as they followed the hound. His bright tongue lolling like a casually held torch, with just one back-glance of one crimson eye, the brute led them through a wide, doorless doorframe, and into a high dark interior that gusted out dank salty breath in their faces.

A cold gray light leaked in here, as if the fog that had swallowed the Hood had now climbed the hills, and its glow was seeping into this gaunt house. They trod a rambling, unpartitioned space, the interior all wall-less, while the outer walls were irregularly recessed in alcoves, nooks, and grottos. In some of these stood furniture, oddly forlorn, bulky antique pieces—an armchair, a settee, an escritoire crusted with ancient papers. These stranded little settings—like fossils of foregone transactions whose participants had blown to dust long since—seemed to mark the passage of generations through this rambling gloom.

Ricky had the disorienting sense they had been trekking for a long, long time. He realized that the stranded furniture had a delicately furred and crusted profile in the gray light, like tidepool rocks, and a cold tidal scent touched his nostrils. Realized too, that here and there in those recesses, there were windows. Beyond their panes lay a different shade of darkness, where weedy and barnacled shadows stirred, and glinted wetly....

And throughout this shadowy passage, Ricky noted, on every stretch of wall he could discern, wooden wainscotings densely carven. The misty glow put a sheen on the sinuous saliences of this dark chiselwork, which seemed to depict bulbous, serpentine knots of tail and claw and thew—or perhaps woven Cephalopoda, braided greedy tentacles, and writhing prey in ragged beaks....

But now the walls had narrowed in, and here were stairs, and up these steep, worn stairs the hound, not pausing, led them. The air of this stairwell was slightly dizzying. The labor of the black beast climbing before them seemed to pull the two men after, as if the beast drew them in an executioner's tumbril. They were lifted, Ricky suddenly felt, by a might far greater than theirs, and Andre, ahead of him, seemed to shiver and quake in the flux of that dire energy. It gave Ricky the sensation of walking in Andre's lee, and being sheltered by his body from a terror that streamed around him like a solar wind.

From the head of the stairs, a great moldy vacancy breathed down on them. They emerged into what seemed a simpler and far older structure. High-beamed ceiling, carven walls…it was no more than a grand passage ending at a high dark archway. The floorplanks faintly drummed, as if this was a bridgeway, unfoundationed. That great black arch ahead…it was inset in a wall that bowed. A metallic wall.

"The tank!" said Ricky. It jumped out of him. "That's that big watertank!"

The hound halted and turned. Andre too turned, gave him eyes of wild reproof, but the hound, raising to Ricky his crimson eyes, gave him a red-tongued leer, gave him the glinty-pupiled mockery of a knowing demon. This look set the carven walls to seething, set the sculpted thews rippling, limbs lacing, beaks butchering, all brutally busy beneath their fur of dust.…

The hound turned again, and led them on. Now they could smell the water in the great tank—an odor both metallic and marine—and the hound's breathing began to echo, to grow as cavernous as Mamma Hagg's had been. Within that archway was a blackness absolute, a darkness far more perfect than the gloom that housed them. As they closed with it, the hound's nails echoed as on a great oaken drum above a jungle wilderness. The beast dropped to its belly, lay panting, whining softly. The two men stood behind.

Within the portal, a huge glossy black surface confronted them, a great shield of glass, a mirror as big as a house. There they were in it: Ricky, Andre, the hound. The brightest feature of their tiny, distorted reflection was the bright red dot of the hound's tongue.

Andre paused for a few heartbeats only. Then he stepped through the arch, with an odd ceremonial straightness to his posture. He gestured and Ricky followed him, seeing, as he did so, that the aperture was cut through a double metal wall that showed a cross-section of struts between.

They stood on a narrow balcony just within the tank, and felt a huge damp breath of the steel-clad lake below them, and gazed into the immense glass that was to afford them their Revelation of the Power and the Glory.…

Andre stared some moments at his reflection, then turned to Ricky. "Now I tell you what it is…you say your name was Rocky?"

"Ricky."

"Ricky, now Ima tell you what it is. I came to see, and be seen by Him. When He really sees *you*, you can see through *His* eyes, and you can live His mind."

"But what if I don't want to live his mind?"

"You can't! You didn't pay the toll! You'll *see* some shit though! You'll see enough, you'll know that if you got any adventure in your soul, you got to *pay* that toll! But that's up to you! Now look, an learn!"

He faced the mirror again, and in a cracked voice he cried, *"Ia! Ia! Ia fthagn!"*

And the mirror, ever so slightly, contracted, and the faintest circumference of white showed round its great rim, and encompassing that ring of pallor, something black and scaly like a sea-beast's hide crinkled into view…and Ricky realized that they stood before the pupil of an immense eye.

And Ricky found his feet were rooted, and he could not turn to flee.

And he beheld a dizzying mosaic of lights flashing to life within the mighty pupil. A grand midnight vision crystallized: the whole San Francisco Bay lay within the black orb, bordered by the whole bright ouroboros of coastal lights.…

He and Andre gazed on the vista, on the bridges' glittering spines transecting it, all their lengths corpuscled with fleeing lights red and white. The two men gazed on the panorama and it drank their minds. Rooted, they inhabited its grandeur, even as it began a subtle distortion. The vista seemed tugged awry, torqued towards the very center of the giant's pupil. And within that grand, slow distortion, Ricky saw strange movements. Across the Bay Bridge, near its eastern end, the cargo cranes of West Oakland—tracked monsters, each on four mighty legs—raised and bowed their cabled booms in a dinosaurian salute—obeisance, or acclaim… While to their left, the giant tanks on Benicia's tarry hills, and the Richmond tanks too in the west, began a ponderous rotation on their bases, a slow spin like planets obeying the pupil's gathering vortex.

Andre cried out, to Ricky, or just to the world he was about to leave, "I see it all coming apart! In detail! Behold!"

This last word reverberated in a brazen basso far larger than the lean man's lungs could shape. And the knell of that voice awoke winds in the night, and the winds buffeted Ricky as though he hung in the night sky within the eye, and Ricky *knew*. He knew this being into whose view he'd come! Knew this monster was the King of a vast migration of titans across the eons of the countless Space-Times! Over the gale-swept universe they moved, these Great Old Ones. Across the cracked continents they trawled, they plundered! Worlds were the pastures that they grazed, and the broken bodies of whole races were the pavement that they trod!

It astonished him, the threshold to which this Andre, night-walking zealot, had brought him. He looked at Andre now, saw the man utterly alone at the brink of his apotheosis. How high he seemed to hang in the night winds! Look at the frailty of that skinny frame! The mad greed of his adventure!

Andre seemed to shudder, to gather himself. He looked back at Ricky. He looked like he was seeing in Ricky some foreigner in a far, quaint land, some backward Innocent, unknowing of the very world he stood in.

"On squid, man," he said, "...on squid, *Ricky*, you get big! All hell breaks loose in the back of your brain, and you can *hold* it, you can *contain* it! And then you get to watch Him *feed*. And now *you'll* see. Just a little! Not too much! But you going to *know*."

Andre turned, and faced the eye. He gathered himself, gathered his voice for a great shout:

"Here's my witness! Here I come!"

And he vaulted from the balcony, out into the pupil—impacted it for an instant, seemed to freeze in mid-leap as if he had struck glass—but in the instant after, was within the vast inverted cone of light-starred night, and hung high, tiny but distinct, above the slowly twisting panorama of the great black bay all shoaled and shored and spanned with light. That galactic metropolis, round its core of abyss, was—less slowly now—still contorting, twisting toward the center of the pupil....

And Ricky found that he too hung within it, he stood on the wide cold air in the night sky, he felt against his face the winds' slow torque towards the center of the Old One's sight.

And now all Hell, with relentless slow acceleration, broke loose. The City's blazing architected crown began to discohere, brick fleeing brick in perfect pattern, in widening pattern, till they all became pointillist buildings snatched away in the whirlwind, and from the buildings, all the people too like flung seed swirled up into the night, their evaporating arms raised as in horror, or salute, crying out their being from clouding faces that the black winds sucked to tatters....

He saw the great bridges braided with—and crumpling within—barnacle-crusted tentacles as thick as freeway tunnels, saw the freeways themselves—

pillared rivers of light—unraveling, their traffic like red and white stars fleeing into the air, into the cyclone of the Great Old One's attention.

And an inward vision was given to Ricky, simultaneous with this meteoric overview. For he also knew the Why of it. He knew the hunger of the nomad titans, their unappeasable will to consume each bright busy outpost they could find in the universal Black and Cold. Knew that many another world had fled, as this one fled, draining into the maw of the grim cold giants, each world's collapsing roofs and walls bleeding a smoke of souls, all sucked like spume into the mossy curvature of His colossal jaws....

It was perfectly dark. It was almost silent, except for a rattle of leaves. The cold against his face had the wet bite of fog....

Ricky shook his head, and the dark grew imperfect. He put out his hand and touched rough wooden siding. He was alone on the porch, no lantern now, no armchair, no one else. Just dead leaves in crackly little drifts on the floorboards as—slowly and unsteadily—he started across them.

He had *seen* some shit. Stone cold sober, he had *seen*. And now the question was, who was he?

He crossed the leaf-starred grass, on legs that felt increasingly familiar. Yes...here was this Ricky-body that he knew, light and quick. And here was his Mustang, blown oak leaves chittering across its polished hood. And still the question was, who was he?

He was this car, for one thing, had worked long to buy it and then to perfect it. He got behind the wheel and fired it up, felt his perfect fit in this machine. Flawlessly it answered to his touch, and the blue beast purred up through the leaf-tunnel as the house—a doorless, glassless derelict—fell away behind him. But this Ricky Deuce...who was he now?

He emerged from the foliage, and dove down the winding highway. There was the fog-banked bay below, the jeweled snake of the Hood glinting within its gray wet shroud, and Ricky took the curves just like his old self, riding one of the hills' great tentacles down, down towards the sea they rooted in....

There was something Ricky had to do. Because in spite of his body, his nerves being his, he didn't *know* who he was now, had just had a big chunk torn out of him. And there was something terrible he had to do, to locate, by desperate means, the man he had lost, to find at least a piece of him he was sure of.

His hands and arms knew the way, it seemed. Diving down into the thicker fog, he smoothly threw the turns required...and slid up to the curb before the liquor store they'd parked near...when? A universe ago. Parked and jumped out.

Ricky was terrified of what he was going to do, and so he moved swiftly to have it done with, just nodding to his recent companions as he hastened into the store—nodding to the Maoris in shades, to the guys with the switchblade cap-bills, to the guys with the crimson hoods and the golden pockets. But rushed though he was, it struck him that they were all looking at him with a kind of fascination....

At the counter he said, "Fifth of Jack." He didn't even look to see what he peeled off his wad to pay for it, but there were a lot of twenties in his change. The Arab bagged him his bottle, his eyes fixed almost raptly on Ricky's, so Ricky was moved to ask in simple curiosity, "Do I look strange?"

"No," the man said, and then said something else, but Ricky had already turned, in haste to get outside where he could take a hit. Had the man said *no, not yet?*

Ricky got outside, cracked the cap, and hammered back a stiff, two-gurgle jolt.

He scarcely could wait to let it roll down and impact him. He felt the hot collision in his body's center, the roil of potential energy glowing there, then poked down a long, three-gurgle chaser. Stood reeling inwardly, and outwardly showing some impact as well....

And there it was: a heat, a turmoil, a slight numbing. No more. No magic. No rising trumpets. No wheels of light.... The half-pint of Jack he'd just downed had no marvel to show like the one he'd just seen.

And so Ricky knew that he was someone else now, someone he had not yet fully met.

"'Sup?" It was the immense guy in the lavender sweats. He had a solemn Toltec-statue face, but an incongruously merry little smile.

"'S happnin," said Ricky. "Hey. You want this?"

"That Jack?"

"Take the rest. Keep it. Here's the cap."

"No thanks." This to the cap. The man drank. As he chugged, he slanted Ricky an eye with something knowing, something *I thought so* in it. Ricky just stood watching him. He had no idea at all of what would come next in his life, and for the moment, this bibulous giant was as interesting a thing as any to stand watching....

The man smacked his lips. "It ain't the same, is it?" he grinned at Ricky, gesturing the bottle. "It just don't matter any more. I mean, so I *understand*. I like the glow jus fine myself. But you...see, you widdat Andre. You've been a *witness.*"

"Yeah. I have. So…tell me what that means."

"You the one could tell me. All's I know is *I'd* never do it, and a whole lotta folks around here, *they'd* never do it—but you didn't know that, did you?"

"So tell me what it *means.*"

"It means what you make of it! And speakin of which, man, of what you might make of it, I wanna show you something right now. May I?"

"Sure. Show me."

"Let's step round here to the side of the building…just round here…." Now they stood in the shadowy weed-tufted parking lot, where others lounged, but moved away when they appeared.

"I'm gonna show you somethin," said the man, drawing out his wallet, and opening it.

But opening it for himself at first, for he brought it close to his face as he looked in, and a pleased, proprietary glow seemed to beam from his Olmec features. For a moment, he gloated over the contents of his billfold.

Then he extended and spread the wallet open before Ricky. There was a fat sheaf of bills in it, hand-worn bills with a skinlike crinkle. It seemed the money, here and there, was stained.

Reverently, Olmec said, "I bought this from the guy that capped the guy it came from. This is as pure as it gets. Blood money with the blood right on it! An you can have a bill of it for five hundred dollars! I *know* that Andre put way more than that in your hand. I *know* you know what a great deal this is!"

Ricky…had to smile. He saw an opportunity at least to *gauge* how dangerously he'd erred. "Look here," he told Olmec. "Suppose I did buy blood money. I'd still need a witness. So what about *that* man? Will *you* be my witness for…almost five grand?"

Olmec did let the sum hang in the air for a moment or two, but then said, quite decisive, "Not for twice that."

"So Andre got me cheap?"

"Just by my book. You could buy witnesses round here for half that!"

"I guess I need to think it over."

"You know where I hang. Thanks for the drink."

And Ricky stood there for the longest time, thinking it over….

ACCESS FANTASY
Jonathan Lethem

THERE WAS A start-up about a half mile ahead the day before, a fever of distant engines and horns honking as others signaled their excitement—a chance to move!—and so he'd spent the day jammed behind the wheel, living in his Apartment on Tape, waiting for that chance, listening under the drone of distant helicopters to hear the start-up make its way downtown. But the wave of revving engines stalled before reaching his street. He never even saw a car move, just heard them. In fact he couldn't remember seeing a car move recently. Perhaps the start-up was only a panic begun by someone warming their motor, reviving their battery. That night he'd dreamed another start-up, or perhaps it was real, a far-off flare that died before he'd even ground the sleep out of his eyes, though in the rustle of his waking thoughts it was a perfect thing, coordinated, a dance of cars shifting through the free-flowing streets. Dream or not, either way, didn't matter. He fell back asleep. What woke him in the morning was the family in the Pacer up ahead cooking breakfast. They had a stove on the roof of their car and the dad was grilling something they'd bought from the flatbed shepherd two blocks away, a sheepsteak or something. It smelled good. Everything about the family in the Pacer made him too conscious of his wants. The family's daughter—she was beautiful—had been working as Advertising, pushing up against and through the One-Way

Permeable Barrier on behalf of some vast faceless corporation. That being the only way through the One-Way Permeable Barrier, of course. So the family, her ma and pa, were flush, had dough, and vendors knew to seek them out, hawking groceries. Whereas checking his pockets he didn't have more than a couple of dollars. There was a coffee-and-doughnuts man threading his way through the traffic even now but coffee was beyond his means. He needed money. Rumors had it Welfare Helicopters had been sighted south of East One Thousand, One Hundred and Ninety-Fourth Street, and a lot of people had left their cars, drifted down that way, looking for easy cash. Which was one reason the start-up died, it occurred to him—too many empty cars. Along with the cars that wouldn't start anymore, like the old lady in the Impala beside him, the dodderer. She'd given up, spent most days dozing in the backseat. Her nephew from a few blocks away came over and tinkered with her engine now and again but it wasn't helping. It just meant the nephew wasn't at his wheel for the start-up, another dead spot, another reason not to bother waiting to move. Probably he thought now he should have walked downtown himself in search of welfare money drifting down from the sky. The state helicopters weren't coming around this neighborhood much lately. Alas. The air was crowded with commercial hovercraft instead, recruiters, Advertising robots rounding up the girl from the Pacer and others like her, off to the world on the other side of the One-Way Permeable Barrier, however briefly. The world of apartments, real ones. Though it was morning he went back to his latest Apartment on Tape, which was a four-bedroom two-bath co-op on East One Thousand, Two Hundred and Fifteenth Street, just a few blocks away but another world of course, remote from his life on the street, sealed off from it by the One-Way Permeable Barrier. He preferred the early part of the tape, before any of the furnishings arrived, so he rewound to that part and put the tape on slow and lived in the rooms as hard as he could, ignoring the glare of sun through his windshield that dulled his view of the dashboard television, ignoring the activities of the family in the Pacer up ahead as they clambered in and out of the hatchback, ignoring the clamor of his own pangs. The Realtor's voice was annoying, it was a squawking, parroty voice so he kept the volume down as always and lived in the rooms silently, letting his mind sweep in and haunt the empty spaces, the rooms unfolding in slow motion for the Realtor's camera. While the camera lingered in the bathroom he felt under his seat for his bottle and unzipped and peed, timed so it matched to the close-up of the automatic flushing of the toilet on his television. Then the camera and his attention wandered out into the hall. That's when he noticed it, the shadow. Just for a moment. He rewound to see it again. On the far wall of the hallway, framed perfectly for an instant in the lens, was the silhouette of a struggle, a man with his hands on the neck of another, smaller. A woman. Shaking her by the neck for that instant, before the image vanished. Like a pantomime of murder, a Punch-and-Judy show hidden in the Apartment on Tape. But real, it had to be real. Why hadn't he noticed before? He'd watched this tape dozens of times. He rewound again. Just barely, but still. Unmistakable, however brief. The savagery of it was awful. If only he could watch it frame by frame—slow motion was disastrously fast now. Who was the killer? The landlord? The Realtor? Why? Was the victim the previous tenant? Questions, he had questions. He felt himself begin to buzz with them, come alive. Slow motion didn't seem particularly slow precisely because his attention had quickened. Yes, a job of detection was just what he needed to roust himself out of the current slump, burn off the torpor of too many days locked in the jam at the same damn intersection—why hadn't he gone downtown at that last turnoff, months ago? Well, anyway. He watched it again, memorized the shadow, the silhouette, imagined blurred features in the slurry of video fuzz, memorized the features, what the hell. Like a police sketch, work from his own prescient hallucinations. Again. It grew sharper every time. He'd scrape a hole in this patch of tape, he knew, if he rewound too many times. Better to have the tape, the evidence, all there was at this point. He popped the video, threw it in a satchel with notebook, eyeglasses. Extra socks. Outside, locked the car, tipped an imaginary hat at the old lady, headed east by foot on West One Thousand, Two Hundred and Eighth Street. He had to duck uptown two blocks to avoid a flotilla of Sanitation hovertrucks spraying foamy water to wash cars sealed up tight against this artificial rain but also soaking poor jerks asleep, drenching interiors, the rotted upholstery and split spongy dashboards, extinguishing rooftop bonfires, destroying box gardens, soap bubbles poisoning the feeble sprouts. Children screamed and giggled, the streets ran with water, sluicing shit here and there into drains, more often along under the tires to the unfortunate neighboring blocks, everyone moaning and lifting their feet clear. Just moving it around, that's all. At the next corner he ran into a crowd gathered staring at a couple of young teenage girls from inside, from the apartments, the other side of the barrier. They'd come out of the apartment building on rollerblades to sightsee, to slum on the streets. Sealed in a murky bubble of the One-Way Permeable Barrier they were like apparitions, dim ghosts, though you could hear them giggle as they skated through the hushed, reverent crowd. Like a sighting of gods, these teenage girls from inside. No one bothered to spare-change them or bother them in any way because of the barrier. The girls of course were oblivious behind their twilight veil, like night things come into the day, though for them probably it was the people in cars and around the cars that appeared dim, unreachable. He shouldered his way through the dumbstruck crowd and once past this obstacle he found his man, locked into traffic like all the rest, right where he'd last seen him. The Apartments on Tape dealer, his connection, sunbathing in a deck chair on the roof of his Sentra, eating a sandwich. The backseat was stacked with Realtors' tapes, apartment porn, and on the passenger seat two video decks for dubbing. His car in a sliver of morning sun that shone across the middle of the block, benefit of a chink in the canyon of towers that surrounded them. The dealer's neighbors were on their car roofs as well, stretching in the sun, drying clothes. "Hello there, remember me? That looks good what you're eating, anyway, I want to talk to you about this tape." "No refunds," said the dealer, not even looking down. "No, that's not it, I saw something, can we watch it together?" "No need since there's no refunds and I'm hardly interested—" "Listen, this is a police matter, I think—" "You're police then, is that what you're saying?" still not looking down. "No no, I fancy myself a private detective, though not to say I work outside the law, more adjacent, then turn it over to them if it serves justice, there's so often corruption—" "So turn it over," the dealer said. "Well if you could just have a look I'd value your opinion. Sort of pick your brain," thinking flattery or threats, should have chosen one approach with this guy, stuck with it. The dealer said, "Sorry, day off," still not turning his head, chewing off another corner of sandwich. Something from inside the sandwich fell, a chunk of something, fish maybe, onto the roof of the car. "The thing is I think I saw a murder, on the tape, in the apartment." "That's highly unlikely." "I know, but that's what I saw." "Murder, huh?" The dealer didn't sound at all impressed. "Bloody body parts, that sort of thing?" "No, don't be absurd, just a shadow, just a trace." "Hmmm." "You never would have noticed in passing. Hey, come to think of it, you don't have an extra sandwich do you?" "No, I don't. So would you describe this shadow as sort of a flicker then, like a malfunction?" "No, absolutely not. It's part of the tape." "Not your monitor on the fritz?" "No"—he was getting angry now—"a person, a shadow strangling another shadow." The chunk of sandwich filling on the car roof was sizzling slightly, changing color already in the sun. The dealer said, "Shadows, hmmm. Probably a gimmick, subliminal special effects or something." "What? What reason would a Realtor have for adding special effects for God's sake to an apartment tape?" "Maybe they think it adds some kind of allure, some thrill of menace that makes their apartments stand out from the crowd." "I doubt very much—" "Maybe they've become aware of the black market in tapes lately, that's the word on the street in fact, and so they're trying to send a little message. They don't like us ogling their apartments, even vicariously." "You can't ogle vicariously, I think. Sounds wrong. Anyway, that's the most ridiculous thing I've ever—" "Or maybe I'm in on it, maybe I'm the killer, have you considered that?" "Now you're making fun of me." "Why? If you can solve crimes on the other side of the barrier why can't I commit them?" The dealer laughed, hyena-like. "Now seriously," he continued, "if you want to exchange for one without a murder I'll give you a credit toward the next, half what you paid—" "No thanks. I'll hold on to it." Discouraged, hungry, but he couldn't really bother being angry. What help did he expect from the dealer anyway? This was a larger matter, above the head of a mere middleman. "Good luck, Sherlock," the dealer was saying. "Spread word freely, by the way, don't hold back. Can't hurt my sales any. People like murder, only it might be good if there was skin instead of only shadow, a tit say." "Yes, very good then, appreciate your help. Carry on." The dealer saluted. He saluted back, started off through the traffic, stomach growling, ignoring it, intent. A killer was at large. Weaving past kids terrorizing an entire block of cars with an elaborate tag game, cornering around the newly washed neighborhood now wringing itself out, muddy streams between the cars and crying babies, ignoring vendors with items he couldn't afford and a flatbed farmer offering live kittens for pets or food and a pathetic miniature start-up, three cars idiotically nosing rocking jerking back and forth trying to rearrange themselves pointlessly, one of them now sideways wheels on the curb and nobody else even taking the bait he made his way back to his car and key in the lock noticed the girl from the Pacer standing in her red dress on the hood of the car gazing skyward, waiting for the Advertising people to take her away. Looking just incidentally like a million bucks. Her kid brother was away, maybe part of the gang playing tag, and her parents were inside the car doing housework Dad scraping the grill out the window Mom airing clothes repacking bundles so he went over, suddenly inspired. "Margaret, isn't it?" She nodded, smiled. "Yes, good, well you remember me from next door, I'm looking for a day or two's work and do you think they'll take me along?" She said, "You never know, they just take you or they don't." Smiling graciously even if a little confused, neighbors so long and they'd never spoken. "But you always—" he began pointing out. She said, "Oh once they've started taking you then—" Awkwardly, they were both awkward for a moment not saying what they both knew or at least he did, that she was an attractive young girl and likely that made a huge difference in whether they wanted you. "Well you wouldn't mind if I tried?" he said and she said, "No, no," relieved almost, then added, "I can point you out, I can suggest to them—" Now he was embarrassed and said hurriedly, "That's so good of you, thanks, and where should I wait, not here with you at your folks' car, I guess—" "Why not, climb up." Dad looked out the door up at them and she waved him off. "It's okay, you know him from next door he's going to work, we're going to try to get him a job Advertising." "Okay, sweetheart, just checking on you." Then she grabbed his arm, said, "Look." The Advertising hovercraft she'd been watching for landed on the curb a half block ahead, near the giant hideous sculpture at an office building main entrance, lately sealed. Dad said, "Get going you guys, and good luck," and she said, "C'mon." Such neighborliness was a surprise since he'd always felt shut out by the family in the Pacer but obviously it was in his head. And Margaret, a cloud of good feeling seemed to cover her. No wonder they wanted her for Advertising. "Hurry," she said and took his hand and they hopped down and pushed their way around the cars and through the chaos of children and barking dogs and vendors trying to work the crowd of wannabes these landings always provoked, to join the confused throng at the entrance. He held on to his satchel with the video and his socks making sure it didn't get picked in this crowd. She bounced there trying to make herself visible until one of the two robots at the door noticed her and pointed. They stepped up. "Inside," said the robot. They were ugly little robots with their braincases undisguised and terrible attitudes. He disliked them instantly. "I brought someone new," she said, pulling him by the hand, thrusting him into view. "Yes, sir, I'd like to enlist—" he started, grinning madly, wanting to make a good impression. The robot looked him over and made its rapid-fire assessment, nodded. "Get inside," it said. "Lucky," she whispered, and they stepped into the hovercraft. Four others were there, two men, two women, all young. And another woman stumbled in behind them, and the door sealed, and they were off. Nasty little robots scurrying into the cockpit, making things ready. "Now what?" he said and she put her finger to her lips and shushed him, but sweetly, leaning into him as if to say they were in this together. He wanted to tell her what he was after but the robots might hear. Would they care? Yes, no, he couldn't know. Such ugly, fascistic little robots. Nazi robots, that's what they were. He hated placing himself in their hands. But once he was Advertising he would be through the barrier, he'd be able to investigate. Probably he should keep his assignment to himself, though. He didn't want to get her into trouble. The hovercraft shuddered, groaned, then lifted and through the window he could see the cars growing smaller, his neighborhood, his life, the way the traffic was so bad for hundreds of miles of street and why did he think a start-up would change anything? Was there a place where cars really drove anymore? Well, anyway. The robots were coming around with the Advertising Patches and everyone leaned their heads forward obediently, no first-timers like himself apparently. He did the same. A robot fastened a patch behind his right ear, a moment of stinging skin, nothing more. Hard to believe the patch was enough to interfere with the function of the One-Way Permeable Barrier, that he would now be vivid and tangible and effective to those on the other side. "I don't feel any different," he whispered. "You won't," she said, "not until there's people. Then you'll be compelled to Advertise. You won't be able to help it." "For what, though?" "You never know, coffee, diamonds, condoms, vacations, you just never know." "Where—" "They'll drop us off at the Undermall, then we're on our own." "Will we be able to stick together?" The question was out before he could wonder if it was presuming too much, but she said, "Sure, as long as our products aren't too incompatible, but we'll know soon. Anyway, just follow me." She really had a warmth, a glow. Incompatible products? Well, he'd find out what that meant. The hovercraft bumped down on the roof of a building, and with grim efficiency the ugly Nazi robots had the door open and were marching the conscripts out to a rooftop elevator. He wanted to reach out and smack their little exposed-braincase heads together. But he had to keep his cool, stay undercover. He trotted across the roof toward the elevator after her, between the rows of officious gesticulating robots, like they were going to a concentration camp. The last robot at the door of the elevator handed them each an envelope before they stepped in. He took his and moved into the cor-ner with Margaret, they were really packing them in but he couldn't complain actually being jostled with her and she didn't seem to be trying to avoid it. He poked into the envelope. It was full of bills, singles mostly. The money was tat-tered and filthy, bills that had been taken out of circulation on the other side of the barrier. Garbage money, that's what it was. The others had already pock-eted theirs, business as usual apparently. "Why do they pay us now?" he whis-pered. She said, "We just find our way out at the end, when the patch runs out, so this way they don't have to deal with us again," and he said, "What if we just took off with the money?" "You could I guess, but I've never seen anyone do it since you'd never get to come back and anyway the patch makes you really want to Advertise, you'll see." Her voice was reassuring, like she really wanted him not to worry and he felt rotten not telling her about his investigation, his agenda. He put the envelope into his satchel with tape and socks. The elevator sealed and whooshed them down through the building, into the Undermall, then the doors opened and they unpacked from the elevator, spewed out into a gigantic lobby, all glass and polished steel with music playing softly and escalators going down and up in every direction, escalators with steps of burnished wood that looked good enough to eat, looked like roast chicken. He was still so hungry. Margaret took his hand again. "Let's go," she said. As the others dispersed she led him toward one of the escalators and they descended. The corridor below branched to shops with recessed entrances, windows dark and smoky, quiet pulsing music fading from each door, also food smells here and there causing his saliva to flow, and holographic signs angling into view as they passed: FERN SLAW, ROETHKE AND SONS, HOLLOW APPEAL, BROKEN SMUDGED ALPHABET, BURGER KING, PLASTIC DEVILS, OSTRICH LAKE, SMARTINGALE'S, RED HARVEST, CATCH OF THE DAY, BUTUAL OF FOMALHAUT, THNEEDS, etcetera. She led him on, confidently, obviously at home. Why not, this was what she did with her days. Then without warning, a couple appeared from around a corner, and he felt himself begin to Advertise. "How do you do today?" he said, sidling up to the gentleman of the couple, even as he saw Margaret begin to do the same thing to the lady. The gentleman nodded at him, walked on. But met his eye. He was tangible, he could be heard. It was a shock. "Thirsty?" he heard himself say. "How long's it been since you had a nice refreshing beer?" "Don't like beer," said the gentleman. "Can't say why, just never have." "Then you've obviously never tried a Very Old Money Lager," he heard himself say, still astonished. The barrier was pierced and he was conversing, he was perceptible. He'd be able to conduct interrogations, be able to search out clues. Meanwhile he heard Margaret saying, "Don't demean your signature with a second-rate writing implement. Once you've tried the Eiger fountain pen you'll never want to go back to those henlike scratchings and scrawlings," and the woman seemed interested and so Margaret went on "our Empyrean Sterling Silver Collection features one-of-a-kind hand-etched casings—" In fact the man seemed captivated too. He turned ignoring the beer pitch and gave Margaret his attention. "Our brewers handpick the hops and malt," he was unable to stop though he'd obviously lost his mark, "and every single batch of fire-brewed Very Old Money Lager is individually tasted—" Following the couple through the corridor they bumped into another Advertising woman who'd been on the hovercraft, and she began singing, "Vis-it the *moon,* it's nev-er too *soon,*" dancing sinuously and batting her eyes, distracting them all from fountain pens and beer for the moment and then the five of them swept into the larger space of the Undermall and suddenly there were dozens of people who needed to be told about the beer. "Thirsty? Hello, hi there, thirsty? Excuse me, thirsty? Yes? Craving satisfaction, sparkle, bite? No? Yes? Have you tried Very Old Money? What makes it different, you ask—oh, hello, thirsty?" and also dozens of people working as Advertising, a gabble of pitches—stern, admonitory: "Have you considered the perils of being without success insurance?"; flippant, arbitrary: "You never know you're out with the Black Underwear Crowd, not until you get one of them home!"; jingly, singsong: "We've got children, we've all got children, you can have children too—" and as they scattered and darted along the endless marble floors of the Undermall he was afraid he'd lose her, but there was Margaret, earnestly discussing pens with a thoughtful older couple and he struggled over toward her, hawking beer—"Thirsty? Oof, sorry, uh, thirsty?" The crowd thinned as customers ducked into shops and stole away down corridors back to their apartments, bullied by the slew of Advertising except for the few like this older couple who seemed gratified by the attention, he actually had to wait as they listened and took down some information from Margaret about the Eiger fountain pen while he stood far enough away to keep from barking at them about the beer. Then once the older couple wandered off he took Margaret's hand this time, why not, she'd done it, and drew her down a corridor away from the crowds, hoping to keep from engaging with any more customers, and also in the right direction if he had his bearings. He thought he did. He led her into the shadow of a doorway, a shop called Fingertoes that wasn't doing much business. "Listen, I've got to tell you something, I haven't been completely truthful, I mean, I haven't lied, but there's something—" She looked at him, hopeful, confused, but generous in her interpretation, he could tell, what a pure and sweet disposition, maybe her dad wasn't such a bad guy after all if he'd raised a plum like this. "I'm a detective, I mean, what does that mean, really, but the thing is there's been a murder and I'm trying to look into it—" and then he plunged in and told all, the Apartment on Tape, pulling it out of his satchel to show her, the shadow, the strangling, his conversation with the dealer and then his brainstorm to slip inside the citadel, slip past the One-Way Permeable Barrier that would of course have kept his questions or accusations from even being audible to those on this side, and so he'd manipulated her generosity to get aboard the hovercraft. "Forgive me," he said. Her eyes widened, her voice grew hushed, reverent. "Of course, but what do you want to do? Find the police?" "You're not angry at me?" "No, no. It's a brave thing you're doing." "Thank you." They drew closer. He could almost kiss her, just in happiness, solidarity, no further meaning or if there was it was just on top of the powerful solidarity feeling, just an extra, a windfall. "But what do you think is best, the police?" she whispered. "No, I have in mind a visit to the apartment, we're only a couple of blocks away, in this direction I believe, but do you think we can get upstairs?" They fell silent then because a man swerved out of Fingertoes with a little paper tray of greasy fried things, looked like fingers or toes in fact and smelled terrific, he couldn't believe how hungry he was. "Thirsty?" he said hopelessly and the man popping one into his mouth said, "You called it, brother, I'm dying for a beer." "Why just any beer when you could enjoy a Very Old Money—" and he had to go on about it, being driven nuts by the smell, while Margaret waited. The moment the grease-eater realized they were Advertising and broke free, toward the open spaces of the Undermall, he and Margaret broke in the other direction, down the corridor. "This way," said Margaret, turning them toward the elevator, "the next level down you can go for blocks, it's the way out eventually too." "Yes, but can we get back upstairs?" "The elevators work for us until the patches run out, I think," and so they went down below the Undermall to the underground corridors, long echoey halls of tile, not so glamorous as upstairs, not nice at all really, the lengths apartment people went never to have to step out onto the street and see car people being really appalling sometimes. The tunnels were marked with street signs, names of other Undermalls, here and there an exit. They had to Advertise only once before reaching East One Thousand, Two Hundred and Fifteenth Street, to a group of teenage boys smoking a joint in the corridor who laughed and asked Margaret questions she couldn't answer like are they mightier or less mighty than the sword and do they work for pigs. They ran into another person Advertising, a man moving furtively who when he recognized Margaret was plainly relieved. "He's got a girlfriend," she explained, somewhat enigmatically. So those Advertising could, did—what? Interact. But caught up in the chase now, he didn't ask more, just counted the blocks, feeling the thrill of approaching his Apartment on Tape's real address. They went up in the elevator, which was lavish again, wood paneled and perfumed and mirrored and musical. An expensive building. Apartment 16D. So he pressed the button for the sixteenth floor, holding his breath, hardly believing it when they rose above the public floors. But they did. He gripped her hand. The elevator stopped on the sixth floor and a robot got on. Another of the creepily efficient braincase-showing kind. At first the robot ignored them but then on the fifteenth floor a woman got on and Margaret said, "The most personal thing about you is your signature, don't you think?" and he said, "Thirsty?" and the robot turned and stared up at them. The doors closed and they rode up to the sixteenth floor, and the three of them got out, he and Margaret and the robot, leaving the woman behind. The hallway was splendid with plush carpeting and brass light fixtures, empty apart from the three of them. "What are you doing up here?" said the robot. "And what's in that bag?" Clutching his satchel he said, "Nothing, just my stuff." "Why is it any of your business?" said Margaret, surprisingly defiant. "We've been asked to give an extended presentation at a customer's private home," he said, wanting quickly to cover Margaret's outburst, give the robot something else to focus on. "Then I'll escort you," said the robot. "You really don't have to do that," he said. "Don't come along and screw up our pitch, we'll sue you," Margaret added bizarrely. Learning of the investigation had an odd effect on her, always a risk working with amateurs he supposed. But also it was these robots, the way they were designed with rotten personalities or no personalities they really aroused revulsion in people, it was an instinctual thing and not just him, he noted with satisfaction. He squeezed her hand and said, "Our sponsors would be displeased, it's true." "This matter requires clearance," said the robot, trying to get in front of them as they walked, and they had to skip to stay ahead of it. "Please stand to one side and wait for clearance," but they kept going down the carpeted hallway, his fingers crossed that it was the right direction for 16D. "Halt," said the robot, a flashing red light on its forehead beginning to blink neurotically and then they were at the door, and he rapped with his knuckles, thinking, hardly going incognito here, but better learn what we can. "Stand to one side," said the robot again. "Shut up," said Margaret. As the robot clamped a steely hand on each of their arms, jerking them back away from the door, its treads grinding on the carpet for traction, probably leaving ugly marks too, the door swung open. "Hello?" The man in the doorway was unshaven and slack-haired wearing a robe and blinking at them as though he'd only turned on his light to answer the door. "They claim to have an appointment with you, sir," said the robot. The man only stood and stared. "It's very important, we have to talk to you urgently," he said, trying to pull free of the robot's chilly grip, then added, regretfully, "about beer." He felt a swoon at looking through the doorway, realizing he was seeing into his Apartment on Tape, the rooms etched into his dreamy brain now before him. He tried to see more but the light was gloomy. "And fountain pens," said Margaret, obviously trying to hold herself back but compelled to chip in something. "I apologize, sir, I tried to detain them to obtain clearance—" said the robot. *Detain, obtain,* what rotten syntax, he thought, the people who program these robots certainly aren't poets. The man just stood and blinked and looked them over, the three of them struggling subtly, he and Margaret trying to pull free of the robot, which was still blinking red and grinding at the carpet. "Cooperate," squawked the robot. The man in the robe squinted at them, finally smiled. "Please," said Margaret. "Fountain pens, eh?" the man in the robe said at last. "Yes," said Margaret desperately, and he heard himself add, "And beer—" "Yes, of course," mumbled the man in the robe. "How silly of me. Come in." "Sir, for your safety—" "They're fine," said the man to the robot. "I'm expecting them. Let them in." The robot released its grip. The man in the robe turned and shuffled inside. They followed him, all three of them, into poorly lit rooms disastrously heaped with newspapers, clothes, soiled dishes, empty and half-empty takeout packages, but still unmistakably the rooms from his tape, every turn of his head recalling some camera movement and there sure enough was the wall that had held the shadow, the momentary stain of murder. The man in the robe turned and said to the robot, "Please wait outside." "But surely I should chaperone, sir—" "No, that's fine, just outside the door, I'll call you in if I need you. Close it on your way out, thanks." Watching the robot slink back out he couldn't help but feel a little thrill of vindication. The man in the robe continued into the kitchen, and gesturing at the table said, "Please, sit, sorry for the mess. Did you say you'd like a beer?" "Well, uh, no, that wasn't exactly—if you drink beer you ought to make it a Very Old Money Lager for full satisfaction—but I've got something else to discuss while you enjoy your delicious, oh, damn it—" "Relax, have a seat. Can I get you something else?" "Food," he blurted. "Which always goes best with a Very Old Money," and meanwhile Margaret released his hand and took a seat and started in talking about pens. The man opened his refrigerator, which was as overloaded as the apartment, another image from the tape now corrupted by squalor. "You poor people, stuck with those awful patches and yet I suppose I wouldn't have the benefit of your company today without them! Ah, well. Here, I wasn't expecting visitors but would you like some cheese? Can I fix you a glass of water?" The man set out a crumbled hunk of cheddar with a butter knife, crumbs on the dish and so long uncovered the edges were dried a deep, translucent orange. "So, you were just Advertising and you thought you'd pay a house call? How am I so lucky?" "Well, that's not it exactly—" Margaret took the knife and began paring away the edges of the cheese, carving out a chunk that looked more or less edible and when she handed it to him he couldn't resist, but tried talking through the mouthful anyway, desperately trying to negotiate the three priorities of hunger, Advertising, and his investigation: "Would you consider, mmmpphh, excuse me, consider opening a nice tall bottle of Very Old Money and settling in to watch this videotape I brought with me because there's something I'd like you to see, a question I've got about it—" The man in the robe nodded absently, half listening, staring oddly at

Margaret and then said, "By all means let me see your tape—is it about beer? I'd be delighted but no hurry, please relax and enjoy yourselves, I'll be right out," and stepped into the living room, began rummaging among his possessions of which there certainly were plenty. It was a little depressing how full the once glorious apartment had gotten. Margaret cut him another piece of cheese and whispered, "Do you think he knows something?" "I can't know he seems so nice, well if not nice then harmless, hapless, but I'll judge his reaction to the video, watch him closely when the time comes—" grabbing more cheese quickly while he could and then the man in the robe was back. "Hello, friends, enjoying yourselves?" His robe had fallen open and they both stared but maybe it was just an example of his sloppiness. Certainly there was no polite way to mention it. There was something confusing about this man, who now went to the table and took the knife out of Margaret's hands and held her hand there for a moment and then snapped something—was it a bracelet?—around her wrist. Not a bracelet. Handcuffs. "Hey, wait a minute, that's no way to enjoy a nice glass of lager!" he heard himself say idiotically cheese falling out of his mouth jumping up as the man clicked Margaret's other wrist into the cuffs and he had her linked to the back of her chair. He stood to intervene and the man in the robe swept his feet out from under him with a kick and pushed him in the chest and he fell, feet sliding on papers, hand skidding in lumps of cheese, to the floor. "Thirsty!" he shouted, the more excited the more fervent the Advertising, apparently. "No! Beer!" as he struggled to get up. And Margaret was saying something desperate about Eiger fountain pens "—self-refilling cartridge—" The man in the robe moved quickly, not lazy and sloppy at all now and kicked away his satchel with the tape inside and bent over him and reached behind his ear to tear the patch away, another momentary sting. He could only shout "Beer!" once more before the twilight world of the One-Way Permeable Barrier surrounded him, it was everywhere here, even Margaret was on the other side as long as she wore the patch, and he felt his voice sucked away to a scream audible inside the space of his own head but not elsewhere, he knew, not until he was back outside, on the street where he belonged and why couldn't he have stayed there? What was he thinking? Anyway it wouldn't be long now because through the gauze he saw the man in the robe who you'd have to call the man half out of his robe now open the door to let the robot in, then as the naked man grinned at him steel pinchers clamped onto his arm and he was dragged out of the room, screaming inaudibly, thrashing to no purpose, leaving Margaret behind. And his tape besides.

SINGING ON A STAR
Ellen Klages

I'M SPENDING THE night with my friend Jamie, my first sleepover. She lives two doors down in a house that looks just like mine, except for the color. I'm almost six.

My father walks me down the block after dinner, carrying my mother's brown Samsonite travel case. Inside are my toothbrush, my bear, a clean pair of panties (just in case), and my PJs with feet. I am carrying my Uncle Wiggly game, my favorite. I can't wait until she sees it.

Jamie answers the door. She has no front teeth and her thick dark hair is held back by two bright red barrettes. My hair is too short to do any tricks. Her mother, Mrs. Galloway, comes out from the kitchen wearing an apron with big daisies. The air smells like chocolate. She says there are cookies in the oven, and we can have some later, and my doesn't that look like a fun game! My father pats me on the shoulder and goes into Mr. Galloway's den to have a Blatz beer and talk about baseball and taxes.

There is only a downstairs, like our house. Jamie's room is at the end of the hall. It has pale pink walls and two beds with green nubbily spreads. Mrs. Galloway puts my suitcase on the bed next to the window, where Jamie doesn't sleep, and says she'll bring us some cookies in a jiffy.

I know Jamie from kindergarten. We are both in Miss Flanagan's afternoon class. We share a cubby in the cloakroom, play outside with chalk and jump ropes, and are in the same reading circle. This is the first time we've been alone together. It's her room, and I don't know what to do now. I put Uncle Wiggly down on the bed and look out the window.

It's not quite dark. The sky is TV blue, and if I scrinch my neck a little, I can see the edge of the swing set in my own backyard. I feel a little less lost.

"It's time to listen to my special record now," Jamie says. She holds up a bright yellow record, the color of lemon Jell-O. I can see the shadows of her hands through it.

She opens the lid of the red-and-white portable record player on her bookshelf. I'm jealous; I'm not allowed to play records by myself yet, because of the needle. Jamie plunks it down on the spinning disk, and the room fills with the smooth crooning of a man's voice:

> *You can sing your song on a star,*
> *Take my hand, it's not very far.*
> *You'll be fine dressed just as you are...*

"We have to go before the song ends," Jamie says. "So we can see Hollis."

Jamie is not this bossy at school. I nod, even though I don't know who Hollis is. Maybe it's her bear. My bear's name is Charles.

Jamie points to a door in the pale pink wall, next to my bed. "We have to go in there."

"Into the closet? Why?"

"It's only a closet sometimes," Jamie says, as if I should know this. She opens the door.

Inside is an elevator, closed off by a brass cage made of interlocking **X**s.

"Wow." I have never been in a house with an elevator before.

"I know," says Jamie.

She pushes the cage open, the **X**s squeezing into narrow diamonds with a creaking groan. "C'mon."

My stomach feels funny, like I have already eaten too many cookies. "Where are we—?"

"Come *on*," says Jamie. "The song's not very long." She grabs the sleeve of my striped shirt and tugs me through, pulling the brass cage closed again behind us. To the right of the door is a line of lighted buttons, taller than I can reach. Jamie presses the bottom button, L.

A solid panel slides in front of the brass cage, shutting us off from the room with the pink walls. There is a clank, and a whirr of motor. I close my eyes. The elevator moves.

In a minute, it stops with another clank and the rattle of the brass cage squeezing open.

"Hi, Hollis," says Jamie.

"Why, hello Miss Jamie," a voice answers. "What a delightful surprise." It is an odd voice, soft and raspy, a bit squeaky, like a not-quite-grown-up boy. I open my eyes.

I don't know where we are. Not in Jamie's house. Not anywhere in our neighborhood. Outside the elevator is a tall room with a speckled linoleum floor and a staircase with a wooden railing, curving up and out of sight. A rectangle of sunlight slants across the floor tiles.

I remember my swing set in the almost-dark. I feel dizzy.

"C'mon," says Jamie. She tugs at my sleeve again. "Come meet Hollis."

I step out of the elevator. The room smells old and dusty, with a sharp tang, like they forgot to change the cat box. At first I don't see anyone. Then I notice a little room under the stairs. The floor inside is bare wood, and a man is sitting on a folding chair, reading a magazine with a flashy lady on the cover.

"Two surprises!" says the man. "What a great day this is turning out to be." He smiles as he closes his magazine, but his voice sounds sad, as if he's about to apologize.

"This is my friend Becka," Jamie says. "She's very good at jacks."

"A fine skill, indeed," Hollis says. "I'm pleased to make your acquaintance."

"Me too," I say.

I'm not sure I mean it.

Hollis looks as odd as his voice sounds. He is not young, and is very thin. The skin under his eyes droops like a bloodhound. His hair sticks out in tufts around his head, like cotton candy, but the color of ginger ale. He's wearing gray pants and a red jacket with a bowtie. On the pocket of his jacket is a black plastic bar that says HOLLIS in white capital letters.

"I want to go up to the roof today," says Jamie. "Will there be trains?"

"A most excellent question," Hollis says. "Let me check the schedule." He pulls back his cuff and looks at his wristwatch. The face is square and so yellowed I can't see any numbers. "Yes, just as I thought. Plenty of time before the next arrivals. And a good thing, too. I'm feeling a bit peckish."

I don't know that word, but Jamie laughs and claps her hands. "I was hoping you were," she says. "But—" She shakes her head. "But you can't leave your post."

"No," he says, even more sad than before. He looks around the empty lobby like he expects someone to appear. "No, I can't leave my post."

"I could go," Jamie says. She sounds as if she just thought of it. But I think they are telling each other an old joke, one I don't know.

Hollis snaps his fingers. "Why, yes you could. You're a big girl." He turns to me. "Are you a big girl too?"

I don't feel very big at all. Too much is happening. But I hear my own voice, telling my mother, "I'm a big girl now," when she didn't think I was old enough for a sleepover. "Yes," I say, louder than I mean to. "I'm a big girl."

"So you are," says Hollis. "So you are." He pulls a green leather disk out of his pocket, about the size of a cookie, with the top all folded over itself, and pinches the bottom. The folded parts open like a flower. When he holds it out to Jamie, I see that it's a coin purse. Jamie takes out two nickels.

"And one for your friend," Hollis says. He holds the purse out to me, and I take a coin. The leather petals refold around themselves.

"The usual?" asks Jamie. She sounds much older here.

"But of course," he says. "Farlingten's best."

Jamie leads the way. The front door of this building is glass and wood, with a transom tilting in at the top. I've never seen one before, but I hear the word in my head. *Transom.* I say it under my breath, and I can taste it in the back of my throat. I've never tasted a word before. I like that.

Out on the sidewalk, a white-on-black neon sign buzzes above our heads and stretches halfway up the tall brownstone building. HOTEL MIZPAH. WEEKLY RATES. This is a noisy place. Cars and trucks honk their horns under the viaduct, and men are yelling about money at a bar next door. I hear a clang and turn to see a green streetcar clattering down tracks in the middle of the street, sparks snapping from the wires overhead. The lighted front of the car says FARLINGTEN.

"What's Farlingten?" I ask Jamie.

"It's where we are, silly."

"Where are we, though?"

She huffs a sigh and puts her hands on her hips. "In *Far*lingten." She seems to think this is enough of an answer and skips a step ahead of me.

I want to go home. I don't know how to get there from this street.

My neighborhood has trees and front yards and driveways and grass. Here all I can see is dirty bricks and stone buildings, black wires crisscrossing everywhere. We come to the corner of the block. Above a wooden rack of magazines and paperback books is a faded green awning that says SID'S NEWS.

"This is Sid's," Jamie says. "It's my favoritest place."

Sid's isn't exactly a store, more like a cave scooped out of the corner, with shelves on both sides. On the left are a hundred different magazines, all bright colors and pictures. My parents only get *LIFE* and *TV Guide*. On the right are rows and rows of cigarettes in white and green and red packs, and boxes of cigars with foreign ladies on their lids. The slick paper and tobacco smell spicy, dry, and a little sour. I almost sneeze.

In front of us, a woman in an orange cardigan, her glasses halfway down her nose, sits on a stool behind a counter full of more candy and gum than I've ever seen in one place in my whole life. Hersheys and Sky Bars, Jujubes and Pay Days, twenty flavors of Life Savers in a rolled-log metal display—and dozens I've never seen before. I think about pirate gold and jewels, and Ali Baba, every treasure story I've ever heard. This is better.

"Wow," I say.

"See," says Jamie.

The woman behind the counter looks up. "Hey, kid. It's been a while."

"Hi, Mrs. Sid. How's business?"

"Can't complain," she says. "Whad'll it be today?"

"The usual." Jamie drops her two nickels onto the rubber OLD GOLDs mat that is the only clear space on the counter.

"Raxar it is. Can't say that I blame you. Two?"

"Three. This is my friend Becka. She's never had one."

Mrs. Sid raises an eyebrow.

"It's her first time here," says Jamie.

"Ah."

I shake my head. "No thanks, I want a Three Musket—"

"You can get those anywhere," says Mrs. Sid. "Try this." She reaches over the counter and picks up a candy bar with a pale, steel-blue wrapper, thicker than a Hersheys, not as thick as a Three Musketeers. On the front, in shining silver letters, it says RAXAR. The *X* is two crossed lightning bolts. "Trust me. You've never had anything like it."

I take the bar and hold out the nickel in my hand.

Mrs. Sid shakes her head. "Keep it, kid. The first one is free." She rings open the cash register and rattles Jamie's nickels into the wooden drawer.

Back on the sunny sidewalk, the silver *X* winks bright and dull, bright and dull as I walk. *Farlingten Confectionary Company*, it says on the side. I start to pull open the paper wrapper.

"Not now," Jamie says. "Hollis doesn't have his yet."

I stop. I'm her guest, so I have to be polite.

When we get back to the door below HOTEL MIZPAH, Jamie puts her hands behind her back. Hollis is waiting by the elevator.

"What did you bring me?" he asks.

"Raxar!" Jamie says, and holds her hands out in front of her, a blue-gray bar flat on each palm.

"Hoorah," says Hollis. "It's the same, forwards and backwards." His voice sounds like he's very disappointed, but he's smiling and his droopy eyes are bright. "Now on to the penthouse."

Hollis hangs an OUT OF SERVICE sign on a nail by the elevator door and holds the brass cage open for us. He presses the very top button, and the elevator clanks and whirrs for more than a minute. I don't know *what* to expect when the doors open, but it's just a hallway, with the same dingy linoleum and stairs as the lobby.

We climb eight steps. At the top is a metal door that Hollis opens with a key. "Watch your feet," he says.

I step over the raised sill out onto a roof of gravel-embedded tar. A stone wall about a foot wide runs along all four sides. My sneakers make crunching sounds as I walk over to the nearest corner. Standing on tiptoe, I can rest my arms on the gritty top, and look out almost forever. It is the highest up I have ever been, and I feel like I'm flying, standing still.

From here, the world is made of boxes—straight-sided rectangles of brown and gray. Walls and streets, windows and doorways, rows of brick and stone ledges on buildings that look so small I could hold one in my hand. Below me are other rooftops with chimneys and water tanks and laundry flapping, and the flat black top of the buzzing MIZPAH sign.

I don't know how long I stand there, taking in all the lines and angles. When I look up, Jamie is waving at me from the opposite wall.

"It's almost time for the train!" she calls.

I crunch over to where she and Hollis stand. There are more boxes on this side, but also trees, in the far distance, and the curve of a river. The light is golden, late-afternoon, as if the city has been dipped in butter.

Jamie points her Raxar bar at me. "When you hear the train, open yours and take a bite."

"Okay." I take it out of my pocket and, like the others, cock my head and listen.

After a minute, I hear the faint rumble of heavy wheels on invisible tracks, and the long, low notes of the train's whistle.

"Now," says Jamie.

I slide my finger under the glued flap. The steel-blue wrapper is heavy paper, lined with a thin foil, and crinkles as I unfold it. The bar inside is the same color as the afternoon light. I bite into one corner of it, and my mouth is flooded with magic. It tastes like toasted butter, malted milk, brown sugar, and flavors I have no name for. The bar is solid at the first touch of my teeth, then crumbles and melts onto my tongue.

I look at the glittering lightning *X*, then at Jamie.

"Well?" she says. There are golden crumbs at the corner of her mouth, and her bar is already half gone.

"It's, it's—it's great," is all I can manage.

"I told you," says Jamie. She takes a huge bite of hers, most of what remains.

The train whistle sounds again, a little closer now, louder.

"What does the train say to you?" Hollis asks me.

"Let's have an adventure," I answer after a moment. I nibble at my Raxar bar. Tiny bites, making it last.

"Ah," he says. It is a long *ah*, heavy with meaning.

"What?"

"That means the people inside are going to the right place. They'll have a fine, merry time there."

"Where are they going?"

"It's different for everyone."

I nod. Another minute and there is only one bite of candy left. I put it in my mouth and hold it in my cheek, like a hamster, letting my new favorite flavor melt away until it is only a memory. Hollis holds his hand out for the empty wrapper.

"What does it sound like to you?" I ask.

He tilts his head, considering. "Like a saxophone," he says. "Mournful. A little tarnished."

"So what does *that* mean?" I lick my lips and find one more golden crumb.

"It means those people are going into the wrong future," he says, shaking his head. "They're all coming to Farlingten, and none of their dreams will ever come true."

My arm gets all goose bumps. "Does Jamie know that?"

"No," he says. "I don't think she does." He reaches over and touches the red barrette in her hair, sliding his hand down to stroke her cheek, the way my mother pets the cat. Jamie is looking out at the trees and doesn't seem to care.

"I'd like to go home, please," I say. My voice sounds very small.

"The light *is* fading," says Hollis. "I suppose it's time."

"Can we stay just a few—" Jamie starts.

"No," he says. "You're not safe here at night." He moves his hand to her shoulder and gives it a little squeeze. "Not yet."

He follows us across the gravel and inside, pausing to lock the metal door behind him. The stairwell is dark after the sunlit roof.

The elevator is waiting for us. Hollis opens the brass gate and pushes a button I hadn't noticed before, a squiggle between the 6 and the 7. Then he steps back out into the hall.

"Goodbye, Miss Jamie," he says, as he closes the gate. "I'll see you again soon." He looks at me. "It was nice to meet you, Miss Becka."

I nod, but I don't look up until the metal panel slides shut, and Hollis is gone.

The elevator clanks and whirrs. I cross my fingers—both hands.

When the door opens, the voice is crooning the last lines of the song:

> *...you can stay put, right where you are,*
> *Or sing your song up on a star.*

But that's not possib—

My legs shaking, I step out of the elevator into the room with the pale pink walls and my game lying on top of the green nubbily bedspread. I am so glad to see Uncle Wiggly. Jamie closes the gate, and then the closet door.

She walks over to the record player, where the yellow disk is now going round and round, hissing like static, and lifts the needle.

"Isn't that the *best* place?" She slips the record into its cardboard sleeve. "We can play your game now, if you—" We hear footsteps in the hall, and Jamie turns to me, her eyes fierce.

"You *can't* tell. Not ever."

"But what if—?"

She grabs my arm, hard. "Promise. Or I can never go back."

"Okay." I pull my arm away. "Okay. I promise." I sit down next to Uncle Wiggly and look out the window.

Mrs. Galloway opens the door and comes in, carrying a plate of cookies so warm I can smell them. A cleaner's bag is folded over one arm. "Who's ready for chocolate chips?"

"I am," says Jamie. She takes two cookies and bites into one.

"How about you, Becka?" Mrs. Galloway holds the plate out to me.

I shake my head slowly. "My stomach feels funny."

"Oh?" Mrs. Galloway sets the plate down on the bed and puts the back of her hand on my forehead. "You don't have a fever," she says. "Do you want some Pepto?"

"I don't think so."

"Hmm. Would you like to go home, dear?"

I nod.

"Well, I'm not really surprised. Five *is* a little young for a big adventure like this." She pats my shoulder. "Let me hang up Jamie's good dress, and I'll walk you back."

She reaches for the knob of the closet door.

No! I want to shout. But when she opens it, nothing's inside except clothes on hangers and three pairs of shoes on the floor.

"The record's over," Jamie says. "And it's dark now." Her voice is cool, matter-of-fact.

"I'll see you in school," I say.

Jamie turns and closes the lid of the record player. "Maybe."

Mrs. Galloway walks me home through the last moments of twilight, and my mother fusses over me and puts me to bed. When she folds my pants over the back of my chair, a nickel falls out of the pocket.

"Where'd this come from?" she asks.

I don't know how to answer that. "Um, Mrs. Galloway. In case the ice cream truck came. But it didn't." I've never lied before. My stomach squirms. Nothing else happens.

"That was nice of her." She puts the nickel down on the bedside table and tucks me and my bear under the covers. "Big day, honey. You'll feel better in the morning." She kisses my forehead.

When she's gone, I pick up the coin. It is smooth and round and nickel-shaped, but the man on it is not Jefferson. On the back, F-A-R-L-I-N-G-T-E-N curves around a picture of an animal that's not a buffalo. I feel goose bumps again and I want to throw it away. But I don't. I think of pirate gold and Ali Baba and butter-light on tall, square stone. I can almost taste a Raxar bar. I get up and put the coin in the box on my dresser, under the felt lining.

Just in case.

In the darkness, lying in bed, even my own room seems strange now. A car drives by. A slanting square of light plays across my ceiling, corner to corner, glass and chrome reflecting the streetlight outside. My closet door leaps into the light for just a moment. I turn my head the other way. But when I close my eyes, I see the **X**s of an impossible elevator and taste *transom* in the back of my throat.

Monday starts the last week of kindergarten. Every day Jamie puts her things in our cubby and sits on my right in reading circle. She watches me, but I don't want to talk to her. At recess I play Red Rover with other kids.

On Tuesday, we return our library books after snack. I wait until Jamie is over by the biographies, and ask Mrs. Gascoyne if she knows where Farlingten is.

"Far-ling-ten? No, dear, not right off hand. But if you want, I can look it up."

Except she can't. There's no Farlingten in the phone book, or on the state map, or even in the big atlas of the whole world. No Farlingten anywhere.

Thursday night, the air is hot and thick. Thunder rumbles far away, but rain hasn't come to our house yet. I toss and turn, sweaty under just a sheet. Through my open window, I can hear the murmur of my parents' voices from the back porch, smell the sweet, acrid waft of smoke from my father's pipe.

Then I hear the music. Not from the hi-fi in our living room, but from outside, a few houses down. I jump, like I've been pinched, and the smooth crooning glides faintly over the distant thunder.

You can sing your song on a star...

It seems to go on forever. I look out my window and wonder about Jamie. I shudder when a train whistles somewhere in the distant darkness, all grays and browns. It does not sound like an adventure.

Jamie is not in school Friday afternoon.

My mother picks me up at three o'clock, because I have a box with my rest rug and paintings and papers to bring home for the summer. We are at the front door when Miss Flanagan calls from my classroom.

"Becka! You left this in your cubby." She hurries down the hall. "I'm glad I caught you," she says, handing me a stiff cardboard sleeve.

It's a record. On the TV-blue cover is a cartoon of a little girl with dark hair. She is sitting with her legs dangling over one arm of a bright yellow star. Across the top, in magic marker, it says BECKA.

I stare at it. That's not how I write my *K*s.

"I've never seen that one before," my mother says. I can hear the question in her voice. She buys all my things.

I can't explain. I don't even know how it got into the cubby. "It was sort of a present," I say after a minute. I'm not sure I want it.

"Who—? Well, never mind. I hope you thanked them." My mother slips it under my rest rug, then puts the box into the back of the station wagon. I can feel it through the back of my neck as we drive.

She pulls into the parking lot of Ackerman's Drugs, six blocks from our house. "I need to pick up a few things," she says. "So I thought we might celebrate with a sundae, Miss First Grader."

Ackerman's smells like perfume and ice cream mixed with bitter medicine dust. The candy counter is next to the red-and-chrome soda fountain. While my mother buys aspirin and Prell shampoo, I look at every candy bar in the display. No lightning bolts. "Do you have a Raxar," I ask the counter man, when he is done making a milkshake.

"Raxar?" He wrinkles his forehead. "Never heard of it."

I'm not really surprised.

When we pull into the driveway, there are police cars parked two doors down. My mother frowns, and carries my box to my room before she walks down to the Galloways' to see what's happened.

I put the record on my dresser, under the box with the nickel.

That night my mother checks the lock on the front door twice after dinner. At bedtime, she tucks me in tight and kisses me more than usual.

"Can I have a record player for my birthday?" I ask.

She smiles. "I suppose so. You're a big girl now."

So you are, echoes Hollis in his odd, sad voice. *So you are.*

"I am," I say. "First grade."

"I know, honey." My mother sits down on the edge of my covers. "But even big girls can—" Her hand smoothes the unwrinkled sheet, over and over. "When you were out playing, did you ever see your friend Jamie talking to a man you didn't know?"

I think, for just a second, then shake my head and keep my promise.

"Well, you be careful." She strokes my cheek. "Don't go anywhere with a stranger, even if they give you candy, okay?"

"I won't," I say. I don't look at the record on my dresser, and I wonder if I'm lying.

QUITTERS, INC.
Stephen King

Morrison was waiting for someone who was hung up in the air traffic jam over Kennedy International when he saw a familiar face at the end of the bar and walked down.

"Jimmy? Jimmy McCann?"

It was. A little heavier than when Morrison had seen him at the Atlanta Exhibition the year before, but otherwise he looked awesomely fit. In college he had been a thin, pallid chain smoker buried behind huge horn-rimmed glasses. He had apparently switched to contact lenses.

"Dick Morrison?"

"Yeah. You look great." He extended his hand and they shook.

"So do you," McCann said, but Morrison knew it was a lie. He had been overworking, overeating, and smoking too much. "What are you drinking?"

"Bourbon and bitters," Morrison said. He hooked his feet around a bar stool and lighted a cigarette. "Meeting someone, Jimmy?"

"No. Going to Miami for a conference. A heavy client. Bills six million. I'm supposed to hold his hand because we lost out on a big special next spring."

"Are you still with Crager and Barton?"

"Executive veep now."

"Fantastic! Congratulations! When did all this happen?" He tried to tell himself that the little worm of jealousy in his stomach was just acid indigestion. He pulled out a roll of antacid pills and crunched one in his mouth.

"Last August. Something happened that changed my life." He looked speculatively at Morrison and sipped his drink. "You might be interested."

My God, Morrison thought with an inner wince. Jimmy McCann's got religion.

"Sure," he said, and gulped at his drink when it came.

"I wasn't in very good shape," McCann said. "Personal problems with Sharon, my dad died—heart attack—and I'd developed this hacking cough. Bobby Crager dropped by my office one day and gave me a fatherly little pep talk. Do you remember what those are like?"

"Yeah." He had worked at Crager and Barton for eighteen months before joining the Morton Agency. "Get your butt in gear or get your butt out."

McCann laughed. "You know it. Well, to put the capper on it, the doc told me I had an incipient ulcer. He told me to quit smoking." McCann grimaced. "Might as well tell me to quit breathing."

Morrison nodded in perfect understanding. Nonsmokers could afford to be smug. He looked at his own cigarette with distaste and stubbed it out, knowing he would be lighting another in five minutes.

"Did you quit?" he asked.

"Yes, I did. At first I didn't think I'd be able to—I was cheating like hell. Then I met a guy who told me about an outfit over on Forty-sixth Street. Specialists. I said what do I have to lose and went over. I haven't smoked since."

Morrison's eyes widened. "What did they do? Fill you full of some drug?"

"No." He had taken out his wallet and was rummaging through it. "Here it is. I knew I had one kicking around." He laid a plain white business card on the bar between them.

QUITTERS, INC.
Stop Going Up in Smoke!
237 East 46th Street
Treatments by Appointment

"Keep it, if you want," McCann said. "They'll cure you. Guaranteed."

"How?"

"I can't tell you," McCann said.

"Huh? Why not?"

"It's part of the contract they make you sign. Anyway, they tell you how it works when they interview you."

"You signed a *contract?*"

McCann nodded.

"And on the basis of that—"

"Yep." He smiled at Morrison, who thought: Well, it's happened. Jim McCann has joined the smug bastards.

"Why the great secrecy if this outfit is so fantastic? How come I've never seen any spots on TV, billboards, magazine ads—"

"They get all the clients they can handle by word of mouth."

"You're an advertising man, Jimmy. You can't believe that."

"I do," McCann said. "They have a ninety-eight percent cure rate."

"Wait a second," Morrison said. He motioned for another drink and lit a cigarette. "Do these guys strap you down and make you smoke until you throw up?"

"No."

"Give you something so that you get sick every time you light—"

"No, it's nothing like that. Go and see for yourself." He gestured at Morrison's cigarette. "You don't really like that, do you?"

"Nooo, but—"

"Stopping really changed things for me," McCann said. "I don't suppose it's the same for everyone, but with me it was just like dominoes falling over. I felt better and my relationship with Sharon improved. I had more energy, and my job performance picked up."

"Look, you've got my curiosity aroused. Can't you just—"

"I'm sorry, Dick. I really can't talk about it." His voice was firm.

"Did you put on any weight?"

For a moment he thought Jimmy McCann looked almost grim. "Yes. A little too much, in fact. But I took it off again. I'm about right now. I was skinny before."

"Flight 206 now boarding at Gate 9," the loudspeaker announced.

"That's me," McCann said, getting up. He tossed a five on the bar. "Have another, if you like. And think about what I said, Dick. Really." And then he was gone, making his way through the crowd to the escalators. Morrison picked up the card, looked at it thoughtfully, then tucked it away in his wallet and forgot it.

✠   ✠   ✠

The card fell out of his wallet and onto another bar a month later. He had left the office early and had come here to drink the afternoon away. Things had not been going so well at the Morton Agency. In fact, things were bloody horrible.

He gave Henry a ten to pay for his drink, then picked up the small card and reread it—237 East Forty-sixth Street was only two blocks over; it was a cool, sunny October day outside, and maybe, just for chuckles—

When Henry brought his change, he finished his drink and then went for a walk.

Quitters, Inc., was in a new building where the monthly rent on the office space was probably close to Morrison's yearly salary. From the directory in the lobby, it looked to him like their offices took up one whole floor, and that spelled money. Lots of it.

He took the elevator up and stepped off into a lushly carpeted foyer and from there into a gracefully appointed reception room with a wide window that looked out on the scurrying bugs below. Three men and one woman sat in the chairs along the walls, reading magazines. Business types, all of them. Morrison went to the desk.

"A friend gave me this," he said, passing the card to the receptionist. "I guess you'd say he's an alumnus."

She smiled and rolled a form into her typewriter. "What is your name, sir?"

"Richard Morrison."

Clack-clackety-clack. But very muted clacks; the typewriter was an IBM.

"Your address?"

"Twenty-nine Maple Lane, Clinton, New York."

"Married?"

"Yes."

"Children?"

"One." He thought of Alvin and frowned slightly. "One" was the wrong word. "A half" might be better. His son was mentally retarded and lived at a special school in New Jersey.

"Who recommended us to you, Mr. Morrison?"

"An old school friend. James McCann."

"Very good. Will you have a seat? It's been a very busy day."

"All right."

He sat between the woman, who was wearing a severe blue suit, and a young executive type wearing a herringbone jacket and modish sideburns. He took out his pack of cigarettes, looked around, and saw there were no ashtrays.

He put the pack away again. That was all right. He would see this little game through and then light up while he was leaving. He might even tap some ashes on their maroon shag rug if they made him wait long enough. He picked up a copy of *TIME* and began to leaf through it.

He was called a quarter of an hour later, after the woman in the blue suit. His nicotine center was speaking quite loudly now. A man who had come in after him took out a cigarette case, snapped it open, saw there were no ashtrays, and put it away—looking a little guilty, Morrison thought. It made him feel better.

At last the receptionist gave him a sunny smile and said, "Go right in, Mr. Morrison."

Morrison walked through the door beyond her desk and found himself in an indirectly lit hallway. A heavyset man with white hair that looked phony shook his hand, smiled affably, and said, "Follow me, Mr. Morrison."

He led Morrison past a number of closed, unmarked doors and then opened one of them about halfway down the hall with a key. Beyond the door was an austere little room walled with drilled white cork panels. The only furnishings were a desk with a chair on either side. There was what appeared to be a small oblong window in the wall behind the desk, but it was covered with a short green curtain. There was a picture on the wall to Morrison's left—a tall man with iron-gray hair. He was holding a sheet of paper in one hand. He looked vaguely familiar.

"I'm Vic Donatti," the heavyset man said. "If you decide to go ahead with our program, I'll be in charge of your case."

"Pleased to know you," Morrison said. He wanted a cigarette very badly.

"Have a seat."

Donatti put the receptionist's form on the desk, and then drew another form from the desk drawer. He looked directly into Morrison's eyes. "Do you want to quit smoking?"

Morrison cleared his throat, crossed his legs, and tried to think of a way to equivocate. He couldn't. "Yes," he said.

"Will you sign this?" He gave Morrison the form. He scanned it quickly. The undersigned agrees not to divulge the methods or techniques or et cetera, et cetera.

"Sure," he said, and Donatti put a pen in his hand. He scratched his name, and Donatti signed below it. A moment later the paper disappeared back into the desk drawer. Well, he thought ironically, I've taken the pledge. He had taken it before. Once it had lasted for two whole days.

"Good," Donatti said. "We don't bother with propaganda here, Mr. Morrison. Questions of health or expense or social grace. We have no interest in why you want to stop smoking. We are pragmatists."

"Good," Morrison said blankly.

"We employ no drugs. We employ no Dale Carnegie people to sermonize you. We recommend no special diet. And we accept no payment until you have stopped smoking for one year."

"My God," Morrison said.

"Mr. McCann didn't tell you that?"

"No"

"How is Mr. McCann, by the way? Is he well?"

"He's fine."

"Wonderful. Excellent. Now…just a few questions, Mr. Morrison. These are somewhat personal, but I assure you that your answers will be held in strictest confidence."

"Yes?" Morrison asked noncommittally.

"What is your wife's name?"

"Lucinda Morrison. Her maiden name was Ramsey."

"Do you love her?"

Morrison looked up sharply, but Donatti was looking at him blandly. "Yes, of course," he said.

"Have you ever had marital problems? A separation, perhaps?"

"What has that got to do with kicking the habit?" Morrison asked. He sounded a little angrier than he had intended, but he wanted—hell, he needed—a cigarette.

"A great deal," Donatti said. "Just bear with me."

"No. Nothing like that." Although things *had* been a little tense just lately.

"You just have the one child?"

"Yes. Alvin. He's in a private school."

"And which school is it?"

"That," Morrison said grimly, "I'm not going to tell you."

"All right," Donatti said agreeably. He smiled disarmingly at Morrison. "All your questions will be answered tomorrow at your first treatment."

"How nice," Morrison said, and stood.

"One final question," Donatti said. "You haven't had a cigarette for over an hour. How do you feel?"

"Fine," Morrison lied. "Just fine."

"Good for you!" Donatti exclaimed. He stepped around the desk and opened the door. "Enjoy them tonight. After tomorrow, you'll never smoke again."

"Is that right?"

"Mr. Morrison," Donatti said solemnly, "we guarantee it."

He was sitting in the outer office of Quitters, Inc., the next day promptly at three. He had spent most of the day swinging between skipping the appointment the receptionist had made for him on the way out and going in a spirit of mulish cooperation—*Throw your best pitch at me, buster.*

In the end, something Jimmy McCann had said convinced him to keep the appointment—*It changed my whole life.* God knew his own life could do with some changing. And then there was his own curiosity. Before going up in the elevator, he smoked a cigarette down to the filter. Too damn bad if it's the last one, he thought. It tasted horrible.

The wait in the outer office was shorter this time. When the receptionist told him to go in, Donatti was waiting. He offered his hand and smiled, and to Morrison the smile looked almost predatory. He began to feel a little tense, and that made him want a cigarette.

"Come with me," Donatti said, and led the way down to the small room. He sat behind the desk again, and Morrison took the other chair.

"I'm very glad you came," Donatti said. "A great many prospective clients never show up again after the initial interview. They discover they don't want to quit as badly as they thought. It's going to be a pleasure to work with you on this."

"When does the treatment start?" Hypnosis, he was thinking. It must be hypnosis.

"Oh, it already has. It started when we shook hands in the hall. Do you have cigarettes with you, Mr. Morrison?"

"Yes."

"May I have them, please?"

Shrugging, Morrison handed Donatti his pack. There were only two or three left in it, anyway.

Donatti put the pack on the desk. Then, smiling into Morrison's eyes, he curled his right hand into a fist and began to hammer it down on the pack of cigarettes, which twisted and flattened. A broken cigarette end flew out. Tobacco crumbs spilled. The sound of Donatti's fist was very loud in the closed room. The smile remained on his face in spite of the force of the blows, and Morrison was chilled by it. Probably just the effect they want to inspire, he thought.

At last Donatti ceased pounding. He picked up the pack, a twisted and battered ruin. "You wouldn't believe the pleasure that gives me," he said, and dropped the pack into the wastebasket. "Even after three years in the business, it still pleases me."

"As a treatment, it leaves something to be desired," Morrison said mildly. "There's a newsstand in the lobby of this very building. And they sell all brands."

"As you say," Donatti said. He folded his hands. "Your son, Alvin Dawes Morrison, is in the Paterson School for Handicapped Children. Born with cranial brain damage. Tested IQ of 46. Not quite in the educable retarded category. Your wife—"

"How did you find that out?" Morrison barked. He was startled and angry. "You've got no goddamn right to go poking around my—"

"We know a lot about you," Donatti said smoothly. "But, as I said, it will all be held in strictest confidence."

"I'm getting out of here," Morrison said thinly. He stood up.

"Stay a bit longer."

Morrison looked at him closely. Donatti wasn't upset. In fact, he looked a little amused. The face of a man who has seen this reaction scores of times—maybe hundreds.

"All right. But it better be good."

"Oh, it is." Donatti leaned back. "I told you we were pragmatists here. As pragmatists, we have to start by realizing how difficult it is to cure an addiction to tobacco. The relapse rate is almost eighty-five percent. The relapse rate for heroin addicts is lower than that. It is an extraordinary problem. *Extraordinary.*"

Morrison glanced into the wastebasket. One of the cigarettes, although twisted, still looked smokeable. Donatti laughed good-naturedly, reached into the wastebasket, and broke it between his fingers.

"State legislatures sometimes hear a request that the prison systems do away with the weekly cigarette ration. Such proposals are invariably defeated. In a few cases where they have passed, there have been fierce prison riots. *Riots,* Mr. Morrison. Imagine it."

"I," Morrison said, "am not surprised."

"But consider the implications. When you put a man in prison you take away any normal sex life, you take away his liquor, his politics, his freedom of movement. No riots—or few in comparison to the number of prisons. But when you take away his *cigarettes*—wham! bam!" He slammed his fist on the desk for emphasis.

"During World War I, when no one on the German home front could get cigarettes, the sight of German aristocrats picking butts out of the gutter was a common one. During World War II, many American women turned to pipes when they were unable to obtain cigarettes. A fascinating problem for the true pragmatist, Mr. Morrison."

"Could we get to the treatment?"

"Momentarily. Step over here, please." Donatti had risen and was standing by the green curtains Morrison had noticed yesterday. Donatti drew the curtains, discovering a rectangular window that looked into a bare room. No, not quite bare. There was a rabbit on the floor, eating pellets out of a dish.

"Pretty bunny," Morrison commented.

"Indeed. Watch him." Donatti pressed a button by the windowsill. The rabbit stopped eating and began to hop about crazily. It seemed to leap higher each time its feet struck the floor. Its fur stood out spikily in all directions. Its eyes were wild.

"Stop that! You're electrocuting him!"

Donatti released the button. "Far from it. There's a very low-yield charge in the floor. Watch the rabbit, Mr. Morrison!"

The rabbit was crouched about ten feet away from the dish of pellets. His nose wriggled. All at once he hopped away into a corner.

"If the rabbit gets a jolt often enough while he's eating," Donatti said, "he makes the association very quickly. Eating causes pain. Therefore, he won't eat. A few more shocks, and the rabbit will starve to death in front of his food. It's called aversion training."

Light dawned in Morrison's head.

"No, thanks." He started for the door.

"Wait, please, Mr. Morrison."

Morrison didn't pause. He grasped the doorknob...and felt it slip solidly through his hand. "Unlock this."

"Mr. Morrison, if you'll just sit down—"

"Unlock this door or I'll have the cops on you before you can say Marlboro Man."

"*Sit down.*" The voice was cold as shaved ice.

Morrison looked at Donatti. His brown eyes were muddy and frightening. My God, he thought, I'm locked in here with a psycho. He licked his lips. He wanted a cigarette more than he ever had in his life.

"Let me explain the treatment in more detail," Donatti said.

"You don't understand," Morrison said with counterfeit patience. "I don't want the treatment. I've decided against it."

"No, Mr. Morrison. *You're* the one who doesn't understand. You don't have any choice. When I told you the treatment had already begun, I was speaking the literal truth. I would have thought you'd tipped to that by now."

"You're crazy," Morrison said wonderingly.

"No. Only a pragmatist. Let me tell you all about the treatment."

"Sure," Morrison said. "As long as you understand that as soon as I get out of here I'm going to buy five packs of cigarettes and smoke them all on the way to the police station." He suddenly realized he was biting his thumbnail, sucking on it, and made himself stop.

"As you wish. But I think you'll change your mind when you see the whole picture."

Morrison said nothing. He sat down again and folded his hands.

"For the first month of the treatment, our operatives will have you under constant supervision," Donatti said. "You'll be able to spot some of them. Not all. But they'll always be with you. *Always.* If they see you smoke a cigarette, I get a call."

"And I suppose you bring me here and do the old rabbit trick," Morrison said. He tried to sound cold and sarcastic, but he suddenly felt horribly frightened. This was a nightmare.

"Oh, no," Donatti said. "Your wife gets the rabbit trick, not you."

Morrison looked at him dumbly.

Donatti smiled. "You," he said, "get to watch."

After Donatti let him out, Morrison walked for over two hours in a complete daze. It was another fine day, but he didn't notice. The monstrousness of Donatti's smiling face blotted out all else.

"You see," he had said, "a pragmatic problem demands pragmatic solutions. You must realize we have your best interests at heart."

Quitters, Inc., according to Donatti, was a sort of foundation—a nonprofit organization begun by the man in the wall portrait. The gentleman had been extremely successful in several family businesses—including slot machines, massage parlors, numbers, and a brisk (although clandestine) trade between New York and Turkey. Mort "Three-Fingers" Minelli had been a heavy smoker—up in the three-pack-a-day range. The paper he was holding in the picture was a doctor's diagnosis: lung cancer. Mort had died in 1970, after endowing Quitters, Inc., with family funds.

"We try to keep as close to breaking even as possible," Donatti had said. "But we're more interested in helping our fellow man. And of course, it's a great tax angle."

The treatment was chillingly simple. A first offense and Cindy would be brought to what Donatti called "the rabbit room." A second offense, and Morrison would get the dose. On a third offense, both of them would be brought in together. A fourth offense would show grave cooperation problems and would require sterner measures. An operative would be sent to Alvin's school to work the boy over.

"Imagine," Donatti said, smiling, "how horrible it will be for the boy. He wouldn't understand it even if someone explained. He'll only know someone is hurting him because Daddy was bad. He'll be very frightened."

"You bastard," Morrison said helplessly. He felt close to tears. "You dirty, filthy bastard."

"Don't misunderstand," Donatti said. He was smiling sympathetically. "I'm sure it won't happen. Forty percent of our clients never have to be disciplined at all—and only ten percent have more than three falls from grace. Those are reassuring figures, aren't they?"

Morrison didn't find them reassuring. He found them terrifying.

"Of course, if you transgress a *fifth* time—"

"What do you mean?"

Donatti beamed. "The room for you and your wife, a second beating for your son, and a beating for your wife."

Morrison, driven beyond the point of rational consideration, lunged over the desk at Donatti. Donatti moved with amazing speed for a man who had apparently been completely relaxed. He shoved the chair backward and drove both of his feet over the desk and into Morrison's belly. Gagging and coughing, Morrison staggered backward.

"Sit down, Mr. Morrison," Donatti said benignly. "Let's talk this over like rational men."

When he could get his breath, Morrison did as he was told. Nightmares had to end sometime, didn't they?

Quitters, Inc., Donatti had explained further, operated on a ten-step punishment scale. Steps six, seven, and eight consisted of further trips to the rabbit room (and increased voltage) and more serious beatings. The ninth step would be the breaking of his son's arms.

"And the tenth?" Morrison asked, his mouth dry.

Donatti shook his head sadly. "Then we give up, Mr. Morrison. You become part of the unregenerate two percent."

"You really give up?"

"In a manner of speaking." He opened one of the desk drawers and laid a silenced .45 on the desk. He smiled into Morrison's eyes. "But even the unregenerate two percent never smoke again. We guarantee it."

The Friday Night Movie was *Bullitt,* one of Cindy's favorites, but after an hour of Morrison's mutterings and fidgetings, her concentration was broken.

"What's the matter with you?" she asked during station identification.

"Nothing...everything," he growled. "I'm giving up smoking."

She laughed. "Since when? Five minutes ago?"

"Since three o'clock this afternoon."

"You really haven't had a cigarette since then?"

"No," he said, and began to gnaw his thumbnail. It was ragged, down to the quick.

"That's wonderful! What ever made you decide to quit?"

"You," he said. "And...and Alvin."

Her eyes widened, and when the movie came back on, she didn't notice. Dick rarely mentioned their retarded son. She came over, looked at the empty ashtray by his right hand, and then into his eyes. "Are you really trying to quit, Dick?"

"Really." And if I go to the cops, he added mentally, the local goon squad will be around to rearrange your face, Cindy.

"I'm glad. Even if you don't make it, we both thank you for the thought, Dick."

"Oh, I think I'll make it," he said, thinking of the muddy, homicidal look that had come into Donatti's eyes when he kicked him in the stomach.

He slept badly that night, dozing in and out of sleep. Around three o'clock he woke up completely. His craving for a cigarette was like a low-grade fever. He went downstairs and to his study. The room was in the middle of the house. No windows. He slid open the top drawer of his desk and looked in, fascinated by the cigarette box. He looked around and licked his lips.

Constant supervision during the first month, Donatti had said. Eighteen hours a day during the next two—but he would never know *which* eighteen. During the fourth month, the month when most clients backslid, the "service" would return to twenty-four hours a day. Then twelve hours of broken surveillance each day for the rest of the year. After that? Random surveillance for the rest of the client's life.

For the rest of his life.

"We may audit you every other month," Donatti said. "Or every other day. Or constantly for one week two years from now. The point is, *you won't know*. If you smoke, you'll be gambling with loaded dice. Are they watching? Are they picking up my wife or sending a man after my son right now? Beautiful, isn't it? And if you do sneak a smoke, it'll taste awful. It will taste like your son's blood."

But they couldn't be watching now, in the dead of night, in his own study. The house was grave-quiet.

He looked at the cigarettes in the box for almost two minutes, unable to tear his gaze away. Then he went to the study door, peered out into the empty hall, and went back to look at the cigarettes some more. A horrible picture came: his life stretching before him and not a cigarette to be found. How in the name of God was he ever going to be able to make another tough presentation to a wary client, without that cigarette burning nonchalantly between his fingers as he approached the charts and layouts? How would he be able to endure Cindy's endless garden shows without a cigarette? How could he even get up in the morning and face the day without a cigarette to smoke as he drank his coffee and read the paper?

He cursed himself for getting into this. He cursed Donatti. And most of all, he cursed Jimmy McCann. How could he have done it? The son of a bitch had *known*. His hands trembled in their desire to get hold of Jimmy Judas McCann.

Stealthily, he glanced around the study again. He reached into the drawer and brought out a cigarette. He caressed it, fondled it. What was that old slogan? *So round, so firm, so fully packed.* Truer words had never been spoken. He put the cigarette in his mouth and then paused, cocking his head.

Had there been the slightest noise from the closet? A faint shifting? Surely not. But—

Another mental image—that rabbit hopping crazily in the grip of electricity. The thought of Cindy in that room—

He listened desperately and heard nothing. He told himself that all he had to do was to go to the closet door and yank it open. But he was too afraid of what he might find. He went back to bed but didn't sleep for a long time.

In spite of how lousy he felt in the morning, breakfast tasted good. After a moment's hesitation, he followed his customary bowl of cornflakes with scrambled eggs. He was grumpily washing out the pan when Cindy came downstairs in her robe.

"Richard Morrison! You haven't eaten an egg for breakfast since Hector was a pup."

Morrison grunted. He considered *since Hector was a pup* to be one of Cindy's stupider sayings, on a par with *I should smile and kiss a pig*.

"Have you smoked yet?" she asked, pouring orange juice.

"No."

"You'll be back on them by noon," she proclaimed airily.

"Lot of goddamn help you are!" he rasped, rounding on her. "You and anyone else who doesn't smoke, you all think…ah, never mind."

He expected her to be angry, but she was looking at him with something like wonder. "You're really serious," she said. "You really are."

"You bet I am." *You'll never know how serious. I hope.*

"Poor baby," she said, going to him. "You look like death warmed over. But I'm very proud."

Morrison held her tightly.

Scenes from the life of Richard Morrison, October–November:

Morrison and a crony from Larkin Studios at Jack Dempsey's bar. Crony offers a cigarette. Morrison grips his glass a little more tightly and says: *I'm quitting.* Crony laughs and says: *I give you a week.*

Morrison waiting for the morning train, looking over the top of the *Times* at a young man in a blue suit. He sees the young man almost every morning now, and sometimes at other places. At Onde's, where he is meeting a client. Looking at 45s in Sam Goody's, where Morrison is looking for a Sam Cooke album. Once in a foursome behind Morrison's group at the local golf course.

Morrison getting drunk at a party, wanting a cigarette—but not quite drunk enough to take one.

Morrison visiting his son, bringing him a large ball that squeaked when you squeezed it. His son's slobbering, delighted kiss. Somehow not as repulsive as before. Hugging his son tightly, realizing what Donatti and his colleagues had so cynically realized before him: love is the most pernicious drug of all. Let the romantics debate its existence. Pragmatists accept it and use it.

Morrison losing the physical compulsion to smoke little by little, but never quite losing the psychological craving, or the need to have something in his mouth—cough drops, Life Savers, a toothpick. Poor substitutes, all of them.

And finally, Morrison hung up in a colossal traffic jam in the Midtown Tunnel. Darkness. Horns blaring. Air stinking. Traffic hopelessly snarled. And suddenly, thumbing open the glove compartment and seeing the half-open pack of cigarettes in there. He looked at them for a moment, then snatched one and lit it with the dashboard lighter. If anything happens, it's Cindy's fault, he told himself defiantly. I told her to get rid of all the damn cigarettes.

The first drag made him cough smoke out furiously. The second made his eyes water. The third made him feel lightheaded and swoony. It tastes awful, he thought.

And on the heels of that: My God, what am I doing?

Horns blatted impatiently behind him. Ahead, the traffic had begun to move again. He stubbed the cigarette out in the ashtray, opened both front windows, opened the vents, and then fanned the air helplessly like a kid who has just flushed his first butt down the john.

He joined the traffic flow jerkily and drove home.

"Cindy?" he called. "I'm home."

No answer.

"Cindy? Where are you, hon?"

The phone rang, and he pounced on it. "Hello? Cindy?"

"Hello, Mr. Morrison," Donatti said. He sounded pleasantly brisk and businesslike. "It seems we have a small business matter to attend to. Would five o'clock be convenient?"

"Have you got my wife?"

"Yes, indeed." Donatti chuckled indulgently.

"Look, let her go," Morrison babbled. "It won't happen again. It was a slip, just a slip, that's all. I only had three drags and for God's sake *it didn't even taste good!*"

"That's a shame. I'll count on you for five then, shall I?"

"Please," Morrison said, close to tears. "Please—"

He was speaking to a dead line.

At five P.M. the reception room was empty except for the secretary, who gave him a twinkly smile that ignored Morrison's pallor and disheveled appearance. "Mr. Donatti?" she said into the intercom. "Mr. Morrison to see you." She nodded to Morrison. "Go right in."

Donatti was waiting outside the unmarked room with a man who was wearing a SMILE sweatshirt and carrying a .38. He was built like an ape.

"Listen," Morrison said to Donatti. "We can work something out, can't we? I'll pay you. I'll—"

"Shaddap," the man in the SMILE sweatshirt said.

"It's good to see you," Donatti said. "Sorry it has to be under such adverse circumstances. Will you come with me? We'll make this as brief as possible. I can assure you your wife won't be hurt...this time."

Morrison tensed himself to leap at Donatti.

"Come, come," Donatti said, looking annoyed. "If you do that, Junk here is going to pistol-whip you and your wife is still going to get it. Now where's the percentage in that?"

"I hope you rot in hell," he told Donatti.

Donatti sighed. "If I had a nickel for every time someone expressed a similar sentiment, I could retire. Let it be a lesson to you, Mr. Morrison. When a romantic tries to do a good thing and fails, they give him a medal. When a pragmatist succeeds, they wish him in hell. Shall we go?"

Junk motioned with the pistol.

Morrison preceded them into the room. He felt numb. The small green curtain had been pulled. Junk prodded him with the gun. This is what being a witness at the gas chamber must have been like, he thought.

He looked in. Cindy was there, looking around bewilderedly.

"Cindy!" Morrison called miserably. "Cindy, they—"

"She can't hear or see you," Donatti said. "One-way glass. Well, let's get it over with. It really was a very small slip. I believe thirty seconds should be enough. Junk?"

Junk pressed the button with one hand and kept the pistol jammed firmly into Morrison's back with the other.

It was the longest thirty seconds of his life.

When it was over, Donatti put a hand on Morrison's shoulder and said, "Are you going to throw up?"

"No," Morrison said weakly. His forehead was against the glass. His legs were jelly. "I don't think so." He turned around and saw that Junk was gone.

"Come with me," Donatti said.

"Where?" Morrison asked apathetically.

"I think you have a few things to explain, don't you?"

"How can I face her? How can I tell her that I...I...."

"I think you're going to be surprised," Donatti said.

✠   ✠   ✠

The room was empty except for a sofa. Cindy was on it, sobbing helplessly.

"Cindy?" he said gently.

She looked up, her eyes magnified by tears. "Dick?" she whispered. "Dick? Oh…Oh God…." He held her tightly. "Two men," she said against his chest. "In the house and at first I thought they were burglars and then I thought they were going to rape me and then they took me someplace with a blindfold over my eyes and…and…oh it was *h-horrible*—"

"Shhh," he said. "Shhh."

"But why?" she asked, looking up at him. "Why would they—"

"Because of me," he said. "I have to tell you a story, Cindy—"

When he had finished he was silent a moment and then said, "I suppose you hate me. I wouldn't blame you."

He was looking at the floor, and she took his face in both bands and turned it to hers. "No," she said. "I don't hate you."

He looked at her in mute surprise.

"It was worth it," she said. "God bless these people. They've let you out of prison."

"Do you mean that?"

"Yes," she said, and kissed him. "Can we go home now? I feel much better. Ever so much."

The phone rang one evening a week later, and when Morrison recognized Donatti's voice, he said, "Your boys have got it wrong. I haven't even been near a cigarette."

"We know that. We have a final matter to talk over. Can you stop by tomorrow afternoon?"

"Is it—"

"No, nothing serious. Bookkeeping really. By the way, congratulations on your promotion."

"How did you know about that?"

"We're keeping tabs," Donatti said noncommittally, and hung up.

When they entered the small room, Donatti said, "Don't look so nervous. No one's going to bite you. Step over here, please."

Morrison saw an ordinary bathroom scale. "Listen, I've gained a little weight, but—"

"Yes, seventy-three percent of our clients do. Step up, please."

Morrison did, and tipped the scales at one-seventy-four.

"Okay, fine. You can step off. How tall are you, Mr. Morrison?"

"Five-eleven."

"Okay, let's see." He pulled a small card laminated in plastic from his breast pocket. "Well, that's not too bad. I'm going to write you a prescrip for some highly illegal diet pills. Use them sparingly and according to directions. And I'm going to set your maximum weight at...let's see...." He consulted the card again. "One eighty-two, how does that sound? And since this is December first, I'll expect you the first of every month for a weigh-in. No problem if you can't make it, as long as you call in advance."

"And what happens if I go over one-eighty-two?"

Donatti smiled. "We'll send someone out to your house to cut off your wife's little finger," he said. "You can leave through this door, Mr. Morrison. Have a nice day."

Eight months later:

Morrison runs into the crony from the Larkin Studios at Dempsey's bar. Morrison is down to what Cindy proudly calls his fighting weight: one-sixty-seven. He works out three times a week and looks as fit as whipcord. The crony from Larkin, by comparison, looks like something the cat dragged in.

Crony: Lord, how'd you ever stop? I'm locked into this damn habit tighter than Tillie. The crony stubs his cigarette out with real revulsion and drains his scotch.

Morrison looks at him speculatively and then takes a small white business card out of his wallet. He puts it on the bar between them. You know, he says, these guys changed my life.

Twelve months later:

Morrison receives a bill in the mail. The bill says:

QUITTERS, INC.
237 East 46th Street
New York, N.Y. 10017

1 Treatment	$2500.00
Counselor (Victor Donatti)	$2500.00
Electricity	$.50
TOTAL (Please pay this amount)	$5000.50

Those sons of bitches! he explodes. They charged me for the electricity they used to...to....

Just pay it, she says, and kisses him.

Twenty months later:

Quite by accident, Morrison and his wife meet the Jimmy McCanns at the Helen Hayes Theatre. Introductions are made all around. Jimmy looks as good, if not better, than he did on that day in the airport terminal so long ago. Morrison has never met his wife. She is pretty in the radiant way plain girls sometimes have when they are very, very happy.

She offers her hand and Morrison shakes it. There is something odd about her grip, and halfway through the second act, he realizes what it was. The little finger on her right hand is missing.

NIGHTBEAT
Neal Barrett, Jr.

THE WAKECHIMES TOUCHED me with the sound of cinnamon. I stretched, turned over, and watched the clockroach play time games against the wall. It marked the spidery minutes in fine script and left crystal duntracks behind.

It was half-past blue, and a lemon moon spilled color into the room. Its light burnished Bethellen's hair to silver and brushed her flesh with coffee shadow.

She stirred once, and I slid quietly away, padded to the shower cage and let cool spicewater bring me awake. There were cocoacubes where Bethellen had left them, but I passed them by and trotted back to the nightroom. My Copsuit sprang from its hollow with a dew-fresh scent, and I let it take me in.

I would have liked to look at myself. A small vanity, but mine own. I take pride in the uniform. It's a Copsuit in the classical cut—basic whipcord in umber and vermilion, sepia pullover, and fringe-leather vest. The jackboots, gloves and chainbelt are traditional indigo. The Marshal's Star of David is cadmium-gold, and the Peacemaker by my side is finest quartz and ivory.

Set. Ready to go, and a last look at Bethellen. She had turned in her sleep to catch the moonvaves. Citron limbs bared to an ocher sea. By morning, I'd taste lemon on her lips.

Outside, the prowlbug hummed to electric life. The moon was high now and a second had joined it—a small saffron tagalong. Lime shadows colored the streetways. The dashglow winked me into service, and I switched the roadlighs and moved along.

The street ribboned over soft hills furred with bonebrake, and through dark groves of churnmoss. Raven blossoms hung from high branches nearly to the ground. I swung the prowlbug into Bluewing, whispered through Speaklow, and coasted down the steep circle to Singhill.

There were people all about. If I listened, I could feel the sound of their sleeping. From Tellbridge I watched the lonelights far away. Not everyone slumbered, then, but all were snug in their homeshells till the day. None would stir before Amberlight polished the world. For that is how it is—the day belongs to us, but not the night.

I have often stopped the prowlbug and dimmed the lights and watched the darklife. In moments, the night fills with chitter-hums and thrashes. A beetlebear stops to sniff the air, pins me with frosty muzzle and razor eyes. For a while there is pink carnage in her heart; then she scutters by clanging husky armor. Jac-Jacs and Grievers wing the dark hollows. A Bloodgroper scatters his kill. There is much to darklife, and few have seen it as it is.

A quarter till yellow. The dashglow hemorrhages, coughs up a number. The prowlbug jerks into motion, whines up the speedscale. Sirens whoopa-whoopa-whoopa through the night, and I switch on the traditional lilac, plum, and scarlet flashers overhead.

There are no strollers to pause and wonder. No other bugs abroad to give me way. Still, there are customs to keep alive, bonds with the past.

The address was nearby. Prowlbug skittered up the snakepath around Henbake. Pressed me tight against the driveseat. Pink lights to port. A homeshell high on Stagperch, minutes away.

Around a corner, and green sparkeyes clustered ahead—nightmates and shadlings hunkered in the streetway. The prowlbug whoopa-ed a warning, and they scattered like windleaves.

They were waiting for me, portal open. A big man with worry lines scribbled on paper features. His handstrobe stitched my path with light-craters to shoo stray nightlings. The woman was small and pretty. Hands like frightened birds. I moved through them up turnstairs past buffwalls to the boy's room.

I'd been there before, but they didn't remember. No-face in a uniform.

CRUCIFIED DREAMS

A child in Dreamspasm is not a pretty sight. I punched his record on the bed-screen, scanned it quickly. Twelve and a half. Fifth Dream. Two-year sequence. No complications. I gripped one bony arm and plunged Blue-Seven in his veins. The spasms slowed to a quiver. I touched him, wiped foamspittle from his cheeks. His skin was cold, frogdank. Waterblue eyes looked up at nothing. The small mouth sucked air.

"He's all right," I said. The man and the woman huddled behind. "Take him in in the morning. Don't think he did internal damage, but it won't hurt to check."

I laid a vial beside the bed. "One if he wakes. I don't think he will."

"Thank you," said the man. "We're grateful." The woman nodded his words.

"No problem." I stopped in the hall and faced them again. "You know he could Secondary."

They looked startled, as if they didn't.

"If he does, stay with him."

They frowned questions, and I shook my head. "Punch in if you like, but there's nothing I can do. He can't have Seven again. And a strong Secondary's a good sign." I sent them a Copgrin. "He's old enough. You could be out of the woods."

They gave each other smiles and said things I didn't hear. The prowlbug was turning all my buttons red and shrieking in the night. I bounded down turnstairs and tore out the portal. No time for strobes and such. If nightlings got underfoot, they'd get a jackboot for their trouble.

The prowlbug scattered gravel, skit-tailed into the streetway. It was wound up and highwhining and I held on and let it have its way. Stagperch faded, and the snakepath dizzied by in black patches. I prayed against sleepy megapedes bunked in on the road ahead. A tin medal for Bethellen. Early insurance.

The dashglow spit data, but I already knew. Bad. Category A and climbing. Name of Lenine Capral and long overdue. First Dream and fifteen.

The Rules say punch before you practice. No way with Lenine Capral. No record, no time, no need. The Dream had her in night-talons. Down on the dark bottom, and nothing for it. Lost, lost Lenine.

I drew the Peacemaker, pressed the muzzle between her eyes. Her body arched near double, limbs spread-eagled. I pulled back lids and looked. Milkpools. Silverdeath darting about. The little shiverteeth nibbling away.

I tossed my jacket aside. Grabbed a handful of hair and pinned her neck where I wanted it. Put the muzzle low behind the ear and up. This time, shock jerked a small arm and snapped it like crackwood. But nothing snapped Lenine.

I couldn't shoot her again. More would burn her skull bone-dry. And nothing in the little glass tubes. Blue Seven was fine for the boy—about as good as mouse pee for Lenine.

Okay. One deep breath and down to dirty fighting. I ripped the sheet away. Stripped her bare. She was slim and fragile, too close to womantime. I spread her wide, and the motherperson made little sounds.

"Out."

The man understood and moved her.

Dreamspasm is a thing of the mind. But that door's closed for helpers. The physical stimuli is to build mental bridges back home. Countershock for young minds. For Lenine Capral, therapeutic rape. Thumb the Peacemaker to lowbuzz and hope this one's led a sheltered life.

Hurt her good.

Whisper uglies in her ear.

Slap and touch and tear. No gentle Peacemaker funsies. Only the bad parts. A child's garden of horrors. Everything Mother said would happen if the bad man gets his hands on you.

Orange.

Red-thirty.

Coming up violet. Cream-colored dawn on the windows.

And finally the sound you want. Lenine the wide-eyed screamer. The violated child awake and fighting. Afraid of real things now. Scared out of Dreamspasm One.

Quickly out and past the hoverfaces. No gushy gratitude here. Mother doesn't thank the Coprapist.

Outside, dawnbreeze turns the sweat clammy cold. A medbug has braved the nightlings all the way from Fryhope. Lenine will get proper patching.

The prowlbug has a homepath in mind, as well it might.

Only I am not ready for Bethellen and breakfast. Both are out of temper with the night's affairs. Instead, I brave the prowlbug's rumblings, move past Slowrush, and wind down to Hollow. The road ends, and prowlbug will duly record that I have violated Safecode and am afoot before the dawn. The nightlings don't concern me. They've fed before Firstlight and bear me no ill.

At the stream I hear their thrums and splashings as they cross back over to find hugburrows for the day.

The stream is swift and shallow and no wider than a childstep. It makes pleasant rillsongs and winds beneath the green chumtrees. It has no name. It is simply the stream that divides the world. Dark from light. Night from day.

There is still nightshadow on the other side. The groves are thick and heavy. I watch, wait, and listen to the stream music.

Timebug says half-past violet. While I wait, I polish dunglasses. Put them on. They help me see what is, and temper what isn't at all.

Wait.

Watch the waterlights.

A blink, a breath and he's there. As if he'd been there all along.

For a moment my stomach does its tightness. But it's not so bad for me. They make teetiny headchanges in policemen. Little slicecuts that go with the Copsuit. But there is still a childmind to remember. Dreamspasms in dark nightrooms.

Through the dunglasses I can see bristly no-color. Hear his restless flickersounds. See him move with the shape of frostfur. Hear him breathe hot darkness. Sense his crush-heavy limbs. Only, I cannot see or hear these things at all.

I wonder if he watches, and what he sees of me. I have to look away. And when I look again, he is gone. Nothing has changed in the thickness over there.

Back to the prowlbug. Ten till Indigo. Amberlight dares the high ridges. Sucks away the darkness.

I imagine him. Thromping and shifting. Dark fengroves away. Safe against the sunstar. All the young darklings purged of manfear. Only fright thoughts now—fading daydemons named Lenine.

What would I say to him if I could? Whatever could be said is what he knows. That the stream divides the world. That there are pinchfew places left to be. That mostly there is nothing left at all. That we have to make do, now, with what there is to share....

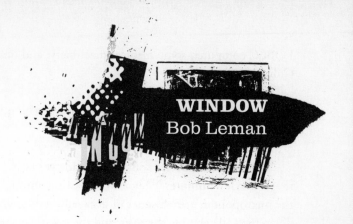

WINDOW
Bob Leman

"WE DON'T KNOW what the hell's going on out there," they told Gilson in Washington. "It may be pretty big. The nut in charge tried to keep it under wraps, but the army was furnishing routine security, and the commanding officer tipped us off. A screwball project. Apparently been funded for years without anyone paying much attention. Extrasensory perception, for God's sake. And maybe they've found something. The security colonel thinks so, anyway. Find out about it."

The Nut-in-Charge was a rumpled professor of psychology named Krantz. He and the colonel met Gilson at the airport, and they set off directly for the site in an army sedan. The colonel began talking immediately.

"You've got something mighty queer here, Gilson," he said. "I never saw anything like it, and neither did anybody else. Krantz here is as mystified as anybody. And it's his baby. We're just security. Not that they've needed any, up to now. Not even any need for secrecy, except to keep the public from laughing its head off. The setup we've got here is—"

"Dr. Krantz," Gilson said, "you'd better give me a complete rundown on the situation here. So far, I haven't any information at all."

Krantz was occupied with the lighting of a cigar. He blew a cloud of foul smoke, and through it he said, "We're missing one prefab building, one

POBEC computer, some medical machinery, and one, uh, researcher named Culvergast."

"Explain 'missing,'" Gilson said.

"Gone. Disappeared. A building and everything in it. Just not there any more. But we do have something in exchange."

"And what's that?"

"I think you'd better wait and see for yourself," Krantz said. "We'll be there in a few minutes." They were passing through the farther reaches of the metropolitan area, a series of decayed small towns. The highway wound down the valley beside the river, and the towns lay stretched along it, none of them more than a block or two wide, their side streets rising steeply toward the first ridge. In one of these moribund communities they left the highway and went bouncing up the hillside on a crooked road whose surface changed from cobblestones to slag after the houses had been left behind. Beyond the crest of the ridge the road began to drop as steeply as it had risen, and after a quarter of a mile they turned into a lane whose entrance would have been missed by anyone not watching for it. They were in a forest now; it was second growth, but the logging had been done so long ago that it might almost have been a virgin stand, lofty, silent, and somewhat gloomy on this gray day.

"Pretty," Gilson said. "How does a project like this come to be way out here, anyhow?"

"The place was available," the colonel said. "Has been since World War Two. They set it up for some work on proximity fuses. Shut it down in '48. Was vacant until the professor took it over."

"Culvergast is a little bit eccentric," Krantz said. "He wouldn't work at the university—too many people, he said. When I heard this place was available, I put in for it, and got it—along with the colonel, here. Culvergast has been happy with the setup, but I guess he bothers the colonel a little."

"He's a certifiable loony," the colonel said, "and his little helpers are worse."

"Well, what the devil was he doing?" Gilson asked.

Before Krantz could answer, the driver braked at a chain-link gate that stood across the lane. It was fastened with a loop of heavy logging chain and manned by armed soldiers. One of them, machine pistol in hand, peered into the car. "Everything O.K., sir?" he said.

"O.K. with waffles, Sergeant," the colonel said. It was evidently a password. The noncom unlocked the enormous padlock that secured the chain. "Pretty primitive," the colonel said as they bumped through the gateway, "but it'll do until we get proper stuff in. We've got men with dogs patrolling the fence." He looked at Gilson. "We're just about there. Get a load of this, now."

It was a house. It stood in the center of the clearing in an island of sunshine, white, gleaming, and incongruous. All around was the dark loom of the forest under a sunless sky, but somehow sunlight lay on the house, sparkling in its polished windows and making brilliant the colors of massed flowers in carefully tended beds, reflecting from the pristine whiteness of its siding out into the gray, littered clearing with its congeries of derelict buildings.

"You couldn't have picked a better time," the colonel said. "Shining there, cloudy here."

Gilson was not listening. He had climbed from the car and was staring in fascination. "Jesus," he said. "Like a goddamn Victorian postcard."

Lacy scrollwork foamed over the rambling wooden mansion, running riot at the eaves of the steep roof, climbing elaborately up towers and turrets, embellishing deep oriels and outlining a long, airy veranda. Tall windows showed by their spacing that the rooms were many and large. It seemed to be a new house, or perhaps just newly painted and supremely well-kept. A driveway of fine white gravel led under a high porte-cochère.

"How about that?" the colonel said. "Look like your grandpa's house?"

As a matter of fact, it did: like his grandfather's house enlarged and perfected and seen through a lens of romantic nostalgia, his grandfather's house groomed and pampered as the old farmhouse never had been. He said, "And you got this in exchange for a prefab, did you?"

"Just like that one," the colonel said, pointing to one of the seedy buildings. "Of course we could use the prefab."

"What does that mean?"

"Watch," the colonel said. He picked up a small rock and tossed it in the direction of the house. The rock rose, topped its arc, and began to fall. Suddenly it was not there.

"Here," Gilson said. "Let me try that."

He threw the rock like a baseball, a high, hard one. It disappeared about fifty feet from the house. As he stared at the point of its disappearance, Gilson became aware that the smooth green of the lawn ended exactly below. Where the grass ended, there began the weeds and rocks that made up the floor of the clearing. The line of separation was absolutely straight, running at an angle across the lawn. Near the driveway it turned ninety degrees, and sliced off lawn, driveway, and shrubbery with the same precise straightness.

"It's perfectly square," Krantz said. "About a hundred feet to a side. Probably a cube, actually. We know the top's about ninety feet in the air. I'd guess there are about ten feet of it underground."

"'It'?" Gilson said. "'It'? What's 'it'?"

"Name it and you can have it," Krantz said. "A three-dimensional television receiver a hundred feet to a side, maybe. A cubical crystal ball. Who knows?"

"The rocks we threw. They didn't hit the house. Where did the rocks go?"

"Ah. Where, indeed? Answer that and perhaps you answer all."

Gilson took a deep breath. "All right. I've seen it. Now tell me about it. From the beginning."

Krantz was silent for a moment; then, in a dry lecturer's voice he said, "Five days ago, June thirteenth, at eleven thirty a.m., give or take three minutes, Private Ellis Mulvihill, on duty at the gate, heard what he later described as 'an explosion that was quiet, like.' He entered the enclosure, locked the gate behind him, and ran up here to the clearing. He was staggered—'shook-up' was his expression—to see, instead of Culvergast's broken-down prefab, that house, there. I gather that he stood gulping and blinking for a time, trying to come to terms with what his eyes told him. Then he ran over there to the guardhouse and called the colonel. Who called me. We came out here and found that a quarter of an acre of land and a building with a man in it had disappeared and been replaced by this, as neat as a peg in a pegboard."

"You think the prefab went where the rocks did," Gilson said. It was a statement.

"Why, we're not even absolutely sure it's gone. What we're seeing can't actually be where we're seeing it. It rains on that house when it's sunny here, and right now you can see the sunlight on it, on a day like this. It's a window."

"A window on what?"

"Well—that looks like a new house, doesn't it? When were they building houses like that?"

"Eighteen seventy or eighty, something like—oh."

"Yes," Krantz said. "I think we're looking at the past."

"Oh, for God's sake," Gilson said.

"I know how you feel. And I may be wrong. But I have to say it looks very much that way. I want you to hear what Reeves says about it. He's been here from the beginning. A graduate student, assisting here. Reeves!"

A very tall, very thin young man unfolded himself from a crouched position over an odd-looking machine that stood near the line between grass and rubble and ambled over to the three men. Reeves was an enthusiast. "Oh, it's the past, all right," he said. "Sometime in the eighties. My girl got some books on costume from the library, and the clothes check out for that decade. And the decorations on the horses' harnesses are a clue, too. I got that from—"

"Wait a minute," Gilson said. "*Clothes?* You mean there are people in there?"

"Oh, sure," Reeves said. "A fine little family. Mamma, poppa, little girl, little boy, old granny or auntie. A dog. Good people."

"How can you tell that?"

"I've been watching them for five days, you know? They're having—*we're* having—fine weather there—or then, or whatever you'd say. They're nice to each other, they *like* each other. Good people. You'll see."

"When?"

"Well, they'll be eating dinner now. They usually come out after dinner. In an hour, maybe."

"I'll wait," Gilson said. "And while we wait, you will please tell me some more."

Krantz assumed his lecturing voice again. "As to the nature of it, nothing. We have a window, which we believe to open into the past. We can see into it, so we know that light passes through; but it passes in only one direction, as evidenced by the fact that the people over there are wholly unaware of us. Nothing else goes through. You saw what happened to the rocks. We've shoved poles through the interface there—there's no resistance at all—but anything that goes through is gone, God knows where. Whatever you put through stays there. Your pole is cut off clean. Fascinating. But wherever it is, it's not where the house is. That interface isn't between us and the past; it's between us and—someplace else. I think our window here is just an incidental side effect, a—a twisting of time that resulted from whatever tensions exist along that interface."

Gilson sighed. "Krantz," he said, "what am I going to tell the secretary? You've lucked into what may be the biggest thing that ever happened, and you've kept it bottled up for five days. We wouldn't know about it now if it weren't for the colonel's report. Five days wasted. Who knows how long this thing will last? The whole goddamn scientific establishment ought to be here—should have been from day one. This needs the whole works. At this point the place should be a beehive. And what do I find? You and a graduate student throwing rocks and poking with sticks. And a girlfriend looking up the dates of costumes. It's damn near criminal."

Krantz did not look abashed. "I thought you'd say that," he said. "But look at it this way. Like it or not, this thing wasn't produced by technology or science. It was pure psi. If we can reconstruct Culvergast's work, we may be able to find out what happened; we may be able to repeat the phenomenon. But I don't like what's going to happen after you've called in your experimenters, Gilson. They'll measure and test and conjecture and theorize, and never once will they accept for a moment the real basis of what's happened. The day they arrive, I'll be out. And damnit, Gilson, this is *mine.*"

"Not any more," Gilson said. "It's too big."

"It's not as though we weren't doing some hard experiments of our own," Krantz said. "Reeves, tell him about your batting machine."

"Yes, *sir,*" Reeves said. "You see, Mr. Gilson, what the professor said wasn't absolutely the whole truth, you know? Sometimes something *can* get through the window. We saw it on the first day. There was a temperature inversion over in the valley, and the stink from the chemical plant had been accumulating for about a week. It broke up that day, and the wind blew the gunk through the notch and right over here. A really rotten stench. We were watching our people over there, and all of a sudden they began to sniff and wrinkle their noses and make disgusted faces. We figured it had to be the chemical stink. We pushed a pole out right away, but the end just disappeared, as usual. The professor suggested that maybe there was a pulse, or something of the sort, in the interface, that it exists only intermittently. We cobbled up a gadget to test the idea. Come and have a look at it."

It was a horizontal flywheel with a paddle attached to its rim, like an extended cleat. As the wheel spun, the paddle swept around a table. There was a hopper hanging above, and at intervals something dropped from the hopper onto the table, where it was immediately banged by the paddle and sent flying. Gilson peered into the hopper and raised an interrogatory eyebrow. "Ice cubes," Reeves said. "Colored orange for visibility. That thing shoots an ice cube at the interface once a second. Somebody is always on duty with a stopwatch. We've established that every fifteen hours and twenty minutes the thing is open for five seconds. Five ice cubes go through and drop on the lawn in there. The rest of the time they just vanish at the interface."

"Ice cubes. Why ice cubes?"

"They melt and disappear. We can't be littering up the past with artifacts from our day. God knows what the effect might be. Then, too, they're cheap, and we're shooting a lot of them."

"Science," Gilson said heavily. "I can't wait to hear what they're going to say in Washington."

"Sneer all you like," Krantz said. "The house is there, the interface is there. We've by God turned up some kind of time travel. And Culvergast the screwball did it, not a physicist or an engineer."

"Now that you bring it up," Gilson said, "just what *was* your man Culvergast up to?"

"Good question. What he was doing was—well, not to put too fine a point upon it, he was trying to discover spells."

"Spells?"

"The kind you cast. Magic words. Don't look disgusted yet. It makes sense, in a way. We were funded to look into telekinesis—the manipulation of matter by the mind. It's obvious that telekinesis, if it could be applied with precision, would be a marvelous weapon. Culvergast's hypothesis was that there are in fact people who perform feats of telekinesis, and although they never seem to know or be able to explain how they do it, they nevertheless perform a specific mental action that enables them to tap some source of energy that apparently exists all around us, and to some degree to focus and direct that energy. Culvergast proposed to discover the common factor in their mental processes.

"He ran a lot of putative telekinesists through here, and he reported that he had found a pattern, a sort of mnemonic device functioning at the very bottom of, or below, the verbal level. In one of his people he found it as a set of musical notes, in several as gibberish of various sorts, and in one, he said, as mathematics at the primary arithmetic level. He was feeding all this into the computer, trying to eliminate simple noise and the personal idiosyncrasies of the subjects, trying to lay bare the actual, effective essence. He then proposed to organize this essence into *words;* words that would so shape the mental currents of a speaker of standard American English that they would channel and manipulate the telekinetic power at the will of the speaker. Magic words, you might say. Spells.

"He was evidently further along than I suspected. I think he must have arrived at some words, tried them out, and made an attempt at telekinesis— some small thing, like causing an ashtray to rise off his desk and float in the air, perhaps. And it worked, but what he got wasn't a dainty little ashtray-lifting force; he had opened the gate wide, and some kind of terrible power came through. It's pure conjecture, of course, but it must have been something like that to have had an effect like *this.*"

Gilson had listened in silence. He said, "I won't say you're crazy, because I can see that house and I'm watching what's happening to those ice cubes. How it happened isn't my problem, anyhow. My problem is what I'll recommend to the secretary that we do with it now that we've got it. One thing's sure, Krantz: this isn't going to be your private playpen much longer."

There was a yelp of pure pain from Reeves. "They can't *do* that," he said. "This is ours, it's the professor's. Look at it, look at that house. Do you want a bunch of damn engineers messing around with *that?*"

Gilson could understand how Reeves felt. The house was drenched now with the light of a red sunset; it seemed to glow from within with a deep, rosy blush. But, Gilson reflected, the sunset wasn't really necessary; sentiment and the universal, unacknowledged yearning for a simple, cleaner time would lend rosiness enough. He was quite aware that the surge of longing and nostalgia he felt was nostalgia for something he had never actually experienced, that the way of life the house epitomized for him was in fact his own creation, built from patches of novels and films; nonetheless he found himself hungry for that life, yearning for that time. It was a gentle and secure time, he thought, a time when the pace was unhurried and the air was clean; a time when there was grace and style, when young men in striped blazers and boater hats might pay decorous court to young ladies in long white dresses, whiling away the long drowsy afternoons of summer in peaceable conversations on shady porches. There would be jolly bicycle tours over shade-dappled roads that twisted among the hills to arrive at cool glens where swift little streams ran; there would be long sweet buggy rides behind somnolent patient horses under a great white moon, lover whispering urgently to lover while nightbirds sang. There would be excursions down the broad clean river, boats gentle on the current, floating toward the sound from across the water of a brass band playing at the landing.

Yes, thought Gilson, and there would probably be an old geezer with a trunkful of adjectives around somewhere, carrying on about how much better things had been a hundred years before. If he didn't watch himself he'd be helping Krantz and Reeves try to keep things hidden. Young Reeves—oddly, for someone his age—seemed to be hopelessly mired in this bogus nostalgia. His description of the family in the house had been simple doting. Oh, it was definitely time that the cold-eyed boys were called in. High time.

"They ought to be coming out any minute, now," Reeves was saying. "Wait till you see Martha."

"Martha," Gilson said.

"The little girl. She's a doll."

Gilson looked at him. Reeves reddened and said, "Well, I sort of gave them names. The children. Martha and Pete. And the dog's Alfie. They kind of look like those names, you know?" Gilson did not answer, and Reeves reddened further. "Well, you can see for yourself. Here they come."

A fine little family, as Reeves had said. After watching them for half an hour, Gilson was ready to concede that they were indeed most engaging, as perfect in their way as their house. They were just what it took to complete the picture, to make an authentic Victorian genre painting. Mama and Papa were good-looking and still in love, the children were healthy and merry and content with their world. Or so it seemed to him as he watched them in the darkening evening, imagining the comfortable, affectionate conversation of the parents as they sat on the porch swing, almost hearing the squeals of the children and the barking of the dog as they raced about the lawn. It was almost dark now; a mellow light of oil lamps glowed in the windows, and fireflies winked over the lawn. There was an arc of fire as the father tossed his cigar butt over the railing and rose to his feet. Then there followed a pretty little pantomime, as he called the children, who duly protested, were duly permitted a few more minutes, and then were firmly commanded. They moved reluctantly to the porch and were shooed inside, and the dog, having delayed to give a shrub a final wetting, came scrambling up to join them. The children and the dog entered the house, then the mother and father. The door closed, and there was only the soft light from the windows.

Reeves exhaled a long breath. "Isn't that something," he said. "That's the way to live, you know? If a person could just say to hell with all this crap we live in today and go back there and live like that.... And Martha, you saw Martha. An angel, right? Man, what I'd give to—"

Gilson interrupted him: "When does the next batch of ice cubes go through?"

"—be able to—Uh, yeah. Let's see. The last penetration was at 3:15, just before you got here. Next one will be at 6:35 in the morning, if the pattern holds. And it has, so far."

"I want to see that. But right now I've got to do some telephoning. Colonel!"

Gilson did not sleep that night, nor, apparently, did Krantz and Reeves. When he arrived at the clearing at five a.m. they were still there, unshaven and red-eyed, drinking coffee from thermos bottles. It was cloudy again, and the clearing was in total darkness except for a pale light from beyond the interface, where a sunny day was on the verge of breaking.

"Anything new?" Gilson said.

"I think that's my question," Krantz said. "What's going to happen?"

"Just about what you expected, I'm afraid. I think that by evening this place is going to be a real hive. And by tomorrow night you'll be lucky if you can find a place to stand. I imagine Bannon's been on the phone since I called him at midnight, rounding up the scientists. And they'll round up the technicians. Who'll bring their machines. And the army's going to beef up the security. How about some of that coffee?"

"Help yourself. You bring bad news, Gilson."

"Sorry," Gilson said, "but there it is."

"Goddam!" Reeves said loudly. "Oh, goddamn!" He seemed to be about to burst into tears. "That'll be the end for me, you know? They won't even let me in. A damn graduate student? In *psychology?* I won't get near the place. Oh, damn it to hell!" he glared at Gilson in rage and despair.

The sun had risen, bringing gray light to the clearing and brilliance to the house across the interface. There was no sound but the regular bang of the ice cube machine. The three men stared quietly at the house. Gilson drank his coffee.

"There's Martha," Reeves said. "Up there." A small face had appeared between the curtains of a second-floor window, and bright blue eyes were surveying the morning. "She does that every day," Reeves said. "Sits there and watches the birds and squirrels until I guess they call her for breakfast." They stood and watched the little girl, who was looking at something that lay beyond the scope of their window on her world, something that would have been to their rear had the worlds been the same. Gilson almost found himself turning around to see what it was that she stared at. Reeves apparently had the same impulse. "What's she looking at, do you think?" he said. "It's not necessarily forest, like now. I think this was logged out earlier. Maybe a meadow? Cattle or horses on it? Man, what I'd give to be there and see what it is."

Krantz looked at his watch and said, "We'd better go over there. Just a few minutes, now."

They moved to where the machine was monotonously batting ice cubes into the interface. A soldier with a stopwatch sat beside it, behind a table bearing a formidable chronometer and a sheaf of charts. He said, "Two minutes, Dr. Krantz."

Krantz said to Gilson, "Just keep your eye on the ice cubes. You can't miss it when it happens." Gilson watched the machine, mildly amused by the rhythm of its homely sounds: *plink*—a cube drops; *whuff*—the paddle sweeps around; *bang*—paddle strikes ice cube. And then a flat trajectory to the interface, where the small orange missile abruptly vanishes. A second later, another. Then another.

"Five seconds," the soldier called. "Four. Three. Two. One. *Now.*"

His timing was off by a second; the ice cube disappeared like its predecessors. But the next one continued its flight and dropped onto the lawn, where it lay glistening. It was really a fact, then, thought Gilson. Time travel for ice cubes.

Suddenly behind him there was an incomprehensible shout from Krantz and another from Reeves, and then a loud, clear, and anguished, "Reeves, *no!*" from Krantz. Gilson heard a thud of running feet and caught a flash of swift movement at the edge of his vision. He whirled in time to see Reeves's gangling figure hurtle past, plunge through the interface, and land sprawling on the lawn. Krantz said, violently, *"Fool!"* An ice cube shot through and landed near Reeves. The machine banged again; an ice cube flew out and vanished. The five seconds of accessibility were over.

Reeves raised his head and stared for a moment at the grass on which he lay. He shifted his gaze to the house. He rose slowly to his feet, wearing a bemused expression. A grin came slowly over his face, then, and the men watching from the other side could almost read his thoughts: Well, I'll be damned. I made it. I'm really here.

Krantz was babbling uncontrollably. "We're still here, Gilson, we're still here, we still exist, everything seems the same. Maybe he didn't change things much, maybe the future is fixed and he didn't change anything at all. I was afraid of this, of something like this. Ever since you came out here, he's been—"

Gilson did not hear him. He was staring with shock and disbelief at the child in the window, trying to comprehend what he saw and did not believe he was seeing. Her behavior was wrong, it was very, very wrong. A man had materialized on her lawn, suddenly, out of thin air, on a sunny morning, and she had evinced no surprise or amazement or fear. Instead she had smiled— instantly, spontaneously, a smile that broadened and broadened until it seemed to split the lower half of her face, a smile that showed too many teeth, a smile fixed and incongruous and terrible below her bright blue eyes. Gilson felt his stomach knot; he realized that he was dreadfully afraid.

The face abruptly disappeared from the window; a few seconds later the front door flew open and the little girl rushed through the doorway, making for Reeves with furious speed, moving in a curious, scuttling run. When she was a few feet away, she leaped at him, with the agility and eye-dazzling quickness of a flea. Reeves's eyes had just begun to take on a puzzled look when the powerful little teeth tore out his throat.

She dropped away from him and sprang back. A geyser of bright blood erupted from the ragged hole in his neck. He looked at it in stupefaction for a long moment, then brought up his hands to cover the wound; the blood boiled through his fingers and ran down his forearms. He sank gently to his knees, staring at the little girl with wide astonishment. He rocked, shivered, and pitched forward on his face.

She watched with eyes as cold as a reptile's, the terrible smile still on her face. She was naked, and it seemed to Gilson that there was something wrong with her torso, as well as with her mouth. She turned and appeared to shout toward the house.

In a moment they all came rushing out, mother, father, little boy, and granny, all naked, all undergoing that hideous transformation of the mouth. Without pause or diminution of speed they scuttled to the body, crouched around it, and frenziedly tore off its clothes. Then, squatting on the lawn in the morning sunshine, the fine little family began horribly to feed.

Krantz's babbling had changed its tenor: "Holy Mary, Mother of God, pray for us...." The soldier with the stopwatch was noisily sick. Someone emptied a clip of a machine pistol into the interface, and the colonel cursed luridly. When Gilson could no longer bear to watch the grisly feast, he looked away and found himself staring at the dog, which sat happily on the porch, thumping its tail.

"By God, it just can't be!" Krantz burst out. "It would be in the histories, in the newspapers, if there'd been people like that here. My God, something like that couldn't be forgotten!"

"Oh, don't talk like a fool!" Gilson said angrily. "That's not the past. I don't know what it is, but it's not the past. Can't be. It's—I don't know—someplace else. Some other—dimension? Universe? One of those theories. Alternate worlds, worlds of If, probability worlds, whatever you call 'em. They're in the present time, all right, that filth over there. Culvergast's damn spell holed through to one of those parallels. Got to be something like that. And, my God, what the *hell* was its history to produce *those?* They're not human, Krantz, no way human, whatever they look like. 'Jolly bicycle tours.' How wrong can you be?"

It ended at last. The family lay on the grass with distended bellies, covered with blood and grease, their eyelids heavy in repletion. The two little ones fell asleep. The large male appeared to be deep in thought. After a time he rose, gathered up Reeves's clothes, and examined them carefully. Then he woke the small female and apparently questioned her at some length. She gestured, pointed, and pantomimed Reeves's headlong arrival. He stared thoughtfully at the place where Reeves had materialized, and for a moment it seemed to Gilson that the pitiless eyes were glaring directly into his. He turned, walked slowly and reflectively to the house, and went inside.

It was silent in the clearing except for the thump of the machine. Krantz began to weep, and the colonel to swear in a monotone. The soldiers seemed dazed. And we're all afraid, Gilson thought. Scared to death.

On the lawn they were enacting a grotesque parody of making things tidy after a picnic. The small ones had brought a basket and, under the meticulous supervision of the adult females, went about gathering up the debris of their feeding. One of them tossed a bone to the dog, and the timekeeper vomited again. When the lawn was once again immaculate, they carried off the basket to the rear, and the adults returned to the house. A moment later the male emerged, now dressed in a white linen suit. He carried a book.

"A Bible," said Krantz in amazement. "It's a Bible."

"Not a Bible," Gilson said. "There's no way those—things could have Bibles. Something else. Got to be."

It looked like a Bible; its binding was limp black leather, and when the male began to leaf through it, evidently in search of a particular passage, they could see that the paper was the thin, tough paper Bibles are printed on. He found his page and began, as it appeared to Gilson, to read aloud in a declamatory manner, mouthing the words.

"What the hell do you suppose he's up to?" Gilson said. He was still speaking when the window ceased to exist.

House and lawn and white-suited declaimer vanished. Gilson caught a swift glimpse of trees across the clearing, hidden until now by the window, and of a broad pit between him and the trees. Then he was knocked off his feet by a blast of wind, and the air was full of dust and flying trash and the wind's howl. The wind stopped, as suddenly as it had come, and there was a patter of falling small objects that had momentarily been wind-borne. The site of the house was entirely obscured by an eddying cloud of dust.

The dust settled slowly. Where the window had been there was a great hole in the ground, a perfectly square hole a hundred feet across and perhaps ten feet deep, its bottom as flat as a table. Gilson's glimpse of it before the wind had rushed in to fill the vacuum had shown the sides to be as smooth and straight as if sliced through cheese with a sharp knife; but now small landslides were occurring all around the perimeter, as topsoil and gravel caved and slid to the bottom, and the edges were becoming ragged and irregular.

Gilson and Krantz slowly rose to their feet. "And that seems to be that," Gilson said. "It was here and now it's gone. But where's the prefab? Where's Culvergast?"

"God knows," Krantz said. He was not being irreverent. "But I think he's gone for good. And at least he's not where those things are."

"What are they, do you think?"

"As you said, certainly not human. Less human than a spider or an oyster. But, Gilson, the way they look and dress, that house—"

"If there's an infinite number of possible worlds, then every possible sort of world will exist."

Krantz looked doubtful. "Yes, well, perhaps. We don't know anything, do we?" He was silent for a moment. "Those things were pretty frightening, Gilson. It didn't take even a fraction of a second for her to react to Reeves. She knew instantly that he was alien, and she moved instantly to destroy him. And that's a baby one. I think maybe we can feel safer with the window gone."

"Amen to that. What do you think happened to it?"

"It's obvious, isn't it? They know how to use the energies Culvergast was blundering around with. The book—it has to be a book of spells. They must have a science of it—tried-and-true stuff, part of their received wisdom. That thing used the book like a routine everyday tool. After it got over the excitement of its big feed, it didn't need more than twenty minutes to figure out how Reeves got there, and what to do about it. It just got its book of spells, picked the one it needed (I'd like to see the index of that book) and said the words. Poof! Window gone and Culvergast stranded, God knows where."

"It's possible, I guess. Hell, maybe even likely. You're right, we don't really know a thing about all this."

Krantz suddenly looked frightened. "Gilson, what if—look. If it was that easy for him to cancel out the window, if he has that kind of control of telekinetic power, what's to prevent him from getting a window on *us?* Maybe they're watching us now, the way we were watching them. They know we're here, now. What kind of ideas might they get? Maybe they need meat. Maybe they—my God."

"No," Gilson said. "Impossible. It was pure, blind chance that located the window in that world. Culvergast had no more idea what he was doing than a chimp at a computer console does. If the Possible-Worlds Theory is the explanation of this thing, then the world he hit is one of an infinite number. Even if the things over there do know how to make these windows, the odds are infinite against their finding us. That is to say, it's impossible."

"Yes, yes, of course," Krantz said, gratefully. "Of course. They could try forever and never find us. Even if they wanted to." He thought for a moment. "And I think they do want to. It was pure reflex, their destroying Reeves, as involuntary as a knee jerk, by the look of it. Now that they know we're here, they'll have to try to get at us; if I've sized them up right, it wouldn't be possible for them to do anything else."

Gilson remembered the eyes. "I wouldn't be a bit surprised," he said. "But now we both better—"

"Dr. Krantz!" someone screamed. *"Dr. Krantz!"* There was absolute terror in the voice.

The two men spun around. The soldier with the stopwatch was pointing with a trembling hand. As they looked, something white materialized in the air above the rim of the pit and sailed out and downward to land beside a similar object already lying on the ground. Another came; then another, and another. Five in all, scattered over an area perhaps a yard square.

"It's bones!" Krantz said. "Oh, my God, Gilson, it's bones!" His voice shuddered on the edge of hysteria. Gilson said, "Stop it, now. Stop it! Come on!" They ran to the spot. The soldier was already there, squatting, his face made strange by nausea and terror. "That one," he said, pointing. "That one there. That's the one they threw to the dog. You can see the teeth marks. Oh, Jesus. It's the one they threw to the dog."

They've already made a window, then, Gilson thought. They must know a lot about these matters, to have done it so quickly. And they're watching us now. But why the bones? To warn us off? Or just a test? But if a test, then still why the bones? Why not a pebble—or an ice cube? To gauge our reactions, perhaps. To see what we'll do.

And what *will* we do? How do we protect ourselves against *this?* If it is in the nature of these creatures to cooperate among themselves, the fine little family will no doubt lose no time in spreading the word over their whole world, so that one of these days we'll find that a million million of them have leaped simultaneously through such windows all over the earth, suddenly materializing like a cloud of huge, carnivorous locusts, swarming in to feed with that insensate voracity of theirs until they have left the planet a desert of bones. Is there any protection against that?

Krantz had been thinking along the same track. He said, shakily, "We're in a spot, Gilson, but we've got one little thing on our side. We know when the damn thing opens up, we've got it timed exactly. Washington will have to go all out, warn the whole world, do it through the U.N. or something. We know right down to the second when the window can be penetrated. We set up a warning system, every community on earth blows a whistle or rings a bell when it's time. Bell rings, everybody grabs a weapon and stands ready. If the things haven't come in five seconds, bell rings again, and everybody goes about his business until time for the next opening. It could work, Gilson, but we've got to work fast. In fifteen hours and, uh, a couple of minutes it'll be open again."

Fifteen hours and a couple of minutes, Gilson thought, then five seconds of awful vulnerability, and then fifteen hours and twenty minutes of safety before terror arrives again. And so on for—how long? Presumably until the things come, which might be never (who knew how their minds worked?), or until Culvergast's accident could be duplicated, which, again, might be never. He questioned whether human beings could exist under those conditions without going mad; it was doubtful if the psyche could cohere when its sole foreseeable future was an interminable roller coaster down into long valleys of terror and suspense and thence violently up to brief peaks of relief. Will a mind continue to function when its only alternatives are ghastly death or unbearable tension endlessly protracted? Is there any way, Gilson asked himself, that the race can live with the knowledge that it has no assured future beyond the next fifteen hours and twenty minutes?

And then he saw, hopelessly and with despair, that it was not fifteen hours and twenty minutes, that it was not even one hour, that it was no time at all. The window was not, it seemed, intermittent. Materializing out of the air was a confusion of bones and rent clothing, a flurry of contemptuously flung garbage that clattered to the ground and lay there in an untidy heap, noisome and foreboding.

SIX MONTHS EARLIER they had captured him. Tonight Harry went into the pit. He and Big George, right after the bull terriers got through tearing the guts out of one another. When that was over, he and George would go down and do their business. The loser would stay there and be fed to the dogs, each of which had been starved for the occasion.

When the dogs finished eating, the loser's head would go up on a pole. Already a dozen poles circled the pit. On each rested a head, or skull, depending on how long it had been exposed to the elements, ambitious pole-climbing ants, and hungry birds. And of course how much flesh the terriers ripped off before it was erected.

Twelve poles. Twelve heads.

Tonight a new pole and a new head went up.

Harry looked about at the congregation. All sixty or so of them. They were a sight. Like mad creatures out of Lewis Carroll. Only they didn't have long rabbit ears or tall silly hats. They were just backwoods rednecks, not too unlike himself. With one major difference. They were as loony as waltzing mice. Or maybe they weren't crazy and he was. Sometimes he felt as if he had stepped into an alternate universe where the old laws of nature and what was right and wrong did not apply. Just like Alice plunging down the rabbit hole into Wonderland.

The crowd about the pit had been mumbling and talking, but now they grew silent. Out into the glow of the neon lamps stepped a man dressed in a black suit and hat. A massive rattlesnake was coiled about his right arm. It was wriggling from shoulder to wrist. About his left wrist a smaller snake was wrapped, a copperhead. The man held a Bible in his right hand. He was called Preacher.

Draping the monstrous rattlesnake around his neck, Preacher let it hang there. It dangled that way as if drugged. Its tongue would flash out from time to time. It gave Harry the willies. He hated snakes. They always seemed to be smiling. Nothing was that fucking funny, not all the time.

Preacher opened his Bible and read:

"Behold, I give unto you the power to tread on serpents and scorpions, and over all the power of the enemy: and nothing will by any means hurt you."

Preacher paused and looked at the sky. "So God," he said, "we want to thank you for a pretty good potato crop, though you've done better, and we want to thank you for the terriers, even though we had to raise and feed them ourselves, and we want to thank you for sending these outsiders our way, thank you for Harry Joe Stinton and Big George, the nigger."

Preacher paused and looked about the congregation. He lifted the hand with the copperhead in it high above his head. Slowly he lowered it and pointed the snake-filled fist at George. "Three times this here nigger has gone into the pit, and three times he has come out victorious. Couple times against whites, once against another nigger. Some of us think he's cheating.

"Tonight, we bring you another white feller, one of your chosen people, though you might not know it on account of the way you been letting the nigger win here, and we're hoping for a good fight with the nigger being killed at the end. We hope this here business pleases you. We worship you and the snakes in the way we ought to. Amen."

Big George looked over at Harry. "Be ready, sucker. I'm gonna take you apart like a gingerbread man."

Harry didn't say anything. He couldn't understand it. George was a prisoner just as he was. A man degraded and made to lift huge rocks and pull carts and jog mile on miles every day. And just so they could get in shape for this—to go down into that pit and try and beat each other to death for the amusement of these crazies.

And it had to be worse for George. Being black, he was seldom called anything other than "the nigger" by these psychos. Furthermore, no secret had been made of the fact that they wanted George to lose, and for him to win. The idea of a black pit champion was eating their little honkey hearts out.

Yet, Big George had developed a sort of perverse pride in being the longest-lived pit fighter yet.

"It's something I can do right," George had once said. "On the outside I wasn't nothing but a nigger, an uneducated nigger working in rose fields, mowing big lawns for rich white folks. Here I'm still the nigger, but I'm THE NIGGER, the bad-ass nigger, and no matter what these peckerwoods call me, they know it, and they know I'm the best at what I do. I'm the king here. And they may hate me for it, keep me in a cell and make me run and lift stuff, but for that time in the pit, they know I'm the one that can do what they can't do, and they're afraid of me. I like it."

Glancing at George, Harry saw that the big man was not nervous. Or at least not showing it. He looked as if he were ready to go on holiday. Nothing to it. He was about to go down into that pit and try and beat a man to death with his fists, and it was nothing. All in a day's work. A job well done for an odd sort of respect that beat what he had had on the outside.

The outside. It was strange how much he and Big George used that term. *The outside.* As if they were enclosed in some small bubble-like cosmos that perched on the edge of the world they had known; a cosmos invisible to *the outsiders,* a spectral place with new mathematics and nebulous laws of mind and physics.

Maybe he was in hell. Perhaps he had been wiped out on the highway and had gone to the dark place. Just maybe his memory of how he had arrived here was a false dream inspired by demonic powers. The whole thing about him taking a wrong turn through Big Thicket country and having his truck break down just outside of Morganstown was an illusion, and stepping onto the Main Street of Morganstown, population sixty-six, was his crossing the river Styx and landing smack dab in the middle of a hell designed for good old boys.

God, had it been six months ago?

He had been on his way to visit his mother in Woodville, and he had taken a shortcut through the Thicket. Or so he thought. But he soon realized that he had looked at the map wrong. The short cut listed on the paper was not the one he had taken. He had mistaken that road for the one he wanted. This one had not been marked. And then he had reached Morganstown and his truck had broken down. He had been forced into six months' hard labor alongside George, the champion pit fighter, and now the moment for which he had been groomed had arrived.

They were bringing the terriers out now. One, the champion, was named Old Codger. He was getting on in years. He had won many a pit fight. Tonight, win or lose, this would be his last battle. The other dog, Muncher, was younger and inexperienced, but he was strong and eager for blood.

A ramp was lowered into the pit. Preacher and two men, the owners of the dogs, went down into the pit with Codger and Muncher. When they reached the bottom, a dozen bright spotlights were thrown on them. They seemed to wade through the light.

The bleachers arranged about the pit began to fill. People mumbled and passed popcorn. Bets were placed and a little fat man wearing a bowler hat copied them down in a note pad as fast as they were shouted. The ramp was removed.

In the pit, the men took hold of their dogs by the scruff of the neck and removed their collars. They turned the dogs so they were facing the walls of the pit and could not see one another. The terriers were about six feet apart, butts facing.

Preacher said, "A living dog is better than a dead lion."

Harry wasn't sure what that had to do with anything.

"Ready yourselves," Preacher said. "Gentlemen, face your dogs."

The owners slapped their dogs across the muzzle and whirled them to face one another. They immediately began to leap and strain at their masters' grips.

"Gentlemen, release your dogs."

The dogs did not bark. For some reason, that was what Harry noted the most. They did not even growl. They were quick little engines of silence.

Their first lunge was a miss and they snapped air. But the second time they hit head-on with the impact of .45 slugs. Codger was knocked on his back and Muncher dove for his throat. But the experienced dog popped up its head and grabbed Muncher by the nose. Codger's teeth met through Muncher's flesh.

Bets were called from the bleachers.

The little man in the bowler was writing furiously.

Muncher, the challenger, was dragging Codger, the champion, around the pit, trying to make the old dog let go of his nose. Finally, by shaking his head violently and relinquishing a hunk of his muzzle, he succeeded.

Codger rolled to his feet and jumped Muncher. Muncher turned his head just out of the path of Codger's jaws. The older dog's teeth snapped together like a spring-loaded bear trap, saliva popped out of his mouth in a fine spray.

Muncher grabbed Codger by the right ear. The grip was strong and Codger was shook like a used condom about to be tied and tossed. Muncher bit the champ's ear completely off.

Harry felt sick. He thought he was going to throw up. He saw that Big George was looking at him. "You think this is bad, motherfucker," George said, "this ain't nothing but a cakewalk. Wait till I get you in that pit."

"You sure run hot and cold, don't you?" Harry said.

"Nothing personal," George said sharply and turned back to look at the fight in the pit.

Nothing personal, Harry thought. God, what could be more personal? Just yesterday, as they trained, jogged along together, a pickup loaded with gun-bearing crazies driving alongside of them, he had felt close to George. They had shared many personal things these six months, and he knew that George liked him. But when it came to the pit, George was a different man. The concept of friendship became alien to him. When Harry had tried to talk to him about it yesterday, he had said much the same thing. "Ain't nothing personal, Harry my man, but when we get in that pit don't look to me for nothing besides pain, cause I got plenty of that to give you, a lifetime of it, and I'll just keep it coming."

Down in the pit Codger screamed. It could be described no other way. Muncher had him on his back and was biting him on the belly. Codger was trying to double forward and get hold of Muncher's head, but his tired jaws kept slipping off of the wet neck fur. Blood was starting to pump out of Codger's belly.

"Bite him, boy," someone yelled from the bleachers, "tear his ass up, son."

Harry noted that every man, woman, and child was leaning forward in their seat, straining for a view. Their faces full of lust, like lovers approaching vicious climax. For a few moments they were in that pit and they were the dogs. Vicarious thrills without the pain.

Codger's legs began to flap.

"Kill him! Kill him!" the crowd began to chant.

Codger had quit moving. Muncher was burrowing his muzzle deeper into the old dog's guts. Preacher called for a pickup. Muncher's owner pried the dog's jaws loose of Codger's guts. Muncher's muzzle looked as if it had been dipped in red ink.

"This sonofabitch is still alive," Muncher's owner said of Codger.

Codger's owner walked over to the dog and said, "You little fucker!" He pulled a Saturday Night Special from his coat pocket and shot Codger twice in the head. Codger didn't even kick. He just evacuated his bowels right there.

Muncher came over and sniffed Codger's corpse, then, lifting his leg, he took a leak on the dead dog's head. The stream of piss was bright red.

The ramp was lowered. The dead dog was dragged out and tossed behind the bleachers. Muncher walked up the ramp beside his owner. The little dog strutted like he had just been crowned King of Creation. Codger's owner walked out last. He was not a happy man. Preacher stayed in the pit. A big man known as Sheriff Jimmy went down the ramp to join him. Sheriff Jimmy had a big pistol on his hip and a toy badge on his chest. The badge looked like the sort of thing that had come in a plastic bag with a cap gun and whistle. But it was his sign of office and his word was iron.

A man next to Harry prodded him with the barrel of a shotgun. Walking close behind George, Harry went down the ramp and into the pit. The man with the shotgun went back up. In the bleachers the betting had started again, the little fat man with the bowler was busy.

Preacher's rattlesnake was still lying serenely about his neck, and the little copperhead had been placed in Preacher's coat pocket. It poked its head out from time to time and looked around.

Harry glanced up. The heads and skulls on the poles—in spite of the fact they were all eyeless, and due to the strong light nothing but bulbous shapes on shafts—seemed to look down, taking as much amusement in the situation as the crowd on the bleachers.

Preacher had his Bible out again. He was reading a verse: "…when thou walkest through the fire, thou shalt not be burned; neither shall the flame kindle upon thee.…"

Harry had no idea what that or the snakes had to do with anything. Certainly he could not see the relationship with the pit. These people's minds seemed to click and grind to a different set of internal gears than those on *the outside*.

The reality of the situation settled on Harry like a heavy, woolen coat. He was about to kill or be killed, right here in this dog-smelling pit, and there was nothing he could do that would change that.

He thought perhaps his life should flash before his eyes or something, but it did not. Maybe he should try to think of something wonderful, a last fine thought of what used to be. First he summoned up the image of his wife. That did nothing for him. Though his wife had once been pretty and bright, he could not remember her that way. The image that came to mind was quite different. A dumpy, lazy woman with constant back pains and her hair pulled up into an eternal topknot of greasy, brown hair. There was never a smile on her face or a word of encouragement for him. He always felt that she expected him to entertain her and that he was not doing a very good job of it. There was not even a moment of sexual ecstasy that he could recall. After their daughter had been born she had given up screwing as a wasted exercise. Why waste energy on sex when she could spend it complaining.

He flipped his mental card file to his daughter. What he saw was an ugly, potato-nosed girl of twelve. She had no personality. Her mother was Miss Congeniality compared to her. Potato Nose spent all of her time pining over thin, blond heartthrobs on television. It wasn't bad enough that they glared at Harry via the tube, they were also pinned to her walls and hiding in magazines she had cast throughout the house.

These were the last thoughts of a man about to face death?

There was just nothing there.

His job had sucked. His wife hadn't.

He clutched at straws. There had been Melva, a fine-looking little cheerleader from high school. She had had the brain of a dried black-eyed pea, but God-All-Mighty, did she know how to hide a weenie. And there had always been that strange smell about her, like bananas. It was especially strong about her thatch, which was thick enough for a bald eagle to nest in.

But thinking about her didn't provide much pleasure either. She had gotten hit by a drunk in a Mack truck while parked offside of a dark road with that Pulver boy.

Damn that Pulver. At least he had died in ecstasy. Had never known what hit him. When that Mack went up his ass he probably thought for a split second he was having the greatest orgasm of his life.

Damn that Melva. What had she seen in Pulver anyway?

He was skinny and stupid and had a face like a peanut pattie.

God, he was beat at every turn. Frustrated at every corner. No good thoughts or beautiful visions before the moment of truth. Only blackness, a life of dull, planned movements as consistent and boring as a bran-conscious geriatric's bowel movement. For a moment he thought he might cry.

Sheriff Jimmy took out his revolver. Unlike the badge it was not a toy. "Find your corner, boys."

George turned and strode to one side of the pit, took off his shirt and leaned against the wall. His body shined like wet licorice in the spotlights.

After a moment, Harry made his legs work. He walked to a place opposite George and took off his shirt. He could feel the months of hard work rippling beneath his flesh. His mind was suddenly blank. There wasn't even a god he believed in. No one to pray to. Nothing to do but the inevitable.

Sheriff Jimmy walked to the middle of the pit. He yelled out for the crowd to shut up.

Silence reigned.

"In this corner," he said, waving the revolver at Harry, "we have Harry Joe Stinton, family man and pretty good feller for an outsider. He's six two and weighs two hundred and thirty-eight pounds, give or take a pound since my bathroom scales ain't exactly on the money."

A cheer went up.

"Over here," Sheriff Jimmy said, waving the revolver at George, "standing six four tall and weighing two hundred and forty-two pounds, we got the nigger, present champion of this here sport."

No one cheered. Someone made a loud sound with his mouth that sounded like a fart, the greasy kind that goes on and on and on.

George appeared unfazed. He looked like a statue. He knew who he was and what he was. The Champion of the Pit.

"First off," Sheriff Jimmy said, "you boys come forward and show your hands."

Harry and George walked to the center of the pit, held out their hands, fingers spread wide apart, so that the crowd could see that they were empty.

"Turn and walk to your corners and don't turn around," Sheriff Jimmy said.

George and Harry did as they were told. Sheriff Jimmy followed Harry and put an arm around his shoulders. "I got four hogs riding on you," he said. "And I'll tell you what, you beat the nigger and I'll do you a favor. Elvira, who works over at the cafe has already agreed. You win and you can have her. How's that sound?"

Harry was too numb with the insanity of it all to answer. Sheriff Jimmy was offering him a piece of ass if he won, as if this would be greater incentive than coming out of the pit alive. With this bunch there was just no way to anticipate what might come next. Nothing was static.

"She can do more tricks with a six-inch dick than a monkey can with a hundred foot of grapevine, boy. When the going gets rough in there, you remember that. Okay?"

Harry didn't answer. He just looked at the pit wall.

"You ain't gonna get nowhere in life being sullen like that," Sheriff Jimmy said. "Now, you go get him and plow a rut in his black ass."

Sheriff Jimmy grabbed Harry by the shoulders and whirled him around, slapped him hard across the face in the same way the dogs had been slapped. George had been done the same way by the preacher. Now George and Harry were facing one another. Harry thought George looked like an ebony gargoyle fresh escaped from hell. His bald, bullet-like head gleamed in the harsh lights and his body looked as rough and ragged as stone.

Harry and George raised their hands in classic boxer stance and began to circle one another.

From above someone yelled, "Don't hit the nigger in the head, it'll break your hand. Go for the lips, they got soft lips."

The smell of sweat, dog blood, and old Codger's shit was thick in the air. The lust of the crowd seemed to have an aroma as well. Harry even thought he could smell Preacher's snakes. Once, when a boy, he had been fishing down by the creek bed and had smelled an odor like that, and a water moccasin had wriggled out beneath his legs and splashed in the water. It was as if everything he feared in the world had been put in this pit. The idea of being put deep down in the ground. Irrational people for whom logic did not exist. Rotting skulls on poles about the pit. Living skulls attached to hunched-forward bodies that yelled for blood. Snakes. The stench of death—blood and shit. And every white man's fear, racist or not—a big, black man with a lifetime of hatred in his eyes.

The circle tightened. They could almost touch one another now.

Suddenly George's lip began to tremble. His eyes poked out of his head, seemed to be looking at something just behind and to the right of Harry.

"Sss...snake!" George screamed.

God, thought Harry, one of Preacher's snakes has escaped. Harry jerked his head for a look.

And George stepped in and knocked him on his ass and kicked him full in the chest. Harry began scuttling along the ground on his hands and knees, George following along kicking him in the ribs. Harry thought he felt something snap inside, a cracked rib maybe. He finally scuttled to his feet and bicycled around the pit. Goddamn, he thought, I fell for the oldest, silliest trick in the book. Here I am fighting for my life and I fell for it.

"Way to go, stupid fuck!" A voice screamed from the bleachers. "Hey nigger, why don't you try 'hey, your shoe's untied,' he'll go for it."

"Get off the goddamned bicycle," someone else yelled. "Fight."

"You better run," George said. "I catch you I'm gonna punch you so hard in the mouth, gonna knock your fucking teeth out your asshole...."

Harry felt dizzy. His head was like a yo-yo doing the Around The World trick. Blood ran down his forehead, dribbled off the tip of his nose, and gathered on his upper lip. George was closing the gap again.

I'm going to die right here in this pit, thought Harry. I'm going to die just because my truck broke down outside of town and no one knows where I am. That's why I'm going to die. It's as simple as that.

Popcorn rained down on Harry and a tossed cup of ice hit him in the back. "Wanted to see a fucking foot race," a voice called, "I'd have gone to the fucking track."

"Ten on the nigger," another voice said.

"Five bucks the nigger kills him in five minutes."

When Harry backpedaled past Preacher, the snake man leaned forward and snapped, "You asshole, I got a sawbuck riding on you."

Preacher was holding the big rattler again. He had the snake gripped just below the head, and he was so upset over how the fight had gone so far, he was unconsciously squeezing the snake in a vice-like grip. The rattler was squirming and twisting and flapping about, but Preacher didn't seem to notice. The snake's forked tongue was outside its mouth and it was really working, slapping about like a thin strip of rubber come loose on a whirling tire. The copperhead in Preacher's pocket was still looking out, as if along with Preacher he might have a bet on the outcome of the fight as well. As Harry danced away the rattler opened its mouth so wide its jaws came unhinged. It looked as if it were trying to yell for help.

Harry and George came together again in the center of the pit. Fists like black ball bearings slammed the sides of Harry's head. The pit was like a whirlpool, the walls threatening to close in and suck Harry down into oblivion.

Kneeing with all his might, Harry caught George solidly in the groin. George grunted, stumbled back, half-bent over.

The crowd went wild.

Harry brought cupped hands down on George's neck, knocked him on his knees. Harry used the opportunity to knock out one of the big man's teeth with the toe of his shoe.

He was about to kick him again when George reached up and clutched the crotch of Harry's khakis, taking a crushing grip on Harry's testicles.

"Got you by the balls," George growled.

Harry bellowed and began to hammer wildly on top of George's head with both fists. He realized with horror that George was pulling him forward. *By God, George was going to bite him on the balls.*

Jerking up his knee he caught George in the nose and broke his grip. He bounded free, skipped, and whooped about the pit like an Indian dancing for rain.

He skipped and whooped by Preacher. Preacher's rattler had quit twisting. It hung loosely from Preacher's tight fist. Its eyes were bulging out of its head like the humped backs of grub worms. Its mouth was closed and its forked tongue hung limply from the edge of it.

The copperhead was still watching the show from the safety of Preacher's pocket, its tongue zipping out from time to time to taste the air. The little snake didn't seem to have a care in the world.

George was on his feet again, and Harry could tell that already he was feeling better. Feeling good enough to make Harry feel real bad.

Preacher abruptly realized that his rattler had gone limp. "No, God no!" he cried. He stretched the huge rattler between his hands. "Baby, baby," he bawled, "breathe for me, Sapphire, breathe for me." Preacher shook the snake viciously, trying to jar some life into it, but the snake did not move.

The pain in Harry's groin had subsided and he could think again. George was moving in on him, and there just didn't seem any reason to run. George would catch him, and when he did, it would just be worse because he would be even more tired from all that running. It had to be done. The mating dance was over, now all that was left was the intercourse of violence.

A black fist turned the flesh and cartilage of Harry's nose into smoldering putty. Harry ducked his head and caught another blow to the chin. The stars he had not been able to see above him because of the lights, he could now see below him, spinning constellations on the floor of the pit.

It came to him again, the fact that he was going to die right here without one good, last thought. But then maybe there was one. He envisioned his wife, dumpy and sullen and denying him sex. George became her and she became George and Harry did what he had wanted to do for so long, he hit her in the mouth. Not once, but twice and a third time. He battered her nose and he pounded her ribs. And by God, but she could hit back. He felt something crack in the center of his chest and his left cheekbone collapsed into his face. But Harry did not stop battering her. He looped and punched and pounded her dumpy face until it was George's black face and George's black face turned back to her face and he thought of her now on the bed, naked, on her back, battered, and he was naked and mounting her, and the blows of his fists were the sexual thrusts of his cock and he was pounding her until—

George screamed. He had fallen to his knees. His right eye was hanging out on the tendons. One of Harry's straight rights had struck George's cheekbone with such power it had shattered it and pressured the eye out of its socket.

Blood ran down Harry's knuckles. Some of it was George's. Much of it was his own. His knuckle bones showed through the rent flesh of his hands, but they did not hurt. They were past hurting.

George wobbled to his feet. The two men stood facing one another, neither moving. The crowd was silent. The only sound in the pit was the harsh breathing of the two fighters, and Preacher who had stretched Sapphire out on the ground on her back and was trying to blow air into her mouth. Occasionally he'd lift his head and say in tearful supplication, "Breathe for me, Sapphire, breathe for me."

Each time Preacher blew a blast into the snake, its white underbelly would swell and then settle down, like a leaky balloon that just wouldn't hold air.

George and Harry came together. Softly. They had their arms on each other's shoulders and they leaned against one another, breathed each other's breath.

Above, the silence of the crowd was broken when a heckler yelled, "Start some music, the fuckers want to dance."

"It's nothing personal," George said.

"Not at all," Harry said.

They managed to separate, reluctantly, like two lovers who had just copulated to the greatest orgasm of their lives.

George bent slightly and put up his hands. The eye dangling on his cheek looked like some kind of tentacled creature trying to crawl up and into George's socket. Harry knew that he would have to work on that eye.

Preacher screamed. Harry afforded him a sideways glance. Sapphire was awake. And now she was dangling from Preacher's face. She had bitten through his top lip and was hung there by her fangs. Preacher was saying something about the power to tread on serpents and stumbling about the pit. Finally his back struck the pit wall and he slid down to his butt and just sat there, legs sticking out in front of him, Sapphire dangling off his lip like some sort of malignant growth. Gradually, building momentum, the snake began to thrash.

Harry and George met again in the center of the pit. A second wind had washed in on them and they were ready. Harry hurt wonderfully. He was no longer afraid. Both men were smiling, showing the teeth they had left. They began to hit each other.

Harry worked on the eye. Twice he felt it beneath his fists, a grape-like thing that cushioned his knuckles and made them wet. Harry's entire body felt on fire—twin fires, ecstasy and pain.

George and Harry collapsed together, held each other, waltzed about.

"You done good," George said, "make it quick."

The black man's legs went out from under him and he fell to his knees, his head bent. Harry took the man's head in his hands and kneed him in the face with all his might. George went limp. Harry grasped George's chin and the back of his head and gave a violent twist. The neck bone snapped and George fell back, dead.

The copperhead, which had been poking its head out of Preacher's pocket, took this moment to slither away into a crack in the pit's wall.

Out of nowhere came weakness. Harry fell to his knees. He touched George's ruined face with his fingers.

Suddenly hands had him. The ramp was lowered. The crowd cheered. Preacher—Sapphire dislodged from his lip—came forward to help Sheriff Jimmy with him. They lifted him up.

Harry looked at Preacher. His lip was greenish. His head looked like a sun-swollen watermelon, yet, he seemed well enough. Sapphire was wrapped around his neck again. They were still buddies. The snake looked tired. Harry no longer felt afraid of it. He reached out and touched its head. It did not try to bite him. He felt its feathery tongue brush his bloody hand.

They carried him up the ramp and the crowd took him, lifted him up high above their heads. He could see the moon and the stars now. For some odd reason they did not look familiar. Even the nature of the sky seemed different.

He turned and looked down. The terriers were being herded into the pit. They ran down the ramp like rats. Below, he could hear them begin to feed, to fight for choice morsels. But there were so many dogs, and they were so hungry, this only went on for a few minutes. After a while they came back up the ramp followed by Sheriff Jimmy closing a big lock-bladed knife, and by Preacher who held George's head in his outstretched hands. George's eyes were gone. Little of the face remained. Only that slick, bald pate had been left undamaged by the terriers.

A pole came out of the crowd and the head was pushed onto its sharpened end and the pole was dropped into a deep hole in the ground. The pole, like a long neck, rocked its trophy for a moment, then went still. Dirt was kicked into the hole and George joined the others, all those beautiful, wonderful heads and skulls.

They began to carry Harry away. Tomorrow he would have Elvira, who could do more tricks with a six-inch dick than a monkey could with a hundred foot of grapevine, then he would heal and a new outsider would come through and they would train together and then they would mate in blood and sweat in the depths of the pit.

The crowd was moving toward the forest trail, toward town. The smell of pines was sweet in the air. And as they carried him away, Harry turned his head so he could look back and see the pit, its maw closing in shadow as the lights were cut, and just before the last one went out Harry saw the heads on the poles, and dead center of his vision, was the shiny, bald pate of his good friend George.

LOSS
Tom Piccirilli

THE LAST TIME I saw the great, secret unrequited love of my life, Gabriella Corben, was the day the talking monkey moved into Stark House and the guy who lied about inventing aluminum foil took an icepick though the frontal lobe.

I was in the lobby doing Sunday cleaning, polishing the mahogany banister and dusting the ten Dutch Master prints on the walls. At least one of them appeared authentic to me—I'd studied it for many hours over the last two years. I thought it would be just like Corben to stick a million-dollar painting in among the fakes, just to show he could get away with it. I imagined him silently laughing every time he saw me walking up from my basement apartment with my little rag and spritz bottle of cleaner, ready to wash a masterpiece that could set me up in luxury for the rest of my life.

And it was just like me to keep wiping it down and chewing back my petty pride week after week, determined to drop into my grave before I'd pull it from the wall and have it appraised. The chance to retire to Aruba wasn't worth knowing he'd be snickering about it for the rest of his life.

I stared at myself in the buffed mahogany and listened to Corben and Gabriella arguing upstairs. I couldn't make out their words from four flights away. He played the tortured artist well, though, and could really bellow like a wounded water buffalo. He roared and moaned and kicked shit all around. He used to do the same thing in college. I heard a couple of bottles shatter. Probably bourbon or single-malt scotch. They were props he occasionally used in order to pretend he was a hard drinker. The journalists and television crews always made a point of saying there was plenty of booze around. I had no doubt he emptied half the bottles down the sink. I knew his act. I'd helped him develop it. For a while it had been mine as well.

Now Gabriella spoke in a low, loud, stern voice, firm but loving. It hurt me to hear her tone because I knew that no matter how bad it got with Corben, she would always stand by him and find a way to make their marriage work.

I kept waiting for the day when his hubris and self-indulgence finally pushed him into seeking out even more dramatic flair and he actually struck her. I wondered if even that would be enough to drive her away. I wondered if I would kick in his door and beat the hell out of him for it, and in a noble show of compassion I would let his unconscious body drop from my bloody hand before breaking his neck. I wondered if she would gaze on me with a new understanding then and fall into my arms and realize we were meant to be together. I often wondered why I wasn't already in long-term therapy.

They owned the top floor of the five-story building. They'd had a fleet of architects and construction crews come in and bang down walls and shore up doorways and put in flamboyant filigreed arches. In the end they were left with sixteen rooms. I'd been inside their place but never gotten a grand tour. I'd mostly stuck to the bathrooms and fixed the toilet when it broke. I imagined the library, the den, the sun room, the bedroom. I didn't know of sixteen different types of rooms. Was there a ballroom?...a music room?...a solarium? I had a passkey to all the apartments in Stark House, even theirs, but I'd somehow managed to resist the temptation to comb through their home.

The other four stories were inhabited by elderly, faded film and television stars, one-hit pop song wonders, and other forgotten former celebrities who'd become short-lived cultural icons for reasons ranging from the noble to the ludicrous. They were mostly shut-ins who every so often would skulk about the halls for reasons unknown or appear, momentarily, in their darkened doorways, maybe give a wave before retreating.

We had the guy who'd invented aluminum foil. We had a lady who'd given mouth-to-mouth to a former president's son after a pile-up on I-95 and saved his life. We had a performance artist/environmentalist who'd appeared on national television after soaking in a tub of toxic waste in front of the Museum of Modern Art twenty years ago. He was still alive even though there was only about 40 percent of him left after all the surgery. He rolled around the corridors with half a face, tumor-packed, sucking on an oxygen tube.

Corben shouted some more. It sounded like he said, "Radiant Face." It was the title of his first book. He was going through his bibliography again. I sat on the stairs and lit a cigarette. The old loves and hates heaved around in my chest. I looked around the lobby trying to figure out why I was doing this to myself. Why I was no smarter than him when it came to bucking fate.

Our story was as flatly clichéd and uninteresting as it was honest and full of bone and pain. To me, anyway. Corben and I had been childhood best friends. We'd gotten our asses kicked by neighborhood thugs and spent two nights in jail trying hard to act tough and be strong and not huddle too closely together. We nearly sobbed with relief the afternoon they let us out. We'd encouraged each other as neophyte novelists and helped one another to hone our craft. I'd taken thirty-seven stitches in bar fights for him, and he'd broken his left arm and gotten a concussion for me. We aced entrance exams to the same Ivy League university.

It was a righteous partnership that went south our junior year in college. We were both getting drunk a lot around then. It had something to do with an older woman, perhaps. I had the memory blocked, or maybe it just bored me too much too care anymore, but I couldn't recall the details. Perhaps she was mine and he took her away, or maybe she was his and wound up on my arm or in my bed. However it played out it released a killing flood of repressed jealousy and animosity from both of us and we didn't see each other again for thirteen years.

We settled in to write our novels. His career caught on with his second book, a thriller about a father chasing down the criminals who stole the donated heart on ice the guy needed for his son's transplant. I liked the book in spite of myself. When it sold to the movies it became a major hit that spawned several sequels. He ripped himself off with a similar novel that dealt with a mob hitman chasing a crippled girl who needed to get to the hospital within thirty-six hours to get the operation that might let her walk again. It aced the bestseller list for six months. Corben got a cameo in the movie version. He was the kindly doctor who sticks the little metal prod in the girl's foot and makes her big toe flinch.

My own books sold slowly and poorly. They received a generous amount of praise and critical comments, but not much fanfare. I brooded and got into stupid scrapes trying to prove myself beyond the page. I couldn't. Corben assailed me in every bookstore, every library, every time I checked the bestseller list. I wrote maudlin tales that sold to literary rags. I won awards and made no money. I took part-time jobs where I could find them. I delivered Chinese food. I taught English as a second language, I ran numbers for a local bookie until he got mopped up in a state-wide sting. I kept the novels coming but their advances and sales were pitiful.

There were women but none of them mattered much. I never fell in love. I wrote thrillers, I wrote mysteries featuring my heroic PI King Carver. I didn't copy Corben but I was surprised at how similar our tastes and capabilities were. I thought my shit blew away his shit.

Thirteen years went by like that, fast but without much action. I lucked into the job as a manager/handyman of Stark House. I lived in Apartment ½ A ½, a studio nearest the basement. So near it was actually *in* the fucking basement. It was the basement. I hadn't sold a novel in almost two years. I kept writing them and sending them to my agent. The rejection letters grew shorter and more tersely formal as time went on. I'd lost what little momentum I might've ever had. Eventually all the manuscripts came back and I stacked them on the floor of my closet hoping I might one day have the courage to burn them.

Maybe I had been waiting for Corben, or maybe he'd been waiting for me.

We used to walk past Stark House when we were kids and discuss the history of the building. It had always accommodated misfits of one sort or another. There were rumors about it a little more cryptic and wondrous than the rumors about every other building.

In the late nineteenth century it had been owned by a family of brilliant eccentrics who'd turned out scientists, senators, and more than a few madmen. A number of murders occurred on the premises. Local legends grew about the shadow men who served the politicians. They said the Stark family carried bad blood.

In the early twentieth century the place had been converted to apartments and became home to a famous opera singer, a celebrity husband and wife Broadway acting team, and a bootlegger who'd made a fortune from prohibition. They said there were secret walls. I searched but never found any. The place still called to life a certain glamour nearly lost through time. The wide staircase bisecting the lobby gave the impression of romantic leading men sweeping their lovers upstairs in a swirl of skirts, trains, and veils. The original chandelier still hung above as it had for over a hundred years and I waited for the day it tore from its supports and killed us all.

I knew Corben would eventually try to buy the building. I was lucky to have gotten in before him. Even his wealth couldn't purchase Stark House outright. When he and I finally met face to face again after all those years, neither one of us showed any surprise at all. We didn't exchange words. We shared similar blank, expressionless features. He must've mentioned something to his wife later on because I caught her staring at me on occasion, almost as if she had plenty of questions for me but didn't want to trespass on such a mystery-laden history.

It made perfect sense to me that I would fall in love with Gabriella Corben virtually the moment I met her.

Upstairs, Corben screamed, "Wild Under Heaven! Ancient Shadows!" I never quite understood what kind of point he was trying to make when he ran through his list of titles. Gabriella spoke sternly and more stuff got knocked over. I heard him sob. It gave me no pleasure hearing it. Finally a door slammed and another opened. The corners of the building echoed with the small sounds of the lurking outcast phantoms slinking in and out of shadow. The old-fashioned elevator buzzed and hummed, moving between the second and third floors. I heard footsteps coming down the stairs, and she was there.

I briefly glanced at Gabriella Corben and gave a noncommittal grin. She moved halfway down the staircase and sat in the middle of the carpeted step, her elbows on her knees, watching me. She wouldn't discuss their argument and wouldn't mention him at all. She never did.

My hidden unrequited love was a secret even from her. Or perhaps not. She was perceptive and understanding and probably knew my heart as well as she understood her husband's, which might've been entirely or might've been not at all. He and I still weren't that different. He was up there screaming out loud and I was down here braying inside.

I went about my business. I did my work. I waited for her to say what she wanted to say and I willed the muscles in my back not to twitch.

I knew what I would see if I dared to look over my shoulder. A woman of twenty-five, comfortable beneath the finish of her own calm, with glossy curling black hair draped loosely to frame her face. Lightly freckled from the summer sun, her eyes a rich hazel to offset the glowing brown of her skin. Her body slim but full, her presence assured. I caught a whiff of her perfume combined with the heady, earthy scent of her sweat beneath it. I must've looked like a maniac, polishing one foot of banister over and over, so damn afraid to turn around.

Where she went a kind of light traveled. She carried it with her. It lifted my heart and left me stunned. It was a feeling I wasn't accustomed to and for a long while I fought against it. I had learned to live with resentment instead of romance. It was my preferred state of being until she came along. Now I burned in silence.

She said, almost sleepily, "You ever wonder what it would be like if you could dig down through all the layers of polish, the paint and wax, peeling back the years, say going in a half-inch deep, to a different time, and see what life here might've been like back then?"

A half-inch deep. Probably eighty years. "I suspect you'd find a lot of the same."

"Really?"

"Life wasn't so different. Maybe you wouldn't trip over a guy who sat in toxic waste in front of the MOMA, but there'd be somebody comparable, I bet."

"What could be comparable to that?"

I shrugged. "A lunatic juggling hand grenades. A World War One vet used to panhandle out front here back in the twenties, and if he didn't make enough coin he'd chase people around with a bayonet. He spooked the neighbors on the other side of the street by flipping around one of those German hand grenades."

She waited but that was all I knew about it. Most tales about real people only had a modicum of interest to them, and no real ending. I didn't want to lose her attention and said, "There's always been plenty of crazy."

"I think you're right. How about the rest of it?"

"The rest of it?"

"Life. Lots of happiness? Beauty? Romance?"

"Sure. This lobby is so nice that there's been a lot of weddings performed right here, at the foot of the stairwell. The publicity shots were gorgeous. They'd have horse and carriages lined up out in the street, and after the ceremony the wedding party would hop in, ride over to Fifth Avenue and down past St. Patrick's Cathedral. If the families of the bride or groom had enough pull, they could get the cardinal's okay to have the church bells ring as the carriages went by."

"That must've been lovely."

Dorothy Parker and one of her lovers used to drunkenly chase each other through the halls of Stark House in the raw, but that didn't quite have the right kind of romance I was going for. "A couple of silent film stars met on the fifth floor back in the twenties. They split their time between Los Angeles and New York and lived next door to each other for a couple of years before ever meeting."

"Which apartments?"

By that she meant, *Which of my rooms?* "I don't know."

"Okay, go on."

"When they did run into each other here it was supposedly love at first sight. They got engaged a week later. The press went nuts with it. They made five movies together too."

"I think I heard about that. Didn't they commit suicide? Jumped off the roof?"

I was hoping to skip that part. Corben had told her more about the place than I thought he might. Or should've. Or maybe she'd been talking to some of the other tenants, though I couldn't figure out which of the shut-ins might actually chat with someone else.

"Yeah, when sound came in. They both sounded too Brooklyn, and no matter what they did they couldn't get rid of the accent."

"Death by Brooklyn," she said. "How sad." She put her hand on the banister and floated it down inch by inch until she'd almost reached the spot I was polishing. She tapped it with her nail. The length of her nail, a half-inch, eighty years. "I've heard there's been even more tragedy as well."

"Of course. Plenty of births, you get plenty of deaths."

"And not all of it by natural means certainly."

"Why do you want to hear about this stuff?" I asked. For the first time I looked directly at her, and as usual, the lust and the ache swept through me. She pulled a face which meant that Corben had been talking up the house history and she wanted a different viewpoint.

"Murder's pretty natural," I told her. "I don't know if that guy ever bayoneted anyone or if the hand grenade ever went off, but there's been a few grudges that ended with a knife or a handgun. One guy pushed his brother down the elevator shaft, and one of the scientists blew himself and his dog to hell mixing up some concoction."

"Scientists?"

"Some scientists used to live here."

"And their dogs."

"Well," I said, "yeah."

"Oh, I see." She chewed on that for a while. I moved up a couple steps, working the banister, easing a little closer. I could see her reflection in the shine. I fought down the primitive inside me trying to get out. Maybe I shouldn't have. Maybe she was just waiting for me to carry her down the stairs. But I didn't make the move.

Gabriella said, "Have you ever considered doing a book about it? The building?"

I didn't want to admit the truth, but she had a way of cooling the endless blazing rage inside me. My loud thoughts softened and quieted, even while I went slowly crazy with wanting her. "Yes, when I was a kid. I've always been intrigued by the building. There's always been a lot of talk, a lot of rumors."

"But you don't want to write one anymore?"

"No."

"Why not?"

It was a good question, and one I wasn't prepared to answer. It took me a while to say anything. "I have my own stories to share, I suppose. I don't need to tell this place's legends and lessons. And it doesn't need me to tell them anyway."

I turned and she smiled at me a little sadly.

I knew then exactly what Corben was doing and what was now ripping him up inside. The damn fool was trying to write a book about Stark House.

A minute later the front door was awash with a blur of black motion, and Gabriella and I wheeled and moved down the stairs together, as one, like I'd seen in a dozen classic films I could name.

Our bare arms touched and I tamped down the thrill that flared through me. She placed a hand on my wrist and my pulse snapped hard. It was odd and a bit unsettling to know that such small, commonplace human actions could still send me spiraling toward the edge. I hadn't realized I was quite so lonely until that moment.

And there it was, the first sighting of Ferdinand the Magnifico, looking dapper as hell in his old-world Victorian-era black suit, lace tie. And this too, our initial meeting with the monkey, Mojo, leashed to his master by a sleek length of golden chain, who hopped around doing a dance in his little jacket and cap while holding his cup out. This also wasn't exactly the grand romance I'd been hoping for, but I'd take whatever I could get.

"Halloo!" Ferdi shouted. Behind him scattered out on the sidewalk stood crates, boxes, and a small assortment of furniture. He must've hired some cheap uninsured movers who would only carry your belongings curb to curb.

Mojo jumped back and forth as far as his chain would allow. Gabriella smiled and said, "Are you certain you can bring an animal like that into this building?"

"Animal!" Ferdi cried. "This is no animal, madam! I assure you! This is my partner, Mojo, a gentle soul no different than you or I, with a heart filled with benevolence and an obligation only to make children laugh!"

She ignored the side of his trunk that stated in bold yellow letters FERDINAND THE MAGNIFICO, and asked, "And just who are you?"

"I am Ferdinand! And this is our new home! Today we move into Apartment 2C of the Stark Building!" He glanced at me, but, like all men, he couldn't keep his eyes off Gabriella for longer than that.

"Nice to meet you, Mr. Ferdinand."

"Just Ferdinand, madam! Are we neighbors? Say it is so!"

"Just Gabriella, Ferdinand," she said. "And it is so, we're neighbors. And this is Will."

"Well then, as you say!"

I bit back a groan. He was the kind of person who shouted everything with a joyous cry. If the decibel level didn't get you, the enthusiasm might. The monkey looked more like my kind of person. He grinned when you looked at him but otherwise just kind of held back, watching and waiting to see what might be coming his way. Printed on the monkey's little hat was the name Mojo. A button pinned to his fire-engine-red jacket read THE WORLD'S ONLY TALKING/WRITING CHIMP. There was a pad with a pen attached by a string in a small bag around his neck.

Mojo pressed his tin cup out to Gabriella. He was insistent. She gestured that she had no cash on her and I pulled a quarter out of my pocket and snapped it off my thumbnail into his cup. I expected him to say thank you, seeing as he was a talking monkey, but Mojo only hopped twice, squeaked, took off his hat and bowed.

"If he talks, why does he have a pad and pen?" she asked.

"He prefers to write!"

"I see," she said. She shot me a look. "Just like Will."

A reference to me, not to her bestselling author husband. It took me back a step. Of course, she was also likening me to a chimp, so maybe it wasn't quite the compliment I had wanted it to be.

"Well hello, Mojo," she said, "how are you today?"

Mojo went, "Ook."

Ferdi lifted his arms and clapped happily. "You see! He says he is fine!"

Gabriella laughed pleasantly and tried again. "It will be very nice having you in the building, Mojo, I hope we'll become great friends."

Mojo did a dance, held out his tin cup, and went, "Ook ook."

Ferdi said, "Bravo, Mojo! As all can clearly hear, you have told them you are delighted to be a new neighbor to such gracious and wonderful people!"

"Why doesn't he write us a note instead?" I said.

"I'm sure he soon shall! But at the moment he is enjoying this conversation so much, he has no need to give letters!"

Gabriella gave me the look again and this time I returned it. We were compatriots, we were sharing a moment. She was laughing and I was smiling. That was good enough. I drew another quarter out of my pocket and tossed it into the monkey's cup. If nothing else, he was a smart chimp. He'd already taken me for half a buck.

"Are you with the circus?" I asked.

"No, nor any carnival! We are our own pair, a team! We have toured Central Europe, throughout Asia, New Zealand, and South Dakota! And now, we arrive here!"

"I'll help with your belongings," I said.

"Wonderful!"

Gabriella swept out past us heading for the door, and the overwhelming urge to touch her rose up in me and made me reach for her, maybe to grab her elbow and turn her to face me, so that I might finally find the courage to say something real and true to her, about myself or about Corben, or perhaps about nothing at all. Just a chance to spend more time with her, even if it was only a few more minutes. When you got down to it I was as needy as Corben, and maybe even worse.

But my natural restraint slowed me down too much, and even before I managed to lift my hand she was already out of reach.

My last image of her:

A gust of wind whirling her hair into a savage storm about her head while she eased out the front door silhouetted in the morning sun, her skirt snapping back at me once as if demanding my attention, a curious expression of concern or perhaps dismay on her face—perhaps the subtle aftereffect of her argument with Corben, or maybe even considering me, for the first time, as a potential lover—moving across the street against traffic. A taxi obscured her, the door finished closing, the chimp chittered, and my secret love was gone.

I thought Ferdi and Mojo might have some friends or fans from New Zealand to help them move in, but they had no one but me. Luckily, they didn't have that much stuff. Mojo really did have monkey bars, a collapsible cage that when put together took up an entire room of the three-bedroom apartment. It was probably my duty to call the landlord and squeal on them. No pets were allowed, much less restricted exotic animals, but I liked the action they brought with them, the energy. Let somebody else rat them out.

We carried everything up the stairs rather than futzing with the tight elevator. It took less than two hours for Ferdi and me to get everything inside and set up.

Ferdi handed me twenty dollars as a tip, but the monkey danced so desperately and kept jabbing his cup at me with such ferocity that I finally gave him the crumpled bill. Ferdi had a real racket going, and I wondered if I could talk him into being my new agent. I could just see him giving hell to my editors, the monkey using his little pen to scribble out clauses on bad contracts. Ferdi asked me to stay and share a bottle of wine with him, but I had a story I wanted to finish.

When I got back to my place I sat at my desk staring at the screen at some half-composed paragraphs that made virtually no sense to me. Being with Gabriella had inspired me, but now the words ran together into phrases that held no real resolve. I didn't know my own themes anymore.

I sat back and stared up at the shafts of light stabbing down across my study, feeling the weight of the entire building above me—all the living and the dead, the bricks and mortar of history growing heavier every year. A hundred and forty years' worth of heritage and legacy, chronicles and sagas. Soon they might crush me out of existence. Maybe I was even in the mood for it.

I had a stack of unopened mail on my bed. I tore into an envelope containing a royalty check for $21.34. I started to crumple it in my fist, but I needed the money. I decided that no matter how Mojo might push me, I wasn't going to give it to him. I picked up an unfinished chapter of my latest novel and the words offended me. I tossed the pages across the room and watched them dive-bomb against the far wall. There wasn't even enough air in here for them to float on a draft. I wondered if Corben was still up there howling. I wondered if Gabriella had returned to him yet or if she was out in the city enjoying herself, taking in enough of the living world for both of them. For all three of us. The claustrophobia started to get to me and I decided to go walk the building.

I hadn't gotten twenty paces from my apartment door when I spotted a man laid out on the tiled floor of the lobby—a shallow red halo inching outward—with an icepick in his forehead that vibrated with every breath he took.

I'd never seen him in the light of day, but I thought it was the guy who'd invented aluminum foil. I couldn't believe he was still alive. Blood and clear fluids lapped from his ears. A wave of vertigo rippled through me and I bit down on my tongue and it passed. I bent to him and had no idea what to do. He was finished, he had to be finished because there was three inches of metal burrowed into his brain, but he was wide-eyed and still staring at me with great interest. He licked his lips and tried to move his hands.

"Jesus holy Christ...." I whispered. I didn't have a cell phone. I started to turn and run for my apartment when he called my name.

"Will."

It was astonishing he could actually see. Death was already clouding his eyes and gusting through his chest. His voice had been thickened by it. It was a sound I'd heard several times before. He sounded exactly like my father when the old man had about three minutes left to go. There was no point in leaving him now. I kneeled at his side. "I'm here."

"I lied," he said.

"About what?"

"I didn't invent aluminum foil. Aluminum foil was first introduced into the industry as an insulating material. It later found diverse applications in a variety of fields."

"What?"

"It can be used instead of lead and tinfoil in other specified applications. The aluminum foil thickness ranges from 0.0043 millimeters to 0.127 millimeters. It comes with a bright or dull finish and also with embossed patterns—"

"Shhh."

"Foils are available in thirty-three distinct colors. In 1910, when the first aluminum foil rolling plant was opened in Kreuzlingen, Switzerland. The plant, owned by J. G. Neher & Sons, stood at the foot of the Rhine Falls and captured the falls' energy. Neher's sons together with Dr. Lauber—oh, Dr. Lauber! Dr. Lauber!—discovered the endless rolling process and the use of aluminum foil as a protective barrier."

The icepick had ripped through his memories. Even if he hadn't invented aluminum foil, he sure knew a hell of a lot about it. I couldn't quite figure why his head was full of all this, but it was probably no worse than thinking about stealing Dutch Master prints and heading to Aruba. I wondered what I would be spouting on about in my last minute if someone stuck a blade into my brain.

I should've offered up some kind of soothing words to send him on his way, but he looked animated and eager to chat despite the fact that his brains were leaking out of his ears and tear ducts. I should've asked him who had done this to him. Instead I said, "Why the hell would you lie about a thing like that?"

"I wanted to meet girls. Forgive me!"

In the hierarchy of sins I thought that lying about inventing aluminum foil in order to meet chicks—which in itself wasn't particularly immoral—just didn't rate very high on the damnation scale. I figured if a priest had been handy, he would've given dispensation without much of a problem.

"You're forgiven," I said. "Who did this to you?"

"Dr. Lauber! Dr. Lauber!"

"Tell me who—"

"God, the things I've done. I once struck my mother. I ran over a dog, someone's pet. I broke the hearts of my own children. I hurt a woman, she bled. I shall surely go to hell. Please, Dr. Lauber!"

"Shhh."

"Dr. Lauber!"

"Close your eyes."

He finally did and died that instant.

The cops questioned me full-tilt boogie. They came around in three teams of two. I got the officer friendlys, the hair-trigger hardcase growlers, and the plaintive guys who just sort of whined at me and wanted me to admit to murder. I told them his last words and they thought maybe he had ratted out the almighty and vengeful aluminum foil powers that be. They quizzed each other about the name Dr. Lauber. They all said it sounded familiar, maybe a hitman working for the syndicate. Maybe a plastic surgeon who'd gone out of his tree. I suspected that if anybody Googled the name they'd find him to be the man who'd discovered the endless rolling process with the sons of J. G. Neher.

The whiners took me down to the station and put me in a holding room with a big mirror, where I stared at myself and whoever was behind it and started to re-evaluate the cops in my novels. I'd been trying way too hard. I'd been breaking my ass creating brilliant detectives who solved crimes with the sparsest clues. But these guys were never going to figure out who'd killed the aluminum foil liar, not unless somebody confessed out of hand just to stop all the bitching.

Eventually they cut me loose and I wandered the streets. I was the guy who had to clean up all the blood off the lobby floor back at Stark House. I didn't want to go back yet. I'd seen death before but not murder. I'd written about it and I recognized how far off I'd been from what it really felt like to be in the presence of homicide.

A certain sense of guilt lashed me as I thought about how close I'd come to walking in on the man being attacked. Maybe two minutes, maybe less. Perhaps I could've prevented it. If only I'd moved a little faster. If only I'd run out into the street to see what could be seen. Maybe I would've spotted a killer rushing away or hailing a cab.

I stopped into a bookstore and bought Corben's latest novel. His dedication read: *To all those who love the mysteries of life and death as much as I do.* It was followed by *And to my wife.*

Not even her name, her lovely name. The bastard pasted her in there as an afterthought. How could she read that and not be appalled? How could he expect her not to be upset? I didn't understand it and knew I never would.

I read the first ten pages leaning against the window of a nearby bodega, and read another twenty walking back to Stark House. I sat outside on the front steps for a half-hour and let the paragraphs slide by under my gaze. I didn't know what the hell I was reading. I was too full of my own anger and past to even see the words. I flipped the pages by rote. I looked at the dedication again and tried to see the substance and meaning behind it. Corben didn't love the mysteries of life. I wasn't sure he loved anything at all. I left the book there and went inside.

The cops had put up little orange cones around the murder scene, with yellow tape cordoning off the area. The tape didn't say "POLICE LINE, DO NOT CROSS" so I tore it down and got my mop, gloves, scouring pads, and sanitizers out of the closet. It took me two hours to do an even halfway decent job of it. I had thought it would take longer. There was still a bad stain. I kept having to stop when my hands started to shake. I didn't know if it was because of all the blood or because I'd been so wrapped up in my own problems that I hadn't seen someone else's desperate loneliness. I'd thought I had it bad, but Jesus, dying with the dry facts of aluminum foil on your lips because you wanted to get laid, it was a whole other level of heartbreak.

Ferdinand the Magnifico and Mojo put on little shows for the neighborhood kids in the garden behind the building. It wasn't much of a garden, but by East Side standards it was practically the Congo. The monkey grunted with certain inflections and Ferdi appeared to honestly believe Mojo was chattering like he was playing bridge with the Ladies Auxiliary Club. Mojo went "ook" and Ferdi, with childish glee, raised his arms out and said, "You see there, clear as the chimes of St. Patrick's! He said, 'I love you.' You heard it yourself! Did you not?" The kids said that they could. They giggled and clapped and tossed pennies and nickels. They chased the chimp and then ran away when the chimp chased them. It brightened the place up.

I didn't quite get how Ferdi made enough to pay Manhattan rent while nickel-and-diming it, but maybe he had tours booked. He could've really cleaned up in South Dakota. It seemed possible. For all I knew Mojo'd sold out Fourth of July at Madison Square Garden.

I'd used three different bleaches and detergents doing additional clean-up work over the course of a week but still hadn't managed to get all the blood out of the tile in the lobby. It had become ingrained, as deep as the aluminum foil liar's guilt.

Something had happened to me that day. My usual brooding and pathos took a left turn into a darker, calmer sea of purpose. I had the increasingly powerful feeling that my life held a greater intent and meaning now, though I didn't know what the hell it might be. I watched the front door. I waited for more murder. I could feel it hovering nearby in every hall. I thought about all the lies I had told to get laid, and wondered if they'd come back to haunt me in the end. What would be my last words? And would they sound dreadfully strange to whoever might be there holding my hand?

The media caught wind that Corben lived in the building and the camera crews started floating around. He showed up on television and made up stories about how close he'd been with the aluminum foil guy. He claimed to have a theory about the killer and said he was working closely with the NYPD to solve the case. They asked if he was afraid of potential retribution. He claimed to own a derringer that he always kept on his person. A lovely reporter asked if he had it on him at the moment. He dared her to frisk him. I watched his last couple of novels bullet up the bestseller lists.

My agent kept calling trying to get me to ride his coattails, or more appropriately the murderer's coattails. He said I should be doing whatever I could to get my last few titles out to the reporters. I should carry my novels around with me, stick them in front of the cameras. I asked him if he knew how stupid that might make me feel. He asked me if I knew how stupid he felt representing an author who still couldn't garner more than a five-grand chump-change advance after publishing a dozen books. It put things into perspective but I still didn't go around clotheslining the reporters and shoving my novels under their noses. My agent quit calling.

My sleep filled with mad laughter and shouting. Some of it was my own. I occasionally startled myself awake making noises. I started smoking more. I wrote more and deleted more. I painted the foyer and caught up on all the minor fix-it stuff that I'd let slide the last several days. I got a closer look at some of my neighbors.

I finally met the lady who had an affair with a famous televangelist's wife and was now something of a lesbian icon. She mildly flirted with me and prompted me to tell her how pretty she was. She seemed insecure and irritable. She told me she wasn't a lesbian at all but had just been fooling around with the wife for the fun of it, but she couldn't admit it in public anymore because of all the money she was making lecturing to various lesbian organizations. She had the televangelist's show playing on a high-definition TV screen with the surround sound turned way up. He seemed to be preaching from every corner of the apartment. It was spooky. I fixed her broken toilet handle and blew out of there.

The toxic waste guy said the old-fashioned elevator didn't accommodate his wheelchair. He was right. The chair was old and wide and well-lived in. He'd been in the building the entire time I'd been there. He was proud of his tumors and tried to show them to me as often as he could, turning his melted, half-eaten face this way and that so it would catch the light from the corridor lamps. He was so pale I could see the blood pulsing underneath his skin. I wondered how long it had been since he'd been outside in the sun. I removed one of the side rails in the elevator and it was a tight fit but his chair squeezed in. We tested it together. His oxygen tube hissed into the hole that used to be his nose. The tank clanked loudly whenever the chair went over a bump. I could just imagine it breaching and the explosion taking out the whole floor. He said thank you and rolled back to his apartment and shut the door.

The former child actor turned gay porno star turned sex therapist daytime talk show host canceled after three months now retired after writing his autobiography wherein he named names, was sued, countersued, and won big cash off a couple of closeted politicians outed and forced to resign needed a couple of his electrical outlets rewired. He interviewed me like I was a guest on his show, asking me a lot of pointed questions about the murder. He wanted to know how finding a corpse had transformed me. I told him I hadn't found a corpse, that the man was still alive when I got there. He wanted to know how I'd been transformed by the discovery of a dying man with an icepick in his forebrain. He wanted to know what I heard, what I smelled, if there had been any aftertaste to the incident. He licked his lips when he said it. He kept looking to one side like he saw an audience there staring at him. I knew he was working on more of his memoirs. When he got to this chapter he'd say that he'd found the aluminum foil liar and the dying man had spoken profound and wondrous lessons of good will.

A couple more days drifted past. I felt eyes on me and found myself constantly looking over my shoulder and checking down the ends of dark hallways. Muffled voices followed me but that was nothing new, muffled voices follow everybody in old apartment houses.

Except I kept hearing my name, or thought I did. For some reason, it made my scalp tighten.

The morning came when I awoke to a knocking—twin knockings—on my basement door. I figured it was the cops doing a follow-up, but instead there was Ferdinand with Mojo, both of them grinning. They were each holding a bunch of paperbacks.

"You are the wonderful writer called Will Darrow!"

"I'm Will Darrow anyway," I told him.

"But why, why did you not let me know this the very day we were introduced? I await the next emergence of your tough guy character, stories of the brutal but heroic King Carver!"

That took me back hard. Mojo pulled on his chain and tugged Ferdi into my apartment. They may have been the first guests I'd ever had inside the place. I said, "You've read my books?"

"Yes, all of them! Will you please sign, yes?"

Mojo extended a novel out to me. It had a cover I'd never seen before, printed in a language I didn't know. Portuguese, maybe? Neither my agent nor my publisher had ever mentioned selling those sub-rights. Or any. My breath caught in my chest and I tried not to think about how much money folks might be skimming. The monkey wouldn't let go of the book. Ferdinand said, "Mojo, give! For signing! He will return it to you!"

A couple of the other books were in the same language, and two more were in a different one. Maybe Swedish. Danish? I had no idea. The rage climbed the back of my neck but there was also a strange sense of pride coming through, knowing people in other countries were reading my work. My hands were icy. I couldn't remember how to spell my name and just scribbled wavy lines inside the books.

"I ask now when shall I be able to tell my friends a new King Carver adventure shall soon be theirs?"

I didn't know what to say. My agent had sent all my recent manuscripts back. I tried to keep faith. "I don't know, Ferdi. But I'll let you know as soon as I finish a new one, all right?"

"That will be stupendous! Will it not, Mojo?"

Mojo went, "Ook."

"You hear, he says—"

"Uh huh."

"—he shall effort to have patience but he excitedly waits for more King Carver!"

"Uh huh."

"Tell me now, how is Miss Gabriella?"

It was the first time I was aware that I hadn't seen her since that day he'd moved in two weeks earlier. A minor twinge of alarm sang through me. "I don't know, Ferdi, it's been a while."

"If you see her, please say that I have inquired about her health!"

"I'll do that."

I handed him the signed books back and Mojo got mad and started hopping and banging his fists against his knees until Ferdi gave him one of the titles. Mojo immediately quieted, opened the book, and his mouth started moving, as if he really could read.

The cops eventually came around again. All three teams, about two hours apart from one another. The nice guys weren't so nice this time. The hardasses not as hard. The whiners still tried to plead with me to tell the truth and come clean about croaking the old man with an icepick. I stuck firm to my story. Nobody hit me with a phone book or a rubber hose. No one asked any new questions or seemed to have any other leads besides me. I started to get a clue as to why there were so many television shows about unsolved crimes. They asked if Dr. Lauber had shown up yet, if I'd seen some guy with a stethoscope and a doctor's bag creeping around the building. Maybe doing illegal abortions in the neighborhood. I blinked and reminded them that abortions weren't illegal. They discussed this amongst themselves for a bit. They invited my opinion but I chose to stay out of it. I stared at them and they stared at me.

I waited to catch sight of Gabriella. I did everything I could do in order to hang around the fifth floor. Fixing hall lights, bracing the handrails, polishing the footboards and wainscoting, polishing the floors. I put an ear to Corben's door and listened for their voices. I heard nothing. There were no more arguments. He'd quit calling out his bibliography. For all I knew they were vacationing in Monaco.

It's sometimes a curse to have an imagination that can draw up detailed visuals. I thought of them entwined after having just made love, now feeding each other wine and caviar. I hated caviar the one time I tried it, but when I thought of romance that's what came to mind. The window open and a cold breeze pressing back the curtains. Moonlight casting silver across the dark. The sheets clean but rumpled. Her crossing the room with a hint of sweat carried in the niche at the small of her back, slowly dripping over the curve of her *derriere*. When I thought of romance I thought there ought to be some French thrown in there too. The bright flare of the refrigerator opening, her body silhouetted the way it had been the last time I'd seen her. The refrigerator door shutting, night vision lost. Total darkness for a moment and then the pressure of her body easing back into bed.

You didn't need a lover to drive you to the rim, you could do it all on your own.

I wore myself down hoping to escape my dreams. I slept heavily but not well. I wrote a lot but not well. I dropped off with my head against the spacebar.

One morning, I found a note slid under my door.

It went six pad-size pages. It stated, in plainly printed block letters much clearer than my own handwriting:

A man made of aluminum foil stepped from my closet and confessed his sins. They were plentiful. His hands are red from a woman's blood. He is terrified because he has not yet met God, and fears he never will, and that God—if He ever existed—exists no more. Dr. Lauber, he said, commands his soul. The Rhine floods across the planets. This is not the afterlife he was hoping for. At the end of our days we all fully expect to meet the creator, and, for good or ill, for Him to speak with us, even if only to judge harshly, perhaps with divine hate. An afterlife without God is one without parameters, without celestial design. Dr. Lauber, the aluminum foil man said, owns us all, though some of us continue to act as if there is such an abstraction as free will. I have come to this belief myself—that none of us are free—some time ago as well. It frightens me, it all chills me so. What say you?

The note was signed: **MOJO**.

You couldn't be better off dead. You were already a phantom in this city. The world spun by filled with the vacuous and the caustic and the fearful. They hunched down inside their coats and disappeared before you really knew they were there. They muttered to themselves and turned away from bright lights and loud noises. I'd raised my voice only once on the street in the past month, and that was hailing a cab. Sometimes I wondered if I'd even know it when my heart quit beating.

The 1976 one-hit-wonder lady who sang "Sister to the Swamp" knocked on my apartment door and asked if I'd repair the broken shower head in her bathroom. She still had an enormous afro and wore the kind of silky, streaming dress that she'd worn on *Soul Train* during the disco years. I got my toolbox and followed her upstairs. She had the gold record mounted on the wall near the window so that the sunlight would send a molten yellow across the room. Everywhere I looked were photos of her with politicians, sports legends, and other musicians popular at the time.

When she spoke I heard very little beside the lyrics to "Sister to the Swamp." The heavy bass rhythm of the song pumped through my head. I got into the tub and worked the shower head until I got it fixed. When I finished, the 1976 one-hit-wonder lady was at the window staring at the rush of foot traffic on the sidewalks below. She held one hand up to the glass like she was trying to find her way through without breaking it. She wanted to go outside. She wanted to sing for the people. I'd seen that haunted need in her eyes and the eyes of the other shut-ins for a couple of years now. I wanted to ask her why she didn't just step outside and do her thing. But even I knew it was impossible. Time had moved on without her and she wouldn't be able to get back up to speed. Her photos and her gold record and the lyrics to her one song were all she had left now. She'd chosen that path and it would have to be enough for her. She said nothing more to me and I grabbed my toolbox and got out of there, back into the world. It felt very much the same on one side of the door as the other.

I got downstairs into my place and sat in front of the computer screen willing the words to come. They wouldn't. Every time I thought of King Carver in Danish a flutter of nausea worked through my guts.

I shut my eyes. I let my fingers move across the keypad on their own. I started typing. Corben and I used to clown around with automatic writing back in college. I did it every now and again when I wanted to clear my mind. I forced my focus to some far corner of my brain and left it there. The typing grew louder.

My hands pounded away. I wondered who the hell was writing Mojo letters to me and why. There had been a craftiness to the note, a kind of witty petulance. It seemed a direct insult to the aluminum foil guy. Someone had done his online research on Dr. Lauber. But to what end? And why send it my way? And why pose as the monkey? A thin shard of fear scraped inside me and my hands seized for a moment. What if the note had come from the icepick killer? Who even used an icepick anymore *except* for killers? This was the fucking age of refrigerator door ice cube makers, baby. Sweat broke across my upper lip. What if the note had really come from Mojo? The paper was the size of the sheets on the chimp's little pad. Why hadn't I seen Gabriella in over a week? My focus snapped back into the keyboard and I felt my fingers type her name. *Gabriella.*

What kind of a damn fool dedicates a book as a codicil to his wife, and does so by simply calling her *My wife?* My thoughts twisted to Corben's book on Stark House. What had he learned about this place that I should know? How far along was he? Who would he dedicate this one to? What if the chimp were dancing up behind me right now with an awl in his little monkey fist?

I opened my eyes and turned around. I was alone. My face dripped sweat. I checked the clock. I'd written for twenty minutes. I scanned the computer screen. Much of it was gibberish with a few random whole sentences found in the muck. I spotted *Death to King Carver* in there among a kind of repetitive bitter ranting about lack of royalties and stolen foreign translations. I'd fallen back into some of the same old traps. It was bound to happen. A few maudlin phrases cropped up. I wrote *Come get me, fucker* and had a partially completed scene of a disemboweling. A filleting blade eased through flesh. There were slithering intestines and someone trying to hold together his fish-white belly with his fingers. I was getting the feeling that my mental state might currently be a bit skewed. *Where has he hidden my love?* Deep among the mire stood out *She speaks.*

It took some of the edge off but not nearly enough. I deleted the file and stared at the blank monitor willing some kind of answers that refused to appear. It didn't matter much. I didn't even know what questions I was asking. I wasn't even sure I wanted to try writing another novel. There didn't seem to be much point anymore. I wasn't as wrecked about not giving a damn as I thought I would be.

I picked up the Mojo note and read it again. I wondered if a man made of aluminum foil might be preparing to step from my closet as well. Why should Dr. Lauber command anybody's soul?

I hadn't talked to Corben on any kind of a significant level in fifteen years. If we passed each other in the halls we would nod and do no more. I had the phone numbers of everyone in the building. I grabbed the phone and called the apartment. I hoped Gabriella would answer. My back teeth hurt because I was clenching my jaws so tightly. Like a love-struck teenager, I thought I might hang up the moment she answered. The phone rang ten times, twelve, thirteen times. Maybe they really were in Monaco.

I hung up and then gave it another dozen rings.

Finally Corben picked up, and with an exasperated growl said, "Who is this?"

"I'm coming up," I told him.

I tossed the phone down and moved out the door on a near-run.

I got to his apartment and we both took an extra moment for what was coming. I stood on one side listening at the door, and I knew he was standing on the other side, his eye to the peephole. We both waited. I had no idea what we were waiting for. I started forward and before I could knock he flung the door open so hard I heard the doorstop snap.

His face, once bordering handsome, had grown into a collision of sharp edges. His high cheekbones were barely covered with flesh. He looked like he'd been ill for days. His jaw line angled back severe as a hatchet. I hadn't seen him for several weeks and I could tell he hadn't been eating. His eyes were feverish, planted too deeply in his head, and he didn't seem able to completely close his mouth. His upper canines prodded his lower lip. I could smell the sourness of his breath beneath the mint mouthwash. His rapid breathing rustled loudly from him.

A lot of the old pain and jealousy sped through my blood. My pulse stormed along. I could feel the veins in my wrists clattering. I wondered if I was as ugly to him as he was to me.

"Where's Gabriella?" I asked.

The question hit him like a rabbit punch. I don't know what he'd been expecting but it sure wasn't that. His face folded into nine variations of anger, indignity, and confusion before it settled into outright surprise. It suited him just swell.

He couldn't come up with anything better than "What?" and he hated himself for it. He got grounded again and the peevish tone thrummed into his voice once more. "Who are you to ask that?"

"Who the hell would I have to be? Where is she?"

"She's not here."

"That doesn't answer my damn question. Where is she?"

His resentful front began to fall apart even faster. He couldn't maintain his outrage. I watched it crack to pieces and the sight startled me. We were getting down deep where the nerve clusters were always on fire for one reason or another. The venom began to seep from me but I held onto that desperate need to see her. He detected it in me and almost took a kind of pity as he said, "She's gone."

"What?"

"It's true."

I took a lunging step toward him and caught hold of myself in time. I looked over his shoulder and hoped he was lying, but I couldn't feel her presence in the slightest. I couldn't smell her perfume, I got no sense of her at all.

"Gone where?"

"I don't know, Will."

The way he said my name tightened my chest. It was almost a whimper, an appeal to friendship. The sound of his own voice angered him and I watched his thin face harden further, his shoulders straightening. I took another step until we were toe to toe. "What the hell are you saying?"

"She hasn't been home since the day the old man was killed in the lobby."

"That was over two weeks ago!"

He steeled himself. "Yes."

"Have you called the police? Filed a missing persons report?"

"No."

"Why not?"

He didn't answer. His eyes softened and he dropped his gaze. He fell back a few steps like he was aiming his ass for the rich leather wraparound sofa I saw in his living room, but he began to stumble. I actually had to reach out and grab his arm to keep him from going over. I shook him hard once but he still looked dazed. The cops should've been called in long before this, but I didn't push the point because I'd lost just about all my confidence in the police anyway.

Corben said, "I can't speak to you now."

"You damn well better."

"I can't. Later. Why don't you come up tonight for a drink? It's been a while since we've talked." He slowly closed the door in my face. I had no idea how I'd gotten out into the hall.

I had three cards from the three teams of cops. I picked up the one from the whiners and started to phone them, but before I tapped out all seven numbers I hung up. I was already a second-rate suspect in a cooling murder case. How smooth would it go down with the police if I called them about Gabriella? They'd question Corben and he was a New York celebrity, a personal friend of the mayor and the governor. He'd slick it over if he wanted, and they'd just have even more reason to presume me guilty of something. I couldn't waste the time. I had to find her. I had to make him crack. I felt it was something I had to do. Something only I could do. Audacity is sometimes its own reward.

Leave it to Corben to call a decade and a half "a while." I decided to play along.

A few hours later we sat in his living room drinking bourbon. From the stink of his breath I could tell he'd been at it for a while before I got there. We skipped fifteen years and anything of substance. I wanted to let my gaze roam his apartment. I'd been in the place many times before. Whenever a toilet clogged. Whenever the garbage disposal backed up. I'd cleaned up Corben's shit for two years, but I'd never been a guest and I'd never spent a minute taking in the personality of his apartment. I wanted to look at the photos with him and movie stars, on the sets of his films. I wanted to get up and hold all his rare nineteenth-century first editions. There were many paintings, mostly small originals done by artists who resided in the world's greatest museums. His tastes were similar to mine and I knew I would find many wondrous, beautiful, awe-inspiring aspects to his home.

But I simply sat and looked at him and waited.

He started off with trivial matters. We discussed our latest works—I mentioned the last manuscript I'd finished and made enough misleading comments for him to think it was still under consideration at my publisher. This one was a grand family drama delving into such an assortment of relationships and secrets and personal mysteries that I had no idea what the hell the story was about. He mentioned his latest bestseller, the one I'd bought and left on the front stoop. He didn't talk about the Stark House book.

He was splitting his attention between our conversation and writing in his head at the same time. He was letting his mind wander the building. The slightest noise made him snap his chin aside. The muscles in his legs jumped. He was trying to kill his interest with booze. He wouldn't be able to stand it much longer.

I started in where I'd left off earlier. "Why didn't you call the police?" I asked.

"We had argued that morning—"

"I know. I heard you."

It did something to him. It got down beneath the layers of his created persona and dragged up his real self. I got a view of my old pal again, the kid he was back in the day before we blew our friendship. He was just a scared boy, alone without his mothering wife to lead him safely through the extent of his own life. He'd been coddled for so long that he'd lost any kind of veneer. His hardshell had cracked badly over the years of his success, and it had let in all his insecurities and reservations and doubts. No wonder he screamed out his titles when he was losing a fight. He couldn't apologize and he couldn't debate. It was all he could defend himself with.

It's sometimes a curse to have an imagination that can draw up detailed visuals, and when you got down to it, he was better at it than me. He had a worse affliction to bear.

"Why are you writing about this building?" I asked.

He reared in his seat but the bravado wasn't there anymore. "She told you that?"

"Not outright. We were talking that day and I got a hint of what you were doing. So why are you doing it?"

He poured himself more bourbon. His hands trembled badly but not out of fear. At least not merely out of fear. Gabriella had been his buffer between him and the rest of the world, and without her he was being rubbed raw. "You know why."

"No, I don't."

"You do!" He sank back into his seat, all knife edges and points. If he moved too quickly he'd slash open a cushion. He frowned and his eyes were already so deep in his skull that they nearly disappeared altogether. He studied me, unsure of just how far to go. Finally his voice leaked words. They fell from his lips so softly I missed them.

"What?"

He said, "You've seen those who share the house with us."

"Seen who?"

"Those who stalk these halls."

"The toxic waste guy bothering you?"

He lashed out and sent a vase sailing across the room where it crashed against the far wall. "You know of whom I speak!"

When his speech patterns grew more gentrified I knew he must be really upset. I tried not to let it get too good to me, but it did. I felt a warmth bloom in my guts. Corben was actually nervous, but not about losing his wife. He'd had dinner at the White House and given signings and speeches to crowds numbering in the thousands, but right here in his own living room he sat trembling before something he couldn't even name.

"What congress have you had with them?" he asked.

I couldn't help it. I burst out laughing. I hadn't laughed in so long that once I got rolling I had a difficult time stopping. Maybe if I'd had more recent congress it wouldn't have been so funny. Corben stared at me in shock. It got me going even harder. Then I thought of Gabriella and the noise died in my throat.

"I came to talk about Gabriella, not any of your nonsense."

"It's not nonsense and you know it!" He reached for something else to throw but there was nothing handy so he hurled his glass. It bounced off the sofa and landed right side up on the floor without breaking. "We heard the stories about this place when we were children."

"We heard stories about every building in the city. The only reason you're so scared of this one is because you live here now. If you were over in Trump Tower you'd be acting the same way."

He shot to his feet, grabbed another glass, poured more bourbon and splashed some on the floor. He hadn't been able to hold his liquor in college and wasn't doing any better now. His voice was already losing its sharpness. "You mock me."

"I ought to mock you just for saying 'you mock me,' asshole. People really let you get away with talking like that?"

He ignored me. He'd started to slip away. "I can't rest. They don't let me sleep. They work their way into the pages and ruin whatever I'm writing. Isn't it the same way with you? Tell the truth. How can you find clarity with all the noise? All the tension and weight of their bearing and closeness."

Even if I had the pity to spare I wouldn't throw any his way. "You've got a beachhouse out in Southampton, a mansion in Beverly Hills, and a villa in Italy, right? So why don't you leave and go spend some time someplace else? Take a trip right after you tell me where your wife is."

"I can't leave, Will. I'm not sure I can ever leave here again. Stark House won't let me go."

"What happened to Gabriella?"

He dropped back into his chair and sat there blankly, withdrawing further into himself, gulping his drink. The ice rattled loudly. He snorted like a pig. A part of me wanted to beat the hell out of him and force him to talk, but I knew it wouldn't do any good. I wasn't going to get any answers from him. He was willing himself to shut down.

"Lay off the sauce," I told him. "I want you clear-headed. I've got more questions and you're going to answer them. We'll talk again soon."

"What was her name?" he asked.

"Who?"

"The one you took away from me in college. Mary? Maggie? Melanie?"

"I don't remember."

"She visits me too," he said. "She's dead but she asks about you. She doesn't remember your name either."

The next afternoon, on the second floor, I saw a young handsome man and a beautifully delicate woman walking up the corridor, holding hands. I'd never seen them before. He was in a tux and tails, and she wore a lace dress that looked straight out of the twenties. They came toward me and the hair on the back of my neck rose. A warm, comforting draft swept across my throat. They both smiled and nodded to me. I couldn't quite get my lips to work but I managed to nod back. I wanted to ask if they'd seen Gabriella but the words wouldn't form. They went to the stairway and began to move down it. I held myself in check for about three seconds and then started after them. I knew what I would see by the time I got there. No one would be on the staircase.

I was wrong. They were still slowly proceeding down it. They murmured back and forth. He said something and she tittered mellifluously. It was a warm and enduring sound. They walked across the lobby floor and out the front door onto the street. Something touched my ankle and I nearly yelped.

Mojo stood at my foot and said, "Ook." The chain that had connected him to Ferdi was gone. He held a piece of paper up to me. I took it.

It was blank.

He chittered and grinned and shoved his cup out against my shin. I tossed him a quarter and he danced back to Apartment 2C.

I went downstairs and stood out on the stoop listening to the world chase itself. Four rapes and two murders had happened in a five-block radius of the building in the last month. There were plenty of suspects but no leads.

I should be looking for Gabriella. I should be beating the piss out of Corben. But I went back to the screen and forced out more sentences. What I wasn't making up I was dredging up. I called up my most shameful moments and laid them on my characters. They all loved Gabriella, they all wanted to smash her husband. I made apologies too late. It was a third-rate redemption at best. I waited for a man made of aluminum foil to climb out of the closet. When it happened I didn't want to jump out of my skin.

I started awakening in the middle of the night to see my old man sitting at the foot of the bed. He always faced away from me, but I recognized his shape, the heft of his hand. When I dared to call to him he hitched his shoulders and began to turn to face me. It was a turn never completed.

Of course he couldn't face me, he was dead. He's been dead most of my life. He wouldn't even recognize me now. I was nine the last time he saw me. Now I look just like the way he did. The heft of my hand is the same. Imagine him now, finding himself at the foot of a stranger's bed, a man he's never met before, who might call out to him, "Dad?" No wonder he vanishes. If it was me, looking back at me, seeing me, a live me facing me, plaintively urging some unknown request of me, I'd run too.

Who the hell wouldn't.

The phone rang and no one was there. It happened more and more.

I kept bleaching the blood stain and finally it faded enough so folks could walk over it again. I got another royalty check, this one for $12.13. In a moment of spite I grabbed the end of it and flicked my lighter. The corner started to brown but I dropped it before there was any real damage. There was no point in ruining what little of mine they were actually sending through. I should be happy the Danes or the Portuguese or whoever the fuck were reading my books. We all make our deals with the devil.

A private investigator hired by the parents of one of the rape victims came around asking questions. He eyed me up good. A handyman with no set hours, no clock to punch. He'd asked around and found out about the murder. He tried to brace me and I held onto my dwindling cool. He lacked subtlety and hoped to push my buttons, whatever they were. He ran out scenarios where I couldn't get laid so I waited in dark hallways and leaped down onto teenage girls. I let him talk the talk because it was for a good cause. I wanted him to hunt down the bastard in the area.

I awoke to laughter outside the basement window. Mojo pressed his face to the glass and waved to me. I saw the feet of boys and girls go by. A breeze blew the stalks of weeds and wildflowers against the pane. I got dressed, took the back door, and went out to the garden.

Ferdi and the kids were following Mojo around, all of them in a line and sort of dancing the Conga. They went around and around while I watched. Mojo's little bag around his neck, stuffed with the pad and pen on a string, bounced as he jumped onto the vines and the lower limbs of a couple of gnarled trees bursting up from brick.

I turned and saw a man with eyes like a dull metal finish. He whispered something I didn't understand. It wasn't English. I thought maybe it was German. My stomach tightened but I could feel myself smiling. The mysteries of life and death, baby, and everything in between.

A sweet moist aroma wafted from him, and suddenly I knew what the Rhine Falls must smell like.

"Nobody uses icepicks anymore," I said. "So he lied. So what? He just wanted to meet girls."

Dr. Lauber held his hands up to show me they were empty. He seemed eager to explain to me that his intent was friendly and forgiving. He said something else I couldn't understand. I approached and the sunlight shimmered off him.

I said, "It wasn't you?"

Dr. Lauber firmed his lips. He shook his head. He reached out to touch me but the touch never came. He had a lot more he wanted to say. The words poured out of him. He had admissions and apologies and declarations to make. We all did. I knew I would die before making all of mine too. It seemed nobody could do any differently. I listened, thinking about Gabriella. By the time the chain of children came around again he was gone.

Mojo skipped by and then the kids, one after the other. As Ferdinand the Magnifico was about to pass, I reached out and grabbed hold of his coat sleeve.

He stopped and faced me. "My good friend, the wonderful writer Will Darrow! Is it not a glorious day!"

"Why'd you do it, Ferdi?" I asked. "Why'd you kill the aluminum foil guy?"

Our eyes locked and I watched the real person slip out from beneath the costume of his caricature. I saw a sorrow and a resolve there that I hoped I would never have to experience. A strength that had been thoroughly hidden and an anguish that would never depart but had been recently muted. He was trying to regain his soul.

He spoke in a quiet voice for the first time since we'd met. "He murdered my wife in Denmark fourteen years ago. You don't need to know the details."

He was right. I didn't.

I knew he'd told me the truth. We can go our whole lives believing we'll recognize the cold hard truth when we hear it, but when it finally arrives it's like nothing that's ever come before. It strikes a chord that's never been hit, and my head somehow rang with it. Ferdi waited for me to make a move. He appeared ready for any judgment.

The aluminum foil liar had told me he'd done terrible things. He had struck his mother. He had broken the hearts of his children. He had made a woman bleed. He didn't think he deserved to be forgiven.

I shrugged and let go of Ferdi's sleeve. He nodded with a slightly accepting, thankful smile. I lit a cigarette and he rushed to catch up to the kids, and the dance continued around the garden.

I saw someone crouched at the foot of my bed. It was my old man again, facing away from me like always. He held his fist up, and in it was clutched a note. I threw the covers aside and walked to him. Maybe now he would talk to me.

But he couldn't turn around, no matter how close I came. Of course he couldn't face me, he was dead. Without looking at me, he stuck his arm out and offered me the note.

It was five pages long and read:

We have come to a spot where the tissue is thinnest and already torn. It is a destiny feared and worshiped. There are those who desire and cannot own, those who die in need. The heart swells and fails. I have seen her, in the depths of this house, in these rooms, lost and at a loss but still retaining that luminescence of life. She is light itself to some. We cannot afford this loss. She haunts the halls eager to reach out to us as we pass. Can you make sense of it? I have tried but I am indisposed by the part I must play. Surely you have heard her in your dreams? Your name called. How bright she is in the dark places. She speaks of you still. She understands your love. It is not too late.

MOJO

When I looked up again my old man was gone. There was a knock at the door. I opened it and there stood Mojo, smiling, holding his cup, his little hat askew. I looked out into the lobby for Ferdinand, but he was nowhere in sight.

I glanced down at the chimp and said, "Okay, Mojo, fess up. I need to hear it. If you really know how to talk, buddy, then now's the time. It'll be our secret, I swear. But this is important. What happens next is going to change the course of a life or two around here, I think." I went to one knee and got in close. He cocked his head and did a dance and put a paw out to touch my nose. "So I want to hear it from your own lips. Talk to me. Did you see it happen? Did you see Corben kill Gabriella?"

Mojo went, "Ook."

I stared at him and he stared at me.

I nodded and said, "Fuckall, that's good enough for me," and went to confront my oldest friend, my only enemy.

I was wired and hot and ready to break bones, but when he opened the door all my rage left me. Almost all of it.

He hadn't shaved or eaten in days. He'd been steadily losing weight and his sternum stuck out like a spike. His eyes had sunken in even further, his lips crusted and yellow, and his breath stank like hell. He hadn't quit the sauce. His sweat was stale and smelled like whiskey and disease. There was a time I would've gloated and been filled with a sick joy. Now I just wanted to know what had happened to his wife.

"I want to talk to you," I said.

"All right."

We sat in his living room again. He hadn't opened a window in ages. The dust swirled in the rays of the sun lancing down through his windows. He'd been drinking too much but I didn't know what else to do for him, so I mixed him a screwdriver. At least he'd get a little orange juice in his system. He looked just a little closer to death than the aluminum foil guy had with the icepick vibrating in his head.

His eyes kept wandering to a spot on the wall behind the couch. I couldn't help riffing on Poe's "Cask of Amontillado" and "The Black Cat." But he wasn't checking the place where he might've stuck Gabriella's corpse and sealed it over with stucco. He wouldn't keep her so close at hand. He was writing behind his eyes.

"I know you killed her," I said.

"You're a fool."

"The monkey saw you do it."

It made him open his mouth so wide that the hinges of his jaw cracked. "What?"

"Mojo told me what you did."

"The chimp…?"

"You shouldn't have left any witnesses. You didn't think the world's first talking writing monkey would tell somebody? He knows his business. Knocks 'em dead in South Dakota."

"I was wrong. You're not merely foolish. You're insane."

The word caught in his throat. He almost didn't get it out. It wasn't an easy one for him to say aloud. I usually had a hard time with it too. Anyone who spends that much time inside his own head had to be extra cautious of tossing words like crazy and insane around. But in this building, in this city, on this day and during this particular conversation, it seemed even more reckless than usual.

"Where is she?" I asked.

He finished his screwdriver and set the glass aside. "Visiting her mother in Poughkeepsie."

I took it in and felt a clash of relief and disbelief. "That's not what you told me. You said you didn't know."

He made an effort to appear embarrassed. Instead he just looked cornered but sly. "I didn't want to admit to it."

"Cut the horseshit."

"You say that to me after telling me about talking monkeys?"

"That's right, I say it to you, asshole."

Corben refused to keep his mind on Gabriella. I backed away a step. His gaze slid over me. It slid over everything. He couldn't keep his focus on any one spot or idea. It was more than just the writing going on in his head. He was tumbling around inside Stark House without moving. I'd never seen him like this before—lost and at a loss. I stopped trying to control the conversation. I would allow him to take the lead.

We sat there and I finally looked all around the place, letting myself take in his riches and treasures. I went from room to room. Holy shit, there really was a solarium. The beauty and the effort and love that Gabriella had put into her home. How could a man not think it was enough? Are any of us ever satisfied? I wondered if I would have so easily been led down the wrong path if I'd had his successes. Become so self-absorbed, so unappreciative. I supposed it could happen to anyone.

We stayed like that for half an hour. I thought he'd forgotten about me, so entwined by himself. I didn't mind waiting. I sat down and felt comfortable in his chair, noting all the small details and touches that were of Gabriella.

"Stark House is haunted," Corben said.

"Maybe," I told him.

His upper lip drew back in a wild leer. He ran a hand through his hair and I realized how thin and gray it had gone. He looked around like he wanted to start kicking shit again. He flung the empty screwdriver glass. It shattered against one of his rare paintings. "How can you say that? How can you still be unsure? You must feel it, Will. Every moment of the day! I can't write anymore. There's no need. The books write themselves. There's always someone else at the keyboard. Even now. Right now, this very minute, in my office. Go look if you don't believe me."

"I believe you," I said.

"I accept my sins and vices, I do, sincerely," he said sounding wholly insincere. "I've done terrible things, every man has, but...but this—I have seen them in the corridors, in the doorways, in my bed—my God, they stare at me. They're the damned. The forsaken."

I shrugged again. I was doing it a lot. "Everyone is, more or less. We muddle through. So what?"

"Doesn't it fill you with black terror?"

"No." I lit a cigarette, got up, and walked around the room.

"How can it not?"

"Why should it?"

Corben glanced up and we went deep into each others eyes. I knew he'd crossed the line. I knew it with all my heart. He'd killed Gabriella, just to see what it felt like. We'd been reading stories about such men since we were kids: the ones who thought they were too good for moral law. He wanted to feel blood run just so he could write about it. And now it was writing itself without him.

I knew something else. He really had loved her—more than anything, more than he could possibly love anything in this life—except for himself and his art. He'd cast himself in the role of villain of his grandest dramatic work. The one that needed no author. He'd learned what he hadn't really wanted to know, and it was destroying him. He'd gone bony but soft.

"Where is she?" I asked.

"I already told you. Stop asking me!"

"What did you do to her?" I asked. "Where did you leave her?"

"You've no right to question me like this!"

I moved in on him. Two great forces worked through me at once—a jealous rage and a wild desire to shove aside the wasted years and have my friend back again. I wanted to save him and I wanted to crush him.

I swallowed heavily and said, "I heard you two arguing that morning. What were you fighting about?"

"I don't have to tell you anything."

"See, now there's where you're wrong."

I hadn't gone soft. I was all nerve-ending and adrenaline. I had dreams I needed to pursue. I still had to learn French. I'd make another stab at trying caviar. I had to track down my foreign rights and royalties. I had to find my love. "Where is she?"

"She's my wife! Who the hell do you think you are?"

"What did you do to her?"

Corben glowered at me, the corners of his lips turned up as if silently asking why I hadn't discovered her body yet, why I hadn't already smashed him to pieces and rammed a steak knife into his belly. Like all of us, he wanted to live and he wanted to die. His need was so apparent it invigorated and disgusted me. I made a fist and drew it back and willed all my hatred, remorse, and broken potential into it. My blood and bone, our lost friendship, our endless understanding of one another. It was no different than any other time I made a fist. Or smiled. Or wrote. Or made love. Or polished the banister.

I dropped my arm to my side, and he cried out, "She's at her mother's house in Poughkeepsie! It's the truth! It's the truth!"

"You're lying."

"She left me!"

"She would never do that."

"She did!"

"You're lying."

"Am I? Maybe I am. Your voice, Will, it sounds so much like mine."

"No, it doesn't."

"Am I only fighting with myself? Sometimes I think I may be the only one alive in this building. I sit here and can almost start believing that you and all the others are only figments, phantoms, that all of you are—"

"Yeah?" I said. I got up close. "Tell me. You ever think that maybe *you're* the only one who's dead?"

The thought had never crossed his mind, but now it did. It hit him like I'd never seen anything hit him before. His eyes widened and his breathing grew shallow. He started floundering in his seat, his hands flapping uselessly. I got another glass and gave him a tall one of straight vodka. He chugged it down until the glass rattled against his teeth.

He stared at me and I stared at him. After a while I got up and left him there alone, receding deeper into shadows of his own making. His eyes implored me as if I could, or ever would, have the capacity to save him. Now as he began fading beyond even my memory until he too had almost completely vanished. I turned around once before I got to his door, and he was nowhere.

Maybe we were both already dead.

There had been a night a few months ago when he and I passed each other on the stairway, and I'd thought that I shouldn't turn my back on him. That he might, right then, decide to draw the derringer he supposedly always kept on his person and pop me twice in the back of the head. The thought had been so strong that I'd watched him carefully as we went by, my hand on a small screwdriver in my pocket, thin enough to slip between his ribs and puncture his heart. We moved on in opposite directions, wary, but alive.

Or so I'd thought. But now, I wasn't so sure.

Perhaps Corben had murdered Gabriella and hidden her under some alleyway garbage not far from Stark House. Maybe he'd tossed her body in the East River or buried her deep in the garden beneath the wildflowers or beneath the brick. Or maybe she actually was up in Poughkeepsie, at home with her mother, calming herself before a time when she might be willing to return to the building and make amends. With him, or only with herself. The dead roam here the way they roam everywhere else—intact, lost, and at a loss. The living were no different. I was no different.

She might eventually come back, for her belongings if not for him. To say goodbye to me if no one else. She might appear in the garden one morning, joining in when the children and Ferdi and Mojo danced together. There were more chances and choices than I'd ever believed in before.

Gabriella might call me tomorrow evening and ask me to come fix her kitchen tap, and I will find her there alone on the fifth floor. She'll have a bottle of wine and a jar of caviar. I won't make faces chewing down the crackers. The window will be open and a cold breeze will press back the curtains. Moonlight will cast silver across the dark. The sheets will be clean but rumpled. I'll do my best to speak French. Total darkness for a moment and then the pressure of her body easing against mine.

Whatever the truth, I would wait for her.

Because, I've been told, she speaks of me still.

She understands my love.

I burn silently. It is not too late.

EDITOR AND AUTHOR BIOGRAPHIES

EDITOR JOE R. LANSDALE is the author of over thirty novels, including the Edgar Award–winning Hap and Leonard mystery series (*Mucho Mojo*, *Two Bear Mambo*), and the *New York Times* Notable Book *The Bottoms*. Over 200 of his stories have appeared in such outlets as *Tales from the Crypt* and *Pulphouse*, and his work has been adapted for *The Twilight Zone* and *Masters of Horror*. Lansdale has written graphic novels including *Batman* and *Fantastic Four* and is the writer-in-residence at Stephen F. Austin State University. He is a tenth-degree black belt and the founder of the Shen Chuan martial art. Joe Lansdale lives in Nacogdoches, Texas, which suits him just fine, thank you very much.

NEAL BARRETT, JR., is the author of numerous novels including *The Karma Corps*, *The Hereafter Gang*, and the Aldair series. His story "Ginny Sweethips' Flying Circus" was nominated for best novelette for both the 1988 Nebula Award and the 1989 Hugo Award. In 2010, he was named Author Emeritus by the Science Fiction and Fantasy Writers of America.

MICHAEL BISHOP is the two-time Nebula Award–winning author of "The Quickening" and *No Enemy But Time*. He has published seventeen novels, and over 120 pieces of his short fiction have been published in seven collections. He has edited seven anthologies including *Light Years and Dark*, which won the Locus Award. Bishop lives in Pine Mountain, Georgia.

OCTAVIA E. BUTLER was the Hugo and Nebula Award–winning author of *Kindred* and the *Xenogenesis* trilogy. She was the first science fiction author to win the MacArthur Foundation Genius Grant. After Butler died in 2006, the Octavia E. Butler Memorial Scholarship was created to help writers of color attend a Clarion writing workshop.

HARLAN ELLISON® has written or edited over seventy-five books, more than 1,700 stories, essays, articles, and newspaper columns; and two dozen teleplays; and a dozen movies. He has won the Edgar, Bram Stoker, Nebula, Hugo, World Fantasy, British Fantasy, and Audie awards as well as the Silver Pen for Journalism from PEN.

JEFFREY FORD is the author of the *New York Times* Notable Books *The Physiognomy* and *Memoranda*. He was mentored by John Gardner, and his short fiction has been collected in *The Fantasy Writer's Assistant and Other Stories* (2003 World Fantasy Award for best collection), *The Empire of Ice Cream*, and *The Drowned Life*. Ford lives in Medford Lakes, New Jersey.

KAREN JOY FOWLER is the author of the *New York Times* bestseller *The Jane Austen Book Club*, later made into a major motion picture, as well as novels and short story collections including *The Sweetheart Season*, *Artificial Things*, and *Sister Noon*. She was a finalist for the PEN/Faulkner Award. She is a co-editor of *The James Tiptree Award Anthology* series. Fowler lives in Santa Cruz, California.

JOE HALDEMAN is a multiple-time Hugo and Nebula Award–winning science fiction author best known for his groundbreaking novel, *The Forever War*, and its sequels. His short stories, including James Tiptree, Jr. Award winner "Camouflage" and Locus Award winner "Graves," have been published in three collections. Haldeman lives in Gainesville, Florida, and Cambridge, Massachusetts.

CHARLIE HUSTON is the author of several crime novels, including *Caught Stealing*, *The Mystic Arts of Erasing All Signs of Death*, and the Joe Pitt Casebooks series. In addition to novels, Huston also writes for Marvel Comics and is responsible for the 2006 revival of the iconic character Moon Knight. He lives in Los Angeles.

STEPHEN KING is the bestselling author of more than forty novels and over 100 short stories, such as *Carrie*, *The Dark Tower*, and "Children of the Corn." He is the recipient of numerous awards, including the Hugo, Shirley Jackson, Bram Stoker, British Fantasy, Horror Guild, and World Fantasy awards. King's work has been made into major motion pictures, such as *The Dead Zone*, *Carrie*, *Misery*, and *The Shining*. He lives primarily in Maine.

ELLEN KLAGES is the author of the Scott O'Dell–winning children's novel *The Green Glass Sea*, *Portable Childhoods*, and *White Sands, Red Menace*. She received the Nebula Award for her story "Basement Magic," and her novella "Time Gypsy" was a Nebula and Hugo Award finalist. She has collaborated on several nonfiction science books for children, and serves on the board of the James Tiptree, Jr. Award. Klages lives in San Francisco.

BOB LEMAN was a science fiction and horror short-story writer. He is best known for the story "Window," which was nominated for a Nebula Award and adapted as an episode of *Night Visions*. All of his work is collected in *Feesters in the Lake and Other Stories*. He was a veteran of World War II, and died in 2006.

JONATHAN LETHEM is the author of numerous stories and novels, including the *New York Times* bestseller *The Fortress of Solitude* and the National Book Critics Circle Award–winning novel *Motherless Brooklyn*. His revision of the comic book series *Omega the Unknown* was nominated for an Eisner Award. Lethem received a MacArthur Fellowship in 2005. He currently lives in Brooklyn, New York, and Berwick, Maine.

DAVID MORRELL is the author of over twenty-five novels. He is best known for the novel *First Blood*, which was adapted into the *Rambo* film franchise. Morrell is the co-president of the International Thriller Writers organization. He was given Comic-Con's Ink Pot Lifetime Achievement Award for his contributions to popular culture. Morrell lives in Santa Fe, New Mexico.

NORMAN PARTRIDGE is the author of four novels and more than seventy-five short stories. His novel, *Dark Harvest*, won the Bram Stoker Award and was voted one of *Publishers Weekly*'s 100 Best Books of 2006. He has also written comics for Mojo and DC Comics. Partridge lives in San Francisco.

TOM PICCIRILLI is the prolific author of over 150 short stories spanning multiple genres. He has written over twenty novels, including four Bram Stoker Award winners such as *The Night Class,* as well as two International Thriller Writers Award–winners, *The Midnight Road* and *The Coldest Mile.* Piccirilli also wrote a Hellboy media tie-in and co-authored a book of literary criticism, *Deconstructing Tolkien.*

MICHAEL SHEA is the two-time World Fantasy Award–winning author of the *Nifft the Lean* trilogy, *In Yana, the Touch of Undying,* and the short fiction collection *Polyphemus.* He has also been nominated twice each for the Hugo and Nebula Award. He lives in Healdsburg, California.

LUCIUS SHEPARD is the author of eighteen novels including *Green Eyes* and *The Golden,* as well as numerous short stories appearing in such collections as *The Jaguar Hunter, The Ends of the Earth,* and *Dagger Key and Other Stories.* His short fiction has won the Nebula, Hugo, International Horror Writers, National Magazine, Locus, Theodore Sturgeon, and World Fantasy awards. He lives in Portland, Oregon.

LEWIS SHINER is the author of six novels including *Deserted Cities of the Heart, Say Goodbye,* and the World Fantasy and Crown Award winner, *Glimpses.* He has published several collections of short stories, including *Love in Vain.* Shiner has made all his short fiction available on the Internet for free under a Creative Commons license. He lives in North Carolina.